WILLOWTREE PRESS, L.L.C.

60,63, 99,123, 198, 207-208, 263,267, 305

CRONE'S MOON

A Rowan Gant Investigation

A Novel of Suspense and Magick

By

M. R. Sellars

E.M.A. Mysteries

CRONE'S MOON: A Rowan Gant Investigation
A WillowTree Press Book

PRINTING HISTORY
WillowTree Press First Trade Paper Edition / October 2004

For information, contact WillowTree Press on the World Wide Web,
http://www.willowtreepress.com

ISBN: 0-9678221-4-9

Cover design Copyright © 2004 Johnathan Minton

Author Photo Copyright © 2004 K. J. Epps

PRINTED IN THE U.S.A.
by
TCS Printing
North Kansas City, Missouri

Books By M. R. Sellars

Praise for M. R. Sellars and the Rowan Gant Investigations:

"Fans of *Hamilton* and *Lackey* will want to religiously follow the exploits of Mr. Rowan Gant."

— Harriet Klausner
Literary Reviewer

"Fans of *Mercedes Lackey's* defunct *Diana Tregarde Mysteries* rejoice— a new witch is in town!"

— Melanie C. Duncan,
The BookDragon Review

"These books should be marketed as controlled substances..."

— Kathleen Hill,
Founder/Moderator,
Pagan Page Turners Book Club

"Hooray for M.R. Sellars, the master of Pagan fiction!"

— Dorothy Morrison
Author of *Everyday Magic* and *The Craft*

"Rowan Gant is a detective in the tradition of *Diana Tregarde* and *Anita Blake*."

— Rosemary Edghill
Author, The Bast Mysteries

ACKNOWLEDGEMENTS

With every book I write, the list of people I feel compelled to thank grows. If I keep at this long enough, the roll call will take an entire volume in and of itself, but I don't mind. True friends are a rare commodity, and those who stick by you are worth more than their weight in gold. The fact that my list keeps growing warms my heart, and thanking those people here is the least I can do. So, without further babbling on my part, (yeah, right. Like I'll ever stop) here are the 'usual suspects' along with a few new additions—

Dorothy Morrison: Gods, what can I say about you my dear friend? You are not only like a sister to me; you are an inspiration—each and every day.

Officer Scott Ruddle, SLPD: The Scotch, Cigars, and back deck are here for you any time my friend.

Roy Osbourn: A character, an invaluable source of information, and hell of a guy. I'm glad to be able to call you friend.

Tammi Nesser: Thanks for letting me borrow your neuroses and phobias— again. Sorry about the whole getting killed off thing.

Trish Telesco: Good friend and author extraordinaire.

A.J Drew: What can you say about the Yeti. He's big, fuzzy, and a great guy. Oh yeah, AJ, be careful what you ask for.

As always, my ever-expanding, long distance family: Mystic Moon Coven.

Duane & Chell: Words cannot express my love for you two.

Angel & Randal: Ditto.

Scott & Andrea: Love you guys too.

All of my good friends from the various acronyms: C.A.S.T., F.O.C.A.S.M.I., H.S.A., M.E.C., S.I.P.A., and S.P.I.R.A.L.

Patrick Owen: Friend and unofficially adopted brother. We've seen some serious sh*t my brother. Good and bad. I couldn't have picked a better person to weather it with.

Tish Owen: Love ya' hon!

Lori, Beth, Jim, Dave, Rachel, Doug, Duncan, Kitti, Edain, Boom-Boom, Kevin, David, Bella, Shannon, Denessa, Boudica, Imajicka, Owl, and probably twenty or thirty more…

My parents: I will never be able to thank you enough for introducing me to the written word. I wish you both were here.

"Chunkee": The man behind the author. You keep saying you have a poor memory, but why is it you know the stories I've written better than I do? Thanks for being there.

Johnathan Minton: The guy who creates the art you buy when you pick up one of my books. All I do is throw some words at the pages in between.

My daughter: For making life an adventure and allowing me to see the world through a fresh set of eyes. Thank you for constantly amazing me.

My wife Kat: Editor, friend, soul mate, keeper of the household, and the one person on earth I cannot live without.

Jim Sellars: My uncle—I am thankful I got to know you again before you had to leave for good.

Styx, Ozzy Osbourne, Loreena McKennitt, Enya, and a host of other artists, that tirelessly (by the magick of the CD player) and unknowingly provide the ambient sound for my office whenever I am writing.

James Young and Tommy Shaw for the song *These Are The Times*. I realize it was written about something wholly unrelated, however each time I hear it I cannot help but think of the relationship between Ben Storm and Rowan Gant.

Firestorm Publicity Services and all that they do to keep me going.

The person who discovered coffee and then decided to turn it into a drink.

The "Don't Be Brothers."

The gang at CAO for producing some of the best cigars a man could ever smoke. Thanks for the tour.

Bucky Katt, Satchel, Wendi, 'The Penguin Mafia', and flying monkeys.

And, as always, everyone who takes the time to pick up one of my novels, read it, and then recommend it to a friend.

For my father,

M. R. Sellars, *Senior*

If, in my lifetime, I am able to be
even half the man you were in yours,
I will truly have accomplished something.

AUTHOR'S NOTE:

While the city of St. Louis and its various notable landmarks are certainly real, many names have been changed and liberties taken with some of the details in this book. They are fabrications. They are pieces of fiction within fiction to create an illusion of reality to be experienced and enjoyed.

In short, I made them up because it helped me make the story more entertaining, or in some cases, just because I wanted to.

Note also that this book is a first-person narrative. You are seeing this story through the eyes of Rowan Gant. The words you are reading are his thoughts. In first person writing, the narrative should match the dialogue of the character telling the story. Since Rowan, (and anyone else that I know of for that matter,) does not speak in perfect, unblemished English throughout his dialogue, he will not do so throughout his narrative. Therefore, you will notice that some grammatical anomalies have been retained (under protest from editors) in order to support this illusion of reality.

Let me repeat something—I DID IT ON PURPOSE. Do NOT send me an email complaining about my grammar. It is a rude thing to do, and it does nothing more than waste your valuable time. If you find a typo, that is a different story. Even editors miss a few now and then.

Finally, this book is not intended as a primer for WitchCraft, Wicca, or any Pagan path. However, please note that the rituals, spells, and explanations of these religious/magickal practices are accurate. Some of my explanations may not fit your particular tradition, but you should remember that your explanations might not fit mine either.

And, yes, some of the Magick is "over the top." But, like I said in the first paragraph, this is fiction...

When the moon is high and new,
kiss your hand to her times two.

When the moon rides at her peak,
then your hearts desire seek.

*When the moon turns to the Crone,
in Saint Louis, don't walk alone...*

Couplets #5-6
The Wiccan Rede
Lady Gwen Thompson, First Printing, Green Egg #69, Circa 1975

Couplet # 7 as written by Rev. Duane Marshall, 2004

Thursday, January 10
Three days prior to the new moon
10:00 A.M.
North of Granite City, Illinois

PROLOGUE:

Her jaw is hurting.

It isn't the only part of her body that is aching by far, but at the moment, it is in the forefront of her mind. She can tell she has been grinding her teeth. There is no doubt about it, because she always does when she sleeps.

Bruxism, that's what her dentist calls it. Pain, that's what she calls it; especially right now. She has a plastic mouth guard she sleeps with that is specially designed just for the affliction, and it helps; but, she knows that considering the amount of pain she is experiencing and the fact that she can't feel it in her mouth that the appliance must not be here.

Thinking about it doesn't help much.

She is beginning to take notice of the laundry list of aches plaguing her body. Her head, her chest, her wrists, her ankles... hell, there isn't an inch of her that doesn't hurt. There are just some parts that are screaming louder than the others.

She starts to move, then flashes on a distant memory. She's not supposed to move? She shouldn't move? She can't move? She tries anyway and finds that option three is apparently the winner. She doesn't know why she can't move, but she decides not to think about it. It just seems easier not to.

It is odd to her that she can remember the word bruxism, but for some unknown reason she can't recall much else. She has no idea how long she has been here. A day? A week? A month? No clue. But what does it matter? She doesn't know where 'here' is.

Come to think of it, she doesn't even know WHO she is. Confusion seems to be the order of business, and she has absolutely no idea why. The only thing she knows for certain is that it is dark, cold, smells odd, and she is hurting.

She lets out a sudden whimper as a glut of visceral fear gives her stomach a hard twist. She has no idea where it is coming from, but it blindsides her. The terror starts winding it's way up from her gut, driving along her spine, and rushes into her brain. She catches her breath as the flush of warmth spreads over her face. She thinks she is going to vomit and swallows hard. She feels a wet tear streaming across her cheek.

A moment later, the fear passes with the same urgency and no more warning than when it had attacked. Again, it seems easier to just forget than to try analyzing it. The question 'why' seems so moot.

She decides to move.

"Oh, that's right," she thinks to herself. "I can't move."

She wriggles her hands, but that only serves to make her wrists hurt more. She tries to move her feet and they hurt too, but there is something more.

She moves her feet again and hears the splashing sound of water. She can feel it against her skin, but it isn't the soothing sensation one would expect. It actually feels as if her feet have been soaking for days.

"Why are my feet in water?" she wonders to herself and then answers the query within the same stream of thought. "Good question. Where am I again?"

She moves her feet and listens closely. Other than the sound of the water, it is quiet.

It's almost too quiet.

She doesn't like that at all. She wishes it wasn't so still. It can't be this quiet.

She stops moving and listens.

Distant footsteps.

Heavy. Deliberate.

She's not so sure she likes that sound any more than the quiet. But she keeps listening.

She feels the fear welling in the pit of her stomach once again and tries to focus on something else.

"Who am I?" she wonders aloud in a barely audible whisper.

Her brain feels scrambled, and even the past few moments seem like a washed out memory from another lifetime. She forces herself to concentrate and begins whispering whatever she can grasp from the disjointed thoughts.

"T..."

"Tee?"

"Tuh?"

"Tay?"

"Two?"

"Two, what?" she wonders.

"Two. Two times one is two. Two times two is four. Two times three is six. Two times four is twelve... Twelve? That's right isn't it? Of course it is. Two times four is twelve. Two times twelve is sixteen... Wait... Sixteen? No... Wait... I'll start over. Two times two is eleven... No, that's not right... What was it I was trying to remember again?"

She gives up. It doesn't seem worth it.

She notices that her mouth tastes funny— strangely metallic.

"That's weird," she murmurs. "Hmph. I can remember what metal is, so why can't I remember what time it is? It sure is dark. Maybe that's why. There's that sound again. Like a motor or something. I wonder what it is?"

The sound grows louder for a moment as a dim light falls across the floor in an ever-widening swath. The luminance chases away just enough of the darkness for her to see the grey concrete floor. A pair of heavy black lines snakes across the filthy surface. She doesn't know what they are, but there seems to be a familiarity about them. She thinks she should know what it is, but she just can't make the connection in her befuddled mind.

Familiar or not, she knows for sure that she doesn't like the look of them.

She hears a low creak of hinges that are in desperate need of oil, and the faint light slowly disappears as the motor-like sound is muffled once again.

A noise comes from above and behind her, and she immediately identifies it. The heavy footsteps are back, but now they are loud. They begin descending into the darkness, coming closer with each deliberate thump.

The cold terror returns, and this time it doesn't go away.

Friday, June 7
Three days prior to the New Moon
7:32 A.M.
St. Louis, Missouri

The television set tossed light out into the room as the picture flickered and changed. The logo of the news station sat prominently in the corner, proudly displaying the network affiliation along with the current time.

It was 7:32 in the morning.

The picture suddenly switched to a shifting, bright background overlaid with an artistic shot of a hovering helicopter, complete with the slow motion blur of its rotors blending into the gradient of colors. The words BREAKING NEWS slashed in bold letters across the screen, and a fanfare of syncopated beats underscored the image.

The screen switched again to a fresh-faced, young reporter holding a logo-adorned microphone. Behind him was a lush scene; leafy trees and dense vegetation disappearing into the unfocused depth of field. It was immediately obvious that he was in a rural or wooded area somewhere.

As he held one hand to his ear, presumably listening in for a cue, he began to speak.

"Thank you Chloe and Russ, I'm on the scene at Rafferty Park overlooking the Missouri River where last evening a jogger made a gruesome discovery. Mike Rickman was coming down this path when he stumbled upon what appeared to be a badly decomposed human arm.

"Authorities were called to the scene and after a thorough search have confirmed finding more remains in a shallow grave well off the path.

"While there has been no confirmation as yet, there has been speculation that the body may be that of Tamara Linwood, the grade school teacher who disappeared from the parking lot of Westview Shopping Mall back in January of..."

The man watching this particular television set this morning might have had an interest in the story had he been able to hear or see it. Unfortunately, he was sprawled on the hardwood floor; face down in a puddle of coffee where his cup had shattered.

He convulsed and postured as the sudden seizure ravaged his

body, forcing him to bite his tongue and writhe as if holding the bare
end of a live extension cord.

CHAPTER 1:

My tongue felt like someone had taken hold of it with a meat-tenderizing mallet or some other equally heinous implement of destruction. Whatever it was that had happened, at the moment, the salty tang of blood was effectively presenting its unmistakable flavor to the few taste buds that remained intact.

My head was throbbing too. Well, maybe not so much throbbing as imploding and exploding all at once. I knew full well that such was a literal impossibility, of course; even so, that was what it felt like all the same. It didn't take long for me to realize that trying to think about it too hard made it hurt just that much worse, so I accepted my brain's knee-jerk comparison as a cold fact and left it at that.

Additional sensations began sneaking in through the tiny fissures in the pain that was hammering my skull; each of them petitioning to be heard, felt, and otherwise experienced to the fullest. Unfortunately, none of those sensations were any more pleasant than the one occupying center stage at the moment.

Given my current inventory of pains, the only somewhat neutral feeling I could identify was linked directly to the right side of my face. In fact, at this very moment, my cheek was reporting back to me that it was firmly pressed against something hard. What that something was, I had no idea, but it was definitely hard... And if my inner ears weren't deceiving me, it was horizontal... Not to mention wet. Overall, it was not an exceptionally painful feeling, but it was most certainly uncomfortable. Still, combining the uncomfortable with the excruciating and then multiplying it by a healthy measure of confusion— well, when you did the math, it all pretty much took on the same properties, none of which could be considered any more desirable than any of the others.

I wondered for a moment if the wet portion of the present feeling was, in part, the blood I thought I tasted. It seemed logical: it was wet, warm, and in the vicinity of my face. Unfortunately, I was forced to abandon the whole idea with urgent haste in order to escape the sharp stab of pain in my skull that the simple act of wondering about it had invoked. Apparently, at this particular moment, my brain wasn't much interested in logic or anything else for that matter.

Between throbs, I noticed that my forehead felt cold. Not just cool but actually flat-out, ice pack cold. It was the only portion of my head that wasn't embroiled in pain at the moment, but judging from the sensation it was announcing to me, that might only have been because it was well on its way to numb. Of course, it hurt to think about that too.

It occurred to me that there was something else just as disturbing as the pain. A pair of something's actually: One, I had no idea what had happened to me in order to bring about this level of agony; and two, I didn't know where I was. If I actually knew the answers to the two questions, I couldn't remember them, and that wasn't good either. I briefly considered the idea that I might be able to obtain one of the answers simply by opening my eyes. However, considering and doing are two different things entirely, and it seemed my eyelids weren't listening to my brain right at this moment.

My vision wasn't the only sense that was nullified either. Up to this point, my auditory nerves had apparently been on vacation somewhere in the land of white noise, as all I seemed to be hearing was a nondescript roar in my ears. The good news was that they now returned from their sabbatical, in a manner much like a radio being switched on and the volume being turned slowly upward. A distant voice began echoing down the hollow tunnel that was my hearing, and even though the simple act of concentrating brought with it an overtone of pain, I strained to make out the words.

The voice sounded male, young, somewhat tinny, and was coming across as no more than a garble of meaningless syllables. The distorted edge of the voice competed for my attention through the warbling hum that still invaded my ear. I swallowed hard and steeled myself for the added aches I feared that I was about to bring down upon myself, and then I concentrated harder.

Another mish-mash of sound worked its way into my ear and with each beat morphed from the unintelligible into a Doppler distortion of noise that whistled past me, only to fade quickly away. I seemed to recognize some of the clamor as words. However, what registered was, "…to be a badly decomposed human arm."

I pondered the incomplete sentence and decided that I was hallucinating, because I just knew the voice couldn't have actually said 'decomposed human arm.'

My addled brain locked in on a piece of the distant voice once again. "…have confirmed finding more remains in a shallow grave well off the path.

"While there has been no confirmation as yet, there has been speculation that the body may be that of…"

The sharp taste of metal suddenly filled my mouth, overpowering the salty blood that had dominated the sense moments before. Every muscle in my body tensed at exactly the same moment, pulling up like rubber bands stretched to their limits and then tugged just a little farther for good measure. I could feel my teeth gnashing against my already tortured tongue once again as my body shuddered uncontrollably through some manner of violent seizure. My face took on a fresh ache as I felt my eyes rolling back in my head.

A vague memory wandered through the maelstrom of my thoughts, and I realized I had been here before. At a different time certainly, and even a different place, maybe. I wasn't sure about the latter, but the fact remained that this was not something new.

I could feel my consciousness starting to flee, and I wasn't so sure that it was a bad thing. However, the split second before it managed to exit, the elastic strands that were my muscles and tendons released. Without warning, they snapped instantly back to relaxed positions— or, as relaxed as they could be under the circumstances. Thankfully, the abuse my tongue was taking from my teeth stopped as well.

I felt limp, weak, and maybe even a bit more disoriented than I had been before if that was possible. I took in a deep breath and laid near motionless; panting as a distant ring echoed in my ears then faded into a low buzz that eventually became a voice.

"… From the Major Case Squad have arrived on the scene and will be taking over the investigation from municipal authorities. Back to you Chloe and Russ."

There it was again, that distant, tinny voice.

This time it had said, "Major Case Squad." Then it said, "Chloe and Russ." Now, these things actually made sense. A by-product of that sense was an answer to one of my earlier questions.

Maybe.

From the sound and content, I thought that what I was hearing might be the audio from a television newscast. A partially revealed memory lumbered through the inside of my skull, and I took hold of it.

I was watching the morning news at home in my living room before heading upstairs to my office and getting to work. I got up from my chair during a commercial break and went into the kitchen. I poured myself a fresh cup of coffee, then turned and went back into the living room.

After that, the remembrance grew a bit fuzzy around the edges. Well, actually it was completely obscured from my view because the real truth was that I had absolutely no idea what had occurred in whatever span of time had elapsed since I had poured that cup of coffee.

Still, maybe I wasn't hallucinating as I'd earlier thought. Of course, if I could get the rest of the memory to come into some kind of focus, I might get a better handle on my current situation.

The thud in my skull was actually starting to subside, for which I was more than grateful. The bizarre in and out thrum, however, continued rumbling in my ear, competing with the sound of the television. I started taking stock of the other sensations and happened across the fact that while my forehead was freezing, my neck was actually warm— very warm. In fact, it was downright hot.

I thought about that for a moment and then realized that there also seemed to be something soft but weighty involved. As I continued pondering this latest sensation, I started feeling pressure against my left cheek that seemed to be moving in time with the warbling hum.

I took another shot at opening my eyes, and slowly my left eyelid responded to the instruction. I looked out of the corner of my eye and found that the majority of my limited field of vision was filled with black fur. The soft pads of a pair of feline paws continued pushing against the side of my face as Dickens, one of our trio of cats, kneaded in rhythm with his own purr.

Some semblance of clarity was beginning to creep back into my head as the various pains began to subside. I rolled my eye forward and saw a close up view of polished hardwood strips stretching out before me, although the tableau was a bit on the fuzzy side. While this was a vastly different angle than to what I was accustomed, I recognized what I was seeing to be my living room floor.

A few inches in front of my face, I could see shapes rising out of the horizontal plane. These were also tinged by blurriness but still identifiable as my eyeglasses and as the fragmented remains of a ceramic coffee mug. I guess that would explain why the side of my head was wet.

Well, at least now I knew where I was, which was a plus. Unfortunately, I also had a nagging suspicion that I knew why I was in my current, uncomfortable position. I felt my stomach do a double flip at the very thought and decided not to go there. Not yet, anyway. Maybe I was wrong, and this had been nothing more than me being a klutz. At least, that's what I tried to tell myself. In the back of my head, I knew better.

I let out a groan and gently shoved the now drooling feline off my neck then pushed myself up to my hands and knees. I let my head hang for a moment and took a deep breath. A chilly draft tickled my bare arms, and the reason behind my semi-frozen forehead became immediately obvious— I had been lying directly in front of the air conditioning vent.

The television was still chattering in the background when I dragged myself to my feet. The newscasters had moved on to another, far less horrific story, and the screen was filled with the image of a hyperactive blonde feature reporter whose actual name escaped me at the moment. Synapses were continuing to fire with fewer misses each time around, so I tried to grasp at the obscured bit of information for no other reason than to take my mind off the things I didn't want to face. But, it didn't help. I could still sense the foreboding tickle growing in the back of my brain, and in the end, all I seemed to remember was that she was named after a state.

I stared at the screen for a moment longer and then gave up. I knew it wasn't important and wasting my time on it would probably just make my headache worse. I reached up and rubbed my palm across the lower half of my face then gently touched my fingertips to my tongue. When I pulled my hand away and had a look, I found blood just as I knew I would.

My tongue still felt like ground meat, and I hadn't yet rid myself of the metallic tang that was invading my mouth. My head was continuing to throb with a dull ache, but other than that, the rest of my body's agonies seemed to have fled as fast as they had arrived. That was both good and bad. Good, of course, because the pain was gone. Bad, because that meant they had been phantom pains. Oh, they had felt real enough at the time, but that was the extent of it. They only felt real. There were no wounds, abrasions, or bruises. There was no physical evidence to explain why they had been there to begin with. And, unfortunately, this lead me back to my earlier suspicion.

My stomach twisted into a knot once again, and I felt a brief spate of nausea come over me. This was exactly the kind of thing that happened whenever I was experiencing someone else's physical pain. And for them, it was real pain, not imagined.

This had been a psychic episode, and it was all too familiar. Sometimes they were the same, and at other times they were vastly different. Usually they came in groups that were so similar as to not be able to tell them apart. But, no matter what, they maintained the common thread of blackouts and migraine-like headaches that seemed to linger forever. The types of phantom pains, odd tastes, auditory anomalies, or anything else always depended upon exactly what was being experienced by the other person.

The last episode I'd had like this one had actually been a series of them, but that had been something like four or five months ago. As abruptly as they had started, they had ended. I'd tried to forget about them, but I couldn't. I knew then that it was only a matter of time before they would return.

The sickening part was that every time this sort of thing happened to me, somebody died. Worse yet, it was usually more than one somebody.

I guess that's what I get for being a Witch.

CHAPTER 2:

I was rinsing my mouth out with warm salt water when the phone rang. I gave a final swish and spit the pink tinged liquid into the basin, then grabbed a hand towel and blotted my bearded chin as I walked out of the bathroom. The electronic warble issued again, making the telephone sound just about as impatient as any inanimate device could be.

"Chill out! I'm coming, I'm coming..." I said aloud, as if a verbal scolding would make it stop. It didn't.

I was still wiping my chin when I rounded the corner into the kitchen and glanced at the caller ID box on the wall. OUT OF AREA and a row of dashes was showing on the liquid crystal display, so I lifted the receiver then allowed it to drop right back into the cradle. I had no interest in dealing with a salesman who believed it was okay to ignore the no-call list, not to mention that I still had that headache.

I continued walking over to the counter and retrieved a mug from the cabinet, then filled it with water from the filtered tap. I had just placed it on the turntable in the microwave when the phone began pealing for attention again. I slammed the door on the microwave shut, then quickly punched in three minutes and hit start before stepping back over to the phone.

OUT OF AREA and a row of dashes displayed yet again, and once more I lifted the receiver then let it drop with a heavy clunk.

The microwave was humming away behind me as I stepped over to the multi-tiered spice and herb rack mounted on the wall and began my search for dried willow bark. The search was going to be a huge pain in and of itself, and that just made my head ache more.

Had I been in charge of the rack, the task wouldn't have been a big deal at all, as everything would be in alphabetical order. My wife, Felicity, however, was the keeper of the herbs, and she had her own way of categorizing the bottles. Little groups of related and semi-related spices, barks, herbs, and teas lined the rack. The organization of such simply defied any explanation I could muster.

However, put Felicity in front of it, and she could easily snatch up a bottle of whatever you asked for without even looking. Unfortunately, she wasn't here at the moment.

The closest I had been able to come in the minute or so I had been looking was in fact bark, but it was cinnamon and not willow. Even though it would have tasted quite a bit better, I desperately needed the salicylic acid, not the flavor. I was dragging my finger slowly across the labeled tops of the myriad of bottles, wondering if I should just give up and take some aspirin, when the phone began ringing once again.

I tried to ignore it, but it wasn't helping me concentrate, so I threw my hands up in a dismissive gesture and let out a heavy sigh. I took the few steps over to the phone and saw the same message as before blinking on the display of the caller ID. Now I was annoyed.

I snatched the phone up from the wall cradle and stuck it to my ear, then barked, "I don't want any!"

I was just getting ready to slam the phone back down when I heard my wife's stern voice issue from the earpiece in a quick stream, "Rowan Linden Gant, don't you hang up on me again!"

I tucked the handset back up to my ear, "Felicity?"

"You don't want any of what?" she demanded.

"Sorry, I thought you were a salesperson," I apologized. "The caller ID is coming up with 'out of area' and no number."

"Ahh," she replied. I could almost see her nodding at the other end. "I forgot to charge my cell battery, so I'm using someone else's. It's an out of state number."

"Oh, okay, makes sense," I replied, then sighed and didn't do a very good job of hiding it. "So what's up?"

"That's why I'm calling YOU."

"Come again?"

"What's wrong?"

"Nothing that I'm aware of," I told her.

"Don't lie to me, Rowan," she pressed.

I tried to circumvent answering the question by placing the burden back on her. "So what makes you think something is wrong?"

"Give me a break, Rowan. You aren't the only Witch living under that roof."

At times I forgot that my wife was prone to psuedo-empathic episodes where I was concerned. Much like I would experience someone else's pain via an ethereal bond, she would see flashes of my torment within her mind's eye. Due to the shifting and uncertain nature of the psychic realm, these images would at times be symbolic or incomplete. The first time it had happened to her, she thought that I was dead.

Thankfully, they didn't happen to her all of the time, and she didn't have to endure the same physical torture as I. If she did, I don't think I would have been able to handle it. The fact that she faced mental pain because of me was enough to make me nauseous just by itself.

Realizing that she was going to get it out of me one way or another, I let out a resigned sigh.

"Remember those seizures I had back in January?" I asked.

There was a brief moment of silence at the other end, and then she spoke quietly, "Not again."

Her comment had been couched as a statement rather than a question, but I answered it anyway, "Afraid so."

"Why, Rowan?" There was almost a pleading tone in her voice. "Why you? Why does this keep happening to you?"

"I wish I knew, honey," I said, reaching up with my free hand to rub my temple. "Seems like we both ask that question a lot every time this kind of thing happens."

"Are you okay?" she asked.

"Headache," I grunted, then added, "Did a number on my tongue again. Broke my favorite coffee mug. But other than that, okay I guess."

"I'm only half an hour away," she informed me. "And we haven't even set up yet. Let me see if we can re-schedule the shoot, and I'll be home within an hour."

"What for?" I returned. "I told you, I'm fine."

"But, Rowan…"

"Really, Felicity, I'm fine," I cut her off. "I'm a big boy, and I can take care of myself. I was just making some willow bark tea when you called."

"You're sure, then?"

"Absolutely. We can talk about it later," I assured her. "Besides, they need you there to make pretty pictures for them."

"I don't know about pretty," she replied. "I'm shooting automotive parts today."

"What, no swimsuit models?" I asked her with a hint of good-natured sarcasm.

"No, but I'm doing a lingerie shoot for the Kathy's Closet chain next week," she answered and then added her own query. "You want to help set up and tear down the backdrops and lights?"

"Yeah, right," I returned with a chuckle to what I thought was a facetious question.

"Actually, I'm serious," she returned. "It's going to be an all day shoot, so I could use the help."

"Yeah, okay, if I don't have a rush job or something for a client, sure," I told her. Then I joked, "But are you sure you really want to get me around all those young models?"

"Doesn't matter," she replied. "I trust you. Besides, you'll be working for me and you'll have to do everything I say."

"Everything?" I asked.

"Uh-huh," she purred and then repeated the word with somewhat exaggerated pronunciation. "Ev-er-y-thing."

"Sounds interesting."

"And, of course, if you don't, then I just might have to take some disciplinary action."

"Again, sounds interesting."

"You never know," she answered with an amused giggle. "By the way, they also offered me a nice discount at their stores."

"No kidding?"

"Uh-huh, so if you do a good job maybe I'll let you take me shopping after we wrap it up."

"That could be fun," I said.

There was a period of silence following my comment and soon there was a palpable sense of seriousness creeping into the void between us. Our momentary lightheartedness disappeared in the wake of the recent verbal distraction.

"You're certain you don't want me to come home, then?" Felicity finally asked, the concern edging her voice once again.

"Positive sweetheart," I told her. "We'll talk when you get home."

"Okay. If you're sure," she said.

"Go make some sexy pictures of carburetors," I told her. "Gear heads need pinups too."

I heard her laugh at the other end of the line, once again breaking through the mantle of seriousness that originally cloaked her.

"And, honey?" I added.

"Yes?"

"Thanks."

"For what? Inviting you to a lingerie shoot?"

"No," I returned. "For everything else."

I could almost feel her smiling when I hung up the phone.

I absently took a sip from the coffee mug and screwed up my face in disgust. Willow bark tea was not the most pleasant drink one could ingest to begin with and being an hour cold didn't help it at all. I suppose that would teach me to look first and then drink. I glared at the cup as if it were at fault, then set it aside and hooked my finger into the handle of the cup I'd been reaching for to begin with— the fresh cup of coffee I had just put on the corner of my desk a few minutes ago.

I took a sip from the new mug and found it to be only slightly less cold. I cocked an eyebrow and shot a glance at the clock in the corner of my computer screen. 10:47 A.M. was staring back at me. The few minutes had somehow expanded into forty-five. I guess I had been a little more preoccupied with my work than I'd originally thought.

I leaned back in my chair. The springs underneath the piece of furniture creaked as it tilted, then I was almost certain that I heard my joints creak as I stretched. I drew in a deep breath then pushed my eyeglasses back up onto the bridge of my nose. As of late, I'd been finding myself allowing them to slip down so I could look at the monitor over the top of the rim.

I knew that meant it was time for a trip to the optometrist. Actually, I'd known it for a while, but I'd been avoiding it. I fully suspected I was going to need bi-focals, and that just meant I was getting old. No one ever wants to admit to aging, and I suppose I was no different.

I looked at the coffee cup in my hand then back at the clock. I mulled it over for a minute and then decided I would go ahead and get one more fresh cup—if there was any left. I was just pushing my chair back from the desk when the phone rang. This time it was my business line, so I didn't bother with caller ID. I simply rolled the chair back in and took the receiver in hand, cutting the device off mid-peal.

"Gant Consulting," I answered.

"Yeah, kin you fix my com-pooter? It's broke." A poorly disguised and all too familiar voice grated from the earpiece.

"No, Ben," I returned without missing a beat. "How many times do I have to tell you? I do custom software and networks, not computer repair."

My cop friend guffawed at what he perceived to be an amusing prank call, and I had no choice but to break into a grin myself. His good humor had a tendency to be contagious, as did his sullen moods; and I'd been on the receiving end of enough of that type of phone call from him to know, so this was a pleasant change.

To be honest, considering what I'd experienced earlier I was surprised to find his tone so jovial. I had been expecting that I would hear from him but figured it would be something I didn't want to hear. That was what always seemed to happen whenever I had one of my episodes.

"So what're you doin'?" he asked.

"Working," I replied. "And for some reason, feeling very old."

"Yeah, funny how it creeps up on ya'," he said. "I remember goin' to bed one night feelin' like a twenty year old. When I got up I had all kinds of old man pains, and I had no freakin' idea where they came from."

"Same here."

"Come on, though," he jibed. "I thought you Witches were immortal."

"Have you been watching sixties sitcom re-runs again?"

"It's the only thing on TV worth lookin' at anymore. Besides, the Montgomery gal is pretty hot."

"Ever wonder why they changed Dicks mid series?" I made an obscure reference to the change of actors from the old show.

"Not really," he replied. "But I have been wondering when you're gonna wiggle your nose and make shit show up outta thin air."

"Not going to happen, Ben."

"Crap. I hate when you tell me that."

As entertaining as the conversation had been, I was still wondering if another shoe was about to drop. "So, what about you? Shouldn't you be out catching bad guys or protecting us from evil doers?"

"Day off," he told me.

"Lucky you," I said, still slightly suspicious. "So what are YOU doing?"

"Talking to you."

"You're in rare form today."

"So sue me. So you wanna do lunch? I'm buyin'."

"You're buying? What's up, you win big at the riverboat?" I chuckled.

"Hell no," he answered. "Lost fifty bucks last time I did that."

"It's a little early for lunch yet isn't it?" I asked.

He came back with a question of his own. "Depends. When'd you get up this morning?"

"Point taken," I replied. "Yeah. Lunch sounds good. I could use a break anyway. What did you have in mind?"

"There's a great little Indian place on Olive, downtown."

"Yeah, been there. I can go for that," I told him. "So you want me to meet you?"

"Nah," he returned. "I'll pick ya' up."

"Okay, so I need to change into something Felicity wouldn't be ashamed of me to be seen wearing in public."

"Well light a fire under it, Kemosabe. It's hot out here."

I wondered for a moment at the comment then said, "Where are you, Ben?"

"Right now? Standin' at your freakin' front door waitin' for you ta' get your happy ass down here and let me in."

His comment was followed by a click as he hung up, and then the doorbell began ringing in a vicious staccato brought about by him leaning on the button. Our two dogs joined in with a chorus of barks and howls as they squared off with the door downstairs in order to protect the house from invaders.

Yeah, I definitely needed a break. I dropped the phone back in the cradle and pushed back, gathering up the used coffee cups before tugging open the office door. As I started down the stairs, I wondered if I should fill my friend in on what had happened to me earlier this morning.

Before I reached the bottom, I had decided it could wait. There was already a niggling feeling in the back of my head that told me Ben and I would be spending a lot of time together in the very near future. Whether he knew it yet or not.

We might as well start off on a happy note; because I already knew what was looming before us would be far from pleasant.

CHAPTER 3:

I wasn't someone you could describe as a big fan of heights. Standing here at this particular moment, looking down through the railing from the top level of the old Peerless-Cross department store parking garage, smack in the middle of downtown Saint Louis, I was reminded of that fact in no uncertain terms.

The honest truth is that for the majority of my life heights had never been much of an issue. I hadn't spared as much as a moment's consideration to the idea of fearing them; at least not any that I remembered. But, of course, that was all before the night when a deranged serial killer had tossed me over the side of the Old Chain of Rocks Bridge somewhere near the middle of its span across the Mississippi river. Now to that, I had given more than just a passing thought. I had dwelled on it. And, to say the least, it was definitely something I wasn't going to forget. Not in this lifetime and probably not even the next.

Fortunately for me, the rope he had been trying to hang me with had held fast. The other bonus was that it had been wrapped around my arm instead of my neck. It was only due to this stroke of blind luck that I had the luxury of being able to recall that night in all of its Technicolor detail.

But that's another story, sort of.

Now, to clarify, I have to point out that I'm not one to panic or go into an immobile stupor due to a fear of heights— not at all. Whenever confronted by the vertical demon, I simply feel an involuntary catch in my throat and then experience that sinking flutter in the pit of my stomach that always precedes the 'fight or flight' adrenalin dump of fear. Of course, it is just about then that said adrenalin does exactly that— dump.

With a sudden flood into my circulatory system, the hormone embarks on an emotionally driven attempt to rescue me from the perceived danger. A few seconds later I, mutter some form of exclamation, the cleanliness of which is directly proportional to the height multiplied by the amount of adrenalin then divided by my heart rate. That accomplished, I remove myself from the situation.

For the most part, all it ever really does is make me tense muscles I don't even remember having and then battle a lingering headache for an hour or two.

"Sudden stop." My friend's deep voice uttered the two simple words from behind and above my left shoulder.

I glanced back without fully turning and questioned him. "Do what?"

"The sudden stop at the bottom," Detective Benjamin Storm returned with an almost jovial undertone. "Ya'know... It ain't the fall that kills ya', it's the sudden stop at the bottom."

It was comments like this one that had long ago convinced me that my best friend, a homicide detective with the Saint Louis City Police, would make the perfect wisecracking cop for a weekly television crime drama. He was loyal, honest, and good at his job. And, as evidenced by his most recent verbal observation, he was inextricably tied to clichés. There were even times when they would season his speech the same way some people salt their French fries— too much. Still, while not always an especially endearing quality, it was a part of his makeup, and I accepted it for the personality trait it was. Of course, accepting it didn't keep me from retaliating against it at times.

Like right now for instance.

"Not actually," I said as I turned, unsure as to whether or not he would take the bait I was about to toss before him.

I put my hand up to shield my eyes against the late morning sun. The sky was clear and the yellow-white globe had already driven the air temperature past ninety, with the relative humidity making it feel as if we were in a Jacuzzi. Worse yet, the hottest part of the day was still to come. Of course, that was just 'Mother Nature's Tourism Bureau's' way of saying welcome to June in Saint Louis, Missouri.

The only thing that made it bearable standing up here on the open concrete deck of the parking structure was the slight breeze rising and falling around us, and more importantly, the fact that a table in an air-conditioned restaurant was waiting for us down at street level.

I tilted my head up to look at my friend's face. While I wasn't the tallest person around, I was still of average height. Ben, on the other hand, took average and built upon it with reckless abandon. He stood a full six-foot-six and carried himself on an enviable broad-shouldered, muscular frame.

The sun silhouetted him so I had to squint in order to make out his angular face. Framing his countenance was coal black hair, worn as long as departmental regulations allowed. His dark eyes gazed out over high cheekbones, revealing little and missing nothing. It was impossible to look at him and not immediately know that he was full-blooded Native American.

"Whaddaya mean, 'not actually'?" he huffed.

And with that, we officially had the 'hook.'

On the fly, I dredged up an old childhood myth and applied my own twist to it. "What I mean is that you're dead before you ever hit the ground."

"Yeah, right."

"Seriously. The fear of falling is so intense that your system overdoses itself on adrenalin. It pretty much shorts out your nervous system and causes you to suffer a heart attack as you fall, end of story. You're a corpse before you ever hit the ground."

I watched his rugged features as his right eyebrow furrowed. I could literally see him rolling what I had said over and over inside his head, trying to get a handle on it.

"Bullshit," he retorted.

The one word comment wasn't exactly what you would call swallowing the 'line,' but I'd known he would be a hard sell.

"Oh yeah." I nodded vigorously as I spoke and offered up a bogus factoid to lend credence to my lie. "It's a known fact. Now, of course, the fall has to be greater than twenty feet for the fear to reach that level and cause your system to dump that much adrenalin."

He cocked his head to the side and gave me an unsure look.

I pressed on. "You know how when you fall you get that bizarre feeling in your gut like you just lost your stomach?"

"Like when ya' top a hill on a roller coaster, you mean?"

"Exactly. Well it's like that, but since you don't fall far enough you don't have the heart attack."

"No way. Hills on roller coasters are way higher than twenty feet." He shook his head as he argued.

"Sure, but that's different. Your subconscious knows you are in a roller coaster."

"You're just yankin' my chain."

"Why would I do that?"

"So what about skydivers?"

"Parachute. Again, the subconscious knows."

The look on Ben's face told me that he was struggling with this sudden contradiction of perceptions. He wasn't stupid by any stretch of the imagination, so I was actually surprised I'd managed to take it this far.

My friend slipped his hand up to smooth his hair and then allowed it to slide down and began to massage the back of his neck. He always performed this gesture when he was thinking hard on a subject.

"Really?" he eventually asked, giving his head a slight nod as he squinted at me.

Now, there was the 'line.' I thought about going for the 'sinker' as well, but I wasn't feeling particularly ornery today, and I doubted my luck would hold out. Besides, it had only been one cliché, not to mention that he was bigger than me and he had a gun.

I gave it a long moment before finally answering him with a simple, "No."

He shook his head and screwed his face into a frown. "Jeezus, Rowan, don't fuck with me like that."

"Hey," I splayed my hands out in a 'don't blame me' gesture. "You're the cop here. Aren't you supposed to be able to tell when someone is lying? Besides, I've never known you to be gullible. How was I supposed to know you'd fall for a line of BS like that?"

"Because it came outta *your* mouth," he replied with a grunt as he stabbed a finger in the air toward me. "I EXPECT everyone else to be lying but not you. And, you got so damn much trivia runnin' around in your head, I just figured maybe you knew somethin' I didn't."

"Well…" I shrugged. "Maybe I do on some stuff. Sudden stops at the bottom, though, not really my area of expertise."

"Yeah, mine either, but I've seen a couple of meat sacks sprawled out on sidewalks. The friggin' stop at the bottom's what did 'em in. Trust me."

"I'll take your word for it," I replied, consciously chasing away the visual his words had conjured, and then I paused for a moment before changing the subject. "So, I may be wrong, but I didn't think we came here to discuss the physics of falling from tall buildings. Or did we?"

"Nope." He shook his head. "But you were the one starin' off into space over here."

"I wasn't staring off into space."

"Yeah, Kemosabe." He nodded. "Yeah, you were."

I didn't issue another rebuttal. It occurred to me that perhaps my earlier self-assessment was in error. Maybe these days heights did make me seize up after all.

"So, speaking of lying, are we at least here to go to lunch like you said when you showed up at my door?"

"Yeah," he answered. "Why would I lie about that?"

"You tell me? It wouldn't be the first time you've used a free meal as a carrot to get me somewhere."

"C'mon, man, I told ya' already. This is my day off."

"I seem to recall you once telling me that you are never really off duty," I reminded him.

"Jeez, what are you, a freakin' tape recorder?"

I merely chuckled in reply.

"Yeah," he continued. "Maybe so, but even when I've done that to ya', I didn't screw ya' over on the deal."

"You sure about that?"

"Hell yes." He waved his index finger in the air to punctuate his comment. "I know for a fact that I still bought chow."

"I wasn't talking about the meal," I said as we began walking along the inclined parking lot toward the glassed-in elevator enclosure.

He ignored the comment. "Well, to be honest, I do have somethin' else I wanna do while we're here, now that ya' mention it. I need to hit *The Third Place* after we eat." He offered the name of the tobacco shop we both frequented with what could have easily passed for reverence. "You good with that?"

"Yeah." I gave him a nod. "I need to have Patrick order me some more *CAO MX Two's* anyway. It'll save me a call."

"You and those damn double maduros," my friend muttered.

"What's wrong with MX Two's?"

"Too strong, white man," he told me.

"Hey, I like what I like."

"Yeah," he said as he tugged open the door to the glass enclosure and motioned for me to go through. "I just wish you'd like somethin' else."

I shook my head as I entered the somewhat air-conditioned waiting area. "What does it matter?"

His matter-of-fact reply came as he followed me through the door. "'Cause I don't like 'em."

"So?" I queried, stabbing the call button for the elevator then looking at him with a puzzled expression. "You aren't the one smoking them."

"Exactly," he replied. "So if you don't smoke the ones that I like, then it makes it kinda hard for me to bum them off ya' now doesn't it?"

"Ohhh, now I get it." I nodded slowly. "You want me to smoke something you like so you don't have to buy any."

"Damn straight," he chuckled. "Cigars are expensive."

"So quit."

My friend looked back at me like I had suddenly grown an extra head. "Yeah, right. I already told ya' once today ta' quit yankin' my chain."

A sickly electromechanical ding announced the arrival of the elevator car. The signal was followed by the scrape and groan of the doors parting down the center with a moment's hesitation then sliding laboriously open. Looking through the widening gap, we could see the car still in motion as it rose the last few inches and then halted with a clunk and a shudder.

"Oh yeah," Ben announced. "This looks real safe."

"You want to take the stairs?" I queried.

"I'm thinkin' maybe yeah," he replied.

"The stairs are outside."

"Yeah, so?"

I held my arms out and glance around. "Hot out there, cool in here. Well, cooler anyway."

"Lemme see... Hot or splattered? Hot or splattered?" He motioned with his hands as if he were physically weighing the two options. "Considering the conversation we just had, I'm not all about splattered if ya' know what I mean. Elevator or not."

"I'm with you on that one."

He stepped back toward the glass door of the waiting area and tugged it open. At that moment, as if cued by some unseen director, our ears were met with what had to be the single most panicked scream I had ever heard in my life to date.

CHAPTER 4:

Training and experience instantly became the primary driving forces behind my friend. With a quick jerk, he flung the door wide and propelled himself through the opening, each of his motions deliberate and purposeful. His head twisted from side to side as he scanned the area. His right hand shifted immediately to his hip and rested on the grip of his nine-millimeter sidearm.

In the few seconds that followed the initial cry, time seemed to expand. Adrenalin injected into my system, this time for reasons wholly unrelated to heights, and in that instant, I experienced a complete lack of coordination. My brain began issuing commands that my body wasn't ready to accept but was forced to execute anyway. In a series of half-stumbling steps I twisted away from the elevator, aiming myself toward the exit. I reached for the door just as it was swinging shut, only to completely miss it with my hand and drive my shoulder against the metal frame instead. Before I could elicit my own surprised yelp of pain, a second scream echoed through the parking structure.

I had believed that the first wail was the most panicked I had ever heard. Without a doubt, the second one made that assessment null and void.

"Gotta be down!" Ben declared, bolting for the stairs at the opposite end of the elevator enclosure.

I ignored the stab of pain in my shoulder and ran after my friend. I apparently hadn't struck the doorframe hard enough to do any actual damage to myself, so it was really nothing more than an annoyance anyway. Ben was already rounding the first landing and taking the stairs in fours by the time I arrived at the top of the flight.

I was coming down from the initial adrenalin rush, and my coordination, while far from perfect, was returning. Still, not being possessed of the expanded stride of the giant Indian in front of me, I grabbed the rail and took the stairs in a more manageable two-at-once pace. I heard him come to a stop below as I quickly rounded the landing and shot down the second flight, hitting the bottom just as a third, more muffled scream sounded.

"Goddammit!" Ben exclaimed. "With the fuckin' echo, I can't tell for sure where it's comin' from!"

Again, a tortured voice cried out, this time with distinguishable words appended to the dire scream. "HELP! Somebody help me, please!"

Ben immediately cocked his head to the side then whipped around and flew by me, shouting, "Next level!"

I stepped back onto the lowest step for a split second to allow him past and then threw myself forward while keeping a firm grip on the handrail, using the momentum to swing me around to the next set of stairs.

Our frantic footsteps were thumping in the stairwell, inciting a disjointed rhythm that resounded through the concrete parking structure. Ben was well ahead of me, and I heard him hit the next level before I even reached the landing. I could hear him shuffling around as he searched for the source of the commotion. A pair of seconds later I bounded off the stairs just in time to see my friend wrapping his large fist around the grip of his pistol and sliding it out of the belt rig.

"Nine-one-one, Row." He called to me over his shoulder as he started across the yellow-striped concrete. "Tell 'em officer needs assistance, code one."

By the time he got the second sentence out of his mouth, he had broken into a dead run.

I pulled my cell phone from my belt and thumbed off the key lock then stabbed in the emergency number. I could hear an immediate click from the device as I placed it to my ear.

"Nine-one-one, what is the nature of your emergency?" came a tinny, female voice.

It occurred to me that at this point that I wasn't exactly sure what the emergency was. I looked up and in the direction Ben had run, looking for whatever he had spied. My friend had covered a fair amount of distance in the few seconds that had passed and was still barreling full tilt up the inclined parking lot. Well beyond him, near the opposite corner, I could see an intense struggle going on between a young blonde woman and an individual who was bear hugging her from behind. They were positioned near the back of a vehicle that was parked in the traffic lane with the trunk lid and driver-side door wide open.

They spun in a circle as the attacker slammed the woman against the side of the car, slipping slightly out of view, so I bobbed and shifted to see around the support pylons. The aggressor in the altercation was nondescript enough to defy identification, but based on stature and what few details I could make out, such as hair length, I assumed the person to at least be male.

They made a half-spin outward then back, bouncing against the rear quarter of the sedan. As they turned, I caught a quick glimpse of the woman's face. For some reason, she looked familiar to me, but at this distance that didn't really mean anything.

"Nine-one-one, what is the nature of your emergency?" the woman at the other end repeated, capturing my attention.

"I'm… I'm not sure," I stuttered and then began spilling the information as quickly as I could. "I'm calling for Detective Benjamin Storm with the city homicide division. He said to tell you 'officer needs assistance, code 1'."

"What is your location, sir?"

The old adage about not being able to look away from a train wreck passed through my mind as I continued staring, frozen in place and mesmerized by the crime playing out in front of me. I forced myself to quickly shift my glance to my friend, checking his progress, and then leveled my gaze back on the fight.

Due to the design of the structure, a low wall and cable barrier separated Ben from them. He was still running up the incline and would need to hook around the end before he would be within close enough proximity to confront the situation. He still had several feet to go before he could even make that turn.

My mind raced as I wondered whether or not we should have come at this from the next level up, but it was too late for that now.

"Sir, your location?" the voice barked from the phone.

"I'm sorry… The old Peerless-Cross department store parking garage, orange level," I replied.

"Is the detective injured?" she asked.

"No. He's trying to stop a carjacking, or a mugging or something, I'm not…"

I was interrupted by yet another scream that sounded vaguely like 'help', and I watched as the young woman broke partially free and suddenly lurched forward. Her attacker managed to maintain a grip on her arm and yanked it hard, knocking her off balance. She fell backward against the car, and as she came to rest against the fender, the man swung around in front of her. Without hesitation, he drew his arm back and landed a fist square into the young woman's face. Her head snapped back, and even at this distance, I could see crimson blood running from her nose.

"Damn!" I exclaimed and then remembering that the phone was still to my ear added, "He just hit her in the face!"

He drew back and hit her a second time then grabbed her by the hair and dragged her to the back of the vehicle. In a rough motion he rolled her into the trunk then slammed the lid shut and raced back to the open driver-side door.

"Sir, can you tell me what is happening?" the operator asked.

The audible thunk was still fading as Ben's authoritative voice boomed outward, ricocheting from the angular surfaces of the garage. "POLICE! STEP AWAY FROM THE VEHICLE NOW!" He was just reaching the corner and beginning to make the turn as he shouted, running with his weapon hand extended and trying to draw a bead on the man next to the vehicle.

"Sir, are you still there?"

"Gods! I think it's a kidnapping!" I exclaimed aloud, making the statement to myself as much as to the 9-1-1 operator.

The attacker had been pre-occupied with the struggling woman and only now noticed Ben barreling around the corner. He ducked quickly into the driver's seat, audibly wrenching the vehicle into gear and gunning the engine even before closing the door.

Tires squealed as the car sped forward, climbing up the incline toward the level above us. Ben slipped out of view behind a support pylon then reappeared on the opposite side, pistol stiff-armed before him and taking aim at the vehicle. I saw him snap his head in disgust as he realized it was too dangerous to take a shot with the victim in the trunk. He followed the tail of the car with his eyes as it screeched into the turn then whipped his gaze around and darted to his right toward the downward corkscrew of the exit lane on the corner of the building.

"Sir?!" I heard the faint but frantic voice issue from the cell phone and realized that I had allowed my hand to drop away from my ear.

I brought the device back up and began speaking, "He just shoved her into the trunk and sped off. Ben is chasing after them."

"Are you still in the parking garage, sir?"

"Yeah," I responded, realizing suddenly that I had to be her eyes. "Yeah, he was heading up, so Ben took off for the exit spiral. He's on foot."

"Sir, we are on the line with dispatch, and they have units responding to your location. I need you to stay with me."

I could hear the roar of the vehicle crossing above me on the next level, revving up then fading as it passed. My view of Ben was obscured by a row of cars occupying the spaces near the center of the level, so I began running up the incline. I was moving slowly at first then began increasing my pace as I tried to get in a better position to see the exit ramp. There was a squeal, another roar, and then the crunch of metal against concrete. Following that, there was nothing.

I broke past the line of cars and stumbled to a halt, directing my gaze through an empty parking space. In the distance, I could see Ben's form in a three-quarter silhouette as he stood at that level's opening to the exit, weapon at the ready.

I started to wonder if the vehicle above had crashed into one of the dividing walls, but then the relative silence was punctuated by the protests of its overtaxed engine as it started down the spiraling ramp.

The car suddenly came into view at the opening, and the tortured wail of scraping metal filled my ears. A pair of bursts from Ben's pistol abruptly punctuated the grating noise as he fired into the windshield of the vehicle.

I watched in horror as the front fender clipped my friend and sent him flying backward. The scrape of sheet metal against concrete began to fade as the vehicle continued down the ramp.

"He's been hit!" I shouted into the cell phone as I began moving once again, breaking into a run toward my downed friend. "Ben's been hit!"

I knew the operator was asking me something because I heard her voice issuing from the speaker, but I no longer had the device to my ear. I pumped my legs and arms as hard as I could, pushing myself up the incline and hooked around the parked vehicles at the end of the row. I had a lot of distance to cover, and I wasn't going to be setting any records for sprinting. By the time I was within forty or so feet of the arc, the exit came once again into view.

Not knowing how hard he had been struck or the extent of his injuries, I was fully expecting to see my friend in a crumpled heap. Instead, I was greeted by the sight of him on his feet, fully upright and very pissed off.

"Fuck ME!" he shouted across the lot as he limped forward. "Sonofabitch!"

"Ben!?" I barely managed to call out against my rapidly shortening breath.

He looked up and saw me running toward him. "Backup, Row. Fuckin' tell me I've got backup comin'!"

I waved the cell phone in the air then sucked in a quick breath and called out to my friend as I continued toward him. "The operator said units have been dispatched."

Below us, the fading sound of the scraping metal had now transformed into the clamor of squealing tires, and out on the streets, angry horns were beginning to blare.

The wail of emergency sirens in the distance was so faint they may as well have been a lifetime away.

CHAPTER 5:

"**N**o, I don't wanna go to the freakin' hospital," Ben's voice carried across the lot as he shouted. He continued walking away from the paramedic but looked back, pointing his finger as he added, "How many times do I hafta tell ya? Now leave me alone and let me do my job."

My friend was disheveled and still moving about with a limp, but other than that, he didn't appear to be seriously injured. But then, this was Ben Storm we were talking about. I'd seen him lie through his teeth to avoid going to a hospital, all because he had a phobia about needles, go figure.

Even though he had relayed a description of the vehicle to the 9-1-1 operator, it had all come down to placement and timing, neither of which factored in our favor. The car was gone before the first police cruiser even arrived on the scene. Between Ben, the parking attendant from the booth downstairs, and me, we had been able to provide miscellaneous details about the sedan as well as a license plate number. Since the car had Illinois tags, officials from that state's patrol division were already in the loop.

I was keeping my ears open for lack of anything else to do. Thus far, from what I had been able to pick up from the various conversations I overheard, there was presently an alert out on both sides of the river but still no sign of the vehicle.

I felt like I should be doing something. I'm not sure what, but that wasn't the point. I hated the idea of being useless with regard to everything that had transpired. But, I suppose being ordered to 'wait over there until we need you' can tend to do that to a person. All in all, I was starting to feel like an extra in a B-movie but without the paycheck or catered buffet lunch.

At the moment, I was watching from the stairwell, sitting on the third step up from the bottom and trying my best to stay out of the way. So far, I had been managing to do so but not without some shifting and shuffling to allow the occasional cop to pass. From what I could see going on in front of me, this was probably the only spot where I was going to have any success whatsoever in the endeavor.

I looked away from the scene long enough to glance at my watch. Somewhere around an hour and a half had slipped past us since this all began: ninety minutes disappearing into history only to be relived by eyewitness accounts, repeated over and over to the point of tediousness. And then repeated again.

Still, even though I had only been asked to tell my accounting a half-dozen times so far, it felt as if I had been in this parking garage just shy of forever. On the other hand, it seemed like the span of interconnected moments had gone by in a sudden blur. I suppose it was yet another of those peculiar stress-induced dichotomies that blindsides you following an unexpected adrenalin rush.

As I watched, I took particular note of the fact that the number of warm bodies occupying the parking garage had increased several fold over what it had been just thirty minutes ago. Now, while I was no expert, unfortunately, I was also not a stranger to crime scenes. The ratio of cops to the singularity of the crime seemed to me like it was already moving beyond overkill. On top of that, something told me there would be even more by the time it was all said and done. There was something more to this than met the eye; even the eye of a witness, or so it seemed.

For the time being, it looked like I was stuck here. Ben was still limping around angrily, but now he was heading in my direction. He had been barking at anyone in a uniform and even some who weren't. This was far from the first time I had ever seen him agitated, but there was something different this go around. It wasn't that this scene felt any more tense than any other I'd been on, just different. There was an overtone of urgency that went beyond any I'd felt before. To me at least, there was even a palpable sense of personal fear coming from the cops on the scene. Not just for the victim but for themselves as well. That was something I had never before experienced at a crime scene, and it bothered me.

I already knew my friend wouldn't be going anywhere for a while. His day off had ended the moment he heard the woman scream. As for me, even if I wanted to get myself a taxi home, I was a witness and I'd already been told that I would need to give a statement. I had thought I'd already done that when I told them what I saw the first six times, but apparently that was not official. When they would be getting around to me again was anyone's guess.

"Hey, Row," Ben greeted me sullenly as he drew himself up against the stairwell railing.

"Hey, Chief," I returned, starting to pull myself to my feet. "You need to sit down?"

He motioned for me to stay seated. "Sit, sit. I'm good."

"You sure?" I asked, stopping mid-rise. "It looked to me like you had a pretty serious limp there."

"I'll live."

I lowered myself back to the step and regarded him for a moment. "The paramedic threatened you with a hypodermic, didn't he?"

"Yeah." He let out something between a laugh and a sigh. "The words 'tetanus booster' got mentioned."

"You probably need one."

"We'll see. Nothin's broke." He gave a slight nod as he spoke, but the expression on his face was saying 'hell no.'

"So much for lunch, eh?" I offered after a moment.

My friend was looking out across the lot, massaging the back of his neck and lost in thought.

I spoke again, "Ben?"

He started and glanced over at me, "What? Oh, yeah. That's a bust for sure. Maybe dinner depending on how this goes."

He brought his hand up to smooth his hair then allowed it to fall back down to his side. He huffed out a heavy breath then addressed me with an added seriousness, "So listen, Row, the Major Case Squad is gonna be runnin' this one."

"Okay," I acknowledged. "That's not a big surprise."

"What I'm tryin' to tell ya' is that Bee-Bee is on her way," he emphasized. "Hell, she's probably downstairs already."

"Bee-Bee," I repeated and rolled my eyes. "Just what I need."

The moniker struck home. It was short for Bible Barb, which was probably the least offensive of the nicknames given to one Lieutenant Barbara Albright. She was a cop and a self-serving bureaucrat all rolled into one package, and she was in command of the MCS.

Like most of those her rank and above, she spent the majority of her time pushing a pencil. But that is where the similarity ended because unlike the others, she had a penchant for getting directly involved. Unfortunately, her involvement was not always a plus.

What had garnered her the various epithets was her self-righteous attitude. That, combined with the fact that she not only wore a badge but also a prominently displayed gold cross around her neck, had earned her the reputation of 'God's Personal Cop.'

She consciously built upon that distinction as well. She wore her badge like a shield and wielded the cross like a sword, using its symbolism like a heavy-handed weapon with which to mete out her own interpretation of justice. To Lieutenant Albright, the laws she was sworn to uphold were but secondary suggestions to the commandments held within the Holy Bible; and she was more than happy to tell you so in no uncertain terms.

While this didn't necessarily make her popular among the ranks, she still had her supporters, and there were enough of them to make a difference. She managed to skirt around various departmental policies and flaunt her religion without reproach. Still, none of this would really matter at all were it not for one simple fact: she absolutely despised me.

While her initial hatred of me began simply because of my Pagan roots and religious practices, my being a Witch was not the only reason for her disdain. Unfortunately, I had no choice but to accept responsibility for a portion of it, as I had been partly responsible for sparking an Internal Affairs investigation of her.

Just a handful of months ago, I had been the object of a

madman's quest to eradicate WitchCraft from the face of the earth. Eldon Andrew Porter had taken the lives of several innocent people in the process, two of them my friends. Before all was said and done, I had come close to losing my own more than once.

During a single day that had been spawned by nothing less than hell itself, far too many things had gone horribly wrong. Information had been leaked; potentially dangerous mistakes had been made, and events that could have only been deliberate sabotage had occurred. All of these things had placed my life in jeopardy at every turn and had almost allowed Porter to escape. I, among a few others, believed that 'Bible Barb' had been responsible for it all.

While in the end she had admitted to using me as the bait to draw Eldon Porter out of hiding, she had been officially cleared of any other wrongdoing and was given nothing more than an administrative slap on the wrist. As for me, I was never fully convinced of her innocence and didn't know that I ever would be.

At the same time, her own convoluted thinking made her believe that I was the root of the problem. She had even commented during a newspaper interview that had it not been for me, at least two of the victims would still be alive. I was already torturing myself over that very fact on a daily basis, and I sure as hell didn't need her fueling the fire for me. I was doing a fine job of that all by myself.

"Look, Row, if it was up to me, I'd get you outta here right now before she gets here," Ben offered. "But we both know that ain't gonna happen."

"Yeah," I nodded. "It's okay."

"If it's any consolation," he added, "I ain't exactly one of her favorite people either."

"Yeah, I know."

He wasn't lying. He had gone toe to toe with her for the sole purpose of defending me and had done serious harm to his career in the process. While my friend was still a homicide detective, Albright had seen to it that he was no longer allowed to work as a member of the Major Case Squad as long as she was in command. That serious blow to his advancement was yet another thing I held myself responsible for, even if he didn't.

"So, I don't want to sound crass," I said. "But what's so important about this particular case that she feels like she needs to get her fingers in it?"

"Nice try," he returned. "But it ain't funny."

I shook my head and looked back at him with a puzzled expression. "What are you talking about?"

"C'mon, Row," he chided.

"No, really."

He arched an eyebrow then cocked his head to the side, squinting while looking at me hard. "You aren't friggin' serious are you?"

"Serious about what?" An audible note of annoyance crept into my question.

"Do you have any clue at all what you just witnessed?" he asked.

"I'm guessing a kidnapping."

"Yeah, and?"

"And what?" I asked, growing more impatient.

He shook his head and gave me an incredulous look. "Don't you ever watch TV?"

"Sometimes. So what?"

"You watch the news, right?"

"Ben, will you just spit it out?" I demanded.

"You're gonna sit there and tell me you didn't recognize the woman who was grabbed?" he asked.

I flashed on a quick memory of the blonde victim and remembered having had a passing thought that I should know her.

I shook my head and shrugged. "Not really. She looked a little familiar, but other than that…"

"She's all over the news," my friend returned, shaking his head as well. "The Gateway Club Telethon, all kinds of charity events… You know, anything with a cause and a donation jar."

"I'm sorry, Ben," I barked the words. "But I still don't know who she is. Now, would you please quit trying to make me feel stupid, and just clue me in?"

"Jeezus, Rowan," he blurted, still shaking his head. "That was Brittany Larson."

I looked back at him, stunned as the name sunk in, and my brain made the connection. "You mean…"

"Yeah, I mean Brittany freakin' Larson," he replied. "The goddammed mayor's daughter."

CHAPTER 6:

Ben was busy going over the turn of events with some other detectives when Lieutenant Barbara Albright arrived. She strode purposefully out of the elevator, headed straight for the door of the enclosure and whipped the door open with a swift yank.

Her low-heeled pumps were clacking out a determined cadence across the concrete decking of the parking lot as she started for the opposite end of the structure. I almost wish I'd had a camera on hand to catch the look on her face when she glanced to the side and saw me sitting on the stairs.

She stopped dead in her tracks, staring at me as her lips drew into a thin frown. After a brief pause, she unbuttoned her jacket and marched toward the stairs, coming to a halt in front of me and placing her hands on her hips.

"Would you mind explaining just exactly what it is that you are doing here, Gant?" She spat the words more as a demand than as a simple question.

She was slight but still altogether imposing just given her attitude. Her appearance placed her somewhere in her mid fifties even with her shoulder length hair having turned prematurely white. She was dressed in a dark grey pantsuit that looked like it came from an upscale department store. Felicity probably could have taken one look and spouted off the name of the designer, but as for me, well, all I knew was that it looked like money was involved.

Her hands, strategically placed to reveal more than just a glimpse of her sidearm, now pushed back the folds of the double-breasted jacket. I'm sure it was an intimidation tactic, probably something learned by all cops, but I had been around this sort of thing far too much. The sight of a gun on someone's hip was old hat to me.

As in my past dealings with her, she was coming across as the mother that every kid on the block was afraid of, and she wasn't planning to do anything to change that opinion. If nothing else, I would say that she was trying to bolster it.

As usual, the gold cross was suspended from a chain around her neck, obvious against the white background provided by her blouse. The breast pocket of her jacket held her badge case, shield flipped outward and prominently on display.

"It's really a simple matter of being in the wrong place at the wrong time, Lieutenant," I answered with forced civility as I rose to my feet.

I was mutely beating back my desire to launch into a string of unpleasantries aimed directly at her. I knew such an act would bring me nothing but trouble, but I was having a hard time explaining that to my subconscious mind.

"Oh, I'm sure that it is," she remarked sarcastically. "Go on. Tell me."

"Lunch," I replied.

"Lunch?" she repeated.

"Yes," I returned, pointing over her shoulder at a group of officers near the actual scene of the abduction; in particular, at Ben's back. "Feel free to ask Detective Storm over there. We were going to lunch and just happened to be waiting for the elevator when it all happened."

"Storm is here, too?" she barked, turning to look in the direction I indicated.

"Yes, as a matter of fact…"

Her hand came up to cut me off as she spoke, "You wait right here."

"Sure," I answered. "I've got no place else to be."

I don't know if she heard me or not because she was already stalking away toward Ben. While I couldn't see her face, I had the distinct impression she was no happier to see him than she had been me.

"That was pleasant," Ben muttered the sarcastic remark as he cranked the steering wheel of his van and backed it out of the parking space.

I didn't wait for the follow-up I knew he was going to utter, "Don't say 'like a root canal', Ben."

"How'd you know I was gonna say that?"

"Experience," I replied.

"Hmmph," he grunted. "So what'd she say to you?"

"She demanded to know why I was here, so I referred her to you."

"Thanks a lot," he told me with no sincerity whatsoever.

"What about you?" I asked. "From where I was, it looked like she was having a meltdown."

"Yeah, pretty much," he answered. "She was just her normal pissy self up 'til she found out I discharged a coupl'a rounds into the vehicle. That's when she lost it."

"What did she expect you to do?"

"Hell, I dunno." He shrugged then cranked the steering wheel to guide us into the downward exit spiral. "Throw myself in front of the fuckin' car I guess."

"You pretty much did," I observed.

"Yeah, well I guess I didn't get run over enough for her liking."

It was just before 2:30 in the afternoon, and the scene had officially been cleared. Skid marks had been measured, paint scrapings had been taken, and photographs snapped from every imaginable angle. None of it seemed to me like it would do any good, but there were procedures to be followed, and my opinion of them amounted to very little— in fact, nothing.

"So what happens now?" I asked.

"You're in for a treat," he returned. "We get to go back to headquarters and tell our stories to some more coppers."

"I was afraid you were going to say that."

The syncopated tone of a cell phone began its rising chirp. I didn't recognize the tone, so I knew it wasn't mine. Ben reached to his side and fumbled the warbling device from his belt, swallowing it in his large hand.

"Storm," he huffed when he got it up to his ear.

As if the mood in the vehicle needed any further darkening, I felt it grow just that much colder in that very instant. A swirling turmoil of pain, anger, and confusion was emanating from my friend, and as I watched him listening to the cell, I saw his shoulders physically droop.

"I know, I know," he finally said. "But have you noticed the news?"

He fell silent for a moment, and his tumultuous emotions became even more tangible.

"Listen, I can't do this right now…" he said into the phone, voice rising slightly. "No… No, I'm not… Look, we'll have to talk about this later… I can't…"

He stopped mid-sentence, pulled the device away from his ear and regarded it with an angered glance. He stabbed the off button with his thumb then threw it into the console between us as he muttered, "Shit."

We had just rounded the last turn of the spiral and now sped down the exit ramp, finally coming to a halt at the booth. Ben flashed his badge, and the attendant nodded as he waved us through.

Remnants of the splintered black-and-white-striped barrier gate were piled off to the side of the concrete island. The metal portion of the lift arm protruded as a twisted stub from the mechanism rendering it totally useless, all of it the visual evidence of the kidnapper's hasty exit.

My friend edged the van forward and after a quick glance in either direction, pulled into the afternoon traffic. I had always made a rule of staying out of Ben's business. If there were something going on in his life he wanted you to know about, he would tell you in his own due time. Asking him before he was ready only served to drive him away and make him bury the subject even deeper.

However, in extreme cases I was known to break my own rules, and this was one of them. I watched him in silence as we navigated the traffic to the corner and then stopped and waited for the traffic signal to turn.

"You okay?" I finally asked.

"Yeah, I'm fine," he answered tersely. "Why?"

"I really couldn't help but overhear..." I let my voice trail off, leaving the rest of the sentence unspoken.

"Sorry about that," he replied. "Forget about it. It's nothing."

"It didn't sound like nothing, Ben."

"I said forget it," he snarled.

We made the rest of the trip to police headquarters in complete silence.

"Where are you?" My wife's voice issued from the speaker on my cell phone.

It was rapidly approaching six P.M., and I was still downtown though fortunately, not sitting on the concrete stairs in the parking garage. I had finally lost count of how many times I had given my accounting of the events and to how many cops I had given it. They eventually concluded that with the exception of a few adjectives and conjunctions, the story was always the same. No more or less information than the previous recitation.

I don't guess I could blame them for trying. I was as aware as anyone else of what can be seen but not consciously remembered.

"What, no hello?" I asked.

"I said hello when I answered the phone," she replied. "Now, where are you?"

"You wouldn't believe me if I told you."

"Try me" came her guarded response.

"Downtown with Ben."

"Tell me you're at a bar, Rowan," she half asked, half instructed, but the tone of her voice told me that she knew that wasn't true.

"Sure," I answered. "It's called Police Headquarters."

"Oh Gods, Rowan," she moaned, then asked, "The seizure?"

"No... Yes... Maybe... I don't know yet" was my response, confusing as it was to us both. "Have you heard about Brittany Larson?"

"How could I not? It's been all over..." she started then stopped herself mid-sentence. "Oh, Rowan, no... What? What happened?"

"Kidnapped as far as anyone can tell right now," I answered. "Although I don't think whoever did it has any qualms about hurting her."

"How do you know that?"

"Well... I kind of had the bad fortune of being a witness to the abduction, and it was a bit violent."

"You what? How?"

I gave her a rundown of the day's events since we had last spoken; all of which had finally culminated in me using my backside to warm a molded plastic chair next to Ben's desk for the past few hours.

The promised lunch had eventually happened sometime around three in the afternoon. Unfortunately, it had taken the form of a stale jelly doughnut and a cup of what the officers of the homicide division referred to as coffee. My personal jury was still deliberating on that point.

I told her about that too.

"So anyway," I continued. "Ben is going to be tied up down here for a bit longer, but they've given me the okay to leave."

"Give me twenty minutes," she replied to the unasked question.

"I'll be waiting outside."

CHAPTER 7:

"**B**ar food?" I said to my wife. "I've been stuck down here all day with nothing but a stale doughnut and bad coffee, and you want me to eat BAR food?"

"It's not 'bar food'," she replied as she dropped the Jeep into third gear and veered onto the Kingshighway exit from westbound Interstate 64. "It's PUB food."

The top was down, and the warm wind was whipping through the open cab of the vehicle. There was still better than an hour of sunlight left in the day, so it was still hot and humid. Fortunately, the temperature had dropped off by a few degrees, so it wasn't quite as bad as it had been earlier in the day; if you liked steam baths, that is. Although, I had to admit the artificial breeze generated by the motion of the Jeep went a long way toward making it tolerable.

"There's a difference?" I asked with a chuckle.

"Aye, and you'll be finding out soon enough, then," she answered, dredging up her inherent Celtic brogue with no effort whatsoever. Truth was, it was probably more of an effort for her to hide it.

Felicity was second-generation Irish-American, but you wouldn't know it to look at her— or especially at times, to hear her. In fact, one would think she had just stepped off an airplane direct from the Emerald Isle.

Her looks were straight out of Celtic myth. She was petite, standing shoeless only slightly more than five feet tall. Her complexion was milky white and smooth like porcelain with the only exception being a light spate of freckles across the bridge of her nose. Bright, green eyes peered out of her doll-like face, and the whole package was framed by spiraling locks of fiery auburn hair that hung down past her waist. If a toy company were to produce a doll to represent Ireland, my wife would make the perfect model for it.

If the looks weren't enough, she was also possessed of the

stereotypical temper that, whether politically correct or not, was so often associated with both the ethnicity and hair color. Fortunately, it wasn't one that was easily ignited although I had managed to spark it on a few occasions.

Growing up, she had spent almost as much time in Ireland as the United States, even attending college there; hence, she was never completely devoid of a light, Irish lilt in her voice. However, get her around her family, get a few alcoholic drinks in her, or wait until she got overly tired, and her guard would drop. The lilt would morph into a thick brogue, replete with slang and colloquialisms the average American was hard pressed to understand. We'd been married better than twelve years, and she still came up with some that perplexed me.

When she really got riled up, she would even mix languages on you. While certainly not fluent in Gaelic, she had more than a passing familiarity with it. That particular vocabulary, however, consisted of innumerable curses and derisive phrases born of the ancient language, and if provoked, she was more than happy to use them.

On the flip side, she even knew a few of the endearments, and I'd had the good fortune to hear them whispered in my ear from time to time.

"I love it when you talk with an accent," I said, shooting her a grin.

"Aye, what accent?" she asked, still laying it on thick and laughing as she spoke. "You're the one with the accent, then."

"Right," I answered. "Midwest plain and dull. So what's the name of this place again?"

"Seamus O'Donnell's."

"Sounds Irish," I joked.

"Well, duh," she returned.

"So it doesn't sound familiar. Have we been there before?"

"No."

"Hmmm. I thought we'd been to every Irish pub in Saint Louis by now."

"They've only been open a few months."

We had made the loop and merged into the afternoon traffic. She sped up to the next intersection, just catching the light before it switched and turned the vehicle to the right from Kingshighway onto Oakland.

"So how do you know this so called 'pub food' is any good if we haven't been there?" I asked, shooting a glance over at her.

Her hair was pulled back, but loose strands were whipping about her face as she looked over and smiled at me. "I said we haven't been there before. I never said that I hadn't been there."

"Oh," I exclaimed playfully. "So you went there without me, did you?"

"Hey, a girl's got to have lunch, doesn't she?" she laughed.

"Yes, I suppose she does," I replied. "So do they have colcannon and Dublin coddle?"

"Among other things, yes they do."

"And Guinness, of course?"

She glanced at me and raised an eyebrow, giving me an unmistakable stare.

"Okay," I held up my hands in surrender. "I know, I know. Stupid question."

"Well, it IS an Irish pub, Rowan," she laughed.

She downshifted as the traffic signal ahead of us winked yellow, and we rolled to a stop at the white line just as it switched over to a glaring red.

Considering the events of the day, I was surprised to find myself in such a good mood. Truth is, even if today had never happened, I still would have been surprised. I hadn't felt this good about life since the first time I'd been cold-cocked by an unwanted ethereal vision of a horrific murder; and that had been almost four years ago.

A far cry from past experiences, my seizure-induced headache had faded relatively quickly. None of the typical creepy sensations that always accompanied these events had plagued me in the least. Even though I could still feel a troubling shadow falling across my life yet again, it was faint and nebulous. Nothing like the dark foreboding that always forced me into a brooding stupor.

I didn't know if it was some sort of artificially conjured euphoria brought on by my wife's contagious good mood, or what. Maybe I was just getting better at keeping myself grounded and centered. As basic a task as that is for a Witch, it was something I'd been having trouble with for some time now. In the end, I simply didn't care what it was, but I knew one thing for sure— I planned to enjoy every minute of it.

I simply felt good. I was truly relaxed and happy for the first time in a very long while.

I felt my wife's fist thump hard against my shoulder as she playfully punched me. "What are you grinning about, Row?"

I hadn't realized that the broad smile had carved itself into my face, but I suppose it was just part of the mood. "Nothing," I replied, rolling my head to the side so I could look at her. "Not a thing."

"Sure, whatever," she replied with her own smile, then asked, "So, did Ben say when he would be getting out of there?"

"Probably in a couple of hours is what he said. Why?"

"Well, it's only a little after six right now, so that would still be early yet," she replied, pulling her hand across her forehead and dragging some of the wild strands of hair from her face. "Maybe he and Allison could join us later for a pint or two."

"I'm not so sure about that," I replied, remembering that I had purposely not told her about the phone call I'd overheard. Truth was, I didn't actually know to whom Ben was talking on the other end, but I had my suspicions. Still, it was best not to start a rumor, even if it was only between us.

"Come on," she urged. "It'll be fun. *The Don't Be Brothers* are supposed to be playing tonight."

"The what?" I asked, furrowing one eyebrow and squinting at her.

"*The Don't Be Brothers*," she repeated. "It's a play on…"

"Yeah, yeah, I get it," I told her as I nodded my head. "I'm just not sure I want it."

"They're really good, Row. I've heard them play before."

"Okay, so speaking of playing, what DO they play?"

She shrugged. "Irish folk songs, what else?"

"You mean Irish drinking songs."

"Of course, they're playing in a Pub."

"So that means we have to sing along."

"Your point?"

"I don't know any of the words, and I doubt if Ben or Allison do either."

"Aye," she said as she shook her index finger at me. "But I do."

"Okay," I gave in, reaching to my belt and grabbing my cell phone. "I'll give him a call, but I don't make any guarantees."

I wasn't actually sure if I would be able to reach him, but I was willing to try. If I was correct, and the earlier call had in fact been from Allison, maybe they had managed to patch things up by now. An evening out might even be just exactly what they needed. After all, it was Friday. They were adults. Their son was old enough not to require a sitter, so that shouldn't be an obstacle. Looking at it that way, there was really nothing to keep them at home.

I thumbed in the speed dial code and put the phone up to my ear. I heard the ringer at the other end issuing from the earpiece, but halfway through the trill it suddenly became muffled. As I listened, a heavy, rhythmic thrum was starting to fill my ears and was effectively dulling the ambient sounds. I glanced around expecting to find a car with a radio blasting heavy metal music somewhere nearby. If that was the source of the noise, however, I couldn't locate it.

When the second ring sounded, a coppery metallic taste began creeping up the back of my tongue, and I instantly tensed. The sensation wasn't new to me, and I desperately feared what I thought it was about to bring. The false sense of security I had felt a few moments ago was now fleeing in earnest.

A tidal wave of déjà vu slammed into me full force, and I knew it was more than just a trick of an overactive imagination. I had been here before, experiencing an unwanted psychic event from the passenger seat of my wife's Jeep. I opened my mouth to warn her of what was about to happen only to have my words halted in my throat by the sound of Felicity's own frightened voice.

"R... Ro... Rowan..." she stuttered, a note of confused terror like I'd never heard from her before was interwoven through the syllables of my name.

I turned my head only to see my wife's normally beautiful face drawn tight into a pained grimace. Her teeth were clenched, and her back began to arch, pressing her body hard against the shoulder belt. A split second later she was shaking uncontrollably. Her head snapped back, thudding against the headrest as her eyes began to roll upward.

The Jeep suddenly lurched forward as her feet slipped from the clutch and brake, her right foot landing momentarily on the accelerator. I dropped the phone, grabbing at the steering wheel as I wrenched the stick shift into neutral. The engine coughed then settled to an idle, but we were still rolling forward.

"Felicity!" I screamed, but she couldn't hear me. I could only barely hear myself as the driving rhythm continued to grow inside my head.

Her body was bucking in violent spasms against the safety harness, and she continued to vibrate with the physical tremor. Her arms were drawn up to her chest, turned inward, and her hands were postured like tight paws, her fingernails digging into her palms.

A trickle of blood ran from the corner of her mouth as she frothed, and I could see that she was biting her tongue. The back of her head continued to slam against the padded headrest, and I mutely thanked the ancients for it being there.

Sharp but distant noises began to invade the heavy beat in my head, and I recognized them as blaring horns. A quick glance forward told me that the traffic signal had switched to green. We were moving forward, rolling by the grace of leftover momentum, but it was far from what traffic would bear. Still, it was too fast for my liking considering the circumstances.

"Felicity!" I called out again, ignoring the futility of the action.

I was struggling to guide the rolling Jeep while at the same time unbuckling my own seatbelt. My first thought was to get my foot on the brake and bring the vehicle to a stop, but I wasn't the most limber individual on the face of the planet, and I wasn't sure I could get around my wife's stiffened legs. In a hostile attempt to assume control of my emotions, a wave of panic began sweeping over me as it elected to challenge my desperate concern for Felicity and move itself into the top position.

A prolonged whimper emanated from my wife as she jerked against the tensed muscles of her body, and I realized it was a scream that couldn't escape. The other realization that struck me square in the face was that the tables had turned. I was helplessly watching her go through all of the things she had stood by and watched me suffer so many times before.

I managed to release the catch on my shoulder harness and twist toward her, levering myself against the back of the seat. As I brought my leg up, my knee cracked hard into the dash, sending a lance of pain through the joint. I barked out an expletive as I pitched forward, and the back of my hand raked against the jangling key ring that hung from the ignition switch.

It was then that I realized the panic had taken over long before I'd ever noticed its icy fingers clawing at my stomach. A brief but welcome stab of lucidity hit me, and the logic it brought along set off a chain reaction in my brain. I reached for the keys and gave them a hard twist, switching off the engine. That done, I quickly wrenched the gear shift into first with a hard shove, doing little good for the transmission but bringing us to a lurching halt.

The dark music was pounding inside my skull as I scrambled from my seat amid the dulled blare of horns. Angry motorists were pulling around our stalled vehicle and speeding off, narrowly missing me in the process. The commotion began to die down only after I could be seen pulling my wife's still-seizing body from the driver's seat.

It was official. I was no longer in a good mood.

CHAPTER 8:

"**L**emme get this straight…" Ben's voice came at me over the cell phone. "Firehair went all *Twilight Zone* this time instead of you?"

Firehair was just one of the nicknames he had for my wife, but it was by far his favorite.

"Yeah, kind of," I answered. "Or maybe in addition to."

Felicity and I were parked diagonally across from one another in a booth at Seamus O'Donnell's. She had pressed herself as far into the shadows of the corner as she could get, and I was keeping a close eye on her.

The pub wasn't my first choice of places to be given the situation, but it was the closest for what she needed. Fortunately, the evening rush had not yet started, so I was able to carry on the phone conversation without yelling over the noise of a crowd or stepping outside.

"What?" he chirped, a note of concern leaping into his tone. "You were both all zoned out in a moving vehicle?"

"No, not exactly," I explained, still trying to get a handle on what had happened myself. "I had some ethereal background noise in my head, but I never stepped over the line. I did that this morning before you came by."

"Whoa, whoa, whoa! Do what?" he barked again. "So you did the la-la land thing this mornin', and you're just now tellin' me?"

"I didn't have anything to connect it with at the time, Ben," I replied. "Then the whole thing with the kidnapping happened… I mean, give me a break."

"So you think it all has something to do with the Brittany Larson abduction?"

"Maybe. I don't know."

"Don't be so goddamned overconfident, Rowan," he chided.

"Cut me some slack, Ben," I replied stiffly. "I'm still a bit rattled.

This kind of thing has never happened to Felicity before. I'm not real happy about it, in case you haven't noticed."

"Yeah… Sorry. You're right," he apologized. "So listen, where are you two right now? Home?"

"No." I shook my head out of reflex as I spoke. "We're in a bar down on Oakland called Seamus O'Donnell's."

"What'd ya' go to a bar for?" he asked, a note of confusion in his voice.

"It was the closest place where I could get her out of the heat and let her rest up," I told him. "Besides, it's actually where we were headed for dinner anyway."

"She doin' okay?"

"Seems to be." I looked across at Felicity. She was still at the far end of the booth but had leaned forward now, elbows on the table, eyes closed, and fingers slowly massaging her temples. "But judging from the looks of her and speaking from experience, she's got a killer headache at the moment."

"What about you?" he pressed. "You gonna go all loopy or anything?"

"Like I actually know when that's going to happen, Ben?"

"Yeah, forget I asked." He huffed out a heavy sigh then muttered, "Jeezus fuck, white man. What am I gonna do with you two?"

"Wish I could help you there, Chief," I told him. "I'm wondering the same thing myself."

"Not what I wanted to hear," he replied. "So listen, stay right where you are. I'm pretty much done here, so I'm gonna shake loose and come down there."

"We'll be waiting."

I thumbed off the phone and clipped it back onto my belt then turned my full attention back to my wife. Her eyes were still closed, and she was carefully working her fingers from temples to forehead and back again. Her lips were parted slightly, and I watched the rise and fall of her chest as she struggled to regulate her breathing. I knew exactly how she felt, and it was killing me to see her like this.

Of course, I suppose now I knew exactly how she felt when the roles had been reversed.

"I'd like to tell you it gets better," I said softly. "But, it's more like you just get used to it."

"*Fek*," she muttered the colloquial Irish profanity.

"Yeah, I know," I agreed.

"How do you do it?" she asked then moaned, still not opening her eyes.

"I wish I could answer that," I replied. "I just do. If it's any consolation, I'd rather not."

"Aspirin," she murmured.

"Let me see if I can get you some," I told her as I started up from my seat.

"Purse. Side. Tin," she told me, exaggerated economy in her selection of verbiage.

I pulled her purse across the table and rummaged about in the side pocket. Under any other circumstances I wouldn't have dreamed of sticking my hand into the carryall. As I had told my wife countless times before, a woman's handbag seemed to me to be a kind of tame black hole: a place where an impossible number of items disappeared and could only be found by the woman who owned the receptacle in the first place. At the moment, hers was definitely living up to that assessment.

"Left. Bottom. Yellow tin." She offered another set of terse instructions.

I pushed my hand deeper into the pocket and finally managed to withdraw the sought after container of aspirin. I sat it on the table and pushed it over to her then started sliding out of the booth as she slitted her eyes and reached for the tin.

"I'll go get you some water," I told her.

"Black Bush," she asserted.

"No whisky with aspirin," I replied. "Water."

"Black Bush," she repeated.

"Water."

She tossed the tin in front of her and it bounced across the table, tablets noisily rattling around inside. Then it slid off the edge and clattered to the floor.

"Black Bush." This time it was a demand.

I knew exactly where she was coming from, and I didn't fault her a bit. The truth was that the aspirin really wouldn't do much good for the kind of headache she had anyway. Not that booze was any better remedy, but it would help take the edge off.

"Shot or rocks," I conceded with a soft sigh.

"Bottle," she replied.

"Slow down," I said to my wife as she drained the tumbler and clacked it back onto the wooden table with a heavy thunk. "That's your second double."

Her hand was still wrapped around the glass, and her head was tilted back, face pointing upward to the ceiling. She drew in a deep breath and then exhaled heavily, puffing out her cheeks as she did so.

"Aye, but I said bottle, not double," she stated as she lowered her gaze down to meet mine.

"Give those a chance to work," I told her. "They aren't even in your bloodstream yet."

She frowned back at me but didn't argue. She slouched down in her seat, and a moment later I felt her sneaker-clad feet slide up onto the bench next to me. She reached up and pressed her palms against either side of her head as if she were trying to squeeze it back into shape.

"This sucks," she moaned.

"I know," I replied.

I was fully aware that the words were of little consolation, but they were the best I had to offer at the moment. I wanted desperately to ask her about the experience. But, she needed some time to come to terms with what had happened, so I didn't broach the subject.

Usually such an ethereal event came with some manner of built-in, albeit obscure, reference to something in the here and now—although, admittedly, mine from earlier this day had held no such prize. Neither had the similar ones I'd suffered through at the beginning of the year.

Patrons were starting to fill the establishment as round one of the dinner rush came upon us. It hadn't reached the point of obnoxious as yet, but the noise level was rapidly approaching that of annoying static. It didn't seem to be bothering Felicity, though.

"You look like shit." Ben's voice cut through the hum of the growing crowd.

I looked up to see him standing over my shoulder, his gaze locked on my wife.

"But you're still a hell of a lot prettier than paleface over here." He jerked a thumb at me as he added the comment.

A waitress sidled up to the table and shot me a questioning look. "Do you folks need anything?"

"I'm good," I replied.

"Black Bush, neat, double," Felicity chimed in.

"Felicity…" I admonished.

"All right then." She cut me off with an annoyed tone lacing her words. "Jamieson, neat, double."

I shook my head and waved my hand in surrender as I looked up at the waitress. "Give her whatever she wants."

"Black Bush," my wife chirped.

The waitress craned her neck and looked up at Ben. "How about you?"

"Beer," Ben told her.

"We have Guinness on tap," she offered.

"No honey." Ben shook his head. "Beer isn't s'posed to be black. Bring me somethin' in a mug that's cold, fizzy, and beer-colored."

"Whatever you say." She shook her head back at him then before she turned and walked away, she added rhetorically, "Do you want me to bring you a straw with that?"

"Friendly place you picked here." Ben made the sarcastic comment as he slid into the booth next to Felicity.

"Aye, you're in a pub, Ben," my wife informed him, still lounging in her seat. "Quit bein' a Colleen."

"She's doin' the accent," he remarked as he looked over at me. "The *Twilight Zone* thing do that to her?"

"Leave me alone," Felicity muttered.

"I'm sure it wore her out, but I think the two double Irish whisky's are to blame," I replied.

"Yeah, okay." He nodded, glancing over at her then back to me. "She's not gonna start talkin' that gibberish is she?"

"*Duairc*," Felicity chimed.

"That answer your question?" I asked.

"She just called me a name, didn't she?"

I shrugged. "Probably."

"I said you're a rude man," she offered.

"Well, at least this time you got the gender right." He shook his head and looked back to me. "So explain it to me. What's up with the squaw doin' the la-la land thing? I thought that was your gig."

"Me too," I answered with a nod. "I'm not sure what's going on there myself."

"Will you quit talking about me like I'm not here, then," Felicity insisted.

"Okay. Chill." Ben jumped the tracks and boarded another train of thought. "So what about this mornin'? What's up with that?"

"Again, I don't know." I shrugged. "The episode was almost exactly like the ones I had back in January."

"You mean when you were floppin' around like a fish outta water when Porter was..." his voice trailed off at the mention of the name.

"Yeah," I acknowledged and finished the sentence for him. "When Porter was trying to kill me."

"Sorry," he said sheepishly. "Didn't mean to dredge that up."

"No problem. It's not something I've managed to forget yet anyhow."

"So I thought those stopped after he was locked up?"

"They did. Until today that is."

Ben frowned hard and stared back at me. Without a word, he reached to his belt and pulled out his cell phone. After an aborted attempt, he managed to key in a number with his thick finger and tucked the device up to his ear. I had a feeling that I knew what he was getting ready to do, and I wasn't sure I wanted to know the answer he was seeking.

"Yeah, Roy?" he said after a moment. "Yeah, it's Ben Storm. Not much, you?... Yeah, so listen, I need a favor. Can you check somethin' for me? Yeah, I need status on an inmate... No, don't have his number, but you'll probably remember 'im. Uh-huh... Name's Eldon Andrew Porter... Yeah, thought you would... Yeah. Not a problem. Yeah, on my cell. Great. Bye."

As Ben ended the call, the waitress came toward the table, expertly maneuvering through the crowd with a drink-burdened serving tray held above her shoulder. In a practiced motion, she swooped it down and plucked a tumbler full of whisky from it then slid the glass in front of Felicity. Next, she placed a pint glass of beer in front of Ben. In a reverse motion, she hefted the platter back up to her shoulder and regarded my friend.

"Cold, fizzy, and well, yellow-colored," she said, reaching with her free hand into the change pouch around her waist and withdrawing a straw. She tossed it in front of Ben and shot him a smile as she walked off. "Enjoy."

"Jeez..." he muttered, shaking his head at me.

"So you don't really think Porter has escaped or something do you?" I asked abruptly, the edginess in my voice was obvious even to me.

"Don't know," he replied. "But we'll know shortly. Roy's an old friend of mine, and he works for the Missouri Department of Corrections."

"But wouldn't there have been some kind of bulletin or alert or something if he'd escaped?" I pressed.

"Depends, Row."

"That doesn't make me feel very secure, Ben."

"Listen, Kemosabe, don't get all worked up," he told me. "I'm just checkin' to be sure. C-Y-A and all that shit."

"Yeah, okay."

I knew that my tone was less than convincing. My friend shook his head then brushed the straw out of the way and lifted the pint of beer. After a long swallow, he rested it back on the coaster and watched it intently as he slowly spun the glass.

"So you said on the phone that you were movin' when Felicity went all la-la," he finally said, bludgeoning the stalled conversation in a new direction with a blunt segue.

"Yeah." I nodded. "Kind of. When she seized, her foot slipped off the brake, and we started into the intersection."

"Not too fast then?"

"Not really I don't guess." I shrugged. "But I still probably didn't do the transmission any favors."

"How so?"

"When I popped it into gear."

"I don't follow."

"To stop the Jeep," I explained. "I switched off the key and then popped it into gear. Kind of an abrupt stop, but it worked."

"I thought you said you weren't movin' too fast?"

"We weren't really. Just rolling more or less."

"Just rollin'?"

"Yeah, why?"

He creased his forehead. "Then why didn't ya' just pull the emergency brake?"

I closed my eyes and hung my head in sudden embarrassment as the mental picture of the Jeep's center console painted itself in my brain.

Ben looked back at me, his face spread into a grin, and I could tell that he was already formulating a wisecrack. Fortunately for me, his cell phone began its low warble, cutting him off before he could utter the taunt. He motioned me to wait and answered it. "Storm. Yeah. That was fast. Yeah. Yeah… You're sure? Okay, thanks, Roy. I owe you one… Uh-yeah," my friend hesitated for a moment before continuing, "Yeah, I'll tell 'er. Bye."

A slightly pained look crept in to replace his grin, and I wasn't sure why, but for some reason, I could tell that it came from something other than the query about Eldon Porter.

I raised an eyebrow and dipped my head at him. "All good?"

"Yeah," he replied as he fumbled to put the cell phone back on his belt, finally giving up and dropping it on the table in front of him. "Porter is locked away safe and sound, preaching to all the other wingnuts in the population."

"Great." I frowned.

"Hey, a coupl'a minutes ago you were getting' ready to panic on me," he observed. "What's up?"

"No I wasn't."

"Yeah, right. What's the deal?"

"Okay, maybe I was," I admitted. "A little. But I guess maybe I was still just hoping for an easy explanation to all of this."

"Yeah." He nodded. "Woulda been nice, but look at it this way; at least he's not on the street."

"True. So since we've ruled that out, maybe it is the Brittany Larson thing after all," I offered with a shake of my head, not really believing it myself. "But that wouldn't explain why I was having the seizures in January."

"No, it wouldn't," he agreed.

I picked up my pint of Stout and took a sip then set it back on the table. The murmur of the crowd was ramping up to a dull roar now, and I looked out of the booth, glancing around at the milling bodies.

Across the way, the bar itself was stacked two deep with people waiting for drinks or simply inhabiting their claimed bit of real estate at the polished, wooden counter. I knew it should be approaching eight, and the band would be playing soon. At that point, we would be unable to carry on any kind of worthwhile conversation, not to mention the fact that I was in no mood for singing along with drinking songs. I suspected that Felicity no longer was either.

I scanned the wall, looking for a clock, and my eyes came to rest on the television set perched on a shelf above the rows of liquor bottles. I watched as a news update filled the screen, absently taking note of the ever-changing price of gasoline.

When the tube flickered and displayed the picture of a twenty-something young woman inset over the shoulder of the anchor, my heart skipped a beat. Beneath the photo was the caption, Tamara Linwood.

Neurons fired in rapid succession, flooding my brain with a not-so-distant memory as I stared at the picture.

Gruesome discovery.
Badly decomposed human arm.
Shallow grave.
Body may be that of Tamara Linwood, the grade school teacher who disappeared from the parking lot of Westview Shopping Mall back in January...

The memory of the phantom metallic tang tickled the back of my tongue, and I closed my eyes. I definitely wasn't going to call it easy, but there it was— the explanation for at least a part of my day.

And, I was absolutely certain that I didn't like it.

CHAPTER 9:

"Tamara Linwood," I said aloud, turning my attention back to Ben.

"Do what?" he asked with a puzzled look.

"Tamara Linwood," I repeated, pointing at the screen across the room. "On the TV."

He twisted in his seat and shot a quick glance over his shoulder. The news anchor had already moved on to the next story, but my friend managed to pick up on what I'd meant anyway. "What? You mean the missing teacher?" he asked. "So, what about 'er?"

"That's why the seizures. She's got to be what this is all about."

"How do you figure?"

"It adds up," I offered. "She went missing in January, right?"

"Yeah." He nodded.

I continued. "And they found her remains this morning."

"That hasn't been confirmed."

"I'm confirming it for you, Ben. Those are Tamara Linwood's remains."

"You sure?"

"They've got to be."

"Listen, Row." He held up his hand and nodded quickly. "I know better than to not believe what you're sayin', but we've been down this road before. I can't just march into my lieutenant's office and announce something based on one of your feelings. Besides, that case belongs to the MCS... And well... you know that situation."

I gave him a frustrated nod. "I know, but they ARE her remains. I'm sure of it."

"How?" he asked.

"I just told you," I replied. "The timing of the seizures. It makes sense."

"To you."

"I thought you believed me?"

"I do, white man," he appealed. "Kinda. I mean I know you're makin' a connection with somethin'… or someone… or whatever the hell, but how do ya' know it's actually her? How do you know it's not someone else who got murdered in January? I hate to say it, but we had a few cases runnin' then besides hers."

"It's a gut feeling, Ben."

"And I can respect that, believe me, but you still don't have any proof. Listen, since we're talkin' about a schoolteacher, look at it this way. It's just like homework from eighth grade math class. Just havin' the answer ain't good enough. You gotta show the work that gave ya' the answer."

"With the ethereal, that is easier said than done," I replied.

"Yeah, I know. But lemme ask you this: So what? So what if they are her remains?"

"Then maybe we can figure out who killed her."

"I'm pretty sure that's the plan whether that's what's left of her or not."

"You know what I mean, Ben. Maybe I can help."

"How? I thought you said your little trips into the *Twilight Zone* hadn't been real informative."

"They haven't," I agreed and then added, "Yet."

"Yeah, and there's the catch. Yet may never happen."

"Come on, Ben. You know how quickly these things can turn."

"Yeah, I do, but which way is it gonna turn? This whole thing might just go away like it did back in January."

I didn't want to admit it, but he had a valid point. Still, for me, there was an overwhelming imperative. The psychic episodes were happening to Felicity now. I simply wasn't willing to stand by and allow that to continue, be it a half dozen more times, or only one. Something had to be done.

"Maybe, but I don't think so. This feels different," I appealed.

"Hate to say it, Row, but…"

"…I've got to give you more than that," I completed the sentence before he could. It was a lament that I'd heard from him more than once, so the lyrics were all too familiar. "Well then," I switched tactics, "How long before they know for sure about the identity?"

"Not my department." He shrugged. "Could be tomorrow, could be next week. Could be never, I guess. Dunno."

"Rowan?" Felicity interjected.

"What's up, honey?" I turned to her. "You okay?"

My wife was still lounged in her seat, arms folded across her chest. Her head was tilted back, and her eyes were closed. She actually looked relaxed for the first time in the past couple of hours.

"We'll need to go before too long, then," she murmured. "I have papers to grade for class tomorrow."

I knew she wasn't fully conscious of what she had just said. I had been in such a state before, myself. She was simply repeating a memory that wasn't even her own. While it was a far cry from the 'work' Ben said I needed to show, in my mind her words served to verify the revelation I had just espoused.

I slowly turned my face back to Ben but didn't utter a sound. I allowed my wife's comment to stand alone as my personal vindication. He looked over at Felicity for a moment then back to me.

"She's teachin' a photography class somewhere, right?" he finally asked, but I could tell from the tone of his voice he already knew the answer.

I just shook my head.

My friend's hand slipped up to his forehead, as if on automatic pilot, then slid slowly back, smoothing his hair. When his fingers came to rest on his neck he spoke. "Okay. Fine. I don't know what good it'll do, but I'll make some calls."

Felicity was still sleeping when the phone rang the next morning. I had just finished filling my coffee cup for the third time and was walking out of the kitchen when the device emitted its annoying demand for attention. I took a step back and plucked the receiver from the cradle without even looking at the caller ID box.

"Hello?"

"I wake you up?" Ben asked at the other end.

"Nope. Neither has the coffee," I quipped.

"That's 'cause you don't make it strong enough. You need some cop coffee."

"I'll pass. I think that cup I had yesterday is what kept me up last night."

"See what I mean?"

"Because it was eating a hole in my stomach," I added.

"Shoulda had another doughnut. They soak up all the bad shit."

"Yeah, right. I'll still take a pass on it."

He chuckled. "Your loss."

"That's a matter of opinion, Ben," I told him then took a sip of my java. "So what's up?"

"You want the good news or the bad news first?" he queried.

"Depends. How bad is the bad?"

"Bad enough. I've been re-assigned to the Major Case Squad."

"I thought that was a good thing?" I questioned.

"Yeah, well, it's the good news too."

"Ooo-kaayyy," I replied slowly. "I'm assuming there's an explanation to go with that?"

"Good news, I'm back on the MCS. Bad news, I'm workin' the Brittany Larson abduction with the Bible Bitch." He offered the matter-of-fact explanation like someone who had not quite come to terms with having been condemned.

"Lucky you."

"Yeah," he agreed sarcastically. "Lucky me."

"So what brought this on do you think?" I asked.

"Who knows?" he replied. I could almost see him shrugging at the other end. "Got the call this morning. I'm thinkin' maybe the fact that Mandalay's the lead agent coulda had somethin' to do with it."

He was referring to Constance Mandalay, a mutual friend and special agent assigned to the FBI's St. Louis field office. It stood to reason that the Federal authorities would have been called in since it was a kidnapping. And, considering that they had worked together before, Constance might well have requested him to be a part of the team from local law enforcement. In a sense, that was slightly amusing itself, because the first time the two had met they had absolutely despised one another.

Still, it was surprising that Lieutenant Albright would be willing to give in, considering her personal mandate regarding Ben's involvement with the MCS; unless, of course, she had her own motives, that is.

"Makes sense," I acknowledged, then voiced my thought. "But, what about Albright?"

"Search me," he replied. "But you'd better bet I'll be watchin' my back. Somethin's hinky with that if ya' ask me."

"Yeah. Good idea," I agreed. "But, hey, at least you're back in the fold. That's good news."

"Yeah, I guess. I'm not so sure I'm all that excited about a Feeb fightin' my battle for me though."

"Look at it as reinforcements," I offered.

"Yeah, sure." He didn't sound convinced.

I decided to maneuver away from what was obviously a sore spot. "So do they have any leads yet?"

"They're workin' on a couple, but I haven't got the full run-down. Headin' in for a briefing in about forty-five minutes."

"What about the car? You got the license plate number, right?"

"Car was found abandoned in North County," he replied. "No fuckin' idea how they got that far without gettin' popped, but they did. Both it and plates were on a hot sheet. Car got jacked in Racine, Wisconsin. Plates were off a van registered to a homeless shelter in Chicago. Both of 'em were stolen weeks ago."

"Great," I offered with a healthy dose of sarcasm. "No evidence though?"

"The crime scene guys have been all over it. Found Larson's blood in the trunk. Some hairs. Plenty of prints but still no hits on

AFIS yet." He referred to the automated fingerprint identification system. "So yeah, there's evidence all right, but this ain't a TV show. Evidence helps convict, not necessarily find."

"Yeah, you've pointed that out before."

"The thing that's got 'em worried right now is that we're comin' up real fast on twenty-four hours, and there hasn't been any contact from the kidnapper yet."

"That's unusual I take it?"

"Yes and no. Usually if you're gonna get a ransom demand, you get it within the first twenty-four."

He didn't have to tell me what it meant if no such demand was forthcoming. My own tortured imagination was taking care of that just fine.

"But there are exceptions, right?" I asked.

"Hell, there're always exceptions," he sighed. "But the odds do a big nosedive if ya' know what I'm sayin'."

"Yeah," I replied. "I know what you mean."

"So listen, Row, there's another reason I called." He proceeded to steer the conversation back onto the original path. "About the whole Tamara Linwood thing from last night."

"Yeah, do you have something?"

"Nothin' you're gonna like," he continued. "I made some calls, but it ain't good. The real deal is I'm not tight with anybody who's workin' it."

"Nobody?"

"Nope. Nobody. The case has actually aged enough with no new leads that it kinda got back-burnered for a while. There're only a coupl'a coppers assigned to it at this point, and they're disciples of her holiness, Bible Barb."

"Okay, so what about the remains? Did they make an ID yet? Wouldn't that get them rolling?"

"They're still waiting for results," he answered. "There wasn't much left, so it might all come down to DNA."

"I seem to remember DNA takes awhile," I remarked.

"Yeah. Could be a coupl'a weeks."

"What about dental?"

"Between you and me?"

"Sure."

"Seriously, Row," he pressed. "What I'm about to tell ya' is not for public consumption."

"I understand, Ben," I acknowledged. "What is it? Did the killer pull her teeth or something?"

"There's no head," he replied succinctly.

"You mean…" I allowed my voice to trail off.

"I mean whoever killed her sawed her head off, and it didn't get buried with the rest of the remains," he answered.

"Gods…" I muttered.

"Yeah."

A memory flitted through my brain, and enough of it made an immediate impression on me to spark a question. "Wasn't there another murder similar to that awhile back?"

"Sarah Hart," Ben answered. "Disappeared from the same parking lot. Remains turned up in a wooded area several months later. No head. That's why that info hasn't been released about the Linwood case yet. Not until we get a handle on it at least."

I let out a heavy sigh. "Haven't we had our quota of serial killers yet?"

"Guess not." His voice held a disgusted tone. "Shit, Row, statistically there are more of 'em out there than you imagine. The connection between crimes just doesn't always get made right away."

"Maybe so, but I still want to know what's making me a magnet for their victims."

"Yeah…" he responded, voice quiet.

I stared at the floor for a moment, listening to the silence that had swollen between us. In the edge of my vision I could see a quarter-sized pentacle resting against my chest. The five-pointed star enclosed by a circle was dangling from a chain around my neck, and I couldn't remember the last time I had taken it off. It was a symbol of man, spirit, and the elements— a symbol of my faith. It was a constant reminder of the path I had chosen long ago and of my identity as a Witch.

At this particular moment, I wished that I could take it off and shed that identity in a bid to stave off the horrors I knew were soon to come. But, as surely as I knew they were coming, I also knew the piece of jewelry was only a physical symbol. I could not change what I was or what I was destined to do that easily. In fact, I doubted I could change it at all.

"So it all hinges on the identity of the remains right now?" I finally asked.

"Yeah," he replied. "The general feelin' is that it's her. They're workin' on that assumption, but until it's official, no one's jumpin' to any wild conclusions. Right now they're workin' a partial print but dunno if that is gonna go anywhere."

"So where does that leave us for now?" I asked.

"That's the thing, white man," he replied. "It kinda leaves us nowhere. Pretty much me working the Larson abduction and you doin' your thing with computers."

"This is really going to heat up if those are in fact Tamara Linwood's remains, isn't it?"

"Yeah. Yeah it is."

"So, what about the seizures?" I asked.

"What about 'em?" he asked rhetorically. "I told ya' the deal on that last night."

"But what if Felicity has another one?" I pressed. "What if I have another one?"

He huffed out a sigh and then said, "There's nothin' I can do, Row. If there was, you know I would. So... So, maybe you two shouldn't be doin' any drivin' for a while."

CHAPTER 10:

"**Y**ou know, you've been avoiding talking about this all day," I said to my wife.

It was now rapidly approaching seven-thirty in the evening, and she was rushing around the house haphazardly stuffing ritual items into her nylon backpack. As usual, she was running late.

Physically, she had bounced back from the episode the previous evening much better than I had expected. In fact, on the outside, if I hadn't been a witness to it, I wouldn't have been able to tell anything had happened. Still, I knew something had to be going on behind those green eyes, and she wasn't being very forthcoming. Scratch that; she was all but denying it.

I had filled her in on the conversation I'd had with Ben, but much to my dismay, she had simply taken it all in with calm detachment. I'm sure it was largely due to the seizure she had experienced, but the radical shift in her personality was disconcerting to say the least.

"There's nothing to talk about," she told me matter-of-factly.

"I know better than that, Felicity," I replied. "Think about who you're talking to. I've been there, remember?"

"Exactly, so you know there's nothing to talk about," she returned.

"Excuse me?"

"Nothing." She shrugged. "I saw nothing. Just like you."

"You must have seen something," I countered. "What about the grading papers thing?"

"I don't even remember saying that, Row."

"But you did, whether you remember it or not."

"Okay, so I said it. Your point is?"

"That you were channeling the spirit of Tamara Linwood," I said. "Or her memories at least, which means recent experiences can't be far behind."

"So?"

"So you have to have seen something, it's just not in your conscious mind."

"Good."

"What do you mean, 'good'?"

"I mean, good. Maybe I don't want it to be in my conscious mind."

I shook my head harshly. "You aren't like that, Felicity. You and I both know it. You aren't going to run from the responsibility."

"Maybe I don't want the responsibility," she spat back. "Did you ever think of that?"

"Do you think I wanted it?" I returned. "It pretty much just got dumped in my lap."

"And it's been fucking up our lives ever since," she stated with enough bluntness to give me pause.

"I haven't exactly got control over it you know," I replied sharply.

"That's not what I'm talking about," she answered.

I shut my eyes and rubbed my forehead for a second before reopening them and letting out a heavy sigh. "You're right. This whole conversation has gotten off track."

She looked back at me wide-eyed, gave her head a slight shake, and shrugged again. "Has it?"

"Yes it has. My original question in all of this is *why*. *Why* is this happening to *you* now?" I submitted. "*Why you* instead of me?"

"Not instead. It happened to you too."

"You're being evasive, Felicity. You know what I'm talking about."

"Coincidence. Sympathy. Destiny." She offered the words in a quick stream and then followed them up with a quick change of subject. "Can you hand me that copy of *Everyday Magic* on the table there?"

I looked at her in silence, inspecting her face carefully. There was something just not right about the way she was acting and moreover, the way she felt to me, and I didn't mean the current argument.

She had erected an ethereal wall about herself, creating a shield against the outside. It was something she had automatically done the moment the psychic episode had ended last evening. I knew it was an act of self-preservation, and it was exactly what any Witch in her position would do. That, in and of itself, was a good thing; but, she was keeping me out as well, and that bothered me.

I kept telling myself that the enforced distance was just because of the newness of the situation and though she wouldn't directly admit it, because of the fear I knew she must be experiencing deep down inside. I had lived with the very same emotion swirling in my gut for long enough to know the pain.

Still, I couldn't help but feel there was something more going on. I just couldn't get it to sit still long enough to peg exactly what it was.

She looked back at me questioningly and raised an eyebrow. "It's right there. Behind you. Please?"

I twisted and picked up the book then slowly handed it to her.

"Thank you," she said as she took the tome from me and then stuffed it into her backpack. She continued flitting about the room as if the previous conversation had never occurred.

I continued watching her and resigned myself to the fact that I wasn't going to be able to pressure her into talking to me about this. I suppose it wasn't all that much different the first time it had happened to me, but that didn't make it any easier to take.

"After what happened yesterday, I'd still be a lot more comfortable if you rode with someone," I finally said.

"Okay," she replied. "I'll ride with you."

"Funny," I told her. "Very funny."

"I was being serious," she answered without looking at me.

I borrowed a page from her current playbook and ignored the comment. "Maybe you should beg off and just stay home. They'll be fine without you for one evening."

"Can't," she told me. "I'm the one giving the lesson tonight."

"So postpone it."

"No."

"Why not?"

"Because I don't want to. Besides, what good is a Coven meeting without a Priestess?"

"Felicity…"

She turned to face me, shuffling things in the knapsack and then zipping it shut. "Come with me."

I shook my head. "You know I can't do that."

"Rowan…" she spoke my name then looked away while chewing at her lower lip. She brought her gaze back to my face and adopted an almost pleading tone. "This was your decision alone. No one in the Coven wanted you to leave."

"I had to," I answered succinctly.

"No you didn't," she appealed. "No one blames you for anything that happened."

"I don't know about that."

"I do," she shot back. "You are the only one to hold yourself in contempt. You had no control over what a crazed maniac did."

"He did it because of me," I replied.

"If it hadn't been you, it would have been someone else who was openly Pagan. You know that."

"But it wasn't someone else. It was me, and he killed them to get to me."

"So?" she spat. "That doesn't make it your fault."

"It's my fault that I didn't stop him."

"You DID stop him."

"Not in time to save Randy or Millicent."

We stood looking at one another. A gelid hush frosted the air between us, expanding out to fill the room. The rhythmic tick-tock of the swinging pendulum on our wall clock clacked dully out of time with my slow breaths as I watched my wife. The passing seconds kept appending themselves to the end of the measure, lengthening the painful silence with each beat. As if pre-ordained to mark the end of the torture, the hammer on the timepiece drew back with a mechanical whir then fell hard, striking a single blow against the chime. The initial sharpness of the bonging sound slowly flowed through the room, softening as it faded to nothingness.

"I have to go," Felicity stated simply, slipping a single strap of the knapsack up over her left shoulder as she brushed past me.

I didn't turn nor even say a word. I heard the deadbolt snap and the door creak slightly on the hinges as she swung it open. I could sense her hesitation as she stood in the open doorway, and I could feel her eyes on my back.

"You know, Rowan," she finally said. "You can stay gone for a year and a day, or you can stay gone forever, it's up to you. But a Coven is family. You know that. You have people... people who are more than just friends that are worried about you. They're your family, and they want to help if you'll just let them."

She grew quiet for a moment, and I slowly turned to face her. She was standing with one hand on the doorknob, staring back at me with a pained sadness in her face.

As I watched her, she swallowed hard then spoke again. "You know... This will never be over until you stop feeling sorry for yourself."

With that, she was gone.

I was still brooding when the dogs began barking at the heavy noises on the front porch. I shushed them as I glanced away from the television to quickly check the clock. Only a little over an hour had passed since Felicity had left, so it didn't seem likely that she was already returning.

I muted the sound on the television and listened closely, wondering if the noise had simply been one of the cats leaping down from the ledge and thudding on the decking of the porch. It wouldn't be the first time such a thing had set off what we affectionately called the 'dog alarm'.

There was nothing but ambient sound for a moment, and I was just about to up the volume again when a scrape and thud sounded. The new thump was followed by the creak of the screen door levering open. The canines stood their ground and renewed their vocal attempt to keep the intruder at bay, our English setter emitting a dangerous sounding growl that was echoed by a throaty rumble from the Australian cattle dog.

A moment later the doorbell rang, sending its harsh tone echoing through the house. The dogs immediately exploded once again into angry barks meant to repel the invader.

I wasn't expecting anyone, and I couldn't imagine who would be dropping in unannounced this late in the evening. Even Ben normally called, albeit at times while he was already standing on the porch, but he called nonetheless.

A paranoid thought raced through my head, and my heart seemed to stop as an artificial hollowness filled my stomach. My subconscious assumed control, and I was gripped by a sudden fear that something was wrong. Given the situation, the first thing that came to mind was that Felicity had been afflicted with another seizure while behind the wheel of her Jeep and that she had been in an accident.

I jumped up from the chair and strode quickly to the door, not even bothering to look through the peephole before unbolting the lock and swinging it open.

The sudden impact of a massive fist against my shoulder was pretty much the last thing I had been expecting.

CHAPTER 11:

I stumbled backward and let out a yelp of pain as I reached for my shoulder. The force of the impact had caused me to spin a quarter turn away from the door. My primal gut reaction was to keep that momentum going until I reached the ninety-degree point and then run as fast as I could in the opposite direction of the threat. However, my socially ingrained, testosterone-induced reaction was to defend my castle.

I quickly recovered my balance and twisted back toward the open door, certain that whomever it was attacking me would be only a hair's breadth from landing another punch. Out of instinct, I brought my arm up to block the expected blow and braced myself against its onslaught. I was already clenching my fists into hard balls, determined that even if I took the first two punches, I was going to give the next three.

I shot a guarded look past my arm in an attempt to see my attacker, expecting to come face to face with some brazen home invader. Instead, I found Ben holding up the doorframe with his shoulder. He stared back at me with a tired grin.

"Howth'hell'are'ya'?" he bellowed, creating a single word from an entire sentence.

"That depends on if you're going to hit me again," I answered, slightly miffed.

"Sorry 'bout that, whyman," he mumbled. "Didn't mean ta' hitcha' that hard. Was jes' s'posed ta' be a frenly punch ya'know."

I rotated my shoulder as I rubbed it with my hand. There was still a good deal of dull pain working its way through the joint, and I winced as it popped. I suppose it didn't help any that he had connected with my left shoulder which was the one Eldon Porter had driven an ice pick into the first time he'd tried to kill me. I'd had surgery to repair the damage that had occurred from both that and the subsequent struggle, but to this day, it still bothered me. I guessed it probably always would.

"I'll live," I told him, my voice still a bit edgy. "Just don't do it again, please."

"Yeah, no prob, Kemonas… Kesomob… Kenomos…"

"Kemosabe?" I offered.

"Yeah, that."

The glazed look in his eyes and the slurred speech were the first two indicators to grab my attention, so I didn't actually need to smell the brewery riding along on his breath to know he was all but obliterated. However, there was no avoiding it. I could only recall having seen him this far gone once before, and that was very early on in his career as a police officer. He was a young, far from streetwise uniform, and he had been the first to respond to a particularly heinous murder-suicide. It had affected him deeply then, and as seasoned— almost even jaded— as he had become now, I was certain that it still did to some extent. Evidence that the old adage about never forgetting your first time applied to just about anything, good or bad.

"Tell me you didn't drive yourself over here," I said, refraining from making any drunken Indian jokes. Sober, I knew he would laugh. In this condition, well, let's just say I didn't want to test any theories.

"'Kay, I won't." He pushed away from the doorframe and stepped in, stumbling over the threshold in the process. "Ya'oughta have somon fis that."

"Gods, you're even more cliché when you're drunk," I muttered.

"Whassat?"

"Nothing." I shook my head and pushed the door open wider as I motioned him in. "Get in here and sit down, Tonto. I'll go put some coffee on."

"I'll hava'beer," he told me as he dropped himself onto the sofa with a heavy thump.

"Don't have any," I lied.

I stepped forward and looked out into the driveway. His van was nosed in diagonally across the double lane of concrete, effectively blocking any entry or exit. I had already made a mental note to at some point get his keys away from him. I appended it to include repositioning the vehicle so Felicity would be able to pull in when she got home.

"Scosh then," he announced.

"Don't have any of that either." I continued down the path of untruthfulness as I closed the door and bolted it.

"Burrbahn?"

"Nope." I was heading for the kitchen now, letting him run down whatever list he could come up with.

"Vokka."

"Can't say as that I have any of that either," I called out.

"How'bout killya?"

I poked my head back out of the kitchen to look at him with a furrowed brow. "What?"

"Killya," he repeated. "Ya'know, killya. Iss Messican."

"No," I replied as I made the connection. "I don't have any Tequila. But I do have coffee."

"Shit," he mumbled.

I stepped back into the kitchen and started the coffeemaker's carafe filling from the filtered tap. While the water was rising, I reached into the cabinet and retrieved the coffee grinder and a bag of beans labeled 'breakfast blend'. I poured a measure of the roasted coffee into the bowl of the grinder, thought about it for a moment and then added an extra handful. I wasn't going to be able to duplicate Ben's 'cop coffee', but I could at least make it a little stronger than usual.

"Yo whyman," Ben's voice boomed through the house. "Wheresa squaw?"

"Coven meeting," I called back.

"Spooky," I heard him say, then pause. "Why you ain't there?"

"Long story," I answered.

"Tell me a shtory."

"Some other time," I said.

After adding the fresh grounds along with a small pinch of coarse salt to the filter basket, I poured in the water and switched the device on. I started to return the grinder and bag of beans to the cabinet but decided against it and left them where they were. I had a feeling it was going to be a long night.

My own earlier introspection was still floating around in the back of my head, but I consciously put it aside for the time being. I had my suspicions about why my friend was currently parked on my couch in a state of advanced inebriation, but my brain was also developing new theories with each passing second. The only way I was going to know for sure was to hear it directly from him.

Still, whatever it was that had brought him to this state, he had sought refuge here for a reason; and it was a good bet that the reason was to talk.

He was loyal to a fault and had been there for me more times than I could count, so the very least I could do was listen and be there for him.

I walked back into the living room to find my friend in a staring contest with Dickens, our black cat, who was perched on the end table quietly inspecting the boisterous human anomaly. As I pulled my rocking chair around to face the sofa, I took the opportunity to look him over myself. The fact that I could see a pistol riding on his hip and his badge clipped to his belt immediately dispelled one of my theories— he hadn't been fired or suspended.

"Coffee will be ready in a few minutes," I offered. "Here's an idea. Why don't you tell ME a story?"

He pointed at Dickens and then looked over at me. "I thing yer cat hase me."

"I think he's confused by you," I replied. "Can't say as that I blame him."

"You confused," he asked, his head bobbing as he tried to focus on me.

"A little, maybe," I returned. "Mainly wondering why you're sitting in my living room totally wasted."

"'Caush I've been drinkin'."

"No kidding. But I've known you a long time, Ben. You don't drink like this."

"New hobby," he mumbled.

"You might want to think about picking a different one."

"Yathink?"

I nodded. "Yeah."

"'Kay, I thought 'bout it," he said almost immediately.

"Yeah, well you might want to try it again when you're sober," I instructed. "So, why don't you tell me what's up."

"Opposite of down," he cackled.

"Yeah, you're a regular comedian," I returned with a frown.

"Oh'yeah," he said suddenly, a distant but serious look washing over his face. "Iss her."

"What?" I asked with a shake of my head.

"Her," he repeated, tossing his hand limply outward in an uncoordinated attempt to point. "Iss her."

I followed the haphazard thrust with my eyes and looked back over my shoulder at the muted television. A news update was playing out on the glowing screen, with a picture of Tamara Linwood inset at the upper corner.

"You mean they identified the remains?" I asked as I turned back to him.

"Uh-huh," he grunted. "Iss her."

I wanted to seize on that point and run with it, but I knew he was in no condition to follow through. I resigned myself to the fact that this was something that would need to be addressed later. How much later was the question.

"I don't think that's why you came here, Ben," I pressed.

"Hellno, I came here ta' visit my friend. You seen 'im? Shortguy, rise a broom." He cackled again.

I was just about to sit back and give up on the conversation when I heard the hissing burp of the coffee pot as it finished its brewing cycle.

"I'm going to go get us some coffee," I told him flatly as I rose.

In the kitchen, I pulled down a pair of mugs from the cabinet and filled them. I started to pick them up then thought about the lack of coordination my friend had just displayed. Figuring that hot coffee and he were not about to mix, I carefully poured a third of his cup back into the pot.

After a quick wipe of the counter with a dishtowel, I hefted the mugs and headed back for the living room. I was beginning to get the impression that Ben was too far on the other side of sober to actually talk about what had driven him to this point. Still, I was hoping that with a little luck, the java might nudge him back in this direction and get him rolling.

Unfortunately, my hopes were immediately dashed when I returned. My friend's head was tilted face upward against the back of the couch, his mouth hanging wide open and his eyes closed. Dickens was draped half across his shoulder and half across the back of the sofa, purring with an in and out warble.

"Ben?" I said aloud.

He didn't respond.

"Ben?" I said again as I sat his cup of coffee on the end table and then gave his arm a nudge.

Nothing.

I let out a sigh and cocked my head, letting my gaze drift out into space. I took a sip of my coffee then walked across the room to the bookshelf and picked up the telephone.

If my suspicions were correct, Ben being trashed stemmed from what little I had overheard the day before. I could well be wrong, but I was guessing that he and Allison were at odds. Still, from the looks of things, he wasn't going to be moving for quite awhile, and there was no reason for her to worry about him when he didn't come home, even if they were angry at one another.

I tucked the device up to my ear and heard nothing but a hollow clicking sound. Puzzled, I tapped the off-hook switch a few times. Still, I heard only the hollowness. I settled it back onto the cradle and with my coffee in hand, trudged back into the kitchen to check the phone there. I found the same thing. Next, I ventured back through the living room, down the hall and into the bedroom. There, I found the reason for the dead line. The phone next to the bed was on the floor, along with everything else that had been on the nightstand. In the wake of the carnage were two lounging cats, Emily and Salinger, glassy-eyed and surrounded by the remnants of a catnip-stuffed toy mouse.

"Hope you two didn't make any long distance calls," I said aloud as I picked up the phone and married it back to the cradle.

After giving the line a moment to reset, I lifted the receiver and got a steady dial tone. As I stabbed in Ben's home number, I mutely wondered how long the phone had been off the hook and if anyone had tried to call.

"Hello?" a familiar voice answered after the third ring.

"Hi, Allison, it's Rowan," I said.

There was an overt silence at the other end then her voice issued again. This time it was a stilted mix of trepidation, confusion, and maybe even annoyance. "Oh, hi, Rowan."

I was taken aback by her tone, but I decided to ignore it and ventured forth. "So listen, I'm sorry to call this late, but I didn't want you to worry. Ben's okay but he'll probably be sleeping here tonight. He's passed out on my couch."

The silence crept in once again.

"Why would I worry?" she finally asked.

"Umm, uhh," I stuttered. "I just thought maybe you might be concerned when he didn't come home."

"He hasn't told you has he?" she asked, her voice audibly softened with a note of understanding now in place of the confusion.

"Allison, he's too drunk to make a coherent sentence," I replied.

I heard her sigh at the other end. "Rowan... Ben and I separated at the beginning of the month. He hasn't lived here for two weeks."

It was my turn to fall silent. In all of my imaginings of what might be wrong, the foremost had been something between the two of them. But, not once did I even consider that it was something this bad.

"Rowan?" she said.

"Yeah. Yeah, I'm here," I answered. "Listen… Allison… I'm…"

"It's okay, Rowan." She stopped me. "I'm sorry I was so cold when you called. I just assumed he'd told you."

"We are talking about the same Benjamin Storm, right?" I asked.

"I know what you mean," she answered.

I stared at the phone, searching for something to say; anything at all would do, so long as it pushed aside the embarrassed silence.

"So, Allison," I finally offered words that no matter how sincere in intent, still sounded tired and overused. "If there's anything Felicity and I can do…"

"Just take care of him, Rowan. God knows someone needs to," she told me, then without another word she hung up.

I pulled the handset away and held it for a long moment, pondering the painful news. I'd known the two of them for what seemed like forever. They had been together ever since we'd met, and the idea of them splitting up now was completely foreign. Even though there was no mistaking what Allison had just told me, I was still having trouble wrapping my head around the concept.

I had just settled the phone back onto the base when the squeal of locked brakes and skidding tires sounded on the street in front of the house. I headed out of the bedroom and back up the hallway, only to be greeted by the dogs bellowing at the door as a frantic pounding began against it.

I rushed to the door, fully expecting to find someone who had just hit an animal, or worse a pedestrian, in front of my house. I twisted the deadbolt and swung the door wide, only to be greeted by RJ, a member of the Coven.

His eyes were wide, and he wore a frightened mask across his features. The moment I saw him, the anguish that made a perpetual home in the pit of my stomach was released in an explosive torrent. Hollowness filled my chest, and my body tensed. The coffee cup left my hand and shattered with an unceremonious crack against the floor, sending hot java and ceramic shards in all directions.

RJ's mouth was open in preparation to say something, but I never gave him the chance.

Words were spewing from my own mouth automatically; the three word sentence came as a guttural bellow. "WHERE IS SHE?!"

CHAPTER 12:

R J didn't even try to compete verbally with my frantic shouts. He simply gestured for me to follow him as he turned and raced back down the stairs and then continued across the front yard. He was only just barely ahead of me when we hit the curb. In a quick motion, he unlatched the side door of the still running mini-van.

In the recently fallen dusk, soft blue shadows ran in oblique lines through the back of the vehicle, muting the interior. A streetlight just up from us painted a harsh glare across the tinted pane of glass to obscure it even more. Still, beyond the swath of reflected brilliance, I thought I could see movement in the back seat.

As RJ wrenched the sliding door back, dim, yellow-white light flooded the inside of the van, emanating from the dome light. The shrouded incandescent bulb struggled to chase away the darkness, while my eyes fought to adjust to the rapid changes in illumination they had been subjected to between the front door and here.

At first, I saw only Cally sitting near the door. When she looked up, I could see the same fear creasing her face that RJ had—and still was— displaying. I could see that she was rocking gently, and when she looked back down, I followed her gaze with my own. Felicity was lying beside her in the seat, body curled into a loose semblance of a fetal position. Her head was resting in Cally's lap, and the young woman had an arm wrapped around my wife's shoulders, holding her fast.

I knelt into the side door of the van and carefully brushed a tangle of hair back from Felicity's face. Even in the dimness, I could see red froth on her lips and a trickle of blood running from the corner of her mouth, evidence that she'd been gnashing her teeth against her tongue during a violent seizure. The crimson trail smeared across her pale skin in an opaque blemish, but other than that, I could see no obvious injuries.

I watched her, my eyes following the rise and fall of her chest as she took slow, even breaths. I relaxed a bit and took in a deep breath of my own. In my throat, I could feel the thump of my heart and imagined that it was only now starting to beat again; although, it didn't seem to be in any hurry to drop back down into my chest where it belonged.

I knew just by looking at her that at least part of my earlier fear had been realized. Still, my mind was already heading in more directions than I could count, so I blurted the first, most obvious, thing that came to mind.

"What happened?" I demanded, shooting quick glances at both Cally and RJ.

"It was just all of a sudden like," RJ answered, voice almost shaking. "We had just gotten started. She was talking to us about Dark Moon spells, and just like that she stopped saying anything. When I looked up, she was staring off into space, all blank ya'know." He waved his hand in front of his face wildly as if trying to illustrate what he meant. "The next thing we knew, she was on the floor shaking and flailing her arms and stuff."

"Gods Rowan, it was like déjà vu or something," Cally added, shaking her head slowly. Her own voice tensed with anguish.

"Yeah, Rowan," RJ agreed. "It was just like what happened to you at Nancy's house a few months ago."

"Dammit." I muttered the word at first, but my voice grew more forceful with each successive utterance. "DAMmit, DAMMIT!"

"Oh man!" RJ suddenly exclaimed. "That's where we were tonight, Nancy's! Is that what it is, Rowan? Is it the house? Is it Randy's spirit or something?"

RJ fired the questions in rapid succession, focusing the last one on Nancy's murdered husband— a victim of Eldon Porter and the very same Randy I had referred to when Felicity had pressed me to go with her earlier.

"No," I replied, still stroking my wife's forehead. "It's not the house, and it's not Randy's spirit. It's probably a spirit, but not Randy's."

"Whose then?" Cally interjected.

"I'm pretty sure it's Tamara Linwood," I answered flatly.

"Oh Gods," she moaned. "You mean the missing schoolteacher that's been on the news?"

"Yeah." I nodded. "I think so, but she's not missing anymore. She was murdered."

"But why is this happening to Felicity all of a sudden?" RJ implored.

"I wish I knew," I said. "How long ago did the seizure start?"

"About forty-five minutes I guess," Cally replied. "Maybe an hour. We tried to call you but the phone was busy."

"Cats knocked bedroom phone off hook," I explained simply. "I just noticed it a few minutes before you pulled up."

"The first one really didn't last long," RJ offered.

"What do you mean 'first one'?" I demanded. "She had more than one?"

"Yeah, she had two," he continued. "The first one just lasted a minute or so. Once she stopped shaking and could talk, we got her up in a chair. We all wanted to call nine-one-one, but she kept saying no, we should call you."

"When we couldn't reach you on the phone, she tried to leave," Cally added. "But we weren't about to let her drive."

"Yeah," RJ echoed. "Good thing too, 'cause we were halfway here when she started shaking all over again."

"Then she just went limp and passed out," Cally said.

My hand was on automatic pilot, still stroking Felicity's cool skin. I felt her jerk slightly, and we all turned our attention back to her when we heard movement against the upholstery. As she began to stir, she let out a low, pitiful sounding moan.

"It's okay, honey," I told her softly. "I'm here."

"*Caorthann?*" The thin whisper of Felicity's voice met my ears as she called my name in Gaelic.

She still hadn't opened her eyes, but she was slowly starting to unfurl from her tight posture.

"Yes, I'm right here," I soothed, brushing the back of my hand lightly against her cheek.

"I'm dead," she whispered again.

"No sweetheart, you're fine. You just had a seizure," I replied softly.

"No," she spoke again, her voice still a thin whisper, then she tried to shake her head but quickly gave up. I could see a tear beginning to glisten in the corner of her closed eyelid. "No, you don't understand. I'm... I'm... Ohhhh...." She moaned.

"Shhhhh." I soothed. "You're okay."

"Rowan... I'm... She's... I'm dead."

"It's okay," I repeated, realizing now what she meant. "Ben just told me that they officially identified the remains."

"No," she insisted, quiet but adamant nonetheless. "No, they haven't found me yet."

I had naturally assumed she was referring to Tamara Linwood, but her objection set my mind racing in yet another direction. It was suddenly apparent to me that she had seen something on the other side; or to be more accurate, this time around she remembered what she had seen.

I could feel my entire face tense as my lips hardened into a frown at the horrific thoughts now invading my already overloaded grey matter.

"Who's dead, Felicity?" I asked.

I was afraid I already knew the name she was going to speak, and I desperately hoped I was wrong.

"Me. I'm dead."

"No, tell me your name." I nudged.

"Brittany," she whispered. "My name was Brittany."

I wasn't wrong.

The episode ended quicker than it began, with Felicity snapping suddenly back into our world without warning or ceremony. She was weak but fully conscious of her surroundings, and that was a good sign.

As soon as she was ready to move, we retreated back into the house. Even though the sun was down, the heat and humidity were still lingering in a suffocating blanket. RJ shut off the van and locked it up while Cally and I tried to help Felicity make the short journey across the yard. I say tried because she was having none of it. The most she would allow was for us to walk alongside her as she slowly trudged. To her credit, she made it into the house under her own power. While I had objected strenuously to her defiant need to go it alone, in the end she won out, mainly because I didn't want to argue with her.

Ben hadn't even changed positions that I could tell, but Dickens had abandoned him— most likely having gone in search of a quieter place to sleep as my friend had begun to snore at a level louder than most gasoline-powered lawnmowers.

In our own bid to escape the noise, after Felicity had cleaned up, we retreated to the kitchen. At least the distance and walls managed to dull the cacophony enough for us to talk.

"Anyone else want coffee?" I asked, holding up the carafe. "It's fresh."

"I'm good," RJ answered.

He had his small frame perched up on one end of our kitchen counter where it ran below the back window. His back was against the frame, and he was in the perfect spot to see anything and everything that was going on. In a way, I guess it was his designated spot and always would be.

Following the murder of their Priestess— a former student of mine— Felicity and I had adopted this young Coven. Our intent had been to point them in the right direction, send them out on their own, and then return to our solitary practice. But, as with all best laid plans, things just didn't work out that way. Unfortunately, I wasn't entirely sure that it had been for the best. Looking back, I wondered if they were doomed by my presence from the very beginning as my involvement with them was born of violence on day one. And, it was a motif that had continued throughout the years.

Until the past few months, we had held almost all of the meetings here. Each time, be it a class, ritual, or Sabbat, for whatever reason, the entire group had invariably migrated to the kitchen. And, every single time, RJ had ended up parked in the exact spot he was now, sitting in the very same half-lotus position while watching with curious eyes and drinking it all in.

It had been five months now since I'd seen him, or anyone else from the Coven besides Felicity for that matter; something that was my own choice as my wife had been so intent on pointing out. But I didn't regret it. At least, I didn't think that I did.

As time wore on, I had once again grown used to practicing The Craft with Felicity alone. I had even managed to get my energies under control and re-focus myself on some of the basics I had seemed to forget in the wake of everything I'd been subjected to, both ethereal and physical.

But, standing here now, there was something oddly comfortable about the sight of RJ and Cally making themselves at home in the kitchen as they'd done so many times before. Felicity was correct. These people were family, and in some small way, even considering the negative circumstances, this was a homecoming.

"I'm going to get some ice water if that's okay," Cally said.

"Yeah, go for it," I replied, breaking out of my introspective trance as her words met my ears. I turned and slid the pot back onto the base then nodded my head toward the cabinets. "Glasses are where they've always been."

"I'll take a Jaim…" Felicity began.

"…Not this time." I cut her off.

"Jaim…" she started again, adding a demanding note to her voice.

"…I said no," I interrupted her again, adopting my own stern tone as I stepped over to the breakfast nook and slid a cup of coffee in front of her. "Not this time. Now take the aspirin, drink the coffee, and try to relax. The caffeine will help, trust me."

"But…"

"No but's." I shook my head. "I've already got Ben passed out on the couch. I'm not going to have you going in that direction too."

"I was gonna ask about that," RJ said.

"What, Ben? Apparently he tied one on," I stated simply. There was no reason for them to know the impetus behind his binge.

"So have you remembered anything else?" I asked, turning my attention back to Felicity.

"Anything else?" she asked with more than a hint of confusion in her voice. "I don't remember anything at all."

"Well you just told me a few minutes ago that Brittany Larson is dead," I returned.

"I did what?"

"Yeah, Felicity," RJ chimed in. "You said, 'She's dead. Brittany is dead.'"

"No…" she muttered, her voice trailing off, not denying that she'd said it but still verbally rejecting that it could be true.

Her hand was covering her mouth, and her head pitched forward as her shoulders drooped.

"It's okay, honey," I told her, resting a hand on her shoulder. "You've done better than me on this one so far."

"For all the good it's done, then," she replied, her voice cracking slightly.

"Mind if I use your phone to call Nancy?" Cally asked in a somber tone. "She and the twins are probably worried sick."

"Help yourself," I replied. "Tell her I'll make arrangements to get Felicity's Jeep as soon as I can."

"Yeah," RJ interjected. "While you got her on the line, ask her if Moonpie Fairybunny bolted or what."

"RJ!" Cally admonished.

"Well what would you call her?" he asked with a shrug.

"Her name is Candee," she replied as she lifted the phone off the wall base and then disappeared around the corner into the dining room.

"Yeah, Candee with two 'e's', don't forget," he called after her, holding up a pair of fingers. "So, I rest my case."

"Moonpie Fairybunny?" I asked.

"A seeker," Felicity answered, speaking toward the surface of the table as she held her head in her hands.

"She's been to the last couple of classes," RJ offered. "Real crystal crunching, cotton-tailed, white-lighter. Enough to make you gag."

"She probably won't even ask to dedicate, RJ," Felicity told him.

"You're probably right. You should have seen her face when you hit the floor," he returned. "I think you scared the crap out of her."

"So what are we going to do?" Felicity asked.

"About Fluffy?" RJ asked rhetorically. "Tell her not..."

"No," Felicity shot back, cutting him off and turning her face up to mine. "About Brittany Larson. What if she really is dead? Shouldn't we tell someone?"

For the first time I could recall, I found myself standing on a very different side of the fence. It was a viewpoint with which I had more than just a passing familiarity but only when it was staring back at me. I had never seen the world from this angle, or at least not in the past few years.

"Honey," I began. "I hate to sound like Ben, but right now we've got nothing to go on. On top of that, you don't even remember saying that she's dead."

"But we have to do something," she appealed.

"I'm not saying we don't," I told her. "But at the moment, our best and only link to the investigation is soused and passed out on our sofa."

"Let's wake him up, then," she pressed.

"Waking up isn't the issue, Felicity. I don't think you understand. He was trashed. And I mean trashed with the proverbial capital T. He's going to have to sleep it off before he can even make a coherent sentence."

"*Foicheallan. Drongair,*" she spat.

"What was that?" RJ asked.

"You've heard her speak Gaelic before," I told him.

"Yeah, but what did she just say?"

"I don't know. Those were a couple of new ones to me."

"He's a useless drunkard" came her retort.

"Settle down, Felicity," I told her, realizing that she was as in the dark about Ben's circumstances as I had been just an hour ago. "He's got his reasons."

"They'd best be good," she remarked with a hard edge to her voice, looking up at me with anger flashing in her eyes.

I certainly understood the turmoil and sense of urgency she was going through. It wasn't like I had been guilty of it myself. However, I didn't want to get into Ben's personal life in front of Cally and RJ.

I looked back at her without a word, hoping that the look on my face would get through to her and that she'd drop the subject for now. She glared back for a moment, and I simply held her stare. I don't know if it was my expression or just the fact that her brain had to be swimming in an untold number of directions, but she moved on, or back as the case may be.

"Fine. So what are we going to do?" she demanded. "Sit around and wait for him to come to?"

"Yes, I suppose so," I returned, trying not to snap at her. I knew all too well how she felt.

"What about Constance?" she declared. "Didn't you say Ben told you she was assigned to the case?"

With the turmoil of the evening, I had completely forgotten about the federal agent.

I nodded assent. "You're right. He did. I'll try to get hold of her as soon as Cally's off the phone. In the meantime, maybe we could try to jog your memory so we have something more to tell her."

She looked back at me and shuddered involuntarily. "I'm not so sure I'm ready for that."

I added, "I can understand that. Truth is I'm not so sure that *I'm* ready for you to do that either.

"You know, something else we could do is put our heads together and try to figure out why this is happening to you instead of me."

Even as I was finishing the comment her face went blank. At first I thought she was about to have an episode, but instead of tensing up, she simply turned her face away from mine. In that instant, the thick ethereal walls she had constructed around herself palpably strengthened.

My own psychic alarms began ringing in the back of my head as it became obvious that she was steeling herself not against the unknown but against me.

"What's going on, Felicity?" I asked.

"Nothing," she returned flatly.

"I don't believe you."

"Nothing's going on," she stated again.

"I know you better than that. You're not telling me something."

Her voice continued to be cold and defiant. "There's nothing to tell."

"Felicity…"

"Fine," she spat, wheeling back to face me. "I've got your answer. I know EXACTLY why this is happening to me."

CHAPTER 13:

I had absolutely no idea where my wife was heading with this, but the sharpness of her present attitude told me it was a place I wasn't going to be happy about. I knew her well enough to tell that her temper was flaring because she had been backed into a corner, or at least that is what she perceived to be happening. The fact that those green eyes were focused so intently on me and no one else was more than just an overt clue that I was the one who had chased her there— they were a proverbial smoking gun.

I ran down a mental list of hastily formed theories but still came up empty. I simply couldn't imagine what she could feel so strongly about keeping secret, given the circumstances. Unless, of course, she was about to issue the blame for her plight directly upon me, and by pushing I was inadvertently forcing her to voice that fact in front of friends. I hoped, however, that such was nothing more than my own insecurities about the pressure everyone had been under and that they were simply bubbling to the top at a less than opportune moment.

I heard Cally re-enter the room behind me and drop the handset back into the cradle as she announced, "The twins are bringing Felicity's Jeep over right now. They can ride back to Nancy's with us."

"They didn't have to do that," I told her evenly without turning away from my wife's molten stare.

"They were already... on... their... way," she replied, voice fading into a stutter near the end of the sentence. "I'm sorry. Did I interrupt something?"

"I guess that depends," I replied as the tension continued to swell. "Were you planning to expand on that last comment, Felicity?"

Faced with the query, my wife backpedaled. "The phone is free. Shouldn't you call Constance," she said. The last part of the statement came not as a question but as an instruction.

"In a minute," I replied. I didn't know if I was only serving to bring myself more grief, but something was telling me not to let this go without an answer. Her attempt to slam the door she had just opened a moment before only steeled my resolve to get it. "What did you mean you 'know EXACTLY why this is happening' to you?"

She made another verbal attempt at escape. "Just forget it."

"I don't think so."

We searched each other's faces for a long moment, and while looking at her, I realized there was something more to this than I had first thought. Something was hiding in the shadows. What I had initially taken for anger alone now held what could have been a hint of embarrassment peeking around from behind the bolder of the two emotional masks.

At the same time, I knew that what she had to be seeing in my face was stark determination. This was very simply one argument my petite, Taurus wife was not going to be able to stampede her way through.

"Okay, fine then," she replied, turning her face away and breaking the stare. "Look in the pantry. Bottom shelf, behind the dog food bin."

Again, I was at a loss as to where exactly this was heading, but at least it was moving forward. I sat my coffee cup on the table then turned and stepped over to the pantry. I swung the tall door open and knelt down in front of the wooden cabinet. I inspected the contents but at first glance saw nothing unusual.

"What am I looking for?" I asked aloud.

"You'll know it when you find it," she replied.

"Behind the dog food bin you said?" I repeated her earlier instruction.

"Yes" came her clipped reply. "On the bottom."

I reached in and pulled a plastic kitchen organizer full of cling wrap and sandwich bags off the top of the clear food bin and set it aside on the floor. Leaning inward and tilting my head away from the next shelf up, I thrust my arm back into the recesses of the cabinet and began groping around. It didn't take long for my hand to brush against something angular that was wedged in behind the dog food container.

It felt roughly like a rectangle as I ran my fingers around in search of a place to grab hold.

Using my free hand, I slid the bin slightly forward then grasped the object and twisted it upward. When I had finally worked it around the other stored items and managed to extricate it from the cabinet, I found myself kneeling on the floor with a shoebox in my hand.

I wouldn't have given the item a passing thought had it not been for the fact that it was purposely hidden. However, that was far from the only reason for suspicion. What immediately caught my eye, as well as my breath, was the length of bright red ribbon tied securely about its girth.

"Gods, Felicity," I murmured as I stood. "You didn't..."

"What did you expect me to do, Row?" she asked, blurting the words, all of which were underscored by a sharply defensive tone. "I've watched you go through too much these past few years. Then when I called home yesterday, and you said it was happening again... I couldn't just stand by and watch. Not again. Not this time."

"You did this yesterday?" I asked, surprise in my voice.

"Yes. When I got home and you weren't here," she said as she nodded. "But I didn't expect it to work as quickly as all that, then."

"Yeah, well we all know you're a hell of a Witch. Guess this just proves it."

"Is that what I think it is?" Cally finally drummed up the courage to ask.

"It's some kind of a binding," RJ interjected before I could answer.

I glanced over at her and nodded. "Yeah. I'm afraid so. And just like any other binding done where strong emotions are involved, it backfired." I leveled my gaze back on my wife as I dropped the box onto the table in front of her. "Unless it was your plan all along to bind this crap to yourself."

"Of course not." She shook her head at me quickly and then screwed her face into a scowl as if I had just made the stupidest comment she'd ever heard. "It was only supposed to bind you *from* the ethereal. It wasn't supposed to bind anything *to* anyone."

"Well, let me ask you this: If you wanted this to all go away, then why didn't you just do a banishing instead? That would seem more appropriate."

"That was my original plan after we got off the phone," she answered. "But then the thing happened with Brittany Larson, and I started thinking... And, I couldn't be sure... And, if I had done a banishing, that could be far more permanent, and..." She kept halting, searching for words to explain. Finally, she gave up trying and simply said, "I just didn't want to close any doors, that's all."

"Even so, Felicity, of all people you know better than this," I admonished.

"Don't lecture me, Rowan Linden Gant," she returned. "It's nothing you wouldn't have done yourself and you know it."

"That's not the point," I told her.

"It is as far as I'm concerned," she countered. "Do you think you're the only one who's allowed to do the protecting?"

She had me there. I shook my head and glanced around the room in resignation. "I never said that. But, to be honest, right now I don't want to argue about this. I know why you did it and I appreciate it, really I do. But," I reached out and pushed the shoebox closer to her, "undo it."

"What if I say no?" she contended.

I sighed. "You know as well as I do that there are ways to get around bindings, especially now that I know about it."

She didn't reply. She knew I was correct.

I pressed forward. "Look, we're both just going to be wasting our energies with this, and that won't do anyone any good. Undo the binding, and let's get back to normal."

She let out a 'hmph' then told me, "In case you haven't noticed, Rowan, our lives haven't been normal for a few years now."

"All right then, status quo or whatever you want to call it, Felicity. Just break the spell. Please?"

She stared back at me in silence for a moment then turned her head slightly to the side and looked past me.

"Cally," she said with quiet resignation. "There are some scissors on the altar shelf in the living room. Could you bring them to me and a book of matches please?"

I gave my wife a thin smile and then said, "Thank you. I'll go call Constance now."

"Mandalay." The federal agent's businesslike voice issued from the earpiece on the telephone amid a rumble of indistinguishable background noises.

I had parked myself in the bedroom so that I wouldn't disturb the magickal workings in the kitchen. On the way through the house, I had taken notice that Ben had finally slumped over to the side and was now snoring at a somewhat lower volume.

Cally had been taking pity on the unconscious cop and was covering him with an afghan at about the time I was making the turn into the hallway.

"Hey Constance, it's Rowan," I replied, as I finished picking up some of the items the cats had scattered. I piled them back on the nightstand before taking a seat on the edge of the bed.

"Oh, hi Rowan." Her voice brightened a notch but remained all business. "I'm just a little busy at the moment..."

"I know, Ben told me you were working the Larson abduction," I interjected before she could rush me off the line. "I wouldn't have called you if it wasn't important. Can you talk?"

There was a brief pause then she replied, "Hold on a second."

I heard shuffling noises, some voices— hers included— and then footsteps. A handful of moments and a few more unidentifiable sounds later, the background noise dropped noticeably.

"I'm back" her voice came again, and then she barreled straight into questions of her own. "So have you talked to Storm recently? He missed a seven-thirty briefing and that's not like him. I've been trying to call him all evening, but I keep getting a message that his phone is turned off and no one picked up at his house either."

I hesitated for a moment before answering. I guess I'd been the lucky one when I got hold of Allison. "Actually, he's passed out on my couch."

"Passed out?"

"Long story."

"Is that why you called?"

"I wish it were," I replied.

"Okay, so what's up?"

"Nothing good I'm afraid."

"What's wrong?"

"Your kidnapping just became a homicide," I offered succinctly.

"How do you…" she started. "No, forget I even said that. So fill me in, what's going on?"

"Well, it gets a little complicated."

"Un-complicate it for me."

"Okay, in a nutshell, Felicity had two ethereal episodes tonight and…"

"Felicity?" she interrupted. "Felicity did the woo-woo stuff? Not you?"

"That's the complicated part."

"Okay, I'll catch up on that later. Go on."

"Well, she had the two episodes, and just before she came out of the second one, she started telling us that Brittany Larson is dead."

"Us? You mean you and Storm?"

"No, me, Cally, and RJ."

"So what about Storm? Was he there or not?"

"He was already passed out," I replied. "That's pretty much why I'm calling you."

"Why is Ben passed out, Rowan?" Her words were more of a demand than a simple question.

It was obvious that him missing the briefing was a sore spot for her, and what she had said was dead on— Benjamin Storm didn't shirk his responsibilities. Unfortunately, this new little tidbit of information just added another layer to my worry over his situation.

I wanted desperately to cover for my friend, and so I tried to think of a feasible way around answering her without telling an outright lie. Unfortunately, I couldn't think of a single thing to say other than the cold truth, and before I knew it, that was exactly what came tumbling out of my mouth. "He's drunk, Constance."

There was a spate of silence on the line, and then her voice issued again, this time with a hard edge. "Wake him up and get some coffee into him, Rowan. I'll be there in half an hour."

Knowing the way she drove, I suspected it would be more like fifteen minutes.

"Okay, but listen, Constance," I appealed. "Go easy on him. He's got just about as good a reason for this as anyone can have."

"Yeah, well he'd better, Rowan because I had to throw some Federal weight around to get him back on the MCS for this investigation."

"Yeah, I think he knows that," I replied. "Or he suspects it at least."

"Well, if he makes me look like a fool then he's going to have someone besides Lieutenant Albright after his ass," she snarled. "And I can be a hell of a lot nastier bitch than she can."

That was it. I'd had enough arguing. I already felt like I was perched atop an inordinately narrow balance beam eighteen hours out of every twenty-four. Between Felicity's binding spell, Ben's marital problems, and now Constance being on the warpath, I felt like what little normalcy I had left in the world was crumbling away beneath my feet, and I wasn't ready to fall quite yet.

My own voice adopted an angry edge, and I replied candidly, "Listen, Constance, I understand where you're coming from, but I seem to remember a certain city homicide detective going to the mat for you when you assaulted a suspect during an interrogation."

There was no way for me to retract the statement, but I'm not sure that I would have wanted to if I could. I had been a witness to her loss of control as well as having been her confidant when she needed someone to talk to about it. I hated to slap her in the face with an incident from the past, but Ben had gone so far as to lie for her, and that was no small gesture from a man who valued honesty as much as him.

Sometimes, I suppose we all need to be reminded of the debts we owe and to whom we owed them.

I could hear her breathing at the other end, but not a single word was spoken for the span of a half-minute.

"Listen, Constance," I finally said. "I'm sorry about that. I didn't mean to…"

"No, Rowan, you're right," she replied, her voice a mix of emotions. "See if you can get him sobered up. I'll get out of here in a few minutes and head over."

"I'll see what I can do," I replied. "Thanks, Constance."

I hung up the phone as I stood and then started out the door on my way to the kitchen to enlist some aid in getting Ben up and about. Whatever curiosity I'd harbored regarding how the process of the un-binding was going was immediately eliminated the moment the rasping pain raked across the back of my neck.

The wall before me became a psychedelic whirlpool spinning at an ever-increasing velocity. My body tensed then jerked as my knees gave way. The burning agony drew itself across my neck once again, halting, then biting anew as it dug deeper into my upper spine.

I was trying to call out for help when the floor suddenly filled my field of vision, only to be replaced almost immediately by indigo darkness.

CHAPTER 14:

I was floating.

Or maybe I wasn't really floating. I had no visible point of reference in the darkness, so I couldn't really say for sure. All I knew for certain was that it felt like I was floating, and I was happily willing to accept that as fact.

I blinked for no other reason than to make sure my eyes were actually open. Again, it felt like they were open, so I took the sensation at face value.

There was little else I could do, and the truth was, I didn't really care.

I was comfortable.

In fact, I don't think I'd ever been this comfortable in all my life.

Since I couldn't see anything, I decided I would just listen.

Actually I wasn't any more interested in listening than I was in seeing, but I did it anyway. Why? I had no idea other than the fact that there was this little nag in the back of my head.

It told me it needed to know something. I don't know what information the nag was after, but it wanted something, and it wanted it now. I tried to ignore it, because after all, I didn't see any point. It wanted to know something, not me.

The nag was on a mission. It told me I needed the information too.

I tried to reason with it. Given that I couldn't see, and for all intents and purposes, I couldn't feel, I didn't really know that I could hear either. So, why bother trying?

The nag wouldn't listen. It wanted me to try hearing in the worst way, and it wasn't going to give up until I did.

I told it no.

It nagged harder and became an annoyance.

I told it to go away.

It wouldn't. Instead, it just kept growing beyond annoyance and became a pain.

A real pain.

Physical.

Tangible.

Now I was no longer comfortable.

I gave up and listened. I doubted that it would do any good, but I did it anyway. I was willing to do just about anything to make the nag go away.

Had I cared, I would have been chagrined when I started to pick up the faint sounds around me, fading slowly in from nowhere to eventually fill my ears with ambient noise. But, I didn't care about such things. I just wanted the nag to go away, so I kept listening.

Cicadas warbled out their song, the buzz rising and falling, fading away, then starting anew.

Okay, I could live with that. Why the nag wanted me to listen to cicadas I couldn't fathom, but if it made the nag leave me alone, I was happy.

But, the nag didn't want to hear the insects. It wanted to hear something else, so I listened harder.

Metal scraping against earth sounded softly in the darkness. How I knew it was metal against earth I couldn't begin to say. I just knew it as simply as I knew two plus two equaled four. It was a fact.

The ambience grew as I listened intently. The cicadas, the metal, the earth, the wind... The crunch of dry leaves began sneaking through, adding themselves to the mix and setting up a rhythm.

Scrape, crunch, thud, warble.

Scrape, crunch, thud, warble.

Underscoring the odd rhythm was an off-key hum, and the nag became very interested in it. I focused on the hum and noticed that it ran in an audible parallel to a severely muffled background of driving bass.

I despised the nag. It was making me take notice of my surroundings, and now I was starting to be curious. I didn't want to be curious. I wanted to be comfortable like before. But, that was slipping further away with each scrape, crunch, thud, and warble.

Now I was noticing that labored breaths interrupted the hum at random intervals, falling in and out of cadence with the crunch and scrape that seemed to be setting the beat.

On the heels of a metallic clunk, a tinny stream of noise masquerading as music suddenly vomited into the blackness. Severe notes, squealing outward from what might have been a guitar, intermixed with the heavy bump of a frenzied drumbeat. In reality, it wasn't very loud at all, but given the disparity of it against the otherwise quiet darkness, it may as well have been a thunderclap.

The nag started down a new path.

It wanted to know about this driving thrum that insisted on being called music. I was just about to appease the annoying little monster when a hot stab of pain shot through my chest.

I felt myself jerked upward, without warning or apology.

Stark, blue-white brilliance exploded in my eyes, hot and fierce like an arc of lightning.

The afterimage of a swirling tunnel and a wooded grove began fading from my retinas.

Blackness.

Crashing luminance, intense and stark.

Nude flesh. Pale, flaccid, and marred.

Blackness.

Again, the impressed image began to fade.

The violent strobe burst, casting a woman's body in harsh light.

Woman. Corpse. Blood.

Blackness.

Scrape, crunch, thud, warble.

Light, coming faster and faster.

Blood. Shoulders. Blood.

Blackness. Light. Corpse. Blackness. Light. Blood. Blackness. Light. Shoulders. Blackness. Light. Head. Blackness. Light. Shoulders. Blackness. Light. Face. Blackness. Light. Brittany. Blackness. Light. Blood. Blackness. Light. Brittany. Blackness. Light.

Headless.
Pain.

Pain.

"...Thirteen, fourteen, fifteen." I heard Cally's steady but frightened voice calling out.

With each number she recited, focused pressure drove into the center of my chest, released, and then instantly repeated. I felt something tightly pinching my nose and something pressed against my mouth. Hot air rushed down my throat, and I was suddenly overcome by a need to cough. I tried, or at least I thought I did, but nothing happened.

I spasmed suddenly and felt my body jerk as I sputtered and gagged. With a heavy wheeze, I drew in a deep breath.

Whatever it was that was trying to smother me let go of my nose and moved quickly away.

I tried to cough again and this time I succeeded.

Then the cough came hard. I felt my shoulders lift from the floor as I sputtered and hacked.

The next breath was easier.

"He's breathing." This time it was Felicity, relief in her tenor.

Soft fingers pressed against my neck, and I heard Cally announce, "He's got a strong pulse."

The clamor of hurried footsteps met my ears, reverberating through the hardwood floor before halting with a heavy thump.

"An ambulance is on the way." RJ's frantic tone now entered the mix of voices.

"Rowan?" A handed patted my cheek lightly as Felicity called my name. "Rowan?"

The back of my neck was on fire, and it felt as though it was creased with an open, festering wound. My head was already starting to throb, and I involuntarily let out a low moan.

There was a frightening image dancing around inside my skull, insisting that I share it. My stomach soured at the very thought of trying to describe the horrific tableau. I wanted nothing more than to chase the vision from my mind and slam the door behind it, but a tickle in the back of my skull said no.

The vision was beginning to fade, and I tried desperately to let it. The tickle objected. It was important even if I didn't want to think so. I had to tell someone before it was lost forever.

"Rowan?" Felicity called again.

"No head," I heard myself whisper.

"What?" she asked.

I felt the warmth of her face near mine as she bent closer.

"No head," I repeated as my short brush with consciousness rushed toward its end. "Brittany. No head."

"His vitals are fine. He's coherent; he knows his name, day of the week, the year, who the President is…" the paramedic was telling my wife, letting her voice trail off as the list grew. "I'm sorry, but there's not much we can do if he refuses to go with us."

Her partner was already loading equipment back into the life support vehicle, which was still lighting up our front yard with its wildly flickering light bar. I hadn't checked, but I was sure that neighbors were standing on porches and peering out from behind their drapes at the commotion surrounding the 'Witch house'. This wasn't the first time we'd provided a light show, and unfortunately, it probably wasn't going to be the last.

As was procedure, a police officer from the local municipality had responded along with the paramedics. He had stepped out onto the front porch himself, and I could see him through the glass of the storm door as he was speaking into his radio.

In sharp contrast to the activity in the immediate vicinity, Ben was still sprawled on the sofa, unconscious and oblivious to everything.

Luckily enough, the afghan Cally had laid over him earlier was still in place, hiding his sidearm and badge, so we didn't have to explain to one cop why another cop was passed out in our living room. Although, there had been some question as to why he was sleeping through the ruckus. We had simply explained it away as us not letting a friend drive drunk, and fortunately, that had been satisfactory.

"But, his heart stopped," Felicity insisted, still trying to convince the paramedic to cart me off to the hospital.

The young woman shrugged and shook her head apologetically. "I'm sorry, ma'am. I've got no proof of that. His EKG looks perfectly normal."

"Felicity..." I started.

"Your heart DID stop, Rowan," Cally pitched her offering into the fray, cutting me off.

I shot her a glance and frowned. I knew she was just being concerned, but at the moment, I needed someone on *my* side not Felicity's. Fortunately, RJ was staying out of the way in the kitchen with the twins, Shari and Jennifer, who had arrived with Felicity's Jeep somewhere in the middle of all this. I'm sure they were hearing the whole story from beginning to end.

Still, if there was a silver lining to the situation at all, at least the seizures were happening to me again instead of Felicity. For that, I was thankful. It also didn't hurt that I was now back on the side of the fence I was used to occupying. For all its pressures and pitfalls, it was still a path I had grown accustomed to walking.

"Look, Felicity, I..." I continued.

"What if I tell you to take him?" Agent Mandalay took her turn at interrupting even though her question was directed at the paramedic. She had already flashed her badge and federal ID when she arrived on the scene moments behind the paramedics, so it was no secret that she was an FBI special agent.

"Is he in your custody?" she asked.

"He can be if that's what it takes," Constance replied.

"Constance!" I appealed again, louder this time. "Felicity! Both of you. All of you. Listen to me. I'm fine."

She turned to face me and shook her head as she shot me a concerned look. "Rowan, what I walked into here a few minutes ago doesn't exactly inspire me to believe that."

"You know what it was as well as I do," I told her, trying to skirt around specifics in the presence of the paramedic. If I started talking about ethereal visions, then she might very well change her assessment of me. I glanced over at my wife and continued. "You too Felicity. Especially you. I don't need to go to the hospital."

"Row," Felicity replied. "Cally and I performed CPR on you. I think I know what I'm talking about."

I looked back at her with pleading eyes and spoke in a deliberate tone. "You know what it was, Felicity."

"I'm not so sure about that."

"I am," I stated, lacing my voice with all the confidence I could muster. "And, I don't need to go to the hospital." Once again I repeated a declaration I had already made over a half-dozen times in the past fifteen minutes.

She stared at me for a moment as if visible evidence that would dispute my claim would suddenly appear. As it was not forthcoming, she finally turned her gaze away and closed her eyes.

"What would you like to do?" The paramedic asked, addressing Agent Mandalay. "Am I taking him or not?"

"It's up to you, Felicity," Constance told my wife. "If you want him to go to the hospital, I'll make it happen."

I didn't say anything more. The two of them had allied with one another almost as soon as Constance arrived. Once that happened, my opinion became instantly moot. Arguing with them had accomplished nothing so far, other than provide fuel for my headache.

Felicity finally let out a heavy sigh, and when she spoke, her normally lilting accent thickened, underscoring her words with a serious edge. "No. If he's wrong, I'll just kill him later, then."

CHAPTER 15:

The shrieking whirr of the blender was biting into my skull as Felicity repeatedly pulsed it on and off. I rubbed my temples and watched on, as in a quick motion, she popped off the lid and added yet another ingredient to her homebrewed hangover remedy.

I slid my hand back around to the base of my neck, brushing it gingerly against my flesh. It was still throbbing, and I wondered if I must have hit something on my way down when I blacked out earlier. What little memory I had of the incident was all but completely out of focus, but I did seem to recall falling forward, not backward. I pulled my hand away and inspected it for blood but found none. Apparently, there was no wound even though it felt like there should be. Whatever it was, I just wished it would go away.

My friend groaned as he opened one eye and looked at me. He was sitting at the breakfast nook, or to be accurate, he was sprawled in a chair next to it. He had one elbow planted against the tabletop, and the side of his face was pressed into his loosely doubled fist.

I was sitting across from him, nursing a cup of coffee and staying out of it. I'd been on the receiving end of the Felicity hangover treatment before, and while it seemed to work, I knew what was in it, and moreover, what it tasted like. I didn't envy him one bit.

Besides, I was too preoccupied to get involved. I was still busy wishing that the aspirin I had taken would actually do some good for my own headache. I knew they wouldn't really, but if they worked their usual chemical magic, they would at least dull it a bit. Eventually.

Agent Mandalay was positioned diagonally across from Ben, standing with her back against the wall and watching him intently. We were down to just the four of us now, Cally and RJ having shuttled the twins back to Nancy's house after helping us re-arrange the vehicles. It was a good bet that they shouldn't be present for what was about to transpire, so we had ushered them out as graciously as we could under the circumstances. Still, we had to promise to give them an update as soon as we knew anything.

"Yo, Kemosabe," Ben eventually croaked, barely loud enough to be heard over the whining blades.

"Yeah?"

"Why you got a freakin' potato in a shoebox?"

I hadn't paid much attention to it, but the physical remnants of Felicity's recently dissolved binding were still adorning the table.

"Leftovers from a spell," I replied.

"What kinda spell? Potato salad or French fries?" he chortled.

"A binding actually."

"Binding. You mean like yer shorts?" He found himself amusing again.

"It's like a magickal version of a restraining order," I offered without acknowledging his attempt at humor. "Basically, it's supposed to keep an individual from doing or saying whatever it is the spell is directed toward."

"'Zit work?"

"Depends," I replied, avoiding the recent details. "Sometimes they backfire."

"Then you make potato salad, right?" he chuckled.

"Yeah, Ben. Whatever."

The pulsing whine of the blender's motor came to a halt, and I looked up to see Felicity pouring a healthy measure of dangerous looking liquid into a glass. In a quick flourish, my wife settled the pitcher back onto the base and quickly dropped the lid onto it before stepping over to the table.

"Drink it," she demanded, planting the full glass in front of Ben. "All of it."

"What is it?" Ben muttered as he turned and gave the glass a one-eyed stare.

"It's an old family hangover remedy," she replied. "Just drink it."

"I'm drunk," he mumbled. "I'm not hung over."

"You're both," she told him. "But you won't be either one after you drink this."

He turned his head farther, and I could tell he was trying to focus on the collection of bottles, cans, and cartons my wife had lined up on the counter during the preparation. He finally gave up and rolled his head back forward.

"What's in it?" he asked, his voice still a gravelly rasp.

"Never you mind what's in it. Just drink."

"No thanks." He closed his eye and slumped down even farther.

"It works, Ben," I offered.

"Mebbe so, but I'll pass."

Felicity pushed the glass closer to him then gave his shoulder a light slap with the back of her hand as she adopted an even more stern tone. "Aye, drink it or I'll be sitting on your chest and pouring it down your damn throat."

"I don't think she's bluffing, Storm," Agent Mandalay offered from her vantage point.

"Yeah, well ah'm fuckin' bigger'n she is," he told her.

"Maybe, but I think she's meaner," Constance returned. "And besides, I've got a pair of handcuffs she's welcome to use."

Ben opened a single eye again, then both. After a moment, he dropped his hand down and pushed himself back up in the seat. He wasn't fully upright, but he was moving in the right direction at least. He wrapped his large hand around the glass and lifted it, inspecting the contents with bleary eyes.

"Bitch," he muttered.

"Which one?" Constance asked with a thin smile.

He looked at her and then cast a wobbly glance up at Felicity who was still standing over him.

"Both of ya'," he replied.

"We love you too," Felicity replied sweetly. "Now drink."

He lifted the glass up to his face and peered into it with one eye then passed it under his nose. He wrinkled his forehead and then put the glass back down as he announced, "Smells like shit."

"Constance," Felicity said.

"Storm," Mandalay returned amid the metallic clink of her

handcuffs slipping out of their case.

"All right, all right," he returned, then picked up the concoction again.

"Just hold your nose," I offered the bit of advice. "And drink it as fast as you can."

"Yeah, right," he sneered back at me, then put the glass to his lips and tossed it back.

Halfway through the first gulp he started to grimace. As the glass started back down, Felicity quickly placed her fingers against its base and forced it back up. He gagged for a moment then swallowed hard and finished the drink.

My wife wrapped her hand around the bottom of the glass then deftly took it from him as he pitched his head back forward and began to sputter.

"JEEZUS! Fuck me!" he exclaimed, waving his hands in the air and working his mouth in an attempt to evict the lingering flavor. "What the hell is that shit? It tastes like somethin' died!"

"It's not that bad, then. It's just egg yolk, tomato juice, brewers yeast, Tabasco, vinegar, salt and a few other things," Felicity returned. "Oh, and a couple of anchovies. Mustn't forget those."

"Jeez..." he continued, face screwed up in disgust. "Fuckin' hairy fish?"

"Fish don't have hair, Ben," I told him.

"Bullshit. Anchovies got hair."

"Those are small bones."

"You call it bones, I call it hair. What're ya' tryin' ta' do, Felicity? Kill me?"

She ignored the question as she began disassembling the blender and washing the various parts in the sink.

"No," Constance told him. "She's trying to wake you up, so *I* can kill you."

"Oh yeah? So what'd I do to you?" he grumbled.

"Briefing. Seven-thirty. Mandatory attendance," she returned succinctly.

If the few hours of sleep combined with my wife's home remedy hadn't sobered him up yet, Mandalay's words did so post haste. A pained look of realization washed over my friend's features as he closed his eyes and dropped his forehead into his palm. "Oh jeezzzz... Fuck me..."

"Yeah, fuck you is right," Constance agreed. "Look, Storm, I'm not even going to ask what your problem is. I don't want to know. Rowan says you've got your reasons, and I'm willing to leave it at that."

Ben shot me a startled glance from beneath his hand, and I just gave him a nod of reassurance as I mouthed the word 'later.'

"Listen, Mandalay," he groaned. "I'm sorry... I"

"That's fine." She held up her hand to stop him. "Like I said, I don't want to know. I've already covered for you, and as far as I'm concerned this never happened. However, things have taken a turn, and I just need you to straighten up and get back on board here. Sooner, not later. As in right now."

"Finally get a ransom demand?" he asked.

She clucked her tongue and took in a breath. "Not exactly."

"What?" he asked, trepidation apparent in his voice.

"Rowan?" She turned the floor over to me.

Ben shot a glance over at Felicity then back to me. "You two go all *Twilight Zone* again?"

"Yeah," I responded. "Unfortunately."

"Aww, Jeezus..." he groaned. "Larson's dead isn't she?"

"If we're right, yeah, she is."

"Yeah, like you've been wrong about shit like that before," he replied with a sarcastic note. "Dammit. When?"

"Our first inkling of it came just a little while after you crashed," I told him. "So about three and a half, maybe four hours ago, I guess. But that doesn't mean it didn't actually happen earlier, or even yesterday."

"I still don't understand what you meant about 'no head' though," Felicity said as she turned to face us and leaned back against the kitchen counter. She began absently drying the freshly washed blender parts as she looked at us.

"What?" I asked.

"That's what you said when you first came to," she replied with a dismissive shake of her head. "Brittany. No head."

The biting pain in the back of my neck suddenly made all the sense in the world.

Just as it had happened with Felicity, the vision had faded away as quickly as it had come, and I didn't even remember uttering the words. In the wake of everything that had happened over the course of the evening, this was actually the first time it had even been mentioned.

I wasn't at all surprised that Felicity didn't understand what the comment meant because I hadn't told her what Ben had confided in me earlier in the day. But, I knew full well what the words implied, and so did Ben and Constance.

My friend slowly moved his hand aside and stared at me. I just stared back.

"You sure that's what he said?" he finally asked without turning.

"Positive," she replied. "Do you know what it means?"

"It means we have a serial killer who just claimed a third victim," Constance announced flatly.

"Hey you three," Felicity said. "I'm obviously not blonde, but maybe I'm having a moment here. A little help, then?"

"Tamara Linwood and Sarah Hart." Ben explained, "Both corpses were found minus their heads."

"Oh Gods…" she murmured softly.

"The initial theory on Hart was that it might have been due to predation," Constance offered. "But then the medical examiner found seven grooved striations on the posterior of the remaining C-six vertebrae. The tool marks lab matched them to a manual hacksaw, most likely with a fourteen TPI bi-metal blade."

"Good memory," Ben said. "I didn't know you were on that case."

"I wasn't." She shook her head. "It came up as an NCIC match when we ran Larson's abduction profile. Secluded parking lot, missing twenty-something-year-old woman, etcetera."

"And you got all that from a NCIC hit?"

"Not all of it." She shrugged. "I had a few minutes this morning, so I read the file."

Ben raised an eyebrow and looked back at her incredulously. "And you remembered all that?"

"Well sure," she replied.

"Jeezus, Mandalay, you're almost as weird as these two."

"I'll take that as a compliment, Storm."

"Well, I hate ta' say it, but we still got another problem," he ventured.

"What's that?" I asked.

"We got no way to prove any of this stuff about Larson is true."

"Unless we can find the body," I offered.

"That's a big 'unless', Rowan," Constance expressed.

"What're ya' thinkin' white man?" Ben queried. "You got that hinky look goin' on."

"I'm thinking that I obviously saw something while I was 'under' so to speak," I explained. "So maybe I saw more than just the 'no head' thing."

"Yeah, but apparently you didn't even remember that, so how are you gonna remember anything else?"

"It's a long shot, but..."

"NO." Felicity's austere voice cut me off.

"What?" Ben turned his head and asked her. "Was he gettin' ready to say he wanted to do somethin' stupid?"

"Yes," she replied, her tone still harsh.

"How do you know what I was going to say?" I asked, slightly annoyed.

"She's married to ya', Kemosabe," Ben huffed with almost a note of pained disgust in his voice. "She knows everything. Even what yer gonna say next."

I sped immediately into an explanation, hoping to overshadow his words and more importantly, his tone. "I was only going to recommend we do a regression."

"Like a past life thing?" Constance asked. "Hypnosis?"

"Similar," I nodded as I answered her. "But instead of past life, I'd just be going to a previous point in my own."

"*Breugadair*," my wife spat, resorting to a Gaelic epithet for liar. "Someone else's *death* is what you mean."

"We don't have much choice in the matter," I contended.

"Rowan, not an hour ago your heart stopped beating for almost two minutes."

"DO WHAT?!" Ben exclaimed, whipping his gaze back around to me.

"You were still passed out," I explained quickly. "Besides, she's making it out to be worse than it is."

"I am not," she defended herself.

"Yer fuckin' heart stopped?" Ben pressed.

"Not according to the paramedics," I said.

"Paramedics?" he exclaimed. "Jeezus H. Christ! What the hell else did I miss?"

"Rowan," Constance said, ignoring Ben's query. "Maybe Felicity is right."

"It's not as dangerous as she's wanting you two to believe," I appealed.

"All right. Fine." Felicity leveled her determined gaze directly on me and pushed away from the counter as she announced, "Then how about if I do it."

CHAPTER 16:

Talking myself into corners was something I excelled at on various occasions. Most especially when it came to trying to convince my wife that I was prepared to handle anything the ethereal world could throw at me. Of course, over the past few years she had seen more than her share of my experiences with such, and she knew better than to believe me. Therefore, it always took some creative explaining to convince her otherwise; or try to at least, because as of late, invariably I would lose the verbal scuffles.

So, getting into the corner was easy. Escaping from it once I found myself pinned was definitely something at which I needed more practice. As it happened, this was rapidly becoming a perfect opportunity for just such an experience. Since my back was now so firmly pressed into the metaphorical niche that it was beginning to take on a similar angular shape, I had nothing to lose by trying.

I blurted the second thing that came to mind, "No way."

I chose the second thing to pop into my head because the first phrase was more along the lines of, 'it's too dangerous.' Quite obviously, echoing my wife's very sentiment would have been equivalent to surrendering my king before the first pawn had been moved. I already wasn't sure that I was going to be able to talk myself out of this one, but I wasn't going to simply give up. I knew my response was less than inspired, but my creative juices were failing me miserably at the moment. Still, I charged ahead, making a bid to break free of the 'rock and a hard place' of my own making.

"Why?" Felicity asked coolly and then baited me with, "Because it's too dangerous?"

"No. Because it wouldn't do any good," I told her. "You didn't see the things that I saw."

"How do you know that?" she asked, crossing her arms beneath her breast. "Neither one of us can remember anything except what the other one said."

"Right," I agreed. "And you didn't mention anything about her being headless."

She arched her eyebrows as she gave her head a slight shake. "So?"

"So I must have seen more than you did."

"Oh come on," she exclaimed. "You don't buy into that any more than I do."

Ben voiced his own observation. "Jeezzz, Row, even I know that's a lame argument."

"You aren't helping," I returned.

"Look," Constance spoke up. "I don't know as much about this as you two do or even Storm for that matter…"

"Hey, you see a broom between my legs?" Ben objected. "Leave me outta this."

"…What I'm trying to ask," she continued, glossing over his interruption. "Is that if it's dangerous for Rowan wouldn't it be dangerous for you too, Felicity?"

"Not as much," she replied.

All bids to get myself out of the corner were immediately null and void. I knew the next words out of my mouth would sabotage my own argument, but I was unable to keep myself from calling Felicity on her comment.

"Okay, so who's blowing smoke now?" I chided.

"All I did was pass out, Rowan," she asserted. "My heart didn't come to a screeching halt like yours did."

"Will you get off that? The paramedics told you I was fine."

"Aye, they did," she shot back. "But I didn't believe it then, and I don't believe it now."

I literally threw up my hands in exasperation. "Okay, so what do we do then? You don't want me doing a regression, and I don't want you doing one either. So where does that leave us?"

"Okay, like I said, I don't really know that much about all this," Constance started in again. "Just what I've seen you do here and there, and, well… It's usually pretty freaking bizarre to be honest… But, that's beside the point. Anyway, here's my idea. What if you still did it, but in a controlled manner?"

"What do you mean by controlled?" I asked.

"Yeah, Mandalay," Ben voiced. "I think I know where you're headin' with this."

"I mean what if you, or Felicity, or even both of you underwent hypnosis by a third party. That way if it gets too weird then you could be snapped out of it right away."

"That's a thought," Felicity said.

Constance shrugged. "We sometimes use various forms of forensic hypnosis with witnesses to help jog repressed or misplaced memories, so why not with you two?"

"She's right," Ben added. "Charlee McLaughlin was tellin' me she used it with a rape victim a few months back. What they got from her was inadmissible in court, but it gave 'em enough to get a decent lead on the asshole. After that, all they had to do was gather evidence."

"The rules of evidence are pretty dicey when it comes to information retrieved via hypnosis," Constance agreed. "But we aren't after that in this case. We're just looking for a location on Larson's remains."

"I'm not sure it would work." I shook my head. "Since the experiences were ethereal to begin with, for all intents and purposes, they took place on another plane of existence."

"But wouldn't the memories still be there?" she asked. "Just inaccessible to the conscious self."

"That's the unknown variable here," I replied.

"But, they could be there, right?" she reiterated.

I pondered the question for a moment. I'd never really given the idea much thought, until now.

"She might have a point, Row." Felicity broke the short silence. "You've always retained memories from psychic episodes before."

"Yeah," I replied slowly. "That's true."

"Aye, so it's worth a try at least," Felicity said.

Mandalay glanced at her watch and looked thoughtful for a

second then said, "I can make a couple of calls. I'm not sure if we have anyone available on this short of notice though. It may have to wait until tomorrow or even Monday."

"But wouldn't there be a better chance of any latent evidence still being intact if the scene is located sooner?" I asked.

"Of course," Ben answered for her. "Fresher the crime scene the better. That's a given."

"Then we need to do this now," I declared.

"Like I said," Constance offered. "I can make some calls."

"I'll go you one better," I said as a vague memory edged into focus. "Ben, your sister performs hypnosis in her psychiatric practice, doesn't she?"

"Yeah, I think she does," he replied with a nod.

"Do you think she'd be up for this tonight?" I asked.

He shrugged. "Hell, she never does anything other than work or sit at home reading, so I don't see why not. One question though."

"What's that?" I asked.

"Actually it's for Mandalay," he replied as he looked over at her. "Say one of these two *Twilight Zone's* us a crime scene. What's the next step?"

Constance wrinkled her forehead and gave a knowing nod. "Guess we'll have to go verify it."

"And after that?" Ben pressed. "Which one of us is gonna tell Albright how we found it?"

"As much as I'd like to do it," she told him. "I'd sure hate to steal your thunder, Storm."

"Yeah, funny. Like I haven't heard that one before."

As it turned out, my friend had been incorrect this go around. His sister had in fact been out to dinner and not holed away in her house reading as he had said she would be. We were lucky, however, as her home number had been forwarded to her service and no sooner had

Ben left a message than she called back. Fortunately, not only was she more than willing to come by the house, she was less than fifteen minutes away.

When Helen arrived, Felicity was in the kitchen starting a fresh pot of coffee, and Constance was hiding away in our bedroom for a few minutes so she could return some calls. Ben was expectantly standing at the open door when she pulled into the driveway. He met her on the sidewalk and immediately renewed the brotherly interrogation he'd originally launched on the phone.

Now that they were in the house, I was standing back and quietly watching the continuation of the small family skirmish that was taking place in my living room.

"I am a grown woman, Benjamin." Helen Storm looked up into her brother's face. Her voice was calm, but the words were underscored with an unmistakable note of no-nonsense finality. "Not to mention that I am your older sister. I can certainly go out on a blind date without your approval."

There was no way one could miss the relationship between the two of them. The family resemblance was more than obvious even though Helen was of average height as opposed to her towering sibling. Both were possessed of the same dark eyes and typical angular profiles. Although in most ways they were the same, Helen's features were far softer. Her pretty face was framed by a cascade of thick, black hair, streaked randomly with strands of grey. The touch of silver was the only visible indicator that she was actually older than her brother.

Having been in some sense a patient of hers, in both official and unofficial capacities, I was used to seeing her in conservative business attire. This evening, however, she was projecting a vastly different outward image via a somewhat flirtatious cocktail dress.

"That's not what I'm sayin', Helen," my friend objected. "There're a lotta nutjobs out… And that dress is…"

"My dress is just fine, dear brother," she replied in the wake of his stammering. "And, I met him at the restaurant so that I would have my own car. I am quite capable of making rational decisions."

"Yeah, but what'd you know about this guy?" he continued. "For all you know he's a wingnut with a…"

"End of discussion, Benjamin," she replied, cutting him off mid-sentence.

He stared back at her and shook his head but kept his mouth shut.

"I'm sorry we interrupted your evening, Helen," I offered, slipping the apology into the mildly uncomfortable void that fell behind her last declaration.

"Don't worry over it, Rowan," she replied as she cast a pleasant smile toward me. "Benjamin sometimes forgets that I do in fact have a social life. The truth is, I was actually considering a trip to the ladies room just so I could page myself. I needed an escape, so as it turns out, your call was serendipitous."

"Escape?" Ben asked.

"He was boring me to tears, Benjamin," she said as she turned back to him. "That's all, nothing more. Stop imagining the worst, please." She cocked her head to the side and gave him a curious stare. "You have been drinking haven't you?"

"What's that got to do with anything?"

"It would certainly explain your mood this evening," she replied. "You are even more overprotective than usual."

"So sue me."

"And would I happen to know what prompted this little binge?" she pressed.

He brushed off the question. "It's not important."

"Yes, I thought as much," she replied with an understanding nod, gleaning untold information from his evasive words. "We should discuss that later. At the moment, however, I seem to recall something being said about a murder investigation and the need for a hypnotist. Well, here I am."

CHAPTER 17:

The flame on the candle reached upward, stretching into a thin tongue as it licked at the air. It undulated in an ever-increasing rhythm until it seemed to almost vibrate then it began to die back downward. I watched intently as the threadlike wisp collapsed into itself to finally become a flickering teardrop of yellow-orange that cast a soft glow into the dimness of the room.

After some discussion as to how a session of hypnosis was to be conducted, as well as detailing our ultimate goal, even Helen agreed that if it worked, there would still be some amount of danger involved. Given Felicity's and my preternatural connection with the other side of the veil, we could very easily springboard from the hypnotic trance state directly into a full-blown ethereal excursion. Helen still felt confident that she could control the situation if it did in fact occur; however, as with anything in life, it was something she could not guarantee with absolute certainty. The fact that there was even a remote chance of slipping past the gates and into the world of the dead was a point of hot contention for my wife and I.

We both agreed that this was something that had to be done. Backing out of it was not even an issue. Given the circumstances, however, neither of us was willing to let the other be a guinea pig. The banter between us didn't last long before Felicity simply insisted that she be the one to go under; or at the very least, that she go first. In her mind, I was only to become involved as a last resort if she was unsuccessful. And, she had every intention of seeing to it that she didn't fail.

I, of course, was dead set against her facing any of this at all. I abandoned my earlier argument, not that it had been getting me anywhere to begin with, and without embellishment told her no, absolutely not; the subject of this experiment would be me, and only me, end of story.

She wasn't ready for story time to be over yet.

As was her stubborn nature, she had just looked back at me in silence like I was speaking an unfamiliar foreign language. After a moment, she said something on the order of, "Damn your eyes, Rowan Linden Gant, if you sit in that chair, you'll never make it under because I'll be slapping you silly." There may well have been a few Gaelic expletives interspersed, but that was the general gist of it, and she said it in dead earnest.

The important thing here is that this was the second time this evening Felicity had threatened to get physical. You always knew just exactly how serious she was whenever she intimated violence. While I figured it was unlikely that she would actually follow through, I had no desire to put it to the test. Manifest proof, yet again, that one should never argue with a redheaded, Irish Taurus when she has already made up her mind. With this one, at least, you simply could not win.

I suppose that one of these days I would wise up and take my own advice in that regard. Maybe.

So, having begrudgingly conceded, I now found myself sitting in our semi-darkened living room, quietly watching my wife begin her journey.

"Don't speak, Felicity. Simply listen to my voice and relax." Helen Storm's soothing tone sounded nearby. "Breathe in deeply and let the air flow slowly from your lungs. Allow it to take with it the stress of the day... Relax... Breathe..."

This was what Helen referred to as the 'Induction,' the process by which the hypnotist starts the subject along his or her way. To me, and I am sure Felicity as well, it was a lesson right out of 'Wicca 101'. Everything she was doing was a basic grounding technique a Witch would use to become centered and connect with the earth before performing magick or ritual. If I didn't know what was actually going on here, I would assume that she was preparing to cast a circle.

"Keep your eyes focused on the flame..." she continued, her voice an even, melodic tenor. "Watch it... Study it... Allow it to become the only thing that you see."

Ben and Constance were in the dining room, still within earshot but physically out of the way so as not to prove a distraction to the process. I, however, was positioned immediately beside Felicity as she reclined in a chair. Proximity was the one concession I had demanded.

I was to be her failsafe. While Helen concentrated on extracting the hidden information, if any, I would watch for signs that my wife was slipping too far across the threshold. It all came down to the fact that whether Felicity liked it or not, I had absolute control over ending the session if I felt it was getting out of hand.

Of course, if it became necessary for me to take a turn concentrating on the flame, she would have the exact same power. Even so, she made me promise not to stop the session needlessly just to get her out of harm's way. I cannot say that I hadn't considered doing just that, but I made the promise, and I would abide by it. My hold card was the fact that we hadn't discussed exactly how far was too far, and it was too late for her to argue that point now.

"Keep watching the flame, Felicity," Helen spoke again. "You are comfortable... You are relaxed... You are at peace with yourself and everything around you... Allow that comfort to fill you from head to toe... Embrace it, and allow it to embrace you..."

I watched the rise and fall of Felicity's chest as it slowed, becoming a barely perceptible movement of her near frozen form. Her face was slack, lips parted slightly and eyes fixed in a glazed stare firmly attached to the glowing tip of the candle. I could physically sense how grounded she was. She had become so disconnected from the conscious mind that even her psychic defenses were quickly falling away. That worried me but not enough to stop the session. I had actually predicted that it would happen before we even started, so even though I was concerned, I wasn't surprised.

I immediately extended my own ethereal shields to surround her as well as myself, effectively negating her sudden vulnerability to the non-physical energies around us. This was a task at which she was far more practiced than I considering that she had done it for me on numerous occasions when I was suffering a psychic episode. Still, it was an ability I possessed even though these days it took a bit more concentration on my part.

"Now, I want you to close your eyes, Felicity," Helen instructed in a quiet voice. "Maintain the image of the flame... See it in your mind's eye... Watch it flicker as if your eyes were still firmly focused upon it... Allow it to illuminate your world as you begin to see a staircase before you, leading downward..."

As expected, my wife was slipping into the trance in record time, undoubtedly due to years of meditation and psychic exercises. Of course, it didn't hurt that Helen was good at what she did. While she had outlined the various stages of the induction for us, it wasn't readily obvious when she moved from one to the next as she did so with such fluid confidence.

The serenity was momentarily broken by the sound of a dull clunk. In reality, it wasn't very loud at all, but in the stillness of the house it echoed heavily. I jerked slightly and looked up across the room to see Ben staring back at me with his own startled expression. His hand was held out toward his coffee cup where it rested on the dining room table as if motioning for it to stop making noise. He tensed and frowned then mouthed the word 'sorry'.

I slowly turned back to my wife and saw that fortunately the sound hadn't affected her in the least.

Helen continued. "When you see the staircase, Felicity, you will raise your right index finger."

Almost as soon as she had finished speaking, my wife's finger arched upward of its own accord and came to rest as if pointing at something in the distance. Consciously, Felicity most likely wasn't even aware that her finger was raised. It was doing so based on something Helen had called an ideomotor response. It was a physical manifestation of the power of suggestion driven by the engine of the subconscious mind.

"Good," Helen announced with a faint note of satisfaction in her voice. "Now, lower your finger. Before we proceed, we will establish this simple boundary. If at any time you hear me say the word 'return', you will immediately come back to this place of absolute comfort and safety. I will then begin counting from one to ten. When I reach ten, you will awaken. You will be calm, relaxed, and you will remember everything. If you understand this, raise your finger again."

Felicity's pale index finger rose on cue.

"Very good. Now I want you to step forward and begin walking down the stairs. As you do so, feel yourself sinking deeper into the sensation of comfort... You will feel as though you are swaddled in a deep, restful sleep, yet you will remain alert... Focused... Aware of your surroundings and of my voice... When you reach the bottom of the stairs, there will be a comfortable chair awaiting you. Take a seat in it, and when you have, lower your finger."

Again, almost before Helen's voice had a chance to fade, Felicity's finger was on the move.

"That was a short staircase," I whispered.

"Sshhhh," Helen shushed me softly, then whispered in return, "There are only as many stairs as the individual requires. No less and no more."

I still thought it was a short staircase even if it was only a visualization. Either that or Felicity had mentally taken them two at a time and at a dead run. But, I kept my mouth shut; Helen was the expert on this, not me.

She paused for a moment after Felicity's finger had fully lowered. I'm not sure whose benefit the brief respite was for, but I desperately needed it myself. As relaxed as my wife appeared to be, in contrast, I was just as tense, if not doubly so. I took the opportunity to draw in a deep breath or two while seeing to it that my own ground was intact and solid.

Finally, Helen began to speak again. "I still do not want you to speak, Felicity, but I want you to open your eyes."

Slowly, her eyelids fluttered upward, but the hypnotically imposed distance was evident in her glassy stare.

"You now see a movie screen in front of you," Helen told her. "Playing on the screen there is a documentary. I want you to watch it closely. I want you to notice every detail... Every nuance... No matter how unimportant it may seem. While you will remember that this documentary is something that was once seen through your own eyes, you are now separate from it. At this moment, you are simply an observer.

"The subject of this documentary is an experience you had earlier this evening when you were teaching a class to your Coven mates. Something happened that only you were able to see but you have now repressed. You will see it once again as you watch this documentary before you. Remember that you are only an observer. Watch… Listen… Remember… Do not speak… When it is over, you will raise your index finger again to let me know."

I watched Felicity's expressionless face as she stared, unblinking into the dim room, looking not at, past, nor even through Helen. For all intents and purposes, we did not exist for her at this moment in time. The mental picture playing out before her was all that occupied her world.

After a long moment, there was a thin, nasal whimper. At first I glanced around, looking to see if one of the dogs had migrated from the bedroom and wanted to be let out. But, when it sounded again, slightly stronger this time, I easily pinpointed it as coming from my wife.

I focused my attention solely on Felicity as I watched her respirations steadily increase. They were coming as a series of rapid, shallow breaths that soon became the palpitating rhythm of loosely harnessed panic. I shot a concerned glance at Helen, and she gently shook her head.

"It is all right, Rowan," she whispered. "This is to be expected. She is fine."

Without a word, I returned my gaze to my wife and watched her shallowly puffing out the breaths as she continued to whimper. Still, she stared straight ahead, attention fixed upon a horror only she could see.

Her eyes were glistening with dampness, and a single tear broke loose from where it had welled and began trickling down her right cheek. It was rapidly followed by another, and then a second stream began flowing from the left. Her body tensed, and the whimpering grew into what sounded like a stifled scream that was repeated not once, but twice.

I was just about to turn to Helen again when Felicity let out a sudden heavy sigh that bespoke relief. I watched on as her body relaxed and her breathing slowly returned to the earlier slow, even rhythm that had accompanied the onset of the trance.

In a single, easy motion my wife stretched her finger upward into the air.

CHAPTER 18:

"Thank you, Felicity," Helen said. "Lower your finger now and relax."

Felicity's face remained slack, but her finger levered back downward without so much as a tremble. Her tension had more than just visibly ebbed; all evidence of it had disappeared but for the tear trails that still dampened her cheeks. For me, however, the expectant silence that fell into step behind her muffled display of anguish was causing my hairs to bristle.

"You should relax too, Rowan," Helen told me.

"Easier said than done," I replied. "Something doesn't feel right about this."

"What's up, white man," Ben asked, still sitting at the dining room table. "You goin' all la-la?"

"No." I shook my head. "Something just feels strange." I paused for a moment and then let out a forced sigh. "I don't know… It might just be me. It seems like nothing ever feels right anymore."

"Well," Helen spoke up, "from a clinical point of view, the session is going very well. In fact, what you just saw should have been the worst of it."

"Should have been?" I asked. "The word *should* doesn't exactly evoke an air of extreme confidence for me, Helen."

"Yes, I understand that," she replied. "Let me explain. What she has experienced will certainly still have emotional consequences tied to it, but at this point it is merely information. She is no longer watching the repressed memory play out; therefore, the connection with it is somewhat dulled. It will not be as intense as re-experiencing it."

"Okay," I replied, trepidation still evident in my voice. "So what now? Do you wake her up?"

"No, not yet," she shook her head as she answered. "Hypnosis is no more perfect than the supernormal incidents that you are prone to,

Rowan. While I have given her a post-hypnotic instruction to remember what she has now re-witnessed, some detail may still be lost upon awakening. What we do now is attempt to retrieve the information by having her recount it to us while still in a trance state."

She leaned to the side and reached for her purse, which she had stowed beneath the edge of the coffee table. After rummaging around for a moment, she withdrew her hand, and in it was a micro cassette recorder. She quickly popped it open, checked the tape, then closed the cover and tested the buttons.

"For an actual forensic hypnosis session, I would have been better prepared," she informed us. "We actually should have been videotaping the entire process, from the initial interview through termination of the session. However, for our purposes, I believe a brief audio recording will suffice."

"This ain't goin' into court if that's what you're talkin' about," Ben offered from across the room.

"Precisely," Helen returned, then momentarily shifted her focus back to me. "Truly, Rowan, you can relax now."

"I'll relax when this is over," I told her.

She gave only a knowing nod as a reply. She was no stranger to the inner workings of my brand of emotionally imbued logic, so she knew she wasn't going to be able to talk me down.

She activated the recorder and laid it on the end table with the microphone directed toward Felicity.

"Now, Felicity," she began. "I want you to speak now, and tell us what you have just seen. Start at the beginning and take your time."

"Candee is arguing with RJ again. She just isn't working out." Even though her face remained blank, Felicity began speaking as if she had been carrying on a conversation with us all along. I immediately noticed a thread of reluctance running through her voice. "There's simply too much friction between her and the others. She doesn't even seem to care how a Coven works. I don't want to talk to her about this, but I'm just going to have to. I need to tell her she should seek another group. Row, I wish you were here to do it. You're so much better at letting people down easy than I am."

I opened my mouth to respond, but before I could get a word out, I felt Helen's hand on my arm. I looked over my shoulder, and she was shaking her head.

I nodded and remained silent.

"Felicity," Helen began. "I want you to move forward in time. You were teaching your class, and by all accounts, you had some type of seizure."

"Yes," Felicity replied, calmly switching the subject. "The class was about Dark Moon magick, and I was going over one of my favorite *Dorothy Morrison* spells with the group. I had just recited the last line where you call to the Crone of Darkness and ask her to allow you to feel the unseen an..."

Her words ended without warning. No stutter, no sound, no nothing. They simply halted mid-breath, leaving an expectant silence in their wake.

"Go on, Felicity," Helen prompted. "It is okay. Just tell us what you remember."

My wife's head tilted forward, slowly at first and then simply fell as if she'd lost consciousness. As her chin touched her chest, her head lolled to the side, and she creased her brow in a display of pain. She rolled her head back upward and allowed it to tilt back, bringing her face up toward the ceiling, then let out a heavy breath.

"Jesus I hurt." The words came out of Felicity's mouth, but the voice was completely unfamiliar.

I turned a hard stare back to Helen and she held up her hand, motioning for me to wait.

"Felicity?" she asked.

I turned back to my wife and watched as she blinked her eyes several times.

The voice came again, louder and defiant. "What, you can't turn on the goddamned lights around here?"

She grimaced visibly and then ran the tip of her tongue across her teeth.

"Fuck," she said. "My tooth's broke."

I felt a sudden closeness and looked up to find that Ben and Constance had moved into the room with us and were watching intently.

"Larson got hit in the mouth," Ben whispered, then canted his head toward Felicity. "Is she doin' what I think she is?"

"If you mean is she channeling Brittany Larson," I returned, "yeah, I think she is."

I shot another glance toward Helen and then turned back to Felicity. I knew something hadn't felt right about all of this, and now that feeling was starting to get worse. Much worse.

My wife's hands were resting on the arms of the chair, and she began to physically jerk and tug as if trying to lift them, but they barely moved. She rotated her wrists as she struggled— stretching her fingers outward and then doubling them back into fists. She pushed herself slightly forward and twisted her shoulders while wriggling in her seat, groaning as she pulled against the unseen bonds. No matter how hard she tried, her forearms remained planted on the rests as if they were actually tied there. She finally let herself fall back into the seat and let out a frustrated shriek.

"Fucking asshole!" the voice burst from her lips as a defiant shout. "Do you have any idea who I am?!"

"Jeezus," Ben muttered. "She's got a pair."

Felicity suddenly jerked her head to the side, pulling it away from something unseen as she sent her eyes searching.

"Don't you touch me," the voice growled. "My father is goddamned Mayor you idiot. Every fucking cop in the state is probably looking for me right now."

Her head jerked backward, and her jaw clenched as her neck began to stretch. A nasal whine came from her nose amid the sound of her choking.

"Bring her back," I demanded, whipping around to face Helen. "Now."

"Yes," she agreed. "I think so. Felicity, return."

My wife's head instantly fell forward then began to slowly tilt back upward. Her chest rose with a deep breath and then settled into her earlier relaxed rhythm. Once again her face was slack.

"No," she said after a moment, her own voice issuing from her lips.

"One... Two..." Helen began counting.

"No," Felicity spoke again, sharpness in her tone. "Not yet. I can't remember it all."

"...Five... Six..."

"NO," my wife insisted, still staring off into space. "We have to know where she is."

"...Nine..." Helen continued.

"NO!" Felicity barked. "I have to go back. I have to..."

She finished the sentence with an agonized cry, which caught in her throat only to be cut off mid scream. Her face suddenly contorted into a pained grimace as her body stiffened, and her hands began posturing inward.

The room filled with the sound of arcing electricity as it started to buzz and snap, and at the exact instant of the first pop, I felt the ethereal defenses I had erected begin falling away. Upon the second, they collapsed inward upon themselves as if caught in a gale force wind.

"RETURN," Helen announced once again, this time with far more urgency.

Blind agony hammered me between the eyes, and I blinked back tears as it screwed inward toward the center of my brain. I felt my own motor control begin to slip as I flopped sideways, almost falling from the armless chair in which I was seated. Something grappled my shoulder in a tight hold, and I looked up to see Ben steadying me.

"*Twilight Zone?*" His words rushed past me in a distorted stream and then began repeating in a hollow echo.

A heavy bass thrum droned inside my head as I reached up with trembling hands in an attempt to contain my exploding skull. I shut my eyes tight and tried to will it away. The one clear thought that kept running through my mind was just let me die.

"ROWAN!" Ben's voice struck my ears again, forcing their way through the heavy metal crescendo that was building in my brain.

"FELICITY! RETURN!" I heard Helen's voice again, and it was edging toward frantic. "RETURN!"

Helen Storm was the calmest, most even-tempered person I had ever met. She didn't get frantic.

Now I was frightened.

"Oh my god!" Agent Mandalay's voice joined the jumble of noises. "Felicity!"

I pitched forward and forced myself to open my eyes. My wife was in the full throes of a seizure; her face was a horrid mask of pain as she shook uncontrollably, gnashing her teeth into her tongue. Pinkish froth was running from the corner of her mouth, and she bucked hard against unearthly restraints. However, that was but one of the torturous images to greet me.

Small, circular wounds had appeared randomly along her bare forearms. They were red and blistered. Oozing and charred. I'd seen pictures of wounds just like them in a brochure from a local women's shelter. The information was about spousal abuse, and the photos were of cigarette burns.

A linear splash of blood suddenly appeared on Felicity's t-shirt just across her left breast, spreading outward as it soaked into the cloth. I watched in horror as yet another burn mark sizzled into view on the back of her hand, appearing right before my eyes.

"JEEZUS FUCKIN' CHRIST!" Ben was yelling. "Helen! Do something!"

"She isn't responding!" Helen returned. "She is pushing herself into it on purpose!"

I was struggling to maintain my own connection with this world, and the visual horror of the torture my wife was now going through only steeled my resolve. I forced a tenuous ground to form once again between the earth and me in an attempt to rebuild my shattered defenses. But, even as I connected, I could feel it making and breaking in a vicious cycle.

Fear was boring upward from the pit of my stomach as I fought simply to keep from slipping any further across the veil myself. I didn't want to think about how far this could go, but my brain rifled through the scenarios anyway. I was intimately familiar with the dangers that came along with channeling those on the other side. At this very moment, each and every one of them was present and accounted for. And, leading the pack, as always, was Cerridwen. The Dark Mother, Goddess of death and rebirth. A deity to whom I had called out on many a Samhain night when celebrating the lives of loved ones long past.

But, in recent years, I had come to despise her and that for which she stood. I knew that I should not, but emotions run deeper than logic, and I could not change the way I felt.

As much as I had denied it earlier, I knew full well that my heart had stopped. Death was something I cheated every time this happened, and I would continue to duck her gelid embrace for as long as I could. But right now, as in times before, the cold bitch was waiting at the other end of this path with open arms, and Felicity was running full speed toward her.

What the darkness offered so freely was meant for me, not my wife, and I simply couldn't allow her to get there first.

CHAPTER 19:

I had a problem, and it wasn't a small one.

The problem being that there was absolutely nothing to stop both of us from dying if this was allowed to progress. Throwing myself into the arms of the Dark Mother, noble as it may seem, did not guarantee Felicity's safety on this plane or any other. Given the situation, she could easily follow me right into death without so much as a pause. There was far more at work here, and while I didn't know exactly what it was, I was determined to win out over it.

This wasn't the time for sacrifice, and I knew that.

What I didn't know was how I was going to make it all stop. Felicity was hell bent on finding an answer, and because of that, she was now caught up in a vortex of her own creation. She had plunged directly into this on purpose, and now I was not only fighting an overwhelming ethereal force, I was pitted against her willful determination as well. The fact is, her doggedness was probably feeding whatever it was she had connected with.

Out of pure reflex, I reached for her hand and clasped my fingers around her gnarled fist. I felt the thread of pure agony arc along my nerve endings as it raced up my arm and exploded through my body. My teeth began to involuntarily gnash as my jaw grew tight, and the sensation of holding onto a bare extension cord ripped into me just as it had the day before.

Amidst it all, however, was a new and different feeling. At first I thought it was my imagination. Nothing more than my senses thrown off kilter by the intensity of what was now happening. But, when the feeling struck for a second and then again for a third time, I knew it was more than a phantom sensation. It was real.

It came first as a tug. Next, it was a sharp jerk pulling against my arm and flowing through to the base of my skull as if some internal wire connected them to one another. Then it became a fierce pull, undulating in time with my on-again off-again connection to the earth.

What was even more surprising was that it made perfect sense to my tortured brain. It was my ground— my connection with the earth— slamming on the brakes as it attempted to shunt the energies harmlessly away. In order to stop this, I was going to have to complete that ground for the both of us and hold it fast. Unfortunately, that was an almost impossible task for me in my current state. Still, I had little choice but to at least try.

I seized on everything I had, reaching deep within myself for the strength to make it happen. I fought to push aside the stabbing pain in my head long enough to visualize a shaft of light extending from myself and deep into the center of the earth. But, just as I feared, each time I would form the vision in my head a fresh lance of agony would pierce me, and I would falter, losing both the connection and the supernatural skirmish in the process.

At some point, I think I let out a scream. I wasn't sure because I don't know that I actually heard it. I couldn't tell you if it was born of pain, frustration, fear, or even a combination of all three. All I know is that whether I heard it or not, I definitely felt it deep within my soul.

I would have assumed that it was only in my mind, but for the fact that behind the deeply felt wail, I did hear Ben cry out my name. A split second later, I felt his hand briefly clamp onto my shoulder, and at that moment, a sizzling electrical pop reported in my ears. Ben's hand immediately jerked away in combination with his expletive-ridden yelp.

In that instant I knew what had to be done. This had grown beyond what I believed it to be. It was no longer a case of me, or even Felicity, stepping across the threshold into the world of the ethereal. The ethereal had come to us. Felicity may have stepped into its domain first, but it was on this side of the veil now. It was a physical manifestation, and it was making itself right at home. If I was to deal with it, I had to approach it as the unwanted houseguest it was.

The arc that occurred between Ben and me was the clue I needed. I was on the right track when I had tried to ground; I just hadn't taken it far enough. I knew now that this could be brought to a screeching halt. All I needed to do was treat it like household electricity— I had to short it to ground and blow its fuse.

"G-g-gr-n-n-d-d," I stammered as I pushed myself out of the chair and fell to my knees next to Felicity.

"WHAT?" Constance yelped.

"G-Ground!" I managed to spit the word out once again, this time without dividing it into a stream of stammered consonants.

Using the arm of the chair for leverage, I pulled myself to one knee and slipped my right arm in behind Felicity's denim-covered knees. I forced myself to release my grip on her hand and worked my left arm partially behind her upper back as she continued to buck and tremble.

"What are you doing?!" Ben shouted at me.

I didn't take time to answer him. I pushed myself upward and tried to pull Felicity along with me, but the awkward angle immediately worked against us. I lost my balance and fell forward, stumbling into the chair, barely catching myself against the opposite arm with my hastily extracted left hand.

I pushed back, breathing heavily as I concentrated on keeping myself from being sucked completely under by the preternatural riptide that was now tearing through my living room. I quickly pulled my right hand free and grasped my petite wife by both wrists then pulled her upward. For her to tip the scale at one hundred five pounds, she had to be fully clothed, soaking wet, and have rocks in her pockets; but at the moment she may as well have weighed ten times that much. She was dead weight with an attitude, and it was taking everything I had just to get her up out of the chair.

"ROWAN!" Ben bellowed again. "What the hell are you doing?!"

"Get back, Benjamin," Helen ordered. "Give him some room."

I threw my gaze in his direction as I dragged Felicity to her feet and steadied her body against mine. His face was a contorted mask of concern, as were Constance's and Helen's. The three of them were frantically moving about, trying to find a way to help but afraid to touch either of us after witnessing the severe jolt Ben had taken. Still, Ben was moving in on me with total disregard for himself, obviously willing to be bitten again if that was what it took.

"Benjamin," Helen declared again. "Move away! I think I know what he's doing. Give him room!"

"G-Ground!" I repeated, forcing the word out past my teeth as my jaw repeatedly clenched and released.

Ben shot a glance at his sister, then at me, but backpedaled as she had ordered. I stooped quickly and planted my shoulder into Felicity's waist while slipping my arm around the backs of her thighs. She was still trembling spastically as I brought myself upright with her body folded over my shoulder. The combination of her weight and the violent jerking sent my sense of balance on hiatus, and I stumbled as I aimed myself toward the front door.

"Door. Get... The... Door..." I managed to chatter through my aching jaw.

Ben was already there, whipping it open and rushing through ahead of us to hold the screen door. I threw myself at the opening and thudded against the doorframe on the way through. I careened forward and staggered onto the porch, just barely catching myself before we tumbled down the front stairs. I steadied myself against a support pillar and grabbed the handrail.

Nothing happened.

Not even a tingle.

I couldn't believe it. I knew that I had to be correct. If I wasn't I had no idea what I was going to do. I looked down at my hand incredulously and realized immediately that the functional metal handhold was coated in plastic— a measure I had paid extra for in order to prevent rust and alleviate the need for painting. Now, it was my bane as it completely insulated me from the metal, negating the ground I was seeking. I instantly despised myself for the decision.

I had to find another piece of non-insulated metal to come into contact with, and I had to find it now. I looked toward the driveway at Ben's van but discounted it immediately. The rubber tires were once again an insulator between the metal and earth ground. I whipped my head to the right and made my decision.

Still gripping the rail, I pushed off and started down the stairs as fast as I could without losing what little balance I had left. I could feel something warm and wet against my shoulder, and I knew without looking that yet another wound had to have appeared on Felicity's pristine skin. I was gripped by the sudden fear that the wounds went deeper than merely the surface.

I hit the sidewalk and continued to my right, tripping over the grooves in the decorative flagstone walk as I hurried toward my new goal. I could hear Ben, Constance, and Helen behind me, but I didn't have time to acknowledge their presence. My vision was beginning to tunnel, and I could feel my own hands beginning to curl into fists as my physical connection with Felicity fought to drag me under.

I continued to stumble forward and eventually lost my footing then fell heavily to my knees. The momentum of my crash carried me forward, and Felicity slid from my shoulder onto the grass. She was still seizing. Even in the darkness, I could see that fresh wounds had appeared on her arms and new, wet stains were spreading across her shirt.

I pushed up onto my hands and knees and looked ahead of myself. The dim, cylindrical vignette that had become my vision stretched out before me, appearing as an unfathomable distance with my objective well at the far end. I knew it couldn't possibly be that far away, but my heart began to sink as I struggled with my now clubbed fists to pull Felicity back up.

I suddenly felt an icy hand pressed against my shoulder. Startled, I swung my head to the side and glanced up into the smiling face of the Dark Mother.

I twisted my head away, daring not to look any longer for fear of giving in and answering her beckoning call. Looking to the opposite side, I slammed my right hand hard against the ground, forcing it to spasm and uncurl. I quickly pushed my left fist into the palm to hold it open then managed to work it around Felicity's trembling wrist as it closed tightly of its own accord. With a guttural scream, I physically threw myself forward, my left arm thrust in front of me as far as I could reach.

When my hand contacted the warm metal of the chain link fence, I was instantly deafened by the cacophonous snap of an electric arc.

Hot, white light flashed, and then my world faded to black.

CHAPTER 20:

Once again we were gathered in the kitchen— all of us except for Helen that is. A self-described chain smoker, once she was convinced that Felicity and I were okay, she had sequestered herself on our back deck for a nicotine fix.

I knew she was blaming herself for what had happened; she had told me as much. I tried to convince her otherwise, but I didn't have much luck. Unfortunately, at the moment, I simply didn't have the energy to force the subject. In the end, we agreed to talk it out at a later date. Still, I hated that she was going to brood over it until then. I knew she would too because that is exactly what I would do if I was in her place.

I felt myself sinking in the chair, probably looking much like Ben had only a few hours before. I was exhausted. My body chemistry was so out of balance I felt like I had been on a weeklong drunk and was only now starting to sober up. If I had any electrolytes left in my system, they were probably cringing behind some obscure internal organ in hopes they wouldn't be obliterated as well.

I tipped a bottle of bright blue sport drink toward the ceiling and drained the remains in a trio of gulps. I was unimpressed by the taste, but then, they were Felicity's choice, not mine. Normally I wouldn't go near them except to move them aside when reaching for something else, but my current state demanded more than plain water.

"Do you want another one, Rowan?" Constance asked as I sat the plastic bottle on the table in front of me and sighed.

I picked the bottle back up and rolled it in my hand until I could inspect the label. Its claimed flavor was 'Berry'. No indication as to what kind of berry except for maybe the color. I hated to tell them this, but it certainly didn't taste like blueberries to me. In fact, it came across more like weak lemonade with a tablespoon of salt and a pinch of sugar added.

"Not really," I finally said. "But I guess I should anyway. It probably couldn't hurt."

"What about you, Felicity?" she asked as she tugged open the refrigerator.

"Not yet," my wife answered, her voice heavily underscored by a Celtic lilt. "Thank you."

"This is fucked up," Ben suddenly blurted.

He had been standing here in the kitchen, observing us in complete silence for the past several minutes. At the moment, his hand was unconsciously working at the muscles on the back of his neck.

"This just ain't even right," he added after a moment.

"You're acting like this is all new to you," I told him.

I knew my voice sounded flat, matter of fact, and emotionless, but it was only because of the exhaustion. It seemed like a struggle even to talk.

"Jeezus, white man!" he exclaimed. "I've seen you two do weird shit before, but this was way outta the freakin' box!"

"What, the stigmata?" I asked, referring to the wounds that had marred Felicity's skin but were now all but completely gone. The only evidence of them having existed being tiny, pinkish scars which were themselves fading away almost as quickly as they had appeared.

"That's a start," he replied.

"You've seen that happen to me before," I told him, languidly holding out my arm. "Remember the Monogram of Christ?"

I referred to a series of puckered wounds that had appeared on my body, each in the shape of the aforementioned symbol and each in conjunction with the death of one of Eldon Porter's victims. They had healed themselves into non-existence just as Felicity's were now doing, but their memory was fresh. Especially after what had been witnessed here tonight.

"Yeah." He nodded vigorously. "And that freaked me out then too."

While I had my arm extended, Constance stepped past Ben and filled my hand with a fresh bottle of the sports drink.

"Thanks," I acknowledged, then turned back to my friend and

shrugged. "Sorry about that." My apology was more out of reflex than any kind of heartfelt remorse.

"Well, what I'm really talkin' about is the friggin' la-la shit flyin' around here." He thrust the index finger of his free hand at himself. "I mean *I* felt it. Me."

"And your point?" Felicity asked, her voice a tired mumble. She was resting her head on the table, using her crossed arms as a makeshift pillow, with her face pointed toward the back wall. She didn't even bother to lift her head when she spoke.

"Well excuse me, 'Samantha'," he retorted, making a sarcastic reference to the old TV sitcom. "Maybe this is old hat for you two, but I damn near got electrocuted by your happy asses."

"Do I look…" Felicity began to reply, but the rest of the sentence was an unintelligible murmur.

"What?" Ben asked.

Felicity turned her head and pressed the other cheek against her arms so that she was facing him even though her eyes remained shut. Then, still with a tired mumble, she repeated, "Samantha was blonde. Do I look blonde to you?"

"Dammit, Felicity!" he barked. "This is serious!"

"I think everybody is aware of that," Constance interjected. "But just look at them, Ben. They're both exhausted. You aren't going to get anywhere by arguing."

My friend ignored her observation and pressed on, aiming his query at Felicity. "So after all this shit, do you at least remember somethin'?"

"Aye, I remember hurting," she muttered. "I remember that somebody hurt me."

"That doesn't get us anywhere now does it?" he snapped.

"Give her a break, Ben," I made a tired appeal.

"Hey," he replied in an annoyed tone. "You're the one that absolutely had to do this right now, so don't come down on me for askin' a question."

"I'm not coming down on you, Ben," I replied. "I'm just saying lighten up a bit."

"I'm just doin' my job."

"Back off, Storm," Constance told him. "Give her some time."

Ben shifted a hard glare quickly onto Agent Mandalay and then snarled, "Yeah, well maybe I just haven't got as much patience as you."

"Chill out, Storm," she returned, shooting him a puzzled expression. "This hasn't been easy on any of us, least of all Felicity and Rowan."

Ben started to reply, a wave of anger flooding his features as his lips parted but then caught himself before any words escaped. He closed his mouth and stood staring at her as he worked his jaw, then without saying anything simply stalked through the kitchen and out the back door, giving it a healthy slam in his wake.

"Damn," Mandalay muttered as she looked after him and then turned to me. "You say you know what's eating him?"

"Yeah," I acknowledged. "But I can't talk about it, Constance."

"Well he needs to get a handle on it," she said. "He's not stable."

"Yeah, I know."

"Just an FYI," she continued. "Jurisdiction for this case is technically still in the hands of the local authorities, and once we prove that this is a murder, the lines are going to get blurred even more. The Bureau will stay involved because of the circumstances, but Albright is going to step up, I'll guarantee it. When she does, I'm not going to be able to cover for him anymore."

"Do you think she'll kick him off the Major Case Squad again?"

"Maybe not. It really depends on the need for manpower, would be my guess. With the victim being the Mayor's daughter, you can bet everyone is going to be pulling duty. A lot of it is going to depend on him."

"Maybe he can redeem himself in her eyes then. He's a good cop, Constance."

"I know he is, Rowan. That's the problem. That's what I mean when I say it depends on him. If he keeps acting like he did just now and doesn't get some help, getting kicked off the MCS will be the least of his worries because he'll probably lose his badge altogether."

That was something I already suspected but really didn't want to hear.

"Helen is still out there, isn't she?" I asked after a moment.

"Yeah," she replied, craning her neck to peer out through the atrium. "I think she's been through about half a pack by now."

"Let him talk with her. I think she knows what's going on with him. She'll get him back on track."

"Are you sure?"

"Pretty sure, yeah."

"I hope you're right, Rowan."

"Me too."

"Listen, Row…" Ben began and then paused.

The forlorn chirp of a single cricket sounded in the wake of his abandoned sentence and then fell silent as well. We were standing at the railing of the deck, looking out into the darkened backyard. The dogs were snuffling about on the lawn, disappearing into the shadows and then reappearing as they wandered into the dim furthest reaches of the outdoor lights.

We had spent many a night out here throughout the course of our friendship. Some of them good and some of them we'd both rather forget. Some simply passing time with a cigar and a drink. Others, pondering horrors I had channeled and trying to get a handle on a case.

Once again, here we were, and I think we both knew that this particular night would be one of those we'd rather forget but simply wouldn't be able to help but remember in painfully graphic detail.

It was pushing three in the morning. I had put Felicity to bed, and after Helen checked in on her, both she and Constance left. There didn't seem to be much else we could do for the time being, and everyone desperately needed some rest.

The carbs in the sports drink had kicked in, giving me not exactly a second wind, but enough energy to at least get up and move. I had pulled down a pair of tumblers and filled them each with ice and a healthy measure of *Royal Salute* before heading out the back door to check on my brooding friend.

He had simply shot a quick glance at me when I sat the drink on the railing next to him but remained silent. It had taken all of five minutes before he finally spoke.

"It's okay," I told him.

"No it isn't," he replied, shaking his head. "I acted like a fuckin' asshole in there."

"Yeah," I agreed. "You did."

"You don't have to agree with me so fast, Kemosabe," he offered with a slight grin.

"It's okay," I replied. "You definitely acted like an ass. But, I think I've probably done the same to you."

"Yeah, you have." His grin spread a little wider. "So, how's Firehair?"

"She's okay," I replied, and then took a sip of my drink. "She crashed awhile ago."

"I guess I'll apologize to her later."

"It's all good. She's got pretty thick skin."

"Yeah, she's a tough one," he agreed. "That's a fact."

My friend looked down at the drink I had poured for him then picked it up and twisted the tumbler back and forth in front of his face. After a moment, he set it back down, this time a full arms length away.

"Thanks, but that's prob'ly the last thing I need right now."

"No problem. I understand," I returned, paused, then asked, "So what now?"

He huffed out a heavy breath. "We keep our mouths shut and hope for a break."

"Not much of a plan," I observed.

"Tell me about it," he replied. "But there's no way we can confirm she's dead, so runnin' off at the mouth'll just cause problems."

"Yeah, I can see that."

We grew quiet again, listening to the ambient sounds of the night. Tires squealed in the distance, and the sound of a roaring engine droned along behind it, eventually fading to nothingness.

"So, where are you staying?" I finally asked.

"Whaddaya mean?" he asked, feigning ignorance.

"We didn't get a chance to talk earlier, Ben," I explained. "I know about you and Allison."

He rubbed his hand across the lower half of his face and sighed heavily through his nose. "How'd ya find out?" he asked. "I run off at the mouth while I was trashed?"

"Not exactly," I replied. "When you passed out, I called your house. I didn't want Allison to worry when you didn't come home."

"Sorry about that," he said. "Guess I shoulda told ya'. Felicity know?"

"Not yet."

"Mandalay?"

"I didn't figure it was my place to tell her."

"Thanks."

I shrugged. "No problem. You'd do the same for me." I paused for a moment, searching for the right words, then said, "You're going to want to talk to her, though. She's returning a favor…" I let my voice trail off.

"Yeah, I know." He gave a short nod. "And I owe her an apology too."

"Probably," I agreed. "So you never answered my question. Where are you staying?"

"'Nother copper in homicide has some rental property down on Tennessee," he told me. "It was vacant, so he's lettin' me have it on a week-to-week."

"You know, you could have come here. We have a guest room."

"Naahh." He shook his head as he uttered the negative. "I think I need some space right now."

"As long as you don't withdraw too much."

"Yeah," he agreed.

"So how is Ben junior handling it?"

"About as well as can be expected I guess."

"What about you? You doing okay?"

He gave an embarrassed chuckle. "Apparently not as okay as I thought I was."

"I'm sure it's a big adjustment," I offered.

"Yeah, you could say that."

"So, I know you've got Helen, but if you need another ear..." I let my voice trail off.

"Yeah, I know. I appreciate it, white man."

"No problem. So... At the risk of prying, is this something you two are going to be able to work out?"

He was just about to answer me when Felicity's terrified scream shattered the newfound calmness of the night.

CHAPTER 21:

J ust as I had witnessed less than two days before, the audible signal
of distress served as a trigger, sending my friend's hand
immediately to his sidearm. His now alert gaze swung instantly in the
direction of the scream. I'm not sure which one of us began moving
first, but I just barely made it to the back door in front of him. In either
case, the dogs had overtaken us, and we were both stumbling over
them as they yapped wildly at the door. I pushed through to the interior
of the house, immediately on the heels of the boisterous canines, and
my friend was at my back, physically urging me ahead at a quickening
pace.

The dogs had left us in their wake, and I could now hear them
whining; the high-pitched noise was interspersed with low growls, and
that punctuated the now random barks. Advancing through the kitchen,
I caught fleeting glimpses of our cats, fur puffed out in panic, as they
darted in opposing directions, two of them literally bouncing from one
another before continuing to individual hiding places.

I hooked through the kitchen doorway, into the dining room, and
then continued through, my arc leading me down the hallway to our
bedroom. I hit the door at as close to a dead run as I could manage in
the short distance. The dogs were already scratching at the barrier,
yelping and growling as they sought to protect their mistress from the
unseen intruder.

Felicity was already splitting the darkness with a third scream.
Of all the noises and exclamations I had ever heard coming from her,
this had never been among them. This was something entirely new and
beyond horrifying. At this moment, it frightened me more than
anything in recent memory. It was a sound that made me painfully
aware that blood could in fact run cold.

I could feel Ben at my back as I burst through the door and
stepped into the darkened room. My gaze fell immediately to the bed
but found only rumpled sheets partially illuminated by the swath of

light that was projecting inward from the hallway. I reached to my side and slapped the light switch on the wall just above the headboard. Brightness leapt onto the tableau, and I brought my eyes up as my ears centered in on the terror-stricken shriek, which was only now beginning to trail off.

Felicity was cowering in the opposite corner, back pressed into the wall next to the bathroom door, hands holding either side of her head as she rocked in a frantic rhythm. Crimson trails were trickling down her arm from her bloody left hand, and an obvious smear blemished her cheek. I launched myself forward, swiveling around the end of the bed and dropping to my knees in front of my wife.

"Felicity?!" I called as I reached out and placed my hands on her trembling shoulders.

My touch proved only to elicit a new round of screams as she began flailing her arms and slapping at me blindly. Her eyes were fixed directly ahead, unblinking and dilated. Upon catching a glimpse of the glassy stare, I was convinced that she wasn't even walking in this world.

"FELICITY!" I called again, grabbing at her wrists as I attempted to defend myself against her unconscious attack. "FELICITY! It's me! Rowan!"

Her head snapped back, and she centered her unfocused stare on my face. Her arms stopped flailing, but she continued to tremble and rock. She sat wordlessly— looking through me more than at me.

I reached out and slowly started to brush back her hair. She flinched and I hesitated.

"It's okay, Felicity," I cooed softly. "It's me. It's Rowan."

Slowly, I pushed my hand along the side of her cheek, lifting her auburn locks, and inspecting her milky skin. I could see no wound on her face, only the smear of crimson.

I continued whispering to her as I took her left hand in mine and turned the palm to face me. Deep gashes were cut into the tips of her index and middle fingers, and they were still oozing thick blood.

"What happened here?" I asked her softly but got no answer.

The dogs were trying to nose their way in for their own first hand inspection, and I could still feel Ben standing behind me.

I began to notice that the room seemed colder than usual, especially since at this hour of the morning the electronic thermostat would still have the air conditioner switched off in energy-saving mode.

I watched Felicity's expression slowly change, recognition dawning in her eyes as she awakened from the dream state. She swallowed hard, and tears began to silently stream across her cheeks. I slipped my arms around my wife and pulled her close as she began to sob, rocking in harmony as I rubbed her back.

I heard Ben shuffle and then step past me into the bathroom. I didn't pay much attention to what he was doing until I heard him slowly mutter, "Jeezus H. Christ."

I continued slowly rocking Felicity but turned my head in his direction and looked up. He was staring at us, and we locked gazes for a moment before he turned away. When I followed his line of sight, I saw the object of his exclamation.

On the large mirror hanging above the double vanity smeared blood reflected in upon itself. Opaque red lines arced in deliberate, if smudged, patterns literally forming what appeared to be a map.

Below it, in unfamiliar, back-slanted writing were the words, FIND ME.

"You never should have done that binding..." I said, a note of sadness filling my voice.

I had just finished rinsing my wife's wounded hand with peroxide for a second time and had now patted it dry. She was still wearing the oversized t-shirt she had been sleeping in, and it was covered with smears and spatters of blood down the left side. I had helped her pull on a pair of jeans and slip her feet into tennis shoes with the intention of taking her to the emergency room, but she would have none of that. She hated hospitals almost as much as Ben and adamantly refused to go even though I was sure she needed stitches. So, it was left up to me to play doctor.

The gashes were fairly deep and somewhat ragged, as she had made them with the sharp edge of a broken drinking glass. Even though I still felt that she should see a doctor, I had to admit that the cuts didn't look nearly as bad as they had before they were cleaned up.

We were in the kitchen where we could both have a seat, and more importantly, I could spread out the first aid kit on the table. At the moment, I was snipping off strips of white tape from a metal spindle.

Ben was behind me, seated in the dining room and comparing a sketch of Felicity's bloody rendering to a road atlas. Unfortunately, the image on the mirror, while obvious in its intent, was a smeary conglomeration of thick lines and devoid of any text labels, save for the 'FIND ME'. Because of that, it was somewhat of a puzzle in and of itself.

Before getting started, he had called Agent Mandalay, catching her just as she was pulling into her driveway. She never even shut off her engine and now, was on her way back here.

"Aye," Felicity returned, her voice surprisingly calm. "Maybe so, but I broke it."

I nodded. "True. But it obviously wasn't a clean break."

I cut a final strip of the surgical tape and stuck it to the edge of the table then snapped the spindle back into its cover. I tossed it back into the box with a slight clatter. Then I reached deeper into the first aid kit and pulled out a small, brown jar then twisted off the lid. I dipped a cotton swab into the homemade comfrey and menthol salve and twirled it for a moment.

Felicity let out a short laugh that came as an abbreviated 'hmph', and then she said, "I wasn't really sure that the spell would work at all if you want to know the truth."

"It didn't, really," I offered. "All it did was suck you into all of this mess."

"Aye, but you were free of the visions for a short time."

"I'm surprised it did that much." I shook my head. "Nothing should have happened at all."

"Why do you say that?"

"Because, I'd already tried it."

"You did?" There was a note of surprise in her voice. "When?"

"Awhile back." I shrugged. "I even tried a banishing."

"Why didn't you tell me?"

"I didn't want to get your hopes up."

"But if you don't believe in the magick, Rowan, then it can't work. You know that."

"I know," I told her. "But you just told me that you had your own doubts."

"Aye." She nodded. "I did at that. But still… You tried to do a banishing?"

"Don't act so surprised. It's not like I want this to keep happening to me you know."

"That's not true."

I stopped twirling the swab. "Excuse me?"

"You see it as a gift as well as a curse."

"I don't know about that."

"I do," she replied. "I can feel it. You certainly don't revel in it, but you see it as your destiny. If it were to stop, you would feel as though you had failed."

She was touching on insights I had thought were completely hidden from view. Of course, I shouldn't have been at all surprised by that. I really knew better than to think I could keep anything from her.

"Pretty amazing," I offered with a sigh, returning to the original subject and hoping she would follow. "A spell that shouldn't have worked to begin with, doomed to certain failure by your own disbelief, and yet you still managed to make magick happen anyway. Lucky you."

I took her hand and blotted the oozing gashes once more.

"Why do you think that is, then?" she asked.

"The Ancients like your accent maybe?" I replied.

"What?" She shot me a puzzled look. "Oh, no, seriously. Why do you think it worked at all?"

"I don't know." I shrugged. "Maybe there's something bigger going on here. We both know I'm probably the last guy to be able to answer that." I pulled her hand closer and retrieved the cotton swab from the ointment. "This is probably going to sting."

The word 'probably' morphed instantly into 'absolutely' as I touched the healing salve to the gashes. She sucked in a startled breath as her face twisted into a grimace. At the same moment, her hand jerked out of reflex, trying to pull away from the sudden burn, but I held it fast.

"I really wish you'd reconsider the stitches."

"No," she forced out between clenched teeth.

I continued gently dabbing the wounds until they were covered, then tossed the swab into the small trashcan next to me.

"There, that should be the worst of it," I said as I started wrapping her fingers with sterile gauze.

I glanced up and saw that her grimace had melted into a thoughtful stare. She was absently chewing at her lower lip, something she tended to do when she was preoccupied. I stopped wrapping for a moment and asked, "You okay? This too tight?"

She snapped out of the shallow trance and looked at me. "What? Oh, no, it's fine. I... Ummm... I was just thinking about earlier."

I went back to wrapping the gauze then glanced up as I said, "Earlier? You mean the hypnosis?"

"No." She shook her head. "Before that. Before I left this evening."

"What about it?"

"What I said about you feeling sorry for yourself," she said hesitantly. "I'm sorry."

I gave my head a slight shake. "Don't be. You were right. I have been feeling sorry for myself."

"No, Rowan..."

"Yes," I interrupted her objection. "I have. Don't get me wrong, honey, it hurt when you said it, but all you did was point out the obvious. I should actually thank you."

"Aye, but I shouldn't have been so mean."

"You weren't really." I grinned. "No meaner than usual, anyway."

She gave her head a dismissive shake, but the corners of her mouth curled into a slight grin.

"Of course," I added as I started applying the tape, "I'm not suddenly all better now just because of what you said. That only happens in the movies. But, I recognize that my own self-pity is a part of the larger problem, so maybe I'm on the right path to do something about it."

"You know you have family who wants to help, then." Her words were a comment as much as a question.

"Yes, I do."

"Hey you two," Ben's voice came from the doorway. "Come look at this for a second. I think I got somethin'"

Felicity was already coming up out of the chair as he finished the sentence, and I had to rise in unison with her as I hastily finished looping the white tape around the gauze.

"Whoa, honey, slow down," I told her as she pulled away and stepped past me, but she wasn't listening.

I knew the sense of urgency she was exuding all too well. She was physically manifesting her desire to get this over with, to make it into a distant memory. I didn't have the heart to tell her that it wouldn't work. Nothing could make it play out any faster than had already been pre-ordained and that speed was something that we'd never be privy to before the fact.

But, what pained me even more was the fact that while I knew the memories would fade somewhat, the distance would never be great enough for her to ever stop running from them.

I pushed back the wave of sorrow brought on by the thought and followed her into the dining room.

"Look at this," Ben was already saying, running his finger along the contours of lines between the sketch and a page in the road atlas. "Right here, this could be the Mississippi River." He drew his hand downward, first on one page then the other. He shot a quick glance at us and then proceeded to motion horizontally. "This here could be Two-Seventy, and this could be Riverview."

I stuck my hand in and traced the same lines. "Sure, but couldn't this also be the Missouri River, this be Highway Seventy, and that be Fifth Street?"

"Yeah," he replied, swishing his fingertip around. "And it could also be the other end of Two-Seventy and this could be Two-Thirty-One. Or it could be Sixty-Four and Fifty-Five for all that matter. But bear with me. Just assume that this is the Mississippi and look here and here." He pointed first to an extra line running perpendicular to the line he had identified as Highway Two-Seventy. "This could be the Chain of Rocks Canal on the Illinois side." He moved his finger back and forth between the sketch and the road map and then dropped his finger onto a small spot on the drawing. "On the mirror, this is pretty much just a bloody fingerprint, so I really didn't pay much attention to it at first, but look at this." He pointed to an identical spot on the roadmap, and at the tip of his finger was a small triangle encompassed by a circle. "This is the tourist info center on the Missouri side."

I glanced back and forth between the two renditions, considering what he had said. The sketch was rough and in reality, just a simplified version of the smears that coated the bathroom mirror. Unfortunately, what we were looking at could be any one of a hundred intersections on the map, not to mention that we were looking only at Missouri. Still, if you did as he said and made certain assumptions, the details could be construed to support his conclusion.

"Tamara Linwood was found in Rafferty Park, right?" I asked. "Near the Missouri River."

"Yeah." He nodded. "And that is southwest. And, Sarah Hart was found in River's Bend Park."

"Northwest," I murmured. "Again, near the Missouri."

"I know, I know," he replied. "You're thinkin' 'So, why dump a body near the Mississippi now. It breaks the pattern.' Well, believe me I'm thinkin' the same thing, but it's still near a river. And, just look at the map."

"But, why so close to the state line?" I mused aloud. "The plates on the car were Illinois, right? Wouldn't that be too close to home?"

"Yeah, the tags were Illinois, but the car was from Wisconsin. Remember, they were both hot, Row."

"I don't know, Ben," I replied. "I can see half a dozen spots on the map that look just like the drawing. What do you think, Felicity?"

My wife had been completely mute through the entire explanation, and even now she didn't reply. I looked over and found her motionless, staring down at the map-covered surface of the table. Her gaze was once again unfocused, and she looked dangerously like she was inches from slipping across the veil yet again.

I reached out and gently placed my hand on her shoulder as I spoke, a thin note of concern underscoring my tone. "Felicity?"

"That's it," she finally said in a soft monotone, her fixed stare still aimed at the table. She reached out and placed the tip of her finger against the map, southwest of the location Ben and I had been discussing. The words next to her lacquered nail read, Woodcrest State Park.

"That's it," she repeated. "That's where I am."

CHAPTER 22:

"**W**oodcrest is gated," Agent Mandalay said, looking at the map. Then she tried unsuccessfully to stifle a yawn.

She had arrived almost immediately following Felicity's announcement pinpointing what she believed to be the location of Brittany Larson's remains. Ben had filled her in on the necessary details, including his pet theory about the rest area on Highway 270. Now, we were all huddled around the table staring at the maps once again.

"Sorry about that," she apologized before continuing. "Anyway, if I remember correctly, they open at seven A.M. like most of the other state parks."

"That's almost three hours from now," Felicity objected.

"I'm sure I could get someone out there to unlock the gate," Mandalay replied. "But I don't think it would be a good idea. This is still just between us, and if you're wrong, the whole thing could blow up in our faces."

"But I'm not wrong," Felicity objected.

"I believe you think that, Felicity," she said. "But are you absolutely sure? You've been through a lot tonight. Both of you. How do you know you aren't misreading it all? The map you drew doesn't look anything like the park you are pointing at."

"I just know I'm not," my wife returned.

"That's not good enough," Constance told her. "You have to remember what, and most especially who, we are dealing with here. My influence with the Major Case Squad is tenuous at best. If we attract attention from the wrong parties, then this could go very sour. Especially if this turns out to be a wild goose chase."

"Besides, Felicity," Ben interjected. "Even if ya' *Twilight Zone* in on the right spot, it's still gonna be dark for a coupl'a hours yet."

She gave him an animated raise of her eyebrows. "So?"

"So, I don't think it'd be a good idea for us to go knockin' around in the woods with flashlights," he returned.

"But we have more than flashlights," Felicity countered. "We have me."

Mandalay forced back another yawn with the back of her hand and then shook her head at my wife. "You're beginning to sound like Rowan."

"Aye, and you're sounding like Ben used to," Felicity replied.

"Just trying to play it safe, Felicity," she told her. "You know how touchy all of this is."

Ben spoke up again. "Like I said, Felicity, even if you go la-la and give us an exact location, we can't see in the dark. The point is, if we go screwin' around out there, we might accidentally fuck up the crime scene and lose a crucial piece of evidence without even knowin' it. It'd be better if we do this at first light."

"He's right," I said.

"I know he is," she replied, resigned frustration seasoning her words as she made nervous motions with her hands. "But, I... I just... I don't know... I just feel like I have to do something."

"I know, honey," I replied. "I've been there, remember?"

"So why don't we look at a map of the park, then?" she proposed. "Maybe the one I drew is on a smaller scale, then."

"That's true, it could be. It would be a starting point at least," Constance agreed. "Do you have one?"

"No," she replied in a dejected tone, then let out a heavy breath as her shoulders drooped noticeably. She turned her back to the table and silently walked into the kitchen.

"I can probably download one from the State Parks or Conservation Department website," I offered, speaking loud enough that I hoped she could hear as well.

"Okay, let's do that," Mandalay gave a nod as she spoke.

"Let's back up for a second. We can go at this from a different angle too," Ben offered. "Row, you got a phone book handy?"

"Sure," I replied, starting toward the bookshelves in the living room. "What for?"

"Woodcrest Park is named after the muni it borders," he told me. "So I'm gonna call Woodcrest PD and see if there's been anything suspicious happen around there in the last day or so."

"Good idea, Storm," Mandalay said.

"Yeah, I have 'em on occasion," he replied with a slight sardonic note.

I returned quickly with the phone book. He flipped it open as he took it from me and then began thumbing his way toward the government office 'blue pages'. "Can I use your phone?" he asked as he searched the hefty book.

"Sure. I'll get it," I replied and then stepped into the kitchen to retrieve the handset. When I came around the corner, Felicity was standing with her arms crossed and leaning back against the counter. She was staring at the floor, her chin against her chest, and she was nibbling at her lower lip once again.

"Are you okay?" I asked.

"Aye." She gave a small nod. "I'm fine."

"Ben is going to call the Woodcrest Police Department," I offered.

"I heard."

"You know, we can probably get a map of the park off the Internet."

"Aye, I heard that too."

"You're sure you're okay?"

She looked up and gave me a weak smile. "I'm fine, Row. Just very, very tired, that's all."

"Here it is," Ben announced behind me. "Row. Phone."

I glanced over my shoulder then back to her. "It's going to be okay," I said as I started backing out of the doorway. "I promise."

"I know," she answered with a nod. "I'll be sure of that."

Ben took the phone from my hand as I turned, and then he began stabbing the number into the handset. A moment later, he tucked it up to his ear and waited expectantly.

"Yeah, good morning," he said suddenly. "My name's Ben

Storm, I'm a detective with St. Louis City Homicide. I need to speak with your watch commander... Yeah... Great, what's his name? Okay, what's her name? Sergeant Michelle Marshall... Great... Thanks... Yeah, it's Detective Ben Storm... Yeah, that's right, City Homicide. Yeah, I'll hold. Thanks."

Ben twisted the handset away from his mouth and reached up with his free hand to massage his neck. After a moment, he canted the receiver back up to his mouth and began speaking again. "Yeah, Sergeant Marshall. Detective Storm. Yeah... I know... Yeah, tell me about it, I'm runnin' on about four hours outta the last twenty-four... Yeah, kinda... So listen, I'm wantin' ta' check if you've had any reports of vandalism or trespassing over at Woodcrest Park the past couple of days?... Really?... When was that?... No kidding... You find anything?... Okay... Yeah... Yeah... No, just a theory I'm workin' on, nothing for sure... No, pretty minor case, nothin' too serious... Yeah... Uh-huh... Yeah..." He looked over at me and rolled his eyes. "Yeah, that's me... Thanks, I think..." He let out a forced chuckle. "Yeah... Well I appreciate it... Sure, if it pans out we'll be sure to let ya' know... Yeah... Thanks... Bye."

He pulled the handset away and pressed his thumb against the off-hook switch.

"Well?" Agent Mandalay asked.

"Park attendant found the gate unlatched when she arrived Saturday morning," he answered. "Chain had been snapped. Prob'ly with a bolt cutter, but there was no other vandalism they could find. Apparently, this happens every now and then. According to the Sergeant, they've caught a coupl'a drunk good ol' boys in the past who thought it'd be a good idea to go fishin' in the middle of the night and broke in so they could use the boat ramp."

"But not this time?" I asked.

"Nope." He shook his head. "But since there was no other damage, they just wrote it off and filed a vandalism report."

He offered me the handset and I took it.

"So what was the eye roll about?" I asked as I started backing slowly toward the kitchen doorway.

"She asked if I was the same Detective Storm that's been on TV with 'that Witch'," he replied flatly.

"Oh."

"Yeah," he grunted. "You're my freakin' claim to fame apparently."

"Sorry about that."

"Don't worry about it," he sighed. "It's not the first time I've been asked, won't be the last I'm sure."

I turned then continued through the doorway and dropped the phone back into its wall base. My mouth was already open to speak to my wife when I looked up and saw that the room was empty. I had been fairly intent on Ben's side of the phone conversation, but I couldn't imagine having missed Felicity coming into the room. Still, it wasn't something I could rule out either.

I glanced around and then turned and called back into the dining room, "Felicity?"

I waited a few seconds but heard no reply. I called out again, "Is Felicity in there?"

"I thought she was in there," Constance called back to me.

I felt my mouth curl downward into a frown as the hair on the back of my neck began to prickle in a wave of gooseflesh. The frightening hollowness that tended to visit the pit of my stomach from time to time announced its arrival, and I knew instantly that something was amiss.

I walked through the kitchen without a word and continued out the back door, through the atrium sun porch, and exited onto the deck. The security floods were still lit, casting illumination across the raised expanse but eventually dissipating as they lost their battle against the darkness a few feet beyond the railing. My wife was still nowhere to be seen.

I frowned harder and advanced across the deck, peering into the night toward the back of the yard. It wasn't unheard of for her to sit on the bench along the side of her potting shed when she wanted some solitude. I strained to see if I could pick out her form amid the faint silhouette of the outbuilding but saw nothing resembling a person at all.

"Felicity?" I called out.

Hearing no reply, I pressed forward and down the shallow flight of stairs to the concrete apron of the driveway leading to the garage.

"Felicity?" I called into the darkness again.

Still, I received no reply.

The hollowness was beginning to gnaw a hole in my stomach, and every sense in my body started advancing toward overload. I turned to my right and walked across the driveway/patio area until I cleared the corner of the house and gazed down toward the street.

Ben's van was off to the side of the drive, having been straightened by RJ earlier after the cop's drunken parking attempt. Past that, I could see the tail end of Constance's sedan where she had parked on the street in front of our house. What was conspicuously missing from the scene was my wife's Jeep.

I spun in place and began a fast walk back across the concrete to the deck then back into the house. As I entered the back door, I looked up at the note board on the side of the refrigerator. Next to it was a line of hooks for extra keys, and the spot reserved for Felicity's spares was empty.

Ben was just pouring himself a fresh cup of coffee as I came in, and he looked up. It didn't take any of his training for him to see that I was distressed. He immediately asked, "What's wrong, white man?"

"Felicity's gone," I told him quickly. "So is her Jeep. I think she's gone out there by herself."

CHAPTER 23:

"Goddammit!" my friend exclaimed. "Hasn't she ever heard of a chain of evidence? If there's a crime scene out there, and she fucks it up, it's not gonna do us any good at all."

"She's not thinking straight right now, Ben," I replied sharply.

Constance apparently heard the commotion and came through the doorway with a puzzled expression on her face. "What's going on?"

"Felicity's gone," I told her quickly.

"Are you sure? I didn't even hear her leave."

"Apparently neither did the dogs because they didn't bark or anything, which is unheard of." I shook my head. "But her Jeep is definitely gone."

"You don't think she..." she began.

"That's exactly what I think," I replied before she could finish the question. "And, we have to stop her."

"Jeezus!" Ben spat. "She's worse than you, white man. At least you wait until I'm not around before pullin' some kinda stunt."

"She doesn't deal well with people being victimized," I told him, impatience growing in my voice. "Especially women."

"Yeah, that's kinda obvious," he shot back, starting toward the phone. "But what the hell does she think she's gonna do out there?"

"Probably the same thing we've been trying to do here. Figure out who is doing this," I explained, growing more agitated with each passing second. "Can we save the why's for later? We've got to stop her."

"What the fuck are you so worked up about, Row?" Ben asked as he snatched the telephone receiver from the wall. "Worst thing that can happen is she screws over the crime scene. I'm the one that needs to be pissed, not you."

"No it isn't!" I snapped. "You saw what happened here tonight. What do you think is going to happen if she manages to connect directly with Brittany Larson's corpse?"

"What? You've done that kinda stuff before," he replied. "I've seen you do it at the morgue."

"Yes, you have," I shot back. "And think about it. Remember what happened? If Felicity hadn't been there to bring me back, I would have ended up being their latest customer."

His eyes widened as the realization hit him. "Jeezus."

"Not my choice of deities," I spat. "But, yeah. Exactly. We have to stop her before she finds the body and tries something stupid."

"Surely she knows what could happen," Constance offered.

"Probably, but like I said, she's not thinking straight," I reiterated. "The way she's been shifting in and out of trances, I'm not even sure she's fully in this world right now."

"Yeah, Detective Storm again." Ben was speaking into the phone. "I need to speak with Sergeant Marshall again... Thanks..." He twisted the phone down and looked over to Constance. "Yo, Mandalay. See if you can figure out the most likely route she would take from here."

Agent Mandalay gave him a quick nod and ducked back into the dining room to check the maps.

"Yeah, Sergeant Marshall," Ben said as he suddenly twisted the phone back up to his mouth. "Listen, I got a situation... Yeah, I wish... So listen, you got someone headed for Woodcrest Park right now and she's intent on gettin' in... No, no, she's a civilian consultant... No, she's just a little overzealous right now... Yeah, I just need you to stop her if we don't get to her first. Yeah, her name is Felicity O'Brien. About five-two, one-ten or so, long red hair. She's drivin' a black Jeep Wrangler, license plates..." Ben looked at me questioningly and motioned for me to give up the information.

I quickly searched my memory but was too preoccupied with worry to form a complete mental picture, so I shook my head and gave him what I could. "V-X-N something."

"Yeah," he continued speaking into the phone. "Partial Missouri plates, V-X-N. That's Victor, X-Ray, November. Got that?"

"Bumper stickers," I blurted as the thought struck. "She's got a Pentacle on the spare tire cover, and on the bumper she has one that says 'Magick Happens'."

Ben repeated the description to the Sergeant. "Yeah... Yeah, she's a Witch too... Yeah... Funny... Uh-huh... Yeah... Okay... Yeah, I'd rather not get into that right now... Yeah, I know... Yeah, but like I said before it's just a theory I'm workin'... Yeah, could be nothin'... Yeah, she's just a little impatient... Yeah, do me a favor; let your officers know she's with us. I don't want her gettin' hurt 'cause of a gung ho rookie. Yeah... Let me give you my cell number..."

"Rowan," Constance poked her head in through the doorway. "Has Felicity been to Woodcrest Park before?"

"Yeah, we both have," I nodded as I spoke.

"Would she be more likely to take Highway Forty, then head south, or get off at Two-Seventy and head south before going west?" she asked.

"Probably Forty," I replied. "But in her present state, who knows."

My agitation seemed to have leveled off for the moment. It wasn't lessening, but at least it wasn't getting any worse. I turned back to Ben and mouthed the words 'hurry up'. He gave me a quick nod and finished the call as fast as he could.

"Marshall will be callin' on my cell if she shows up out there," he offered as he hung up the handset then glanced over at Mandalay. "Whaddaya got?"

"Only one road leading in to the park, and that's Piper Valley. From here she can come at it one of three ways. Out Forty to Millstone which eventually turns into Piper Valley; or Two-Seventy to Woodsbend which intersects Piper Valley just before the park entrance. The third option would be to take Two-Seventy to Forty-Four then up Woodsbend from the backside of the park. But that would be going out of the way."

He looked over at me. "Row?"

"Could be any of the three," I returned. "It all depends on what's driving her."

"Okay, lemme think." He huffed the word out as he smoothed his hair back then brought his hand to rest on his neck. After a pair of seconds he spoke again. "Mandalay, you take Forty, Rowan and I will take Two-Seventy. Sound reasonable?"

"That would be my call," Constance replied.

"What about Forty-Four?" I appealed.

"We gotta rule that out," he answered quickly. "Too far outta the way to make sense."

"But we don't know for sure," I pressed. "I can take my truck and…"

"Fuck no," he cut me off. "One loose cannon is enough right now. I don't need you runnin' around all *Twilight Zone* too. Besides, Woodcrest PD is gonna be lookin' for her too."

"Dammit, Ben, she's my wife."

"No shit," he snapped back. "I was there, remember? You ain't goin' off alone, end of story. Now lock it up and let's hit the road. Maybe we can catch up to her before she pulls another Rowan."

Neither of us had said a word since getting into the van. I don't know if it was because discussing the possibilities only served to make both of us sick to our stomachs; or, if it was simply because there was nothing more left to say on the subject. In any case, silence had become the rule, and we were making no move to break it.

We were winding down Woodsbend Road toward Piper Valley, shrouded in darkness by the tall stands of trees on either side of us. Technically, we were cutting through one edge of the park itself, even though there was a sparsely populated residential area to our right. Still, there was no actual access to the interior roads until one went through the main entrance at the end of Piper Valley, so that was where we were headed.

Slightly better than twenty-five minutes had passed since we had set out from my house, and I still hadn't relaxed. In fact, the closer we came to the park without any sign of Felicity the more stressed I became. Now that we had all but arrived, I had become a knot of nervous energy with no place to go.

Every muscle in my body was aching, almost certainly from being tensed for what seemed like forever. My head was throbbing, and while I suspected that some of it was ethereal in nature, a good portion was nothing more than plain old stress combined with a lack of sleep.

I was almost certain that I was going to have a bruise across my chest from where I had been straining against the safety harness. I had been pitching myself forward every time we spied a set of taillights, and then I would remain there, staring intently through the windshield until we came close enough to identify the vehicle we were approaching. Invariably, when the necessary details came into view, it would not be Felicity's. I would then slump back into my seat, even more agitated than I had been the moment before. But, even sitting back, I couldn't force myself to relax because we would almost immediately spot yet another pair of red, glowing pinpoints in the distance, and I would begin the cycle anew.

Ever since we had exited the highway and continued our trek along the serpentine, downward slope of Woodsbend, we had been the solitary vehicle in the darkness. There was nothing for me to crane my neck or strain my eyes to see, except the reflective dividing line down the center of the asphalt before us. Still, proximity to the park kept me wrapped so tight that I felt as if I was about to burst out of my own skin at any moment. And, I almost did just that when Ben's cell phone chirped then moved immediately into its ever-increasing warble.

"Storm," he said after fumbling the device off-hook and placing it to his ear. "Yeah... Yeah... Okay... Yeah, I think we're pretty close right now... Uh-huh... Thanks..." He reached over to the passenger seat and handed me the cell phone. "Hang that up, will'ya?"

"What?" I demanded as I took it, thumbed it off, and then dropped it back into the center tray. "Who was that?"

"That was Marshall," he replied. "She says they found Felicity's Jeep on the shoulder of Woodsbend."

"Is she okay?" I asked with a note of relief.

"All they found was the Jeep, Row," he replied, keeping his voice as businesslike as he could. "We should be comin' up on 'em in just a sec…"

The phone began warbling again, and Ben repeated his earlier grope. "Storm… Yeah, Marshall just called me… Yeah, be there in a minute… Bye."

He handed the phone to me again, this time without a word, and I simply disconnected the call. My fleeting moment of relief had now become alarm. "Who was that?"

"Calm down. It was Mandalay. She just got there."

"Ben, if Felicity isn't with her Jeep, she's already in the park," I told him.

"Yeah, Row. I know."

"Then we've got to get in there," I implored.

"We're workin' on it, Row. Calm down."

We continued down the sloping road, easing slowly into a particularly tight bend of which we had been forewarned by a yellow caution sign emblazoned with a sharply twisted arrow. As we started into the switchback, we could see an undulating glow against the trees. The farther into the turn we went, the brighter and more frantic they became. Finally, we hooked around the opposite side of the angle and were greeted by flickering emergency lights atop a patrol vehicle.

Ben slowed the van and brought it to a halt behind the squad car then levered it into park and switched off the engine. I was already unbuckling my safety belt before we had come to a complete stop.

Ben grabbed my arm as I began to shoulder the door open. "Let me and Mandalay do the talkin'. Understand?"

"Yeah, whatever," I answered absently.

"I'm serious, Row," he told me.

"Yeah, fine," I barked back. "Let's just find Felicity before it's too late."

"That's the plan, Row."

The bright beam of a flashlight hit Ben as soon as he was out of the vehicle and then slid over into my face, effectively blinding me. Ben called out to the uniformed officer as we walked toward the Jeep. "Detective Storm. I'm the one who called."

The light came down out of my eyes, and I blinked to re-acclimate my sight to the darkness. I could hear Agent Mandalay talking to the officer and verifying our identities.

"You the one who found it?" Ben asked, continuing forward.

"Yeah," the officer said as we approached. "Found it a few minutes ago, just like this.

The door of the Jeep was hanging open, and though the engine was switched off, the keys were still in the ignition. The officer shone the flashlight around the interior of the vehicle and then aimed it toward the nearby tree line.

He nodded toward the point no more than a dozen feet away where the light fell against a chain link fence, then played it upward to the strands of barbed wire across the top. There, hanging across the barrier was what looked to be one of the floor mats from the Jeep.

"Looks like your suspect might have gone over the fence there." he said.

"Suspect!" I blurted, starting forward.

Ben's hand clamped onto my shoulder and pulled me back. He stepped forward himself, interposing his huge frame between the officer and me.

Agent Mandalay was already on the defense. "She's not a suspect."

"Listen," Ben spoke, voice calm but adamant. "Let's get one thing straight right now, she's a consultant, and if she gets hurt I'm holdin' you responsible."

I'd had enough. Standing here bantering with the Woodcrest cop wasn't accomplishing anything other than raising my ire. Not to mention, every moment that passed was taking Felicity closer to a possibly fatal decision, if she hadn't arrived there already.

I glanced around and saw that the three of them were intent on one another at the moment, so I began moving toward the fence.

Behind me I could hear the officer talking to Ben. "Yeah, okay, so what's a consultant doing trespassing in a state park in the middle of the night?"

"Makin' my life hard, obviously," Ben returned.

"What case are you working anyway?" the cop demanded.

"Nothin' that concerns you right now," Ben shot back.

"It's got to be something big," the officer pressed. "A city homicide detective and a Fed out here in the dark…"

"Look, Officer…" Constance started.

"Martin," he replied.

"Officer Martin," she continued. "We're working against the clock here, and we don't have time for this. Now, has anyone gone in?"

I was only a few steps from the fence now, and I knew that I was going to be discovered at any moment. I was going to be very hard to miss when I started climbing.

"Not yet," the officer replied. "Dispatch is sending a car to the main gate."

"Good, I'll go meet them," Constance announced. "Storm, why don't you and Rowan…"

The moment I heard my name, I knew my time was up. I took the last two steps at a run and launched myself up onto the fence. Twining my fingers into the metal links, I kicked the toes of my shoes into the small holes finding any kind of hold I could as I scrambled to pull myself upward.

"Rowan!" Agent Mandalay exclaimed, obviously noticing me.

"Jeezus H. Christ!" came Ben's bellowing voice amid the sounds of them starting to move. "Rowan! Stop!"

My only saving grace was that they were stunned enough by my action not to have started moving immediately. The delay, brief as it was, allowed enough time for me to put distance between the ground and me.

By the time they reached the fence, I was already pitching my waist over the rubber mat and rolling forward. I wasn't about to win any medals for my dismount, but I still managed to drop myself to the ground on the opposite side with only a minor stumble.

As soon as I gained my footing, at my back I could hear Ben's exclamation, "Goddammit, Rowan, STOP!"

My gut reaction was to simply start running as fast as I could in the opposite direction of the fence. I looked forward into the woods, following the filtered beam of the uniformed officer's flashlight that was apparently aimed at my back. I hesitated and then took a step toward the dense thicket.

"Dammit, white man, I said STOP! What the hell are you doing?" Ben yelled at me through the fence.

I froze and cast a glance back in his direction.

"She came in this way, Ben," I shot back. "She had to have a reason."

I couldn't see his expression. The flashlight was aimed at my face, and the glare blinded me to any details. Ben was a massive silhouette against the chain link, flanked by the smaller shadows of Agent Mandalay and the patrol officer. I held up my hand in an attempt to block the light.

"Wait up," my friend finally said with a heavy sigh, then turned to the Woodcrest officer. "Gimme the flashlight." Surprisingly, the officer didn't argue and instead simply handed over the multi-cell *Mag-lite* without a word.

"You stay here," Ben instructed him as he switched off the light and tucked it into his belt. "Mandalay, you meet the other uniforms at the main gate and work your way in. If you find her first, call me on my cell."

"How will you know where you're going?" Mandalay asked quickly.

"Hell if I know," Ben spat as he hoisted himself onto the fence and began to climb. "Ask Rowan."

CHAPTER 24:

The bulk of the nearly two thousand acre park was a woodland refuge, bordered along the western edge by the Missouri River. Taken in that context, finding a solitary, petite, redheaded woman amid it all presented itself as an overwhelming task. Fortunately, we knew where she had entered, and she probably had no more than a thirty-minute head start. We hoped.

The thing that kept gnawing at me, however, was what she could manage to bring upon herself in those thirty minutes. I quickly found myself dwelling on the possibilities and had to force them out of my head at regular intervals, lest I become literally paralyzed by a fear of what might be. The thoughts were already playing hell with my confidence. The last thing I needed was to have an emotional meltdown before we even found her.

I didn't have a solid idea of where to go from here. For all I knew, she could have simply plunged directly into the woods; or she could have followed the fence line and entered them elsewhere. However, it seemed logical that if she had taken the time to scale the fence at this specific point, walking the fence was probably the least likely of the options. So, I decided to take the straight-line approach and set out into the tree line.

I had been to the park enough times to know that it was segmented along one small portion by a railroad that was still in use. And, as I recalled, the railway ran through the edge of the park we had just entered. Something told me the tracks were where Felicity was heading. I don't know why the rail line popped into my head, or even why it would have been the destination of the killer. But at this point, intuition was all I had going for me, and I wasn't going to doubt it. Not yet, anyway.

The first fifty yards of our trek had been uphill, and with me in a frantic lead, we had topped the ridge quickly. Still, even with fear and adrenalin driving me, I was winded, and so was Ben.

The night had only allowed the air temperature to dip into the mid-eighties, and with our proximity to the river, the humidity was making it feel more like the high nineties. I was already drenched in sweat, and I suspected Ben was as well. Even though he was certainly in better shape than me, the closeness of the air combined with the upward sprint was enough to open anyone's pores wide.

"Jeezus, white man," my friend huffed as we came to a halt atop the rise. "Can't you two do anything the easy way?"

I ignored the question. I was pretty sure he didn't really want an answer, and besides, I was far too busy to talk. I was standing as still as I could manage, reaching out for my wife with every earthly sense I had available. My eyes were searching for shadows in the harsh beam of the flashlight as I played it across the landscape before me. All the while, I was listening for telltale sounds of movement; or even, goddess forbid, a distant scream. Every now and then, I would take a moment to concentrate on breathing in hopes of catching a whiff of her perfume. Unfortunately, I was yielding no results.

Of course, I wasn't stopping at the physical. On a preternatural level, I was sending feelers out far ahead; but, thus far, I was having no more luck in that arena than the other. I'm sure my now rampant fear for Felicity's safety was clouding my ability to sense anything outside the scope of the mundane, but still, I truly believed that I should have felt something. The fact that I couldn't only served to frighten me more.

Sunrise was now less than forty minutes away. A quick glance upward through the small gaps in the trees showed that the sky was beginning to pale with the first inkling of the approaching dawn. Still, the canopy of foliage overhead was containing the darkness as if it were a black fog— hugging it close to the ground and obscuring the landscape.

"This way," I said after a moment, aiming the flashlight down a gradual slope.

"You sure?" Ben asked.

"As sure as I can be at the moment," I returned, my voice edgy.

We started downward, stumbling as we worked our way through the murky forest, thick undergrowth hindering our every step.

"It's gonna be okay," Ben told me. "Felicity's not stupid, Row. She's not gonna do anything that'd get her hurt."

"It's not her doing the something stupid I'm worried about," I explained. "It's whatever she's tapped into. The spirits of the dead don't always have the living's best interest at heart."

We continued in silence for a moment. I could tell he was chewing on what I had just said.

"Are you sayin' Larson's ghost would try to hurt her?" he finally asked.

"Probably not on purpose, butsssppptt..." I replied, sputtering suddenly as a low hanging branch caught me across the face, then barked an exclamation. "Dammit!" I stopped, reached up and pushed the near invisible trap out of my way, then continued my answer as I forged the path. "Like I was saying, not on purpose. But, tortured souls are in search of one thing, and that's closure. Since conduits into this world are few and far between, they tend to clamp on and not let go... The results aren't always pretty."

"Like what happens to you," he grunted.

"Yeah," I returned with a sigh. "Like what happens to me."

The foliage seemed to be thinning, and the slowly increasing greyness could almost be visibly detected filtering into the darkness before us. As I forced my way through the thicket, I tilted the flashlight up then panned it around and saw its focused beam disappear into nothingness. Pressing forward, I crunched through the carpet of fallen leaves and aimed myself in what I imagined to be a straight line.

After several steps, the landscape began to lighten more noticeably even if it was still a muddy twilight. Pushing through the brush, I continued down the incline and soon found myself unceremoniously sliding the last few feet down a vastly sharper drop. Fortunately, I didn't fall far, landing in what at first appeared to be a shallow clearing.

I heard Ben skidding down the slope behind me and twisted out of the way just in time to avoid being run over by him as he stumbled out into the open space. I quickly panned the light around, trying to get my bearings and realized that we were standing on a service road.

It was somewhat overgrown and didn't appear recently traveled, by vehicle at least. I tilted the flashlight down and scanned the ground, looking for any sign that Felicity might have come through. I harbored no belief that I would find anything so obvious as footprints, but at this point, I was willing to accept anything The Ancients would see fit to bestow upon me.

Their gift came in the form of an audible clue, although it was connected not with her directly but with my own pet theory about where she would be heading. I listened closely as in the distance a low rumble was beginning to build in both volume and tempo. Unfortunately, the sound was echoing through the woods in a haphazard pattern.

"Whaddaya think?" Ben asked.

"Sounds like a train," I replied.

"Yeah, but I mean, which way?"

I sighed and shook my head. Then I pointed the flashlight to my right and began to speak, my tone unsure, "Well, it looks like the road curves up ahead there. Assuming we followed a relatively straight path coming over the ridge and didn't get turned around, that should take us deeper into the park and toward the train tracks. I'm guessing that's where she'd be heading."

"Why's that?" he asked.

"I don't know. Just a feeling."

"Okay. I'm good with that."

"Of course, as I recall, the tracks curve," I added, second-guessing myself. "So she might have gone back the other way. That is if she came through here at all."

"So whaddaya wanna do?"

"I'm pretty sure we kept on a straight course," I finally said, a tremor of uncertainty still underscoring my words. "If nothing else, going right should take us farther into the park. I think."

"Then let's go," he urged.

We started walking, and I twisted my wrist up then pressed the backlight button on my watch. The blue glow lit the dial, and I peered quickly at the numbers. "Five-thirty," I said over my shoulder. "If she was being guided by some ethereal force, then she knows exactly where she's going and has probably had plenty of time to get there by now."

I was amazed at how calm my voice suddenly sounded because internally I was a wreck. My stomach was twisted into a double knot, and nausea had become a constant companion. A sickly sense of dread was raping my spine and wrapping its cold fingers around the back of my brain.

The only thing that kept me from completely losing my sanity at this very moment was the fact that I had not felt anything happen on an ethereal level. Felicity and I had a very tight connection with one another and would often share experiences as if we were one person. At the very least, I was sure I'd be able to feel it if she was already in immediate danger.

At least, that is what I kept telling myself.

The buzzing annoyance of myriad insects was beginning to fill the air, and we both found ourselves randomly slapping at mosquitoes. Birds had begun to chirp their staccato songs to greet the onset of morning, and I could hear squirrels chittering in the branches above.

The distant rumble of the train was coming closer, but I still couldn't pinpoint a direction due to the echo, and that made me even more unsure of my choice. We continued along the unused service road for several yards before I began to slow my pace, eventually coming to a complete stop.

"What's wrong?" Ben asked. "You goin' la-la?"

"I don't know, Ben," I replied, my agitation growing rapidly. "I don't know if… I'm not… I'm just not sure we're going in the right direction."

"You wanna turn around?" he asked.

"Gods, I just don't know," I replied, fear suddenly bubbling to the top in an attempt to overtake me.

"Just calm down, Row," he told me, then looked upward. "Sun'll be up in less than twenty minutes. It's already gettin' light, so why don't we do this. You keep goin' this way, and I'll backtrack and go the other way."

I shook my head. "I still don't even know if she actually used this road, Ben."

"Listen, Row, I know you're upset, but you gotta get a handle on it," he said. "I'm tellin' ya', man, we're gonna find her and it's gonna be okay."

"How can you know that?" I snapped.

"Because I'm tellin' ya that's how it is," he responded in a stern voice. "It's gonna be all good, Rowan. Now go."

He turned and started back down the service road, heading quickly away from me through the overgrowth. I watched after him for a moment then swallowed hard and mutely kicked myself for the display of emotion. Where Felicity's safety was concerned, I had a hard time being rational, and he was correct— I had to stop letting it get the best of me.

I turned in the opposite direction and started up the road, pressing forward into the almost ninety-degree curve, my head down to follow the spot of the flashlight along the ground. I stepped carefully around a deep rut and continued walking until I rounded the bend.

When I looked up, the road stretched out before me in a straight line, and the overgrowth was knocked down as if the pathway had been frequented far more recently. In fact, it even looked somewhat maintained. In the distance, the lane passed beneath a short train trestle and beyond that, disappeared into the forest.

I was mentally debating whether or not I should call Ben back this way when I focused on something slumped against a tree along the roadside, just before the trestle.

My heart froze in my chest, and the sudden onset of blind panic made my skin prickle hot then cold. The flashlight struck the ground with a thud, its beam now directed against a clump of tall grass off the side of the road. I felt a heavy thump in my chest as my heart reacted to the dump of adrenalin, and my legs began pumping hard against the ground.

I wasn't sure if I heard myself screaming or if it was simply the whistle of the oncoming train as I sprinted madly toward Felicity's motionless form.

CHAPTER 25:

What I heard wasn't just me screaming, nor was it only the whistle of the train. It was both. A pair of disharmonic tones blended into a single horrific chord. I don't know what it was that I was screaming, but my guttural shriek had joined with the blast of the air horn to shatter the pre-dawn calm.

It could have been the word 'no'. It could have been Felicity's name. I might have been calling for Ben. A flagrant curse aimed at the Dark Mother wasn't out of the realm of possibility either. Perhaps it was even all of them at once, I really cannot say.

The simple fact was that the chilling wail was just exactly that— an unintelligible cry of lament in a single drawn out breath. I suppose the second round would have been just as terrifying to hear as the first had it not been drowned out by the now overwhelming roar of the approaching freight train.

My heart was pounding as I drove myself forward— covering the distance between Felicity and me with a burst of speed that could only have been the product of an adrenalin surge. I started backpedaling as I drew near, trying to bring myself to a stop. In the end, I literally fell in front of her, hitting the ground hard and scrambling the last foot or so on my hands and knees.

As I crawled, my ears were filled with the thunder of the diesel engine. The cacophony was punctuated by the rhythmic clack of the locomotive wheels against track as the southbound freight train started across the trestle above.

Slipping my arms behind my wife's back, I pulled her up and hugged her close. Hot tears were already streaming down my face as every ounce of the fear and dread I had been holding at bay was now bleeding out of me in an emotional hemorrhage.

Her body was warm to the touch and I buried my face against her neck, stroking her hair as my own body shuddered in an off-kilter cadence with my heavy sobs. My very soul was rending itself into nothingness as I spiraled into darkened despair. I couldn't even find the energy to curse Cerridwen for taking her from me, nor myself for allowing it to happen.

All I could do was cry.

The last thing I expected to feel were her arms slowly wrapping across my back.

In my head, I could have sworn I heard the lilting Celtic tone of her faint voice saying, "Aye, Rowan, it's okay…"

My first thought was that she had now joined the voices of the dead. It only stood to reason that she would speak to me from beyond the veil. And, of course, the whispers of those on the other side had become such an integral part of my life these past few years that I was rarely surprised when they made themselves known.

My second thought, when I considered the pressure I believed I felt against my back, was that the inevitable had arrived without delay. I had stepped over the edge and was officially insane.

I continued to hold her tight, letting the world around me be swallowed by the riotous noise from above. It didn't even cross my mind that she was actually alive and well until the train had finally passed, and I could actually hear her complaining.

"Row, please," she said, her voice a strained whisper. "I can't breathe."

I loosened my grip and pulled away from her. She was staring back at me with her eyes wide. Her tired expression displayed the cumulative fatigue of the past few days, but she still managed to cock her head to the side and give me a look of concern. She sucked in a deep breath and quickly huffed it back out.

"Thank you," she said.

"I thought you were gone…" I said, wiping the back of my hand across my eyes.

"Aye," she returned with a slight nod. "I got that impression."

"Oh Gods…" I whispered, reaching out and gently brushing her cheek.

"It's okay, Row." She gave me a weak smile. "I'm fine. Really."

"Told ya', white man." I heard Ben's voice come from behind me, and I quickly glanced back over my shoulder.

My friend was standing in the middle of the service road looking down at us. He was nervously fidgeting, wringing his hands around the length of the flashlight I had dropped, and he had apparently retrieved. His expression was a mix of relief and discomfort all at once, and he looked away as if embarrassed to have witnessed my unchecked emotional outburst.

I forced out a hot breath and then sucked in a fresh one in an attempt to relax. I continued to wipe my eyes as I sniffed, somewhat chagrined myself. "How long have you been there?"

"For a bit," he said softly. "Caught up to ya' right after ya' started screamin'."

"I'm surprised you heard me."

"Jeezus, Kemosabe, who couldn't? You were louder than the fuckin' train," he told me with a half-hearted chuckle. I'm sure the joke was to ease his apparent discomfort as much as mine.

I let out a clipped laugh as well. "Yeah... So... I guess I looked pretty ridiculous."

"No," he replied with a slow shake of his head. "You looked pretty much like any guy would if he thought he'd just lost everything he had to live for."

The level of understanding Ben was displaying was a testament to the depth of our friendship. I knew full well that he wasn't one for overt displays of tenderness or sharing of vulnerabilities, so I appreciated his words even more.

"Thanks, Chief," I told him.

"It's all good, Kemosabe," he replied, raising a hand and smoothing back his hair. "So ya'think we can change the subject before this gets all touchy feely?"

"Afraid you'll damage your reputation with the woodland creatures?" Felicity quipped.

"Maybe," he grunted. "So what's up with you? Ya' damn near gave us all heart attacks."

She shrugged. "Aye, sorry about that."

"So what did happen?" I asked, turning back to Felicity. "Why are you just sitting here?"

"Waiting for you," she replied. "I knew you wouldn't be too far behind."

"Look at this," Ben said, shoving a wrinkled piece of paper over my shoulder.

I took it and glanced at the scribbles. It was the map he had copied from Felicity's bloody rendition.

"Turn it the other way," he instructed, motioning with his finger.

I followed his direction and rotated the paper, then looked carefully at the scrawl of lines. My friend reached over my shoulder and indicated several points on the homemade map.

"Service road, railroad tracks…" he allowed his voice to trail off.

I looked up from the paper and at Felicity. "Did you find…"

She was already nodding before I could finish the question. "Aye, there's a grave on the other side of the tracks. A few yards off the road."

"Did you disturb anything?" Ben asked, shifting into his official cop persona.

"No." She shook her head. "I haven't even been over there."

"Then how do you know for sure…" he began, then caught himself. "Forget it. Forget it."

"Not that I'm complaining," I said. "But I was certain you would try to connect with her. Why didn't you?"

"I would have, but she wouldn't let me," she replied. "She remembered me, Rowan."

"She what?"

"Brittany and I went to elementary school together," she replied. "I'd almost forgotten that myself, but she didn't. She told me she couldn't allow an old friend to be hurt. All she wanted was for me to find her."

Behind me, I heard Ben softly whistling the theme from the television show, *Twilight Zone*.

"Hey! You wanna get off my ass?" Ben's angry shout echoed through the woods as he stared down at Lieutenant Albright. "It's not like I'm the one who killed 'er ya'know!"

"Don't take that tone with me, Detective Storm," she spat in return.

"Both of you need to settle down," Constance interjected.

"I don't see where you have much say in this, Special Agent Mandalay," Albright announced as she brought her angry gaze to bear on Constance. "This is no longer an abduction, it is a homicide investigation."

True to what Constance had told me earlier, Lieutenant Albright was well on her way to reclaiming this case. It was obvious from her display that in her mind, you were either with her or against her. And, the four of us were already marked as against. Of course, I'm sure we had been tagged as such all along.

"The Bureau still has an interest in this, Lieutenant," Constance returned. "The fact is you have a serial killer on your hands."

"Be that as it may, you have no business interfering with my command," Albright snipped.

"I'm not trying to interfere with anything," Constance replied with a shake of her head. "I'm simply telling you that standing here yelling at one another isn't getting any of us any closer to solving this crime."

"I still want to know what THEY are doing here." Albright shrugged off Mandalay's observation and shunted the conversation into a different direction as she gestured at Felicity and me.

"They're why we found the body," Ben returned stiffly.

"What are you, Storm, some kind of lap dog? Do you just let these two lead you around by the nose?"

"I'm a cop," he retorted. "Unlike someone I could mention."

"And what is that supposed to mean?"

My friend shook his head and looked away. "Just forget it."

"No," Albright snarled. "I want to know just exactly what you were implying."

"Okay, you wanna know…" Ben replied, thrusting a finger at her.

"Storm…" Constance warned.

"No, Mandalay, she says she wants ta' know." He shot a glance her way then looked back to the lieutenant. "It means if you'd quit fuckin' around playin' politics, maybe the Major Case Squad could get back to doin' police work like it's supposed to."

"I see," she returned with a cold chill in her voice. "And you call what you have been doing 'police work'?"

"Yeah, I do."

"Considering your entourage, I would say that is a matter for debate."

"Yeah, well who just found Larson's body?" he chided.

"That is a good question, Detective," she answered. "An even better question would be, just exactly how did your little group find the body?"

He shook his head. "You don't really wanna know that."

"Oh, but I do, Detective," she told him as she crossed her arms and nodded her head. She didn't hide her sarcasm. "I do."

"Listen, I'm not goin' there with ya' right now, 'cause you're not gonna believe it if I do."

"WitchCraft, then," she replied, spitting the word as if it was a bad taste in her mouth.

"Yeah, whatever. I'll take any lead I can get if it helps me get an asshole off the streets."

"Even if that lead could compromise the investigation?"

"There's nothin' compromised here," he snapped.

"Are you certain of that?"

"Yeah, I am. Besides, who are you ta' lecture me on compromisin' an investigation anyway?"

"What is that supposed to mean?"

"Let's just say I sure as hell don't try ta' help the assholes of the world escape."

A hush fell between them as Ben all but hung her name on the verbal accusation. My friend was among the few who thought she had simply managed to dodge a bullet when Internal Affairs had cleared her of any wrongdoing in the Eldon Porter debacle. However, I was beyond shocked the he had just made his opinion so blatantly public.

The two of them stood staring at one another, Albright's jaw working as her mouth curled into a hard frown.

"Excuse me, Lieutenant?" a crime scene technician edged into the envelope of the standoff.

"What is it?" she barked without shifting her glare from Ben.

"The medical examiner just arrived," the technician answered with a bit of trepidation. "You said you wanted to know when she got here."

"Thank you," she returned evenly. "I will be right there."

She continued staring at Ben, and he at her, as the crime scene tech made a hasty retreat. After a long measure, she looked away for a moment, then back to my friend as she placed one hand on her hip and pointedly stabbed the index finger of her other at him.

"We will discuss this later, Detective Storm," she forced the words between her clenched teeth. "But right now I want you as far from this crime scene as you can get. Do I make myself clear?"

"Yeah," he spat. "As a freakin' bell."

She didn't stop there. "And, I want you to take your damnable Satan worshippers with you before I have them arrested for trespassing."

CHAPTER 26:

The morning sun was filtering through the green canopy of the trees and had already set about the task of bringing on the heat of the day. Even with a slight breeze, it was starting to get hot out here, and the sun was far from the only reason. The two detectives were squared off, their tempers swelling outward with a palpable hatred for one another. I watched on as Ben stared back at Lieutenant Albright, painfully silent in the wake of her voiced threat.

My friend was ready to fight; there was no doubt about that. While the lieutenant was certainly guilty of repeatedly baiting him, for all intents and purposes, he had taken the first swing. It was clear from his current stance that he was planning to finish this without regard for the price it may cost in the end.

I continued watching as he worked his jaw and slid his palm across his chin then allowed his arm to drop to his side. His hand clenched and unclenched repeatedly, and I recognized the motion to be a precursor of him working into a rage. Following the visual cue, I took hold of his arm and then gave him a healthy nudge just as his mouth opened. When he glanced over at me, anger in his eyes, I simply shook my head and mouthed the word 'no.'

"Is there something you wanted to say, Detective?" Albright spat, daring him to cross the line.

Ben continued looking at me, and I shook my head again. I knew full well that what had just set him off was her verbal assault on Felicity and me. I didn't like it any more than he did, but I'd grown jaded to such insults over the years. Moreover, I wasn't going to let him jeopardize his career any more than he already had, especially on our account.

"No, Lieutenant," he finally growled as he turned back to her. "Not a damn thing."

"Good," she retorted and then looked over at me. "Mister Gant, I expect you to be available for questioning." She shot her glance at

Felicity then added, "That goes for both of you."

"Whatever you say, Sheriff," I told her with my own injection of sarcasm. "Don't leave town. Got it."

"Crack jokes if you want, Mister Gant," she retorted. "But, make no mistake, as far as I am concerned, both you and your wife are suspects."

"You have got to be kidding me" was my incredulous reply.

"By procedure, maybe," Constance interjected. "But, that's ludicrous and you know it."

"Is it?" Albright queried. "How did they know where to find the body?"

"We already covered that," Ben told her.

"Did we?"

"Oh, gimme a fuckin' break," he snarled.

"I am," she replied. "I'm not bringing you up on charges right this minute. Now get out of here. All of you."

"I'll be staying, Lieutenant," Mandalay announced in a cold tone.

"I see no reason..." Albright started.

"I will be staying, Lieutenant," Constance repeated, emphasizing the words as she cut her off. "If there is a problem with that, we can contact the Bureau field office, and I'm sure the SAIC can give you several reasons for me to be here."

The lieutenant regarded her silently for a moment, then sighed and motioned toward us. "Suit yourself, Agent Mandalay, but I am still lead detective, and I want these three out of here now."

"I'll take care of it," Constance told her evenly.

"See that you do."

"One more thing, Lieutenant," Mandalay replied in a careful but frosty tone. "I suggest that you don't push me. I'm the last bitch you want to cross right now."

"Yes, I am sure that you are," Albright returned in her own cold voice and then paused before adding, "A bitch."

They stared at each other for one of those time-warped moments that lasts only a few brief seconds but feels like an eternity to everyone within its sphere of influence. Albright finally turned and headed away from our small clutch.

At first, she retreated without a word, but after a few steps, she paused and called back over her shoulder, her voice thickly frosted with sarcasm. "By the way, I had Miz O'Brien's Jeep towed and impounded as possible evidence. I do hope it won't be an inconvenience."

"*Fek tù saigh*," Felicity calmly issued the curse of mixed colloquial Irish and Gaelic.

This wasn't the first time my wife had launched that particular phrase at the lieutenant and at one point, had even supplied her with the English translation. Apparently the meaning of the foreign words had stuck with Albright ever since, as evidenced by her reply.

"Funny you should say that, Miz O'Brien, because it is *exactly* what I was thinking." She made the comment with an air of satisfaction and then continued on her way.

The lieutenant's haughty attitude told us that as far as she was concerned, she had come out on top this go around, and truth be told, she had. However, whether she wanted to admit it or not, this was merely a single skirmish, and the war was far from over. Still, it took everything I had to stand there motionless and not say a word, and I'm sure the same was true for everyone else. In fact, I could tell by looking at Ben that he was struggling just to contain himself; and, though I'd seen him angry a number of times before, the darkness of the emotions seething from him at this moment actually worried me.

Right or wrong, the fact remained that there was nothing we could do; at least, not with a head-on approach, and not at this particular moment. It was beyond obvious that any further confrontation would only make the situation worse, so we stood our ground and kept silent.

In the end, it still took some swift talking from Constance, as well as Felicity and me, to convince Ben not to go after the lieutenant. While I doubted he would resort to physical violence, I knew for a fact that his mouth would get him into more trouble than he needed at this point in his life.

I can't say that I blamed him. Albright was deep under everyone's skin, not just his. I even caught myself having some intensely dark thoughts about the woman and had to mentally back away from the ill wishes for fear I might inadvertently manifest one or two of them. I glanced over at Felicity and couldn't help but notice that even at a distance, she was systematically vivisecting the lieutenant with a razor sharp stare. I have to admit that the intensity of her gaze made my spiteful ruminations appear pleasant in comparison. Mandalay was probably the calmest of our small group, but even so, almost everything that came out of her mouth was clipped and official, no matter to whom she was speaking.

However, what really stood out to me was the mood of the cops working the scene. I certainly wasn't about to diminish how horrific this crime scene was. They were all nightmares in the making. Still, over the past few years, I had worked some that were far worse than this. I thought I knew what the atmosphere should be like, and this wasn't it. Considering that these men and women were veterans whose experiences were sure to overshadow mine in both volume and intensity, I was somewhat taken aback by their overall tenor. The emotional climate in this corner of the park had been barreling downhill since the arrival of the first uniformed officer, and that pace had been quickening. It had now progressed far beyond any level of edginess I would have expected.

At first, I assumed the air of discontent was simply due to the fact that they were working such a high profile homicide. Let's face it; this wasn't Jane Q Public, this was the daughter of the Saint Louis city mayor. There was bound to be more than the average amount of pressure on these cops. But, as I watched, it became clear that there was more at work here. While it might have gone unnoticed by a casual observer, paying attention to the various interactions between crime scene technicians and Major Case Squad detectives told a story. And, the story was that wherever the tension was greatest, Albright could be found at the center, pulling the strings.

As irritants go, she was at the top of the scale and virulent to a fault.

My concentration on the scene was shattered by a hard nudge against my shoulder, and I broke my stare away to glance up at my friend.

"Huh?"

"I said, c'mon," he voiced, apparently repeating himself. "I'm takin' you two home."

Sleep was a welcome commodity to us all, although for me, it was nowhere near as restful as I would have liked. Even though my conscious mind knew Felicity was safe and was lying beside me in the bed, my subconscious had elected to unload the emotional baggage of the past few hours.

My slumber was plagued with more than one nondescript, but horribly intense, dream of loss and despair: each cycle driving me upward into wakefulness, only so I could dry my dampened cheeks on the pillowcase then roll over and repeat the process, or so it seemed. I'm not sure how long it took before I fell into something resembling actual sleep, but in the end, even that was shallow and fitful. I suppose that is why I'm the one who heard the noise.

I'm not sure which sound I heard first, the dogs barking or the banging on the door. In either case, there was enough racket to pluck me out of the twilight sleep I'd finally become semi-comfortable with and deposit me face first into the harsh world of the awake.

I opened one eye and saw that the bedroom was dimly lit by sunlight that was forcing its way between the slats of the closed mini blinds. I lifted my head and cast my monocular glance in the direction of the clock and saw that it was 3:43 in the afternoon. I closed my eye and let my head fall back onto the pillow then listened for a moment. All I heard were the muffled reports of various Sunday afternoon outdoor activities— children playing, lawnmowers running in the distance, an occasional car passing by, the usual stuff.

I struggled to think about it for a moment. Firstly, there was nothing more than ambient noise meeting my ears. Secondly, I really didn't want to get up yet. And, thirdly, Ben was in the living room. We had convinced him not to drive, since he was surely as tired as we both were, so he had crashed on the couch. It stood to reason that if there had been any such noises as barking dogs and door banging, he would have heard it first and gotten up. My foggy brain tallied the column and then decided that since I wasn't hearing anything now that I hadn't actually heard anything before.

Besides, considering the abnormally busy expressway running between my conscious and subconscious, whatever it was I thought I'd heard couldn't be real anyway. It was most likely yet another dreamlike terror come to wreak havoc upon my already abused psyche. I'd had more than enough of that and didn't plan on dealing with any more, so I simply rolled over and pulled the pillow up over my head.

I didn't even have a chance to get comfortable when the banging sounded again and was followed by our doorbell ringing in a rapid staccato. The entire disorganized symphony was underscored by the dogs wildly yapping and growling. This time, however, there was an added thud as Ben's feet hit the living room floor, and I could hear him muttering something. While I couldn't make out the actual verbiage, I had a fairly good idea of the content because I was considering a few expletives myself, and I'm pretty sure they were the same ones.

"Aye," my wife mumbled in a tired voice. "Who do you think it is?"

"Who knows," I muttered.

"Are you going to get up and see?" she asked.

"Let Ben get it."

"That would be rude. It's not Ben's house, then."

"He's family."

"Rowan."

"He's closer to the door."

"Rowan…"

"All right, all right..." I was already moving as I spoke the words.

I sat up on the edge of the bed and let out a yawn as I rubbed my eyes. After a quick stretch, I slid on a pair of pants and then pulled a t-shirt over my head as I trudged around the end of the bed toward the door. I could hear movement and voices out in the living room and knew that Ben had already answered the door, so I didn't rush.

"Listen," I said. "He already got it."

"Go and see who it is," my wife mumbled as she rolled over on her side.

"Why me and not you?"

"Because you're already up," she muttered.

"Yeah," I huffed. "Because I'm already up. Go figure."

I was just reaching for the door handle when there was a hard knuckled rap on the bedroom door.

I followed through, giving the handle a twist and then swung the wooden barrier open. As expected, I was greeted by the disheveled countenance of my friend. His clothing was rumpled, and his hair was protruding from his head at odd, pillow-induced angles. He was standing there massaging his neck and staring at me with surprisingly clear eyes. Even though his outward appearance bespoke of recent intimacy with sleep, he was obviously far more alert than I.

"You two better get cleaned up," he said simply. "Mandalay's here. Looks like 'Bible Barb' wants you both downtown."

CHAPTER 27:

"Constance, why don't you go home and get some sleep, then," Felicity said.

We were all seated in an interview room at St. Louis City police headquarters. This wasn't the first time I'd been in one and probably wouldn't be the last unless my life made a very drastic change and dead people suddenly stopped talking to me. Unfortunately, I didn't see that happening any time in the near future. Still, this was a bit different. I was used to being on the metaphorical other side of the table. Being the interviewee was yet another new experience to add to my résumé.

We were waiting for Lieutenant Albright to arrive and had been for better than fifteen minutes. I knew that making us wait was nothing more than a stalling tactic intended to set a mood. It was a blatant textbook attempt to make us nervous and give her an upper hand. What she failed to realize was that not only was there nothing for us to be nervous about, we were still simply too tired to care.

"Maybe when this is over," Mandalay returned in a spent voice.

She was slouched in a chair, head tilted back and eyes closed. She hadn't had the same luxury of sleep as had we, and in the past quarter hour, she had nodded off at least once.

"You look like hell, Constance," I said.

"Yeah, probably," she agreed, then chuckled. "But have you looked in a mirror lately, Rowan?"

She was correct. We had done our best to get ourselves together, but both Ben and I were just to the other side of folded, spindled, and mutilated. Not the good side, mind you. Even Felicity was showing some signs of wear around the edges, and that was unusual when you considered that she always looked like a perfect china doll even when she had just crawled out of bed.

The ragged FBI agent tilted her head down with a yawn then slowly pushed herself upright in the chair. She gave us a sleepy glance and then spoke again. "So, did you manage to get hold of your attorney?"

"She wasn't in," Felicity answered. "I left her a message though."

"You said when you picked us up that we weren't being charged with anything," I offered.

"Not that I'm aware of," she replied. "Like I said, she didn't tell me what this was about. But, I'm not putting anything past Albright. I really think your attorney should be present for this."

"I'm sure she'll call as soon as she picks up her voice mail," Felicity offered.

"Well, until then, I'm staying," Constance replied.

"I know you have a law degree, Constance," I told her. "But wouldn't that be a conflict of interest?"

"Fuck it," she replied. "Friends don't let friends get railroaded."

"You've been hanging around Ben too long," I quipped.

She nodded. "Yeah, tell me about it."

"'Bout time ya' learned ta' speak English," Ben said. "I knew I'd rub off sooner or later."

"Wouldn't having an attorney here just make us look like we were trying to hide something?" my wife asked, still dwelling on the earlier thread of the conversation.

"It doesn't matter with this bitch, Felicity," Mandalay replied. "She's got it in for you two. That's all there is to it."

"Ya'know she's prob'ly on the other side of the window listenin' in right now," Ben said.

"Yeah," Mandalay agreed. "She probably is. So what?"

"So she prob'ly just heard ya' call 'er a bitch."

"Good," she replied as she twisted in her chair and looked toward the one-way glass. I watched her reflection as she stuck out her tongue and then twisted back around to face us. "I sure as hell wouldn't want her to get the wrong idea."

"I think you've made your position clear," I said, surprised by the somewhat juvenile display but writing it off to her lack of sleep.

Mandalay gave a tired chuckle. "We can only hope."

"Jeez, Mandalay," Ben said. "I'm likin' you more every day."

"Cool it, Storm," she replied. "You're a married man."

"Yeah, at the moment maybe."

"Aye, what's that supposed to mean?" Felicity asked, puzzlement in her voice.

"You still haven't…" He waved his finger between Constance and Felicity but directed the unfinished query at me.

I shrugged. "When have I had time?"

Mandalay visibly straightened in her chair and cocked her head to the side as she focused her gaze on Ben. "Is that it? Is that why you've been so flaky, Storm? Are you and Allison…"

Her question was interrupted as the door to the interview room swung open, and Lieutenant Albright followed it inside. A stack of files, several inches thick, was tucked in the crook of her arm, and she held them close as if they were a prized possession.

"I'll tell ya' later," Ben offered quietly to Constance and Felicity and then turned his attention to Albright.

The lieutenant was still wearing the scowl that seemed to be a permanent adornment for the lower half of her face, but there was definitely something different about her. I couldn't put my finger on it at first, but unless I missed my guess, she was ruffled.

I suppose it could have been that she actually had overheard Mandalay's epithet, but that sort of thing had never seemed to faze her before. This was something different, and you didn't have to be a Witch to feel the chaotic energy emanating from her.

She half-turned, pushed the door shut, then strode purposefully over to the table and simply glared at me. She opened her mouth to speak, hesitated, then closed her mouth and found a way to frown even harder than before. After a moment, she angrily tossed the file folders onto the laminated surface.

Crime scene photos, notes, and official reports peeked out of their manila sheaths as the folders slid a few inches and partially spilled their contents.

"These do not leave the building," Albright announced. The deliberate control she was exercising on her voice was plainly audible.

"Okay" was all I could think of to say.

I glanced down at the photos and caught a quick glimpse of a headless female corpse paper-clipped to an autopsy report. A similar photo was protruding from one of the other folders as well.

"Understand right now that I am against this," she continued. "However, the mayor seems to think we should utilize your so-called talents regarding these cases. I did my best to convince him otherwise, but his emotions are getting the better of him at the moment. I am sure he will eventually come to his senses."

I don't suppose I was surprised by the callous attitude she was displaying, but that didn't keep me from finding it utterly abhorrent. I had plenty I wanted to say to her in response, but I knew starting yet another argument would accomplish nothing, so I picked the most innocuous of the replies that flitted through my head. "So Felicity was right. Those were Brittany Larson's remains."

"Yes" was her monosyllabic response.

"And because of her, you have a very fresh crime scene," I pressed, unable to help myself.

She hesitated and then replied again, almost choking on the word. "Yes."

Without thinking, I allowed my next thought to escape in the form of audible words. "You know, where I come from people say thank you."

She leaned forward, placing her hands on the table and locking her gelid gaze on me. "Do not patronize me, Mister Gant. Trust me, if it were not for the fact that one of the victims is his daughter and that you found her body by whatever godless means your kind employs, I can guarantee you that this would not be happening."

"Godless? Our kind?" I started. "Look, I've got no idea what I did to you that makes you hate me so much, and honestly, I'm not sure I want to know."

She simply continued glaring at me without a word.

Getting no response, I resumed speaking. "And, apparently you aren't going to tell me anyway... Well, Lieutenant Albright, if it's any consolation at all, I'm not particularly excited about having to work with you either."

"Understand, Mister Gant, that we are not working with one another." She placed more than the lion's share of emphasis on the word 'not'. "We are simply working on the same case whether we like it or not. And, I for one, do not."

"Then I guess we'll just have to make the best of it for the duration," I offered flatly.

"Rest assured that with the exception of locking you in a cell, something I would relish mind you, I would just as soon have no contact with either of you whatsoever."

"Aye, the feeling is mutual," Felicity snipped.

"And, as for you..." Albright began, looking over at my wife.

"Fine," I interjected before the two of them could go at it full force. "I think we all agree that we don't much care for one another, so let's drop all the bullshit here and now. What, exactly, is it that you want from us?"

"Review the files, strike whatever deal with Satan you usually make, and then find the killer," she said, ticking off the short list in a perfunctory fashion.

"Just like that," I replied.

"Is that not how you normally do things?" she spat sarcastically.

"Well, for one thing," I replied. "Satan is a Judeo-Christian entity. He's your boy not ours. But, I doubt I can convince you of that."

"Spare me your double-talk, Mister Gant," she growled. "I have dealt with devil worshippers before, and you cannot fool me."

"I'm not trying to fool anyone, Lieutenant."

"The wicked worketh a deceitful work: but to him that soweth righteousness shall be a sure reward. Proverbs, chapter eleven, verse eighteen."

The hair rose on the back of my neck, and I felt a cold chill run up my spine as the words struck my ears. The last person to quote Bible passages to me had been Eldon Porter, and he was trying to kill me. I had been convinced for months that Barbara Albright was intent on the same end, though perhaps not in such a blatant way as he. This just served to cement my belief in that fact.

"I've read your book," I told her. "I don't need a Bible lesson."

She didn't let it go. "Set thou a wicked man over him: and let Satan stand at his right hand…"

"…When he shall be judged, let him be condemned: and let his prayer become sin," I replied, continuing the verse for her just as I had done when confronted by Porter. "Let his days be few; and let another take his office. Let his children be fatherless, and his wife a widow. Shall I continue? Book of Psalm. Chapter one-oh-nine. I already told you, I know the drill."

Her voice moved up a notch. "Do not mock me!"

"Yeah, whatever."

"Just make it happen, Gant!"

Albright had been flustered when she entered, but she was practically livid now. As if I didn't already press all the wrong buttons in her life, I'd obviously just found one labeled do not touch.

"Look, it ain't like that, Lieutenant," Ben spoke up in a well-intentioned attempt to defuse the situation.

"I was not speaking to you, Detective Storm," she snapped, turning her hard stare on him.

"He's right," I said. "That's not how it works."

"I don't care how it works," she replied, and then turned back to face me before continuing, her voice still a mark or two above the necessary volume for the small room. "In fact, I don't even know if I believe that it works. All I do know is that the mayor insists that you be brought into the loop, and that is what I am doing. From this point forward, I expect you to stay out of my way."

"With pleasure," I told her.

"Good. I am glad that we understand one another."

"So," I asked. "Since I'm obviously persona non grata, what do you want us to do if we come up with something?"

She regarded me silently for a moment, boring a hole through me with her stare, then pushed back from the table and stood fully upright. She reached into a pocket on her jacket and withdrew a rectangular, gold-tone case. Flipping it open, she slipped a business card from it and tossed it onto the table before me.

"You can leave any information you have on my voice mail," she said tersely. "Make certain that you do not waste my time, Mister Gant."

"Yeah," I grunted. "Wouldn't dream of it, Lieutenant."

She turned on her heel and started purposefully toward the door. Before she'd made it two full steps, my wife spoke up.

"Lieutenant Albright," Felicity called out, a demanding note in her voice.

The lieutenant stopped and turned to face her, then snarled, "What is it, Miz O'Brien?"

"I'll be having my Jeep back now," Felicity stated, staring coldly at the woman and not even bothering to pretend her words were a request.

Albright was noticeably annoyed by the demand. She looked at my wife as if she were sizing her up for a fistfight, then finally returned sharply, "Have Detective Storm show you to the impound lot."

That said, she wheeled around and left the interview room, slamming the door in her wake.

Ben looked over at me. "Jeez, white man. You sure got under her skin that time."

"Bible verses," I muttered.

"Yeah, Rowan," Constance spoke up. "Are you sure you didn't memorize the whole book?"

"No, like I've said before, just the passages regarding Satan and WitchCraft," I replied. "Those are the ones that get thrown in my face. But that's not my point."

"Okay." Ben shrugged. "What gives?"

"She just justified her actions to me with a Bible verse, Ben," I replied. "And then got upset when I was able to quote them back to her."

"Yeah, I noticed. So?"

"Yeah, so tell me, who else do we know who does that?"

"Eldon Fucking Porter," he replied slowly, his eyes lighting with realization as he reached up to massage his neck. "Sonofabitch."

Thursday, October 3rd
Three days prior to the new moon
3:19 P.M.
St. Louis, Missouri

CHAPTER 28:

A few days shy of four months had passed, and any lead connected with Brittany Larson's murder had long since gone cold. To be honest, absolutely frigid was a more accurate description.

The case had started its death spiral in the hours immediately following the postmortem on the young woman's remains. As fresh and undisturbed as the crime scene had been, it had revealed nothing to police other than the fact that they had a dead body on their hands and that said remains had been intentionally buried in a shallow grave.

The only hopes left in that empty wake were the autopsy results along with the off chance that someone had witnessed something and that they would come forward. The latter option quickly became the center of an official media blitz that rivaled almost any ad campaign you could imagine: everything from regular television appeals, radio spots, constant mentions on the nightly news, and full-page ads in the metropolitan newspaper. Calls came in to the Major Case Squad at a steady rate for the first few days and even ballooned in volume at one point before tapering off to a modest trickle. Unfortunately, each potential lead consisted only of attention seekers and frustrating dead ends.

As to the postmortem, there were clues to be had, most definitely. However, they were only indicators as to what had occurred during Larson's final few hours of life; and eventually, what had brought about her death. Unfortunately, they were not the kind of telltale signs needed to help identify her killer or even convict him, should he be found. There were no fingerprints, no foreign hair or traceable fibers, nothing.

What the autopsy did reveal, however, was that she had been brutally tortured; and, the laundry list of things that had been done to her read like a script from a bad 'hack and slash' horror flick.

Ligature marks on her forearms, wrists, and calves, along with patterned bruising showed that she had been bound, possibly in a chair, for several hours. Hypostasis of the blood in her lower extremities showed that she had died in that position and remained there for some time before being moved. Deep cuts and punctures scored her torso, most having occurred while she was still alive, although some well after she had expired. Her breasts had been severely mutilated, and she was pockmarked with well over one hundred cigarette burns of varying degrees. I don't suppose any of these came as a great surprise to us considering the stigmata that had displayed across Felicity's body the night she channeled Larson. Still, the photos were more than just a little hard to take.

There was vaginal and anal tearing, indicating that she had been violently raped, but there was no trace of semen whatsoever. This lead the investigators to believe that either there had been no ejaculation, a condom had been used, or more likely, due to the amount and nature of the trauma, that the penetration had been performed with a foreign object. Conspicuously absent from the trauma was bruising, which meant she had been defiled post mortem, a small consolation for her.

Another of the glaring observations was, of course, the fact that her head was missing. This, and the fact that hacksaw marks were found on the exposed vertebrae instantly tied her homicide to those of Tamara Linwood and Sarah Hart. That was something we had all suspected, and in fact known in our own way, but the physical evidence simply proved us out.

The final bulleted point in the report was also one of particular note. There were various torn ligaments and ruptures within striated muscle tissues. These, coupled with several blistered marks on her skin that were consistent with electrical burns, told a gruesome tale in and of themselves.

There had been deeper dimension to her senseless torture— an added layer that had racked her both mentally and physically. And, it provided an explanation for the ethereal electrical storm my wife and I had endured and barely survived.

In the end, the listed cause of death was asphyxia. The notes explaining the possible cause outlined that various indicators pointed to the fact that it may have been due to prolonged high-voltage current passing through the thoracic wall— the result being violent spasms of the intercostal muscles and diaphragm.

In short, she had been electrocuted into suffocation but not before enduring many hours of unimaginable agony.

The report had been a horrific chore for me to read. Even as jaded as I had become these past few years, simply reading what had been done to this woman made me physically ill. The darkness one had to possess in their very soul to do such a thing to another living being was unfathomable to me. Equally distressing was the fact that I realized whoever had done this had done it not out of anger or spite, but because he enjoyed it. It brought him pleasure in the most intimate sense, and that very concept sent bile rising in my throat.

I had to set the folder aside on more than one occasion that day we spent at Police Headquarters. I simply had to place some distance between it and me for a while before I could gather the stomach to continue with the next page. Even avoiding the autopsy and crime scene photos after the first glance through didn't give me any relief. The words on the page were enough by themselves to spark violent images in my head that I was certain would drive me insane.

One of the things that pained me as well was the fact that I couldn't convince Felicity not to read it. She wasn't content to hear my carefully edited version of the postmortem. She had to see it for herself, and when she did, she alternated between sorrowful tears and raging fits of anger with each clinically descriptive paragraph she digested. Before it was over, we were both inhabitants of an emotional wasteland: disgusted, overwhelmed and spent, prone to moodiness and withdrawing rapidly from the world. Had it not been for a number of sessions with Helen Storm, my wife and I would surely have imploded. I already had a healthy respect for Ben and anyone else with a badge for that matter. What I saw in this report just made me admire them that much more. How they could face this sort of thing and not simply crack, I would never understand.

On top of it all, there was a secondary driving force that kept us going. We both knew that Brittany Larson was but one of the victims. There were at least two others who had been put through the same horrors we now beheld in black and white. And, the truth was that no one knew if it stopped there. The police had a list of names that shared some very simple traits: women who were young, pretty, and more to the point, missing. Fortunately, by the blessings of The Ancients, that list was very short. Still, it existed and that was a horror in itself.

As if utter failure on a mundane level weren't bad enough, it just got worse. True to what I had told Lieutenant Albright that first day in the interview room, it simply didn't work the way she wanted. The winds of the ethereal plane could be as fickle as the doldrums and at times, even more unforgiving.

And, this go around, that is exactly what they were. Not only had it not worked the way she wanted, it had not worked at all. Magick, it seemed, had forsaken us.

Of course, this only served to fuel the lieutenant's crusade against me, and it wasn't long before she managed to sway the mayor back to her way of thinking. After less than two weeks, we were unceremoniously banned from any involvement with the investigation. Felicity and I were out, Ben was quickly reassigned back to the city homicide division, and some thirty-odd days later special agent Mandalay had no choice but to move on to more pressing FBI business.

To our chagrin, any and all ethereal contact between the spirit of Brittany Larson and Felicity had abruptly ended the moment my wife had located her decapitated corpse. Not that we hadn't tried our best to reestablish the connection, but in some ways I was relieved that we hadn't. After what we had been through, I was particularly gun-shy about Felicity setting foot into that realm ever again. I knew there was no way I could stop her, but each day that she didn't cross the veil was a day I didn't have to worry about her on that level.

Having been the one in the hot seat to begin with, I opened myself to the darkness, literally calling out to and inviting in the voices I so often wanted to quell in the worst way. Much to my surprise, those who inhabited the other side of the dark curtain were even eschewing contact with me for a change. If they were talking, it wasn't to me.

As far as I could tell, all was quiet in both worlds, and I began to ponder the idea that it might actually be over. I wondered if my bane had truly disappeared and that the past few years had been nothing more than a bad dream. And, as much as I hated not being able to help find the killer of those three women, having my own voice be the only one to inhabit my skull was a welcome and restful change.

At the same time, as much as I had begun to consider the unwanted psychic events as a now distant memory, I knew I could never be so lucky. I had stared directly into the face of evil on a hot summer night a few scant years ago and at that moment, knew that it was my destiny to do so again and again.

Because of that, I wasn't terribly surprised when I awoke one gentle autumn afternoon, completely disoriented, lying in a crumpled heap in the backyard; with a metallic taste in my mouth, my tongue feeling like freshly ground hamburger, and my wife's concerned face staring down into mine.

CHAPTER 29:

"**Y**ou're okay?" Felicity asked as she pushed a glass of salt water into my hand and picked yet another crumbling leaf from my hair.

Her words ran past me, stretching into a drawn-out, half-speed playback. I considered the question then nodded for lack of anything else to do.

"Then I'm calling Ben," she told me in her full-fledged 'don't you dare argue with me' voice.

It took a few seconds for the meaning of her words to register. My nerves were so jangled that I seemed to be lagging at least a half step behind everything going on around me. I suddenly noticed that she was no longer in front of me and that somehow my mouth was now full of salt water. I looked to the side and saw that she was across the room. She already had the phone in her hand and was stabbing at the buttons with her dainty thumb. I gave what I thought was a quick swish, twisted my head to spit the mouthful of salt water into the kitchen sink, dribbled a good portion of it down my shirt, and then turned back to her and nodded.

"Othay," I said, pushing the half-intelligible word past my swelling tongue. "Buth thhith maith be nutthin. Juss enethy baglath"

My response was completely moot. She was already asking whoever had answered the line if she could speak to Detective Benjamin Storm. I kept quiet and took another swig of the warm brine then began to swish it around again as I watched my wife impatiently shuffling in place with the phone up to her ear. My brain was having trouble processing the image, and what I got was more along the lines of a fuzzy pair of Felicity's dancing in the air before me. I blinked hard and shook my head, trying to get a grip on reality.

"Fek!" she spat after a moment, then pulled the phone away and thumbed the off-hook switch. "Voice mail."

I spit again, managing to hit only the sink and not my shirt, then asked, "Ovit or tell?"

"What?"

I had made a serious mess of my tongue this time around. Worse than the times before and that didn't bode well. What I had just tried to tell her was that this might be nothing at all. That it might be nothing more than an energy backlash a few months in the making. An ethereal echo created by all of our attempts to reconnect with Brittany Larson. It wasn't out of the question. Felicity and I had put every ounce we could spare into the attempts, and then some, so backlash was a very real possibility. Put simply, there were times that casting undirected energies upon ethereal waters was much like gambling. In some cases, however, it could be a not quite practiced, side-armed fling of a boomerang; and, if you turned your back on it you ran the risk of getting cold-cocked.

But, that wasn't what was happening now. Even though I had said it aloud, I didn't believe it at all. And, it was obvious that my wife didn't either. I knew I was just trying to convince myself that this couldn't be starting again— so much for trying to be reassuring.

I was now fighting a headache that had positioned itself at the base of my skull, and I knew right away that it wasn't going to be responding to aspirin, willow bark tea, or any other remedy I could cook up. But at least I was starting to be able to see straight even if it was taking a lot of concentration.

I struggled with my aching tongue and tried again. "Ovfith or t-thell?"

"Office," she replied, finally grasping my words.

"Thry hith tell."

"That's what I'm doing, Row," she returned, waving the phone at me. "Are you sure you're okay?"

"Ah thnno," I mumbled.

"Aye, sorry then. Wrong number," I heard her say, then she spat, "Dammit, I can't remember his cell number."

"Thith, tthedro…" I started. "Tho. Ith fife, thefthn…" After the second try, I realized I was in no condition to extract the number from my scrambled grey matter. Fortunately, I was still possessed of enough lucidity to notice the caller ID box on the wall. I shook my head and pointed to it. "Thayre. Theck thh calther Idee."

She was getting better at understanding my new language, and she immediately began scrolling through the numbers until she hit what she was searching for. With a quick flourish, she tapped in the seven digits and tucked the handset back beneath her mane of spiraling auburn curls.

She began her impatient shuffle once again, and I watched her as I fumbled with the cap on a bottle of aspirin. I knew it wouldn't help my head, but maybe it would do some good for my tortured tongue.

"Aye, Benjamin," she said suddenly. "It's Felicity. No, this is important. Row just had another seizure... Yes, just like before... Not ten minutes ago... Yes..."

I watched on as she paused, obviously listening to him. Her face grew hard and her lips curled into a frown. After a moment she spoke again. "When?... No... We haven't even had the TV on for two days now... Aye... Yes... He seems to be okay at the moment, I think... Rattled... No... No, not yet... Yes... Okay... Should I call her?... Yes... Okay then, we'll be here."

She hung up the phone without even telling him goodbye. When she turned back to me, there was an even thicker layer of concern overlaying her features.

"Whathh?" I asked, not sure I wanted to know.

"He's on his way," she said. "He wants me to call Constance."

"Ah kinna gotthh thaa," I replied. "Whath-elth?"

She shook her head and looked away for a moment before locking eyes with me once again. "He says the Major Case Squad is already working a scene. They found another body, Row. Just like before. Shallow grave, near the Missouri River, no head."

I looked back at her and closed my eyes as I slowly shook my head. A wave of nausea welled up in my stomach, bringing its thin burn up to my mid-chest.

Even though I had known in my heart that this wasn't backlash, and even though I had known that this was going to happen again, I had still hoped I was mistaken. Right now, I would have given just about anything to be wrong.

If all this weren't enough, I was also directing anger inward at myself. I didn't know if it was because I had tried too hard or not hard enough. Or, if perhaps it were all because I had begun to take comfort in the fact that the dead had stopped speaking to me, and due to that, had ignored a sign I normally would have picked up. Whatever the reason, I knew it must be my fault that I had only now heard the voice from beyond the veil. Only now, finally choosing to listen, after she was already dead and there was no way to save her.

I beat back the desire to vomit and opened my eyes. Felicity was still staring at me, her face stricken with the same pained mask I'd seen her wear four months ago.

"Dammit," I spat.

It was the first clear thing I'd said in the past fifteen minutes.

"Whoa, back up, Kemosabe," Ben told me, waving his hand to indicate that I should calm down. "You're makin' assumptions, so lemme just tell ya' what's goin' on."

"I already know what's going on," I returned.

Fortunately, the combination of salt water, aspirin, and ice had taken the swelling in my tongue down enough to allow me to communicate normally by the time he had arrived. The lingual organ still had a tendency to get in the way of my teeth from time to time, but at least I was intelligible for the moment.

My friend had barely made it through the front door when I started in on him, all but babbling about what had transpired. The anger I had internalized had grown beyond my limits and was now venting back into the world as I outwardly berated myself for obviously missing something. Of course, what I was missing right now was the fact that he needed me to be quiet and let him talk.

"No, you don't," he replied. "There's more goin' on here than ya' know."

"I know another woman is dead, Ben, and it's my fault!" I appealed.

"No, it ain't. Now do you wanna shut up and listen to me for a sec?" he barked.

I started to form a comeback, then decided against it. Ben had a look on his face that told me he was starting to lose his patience, and I knew that if he did, it wouldn't be pretty. So, instead of a trite objection, I simply said, "Fine. Tell me what's going on."

"Okay," he replied. "First off, we've got a bit of a misunderstanding here. What was found today was skeletal remains. Not a fresh body."

"So this happened some time ago then?" Felicity interjected.

He nodded. "Yeah. Matter of fact, the medical examiner is estimating somethin' like two years, but that's not a definite until they run some tests. However, the skull is missing, and there are saw marks on the vertebrae. So, add it all up, and it's a good bet we're dealin' with the same asshole."

I still wasn't finished being angry with myself, so I spat, "Well, then I should have picked up on it two years ago then."

"Give yourself a fuckin' break, Row," Ben offered with an impatient shake of his head. "Who knows? You were prob'ly all *Twilight Zoned* 'bout somethin' else when this one happened."

"That's no excuse," I grumbled.

"Yeah, well deal with it," he replied. "I need ya' focused right now."

"What for? I snipped. "She's already dead."

"Listen, drop the attitude before I kick your sorry ass around the block," Ben said. "I already told ya' you don't have the whole story yet, and your not givin' me a chance to tell it."

I wanted to fire off a retort, however, he was dead on the mark; so I kept my mouth shut and sat stewing in my own self-loathing.

"Gods," Felicity said. "Don't tell me there's more."

"Sorry, but there is," he continued. "And, the way I got it figured the remains they found ain't why you're goin' la-la all of a sudden, Row."

"What then?" my wife asked.

He sighed and then gave his neck a quick rub. "This has been all over the news today, so I'm surprised you haven't heard about it. At around seven forty-five this morning, one of the security cameras on the parking lot at Northwoods Mall caught somethin'. A young woman was abducted while she was on her way in to work. Went down pretty much the same way we witnessed it happen with Larson, white man. And, from what I saw on the tape, it was probably the same shithead doin' it."

"Oh Gods," Felicity moaned.

I knew exactly how she felt. I was just too busy trying to ward off a sudden wave of nausea to be able to speak.

"Yeah, well," he continued. "The security guard who monitors the cameras was just comin' outta the crapper, so he only caught the tail end of it happenin'. He called nine-one-one, but by then it was too late."

"Great," I muttered sarcastically.

"Yeah," he returned and then paused for a moment. "The tape wasn't the best. Got a make and model on the car but no tags. Doesn't matter though 'cause it's prob'ly hot like last time. Nothin' real clear on the bad guy either. Just average height, dark hair, and stocky build; again, pretty much the same as with Larson."

"So, who was the woman?" I asked. "Do you know?"

I'm not sure what made me ask the question. It may have simply been the desire to hang an identity on the abductee. Perhaps it was a need to make her into something more than a nondescript entity, especially since I was apparently feeling her pain. Still, judging from the tickle in my brain, there seemed to be something more driving me when I spoke the words.

He gave a nod. "Yeah. One of the other security officers managed to ID her as the manager of the Kathy's Closet store there in the mall. Her car was…"

"Wait a minute," Felicity cut him off, a deeply concerned look washing over her face. "Kimberly was abducted?"

Ben gave her a slightly confused glance while reaching into his pocket and pulling out his small notebook. He quickly flipped it open and glanced down. "Yeah. Kimberly Forest. You know 'er?"

"Aye, Kathy's Closet is one of my big accounts," Felicity replied. "I shoot all of their catalogs, and Kimberly has done some of the fill-in modeling. We got to know one another the past couple of years."

"Fuck me," Ben muttered. "I'm sorry, Felicity. I didn't know she was a friend."

"No," I announced on the heels of his comment.

"No, what?" he asked.

"No," I repeated, looking over at Felicity. "I know exactly what you're thinking, and you aren't going to do this."

"Aye, and you're going to stop me?" she asserted.

"If I have to."

"Try it," she challenged, her voice taking on a hard edge.

"Jeezus H. Christ, will you two stop it!" Ben interrupted sharply. "I ain't got time for this crap. Look, we got a missin' woman and no real leads except for your freaky-ass hocus-pocus shit."

We both looked back at him as he paused. There was a mix of pain and anger in his face, and even though his voice was harsh, it was underscored with a faint pleading tone. He was looking for help, not conflict.

He cleared his throat then lowered his voice and continued. "Now, if this sick fuck follows the same time frame as he did with Larson, Kimberly Forest is gonna be dead inside of twenty-four hours. That doesn't leave us much time."

"You're right, sorry," I apologized.

"Listen," he said. "I wasn't even gonna call you. I know what you two have been through, and I hate the thought of draggin' ya' through it again. But… But, since you called me…" He allowed his voice to trail off, staring back at me with an apologetic look.

"It's okay," I told him. "We all knew I'd end up in the middle again. It was only a matter of time."

"So, do ya' think you can help?" he asked. "Or is this just gonna put ya' through hell for nothin'?"

"I don't know. This seizure was just like before, Ben," I explained. "I don't remember anything."

"Shit. Not what I wanted to hear."

"I know, but I'm not going to give up yet."

"Row, after what happened a few months ago…" he began.

"The hell is going to happen anyway, Ben," I told him. "Look at what just occurred. Why Felicity called you. There's nothing I can do to stop it, so I might as well try to use it to our advantage."

"How you gonna do that if you don't remember anything?"

"We'll just have to try it again," I offered.

"Try what? You mean the hypnosis?" Felicity asked. "Like last time."

"Maybe," I replied. "Or maybe something more direct."

"Rowan, what are you thinking?" Felicity asked. I could tell she was already preparing her own veto for my yet to be announced course of action.

"Psychometry" was my single word response.

"What the hell's that?" Ben asked with a harrumph. "Math for Witches?"

"Psychic impressions from physical contact," Felicity explained.

He nodded. "So you mean like when you go all la-la from touching a victim's body?"

"Exactly," I replied. "But it's also like when I 'see' things at crime scenes just by being there."

"Okay, so that's what ya' call it." He raised an eyebrow and gave his head a quick, sideways cant. "So you wanna go to the site of the abduction?"

"For starters."

"And if that doesn't work?"

"Let's cross that bridge if we get to it."

CHAPTER 30:

"So whaddaya need to do, Row?" Ben asked as he nosed his van into a parking space, levered it into park, and then turned in his seat to look back at me.

Felicity was sitting directly behind him in the back seat, and I was on the passenger side near the door. Agent Mandalay was in the front with him, riding shotgun. She had returned Felicity's call just as we were getting ready to leave, so we had waited for her arrival before making the trek to the Northwoods Shopping Mall.

"Where did the abduction actually take place?" I asked.

"Let me see," he murmured, then began counting to himself as he lazily gestured out the window with his finger. "...Four... Five.... Six... That one. That should be it, right over there." He pointed through the passenger side of the windshield. "See that light standard? That should be the one she was next to when she was grabbed."

I followed the line of his arm to the large concrete footing and towering light post some thirty to forty yards away in the opposite row.

"You don't know for sure?" Felicity asked.

"I'm not actually workin' this case," he reminded her, then pointed out the passenger side window. "I know for sure it was on this lot. There's the Kathy's Closet store, over there, and that is the row Ackman said she was parked in. Right now I'm just goin' by what I was told and the tape they showed me when I was asked to ID the shithead."

"If you aren't on this case then what are you really supposed to be working on, Storm?" Mandalay asked.

"Last week's gang shooting," he replied absently. "And about five more unresolved gang shootings. What about you?"

He leaned forward and sent his eyes searching.

"Miscellaneous bureaucratic paperwork," Mandalay admitted, then continued her own line of questions. "So where does your lieutenant think you are right now?"

"Day off," he explained, his attention still directed elsewhere. "Had ta' go see my lawyer. But, they called me in to look at the tape so I asked a few questions, and now I'm here."

"Unofficially, of course?" she half-asked, half-stated.

"Well sure."

My friend stopped scanning and cocked his head, then pointed again, this time to a different post. "If I'm rememberin' the angle right, that should be the security camera over there. It's an older system, so like I said, the picture wasn't the best."

I panned my gaze across the muted tableau. It looked dull and flat. Even the more brightly colored vehicles congesting the parking lot seemed subdued under a dusky grey film. Sunset was less than two hours away, and with the overcast skies already blocking a good percentage of the light, perceived nightfall would be coming even sooner than usual.

I don't suppose it made any difference one way or the other, whether it was day or night, with maybe one exception: We knew Brittany Larson's body had been buried under the cover of darkness, and you can bet the others were as well. Since Kimberly Forest had been in the hands of the very same sadistic bastard for a little better than eight hours, I had to wonder if she was even still alive and if we should be staking out wooded areas near the Missouri River instead.

The harsh reality was that we really had no way to know how much time she had left. With the exception of what had happened with Brittany Larson, we had no actual evidence of the lag time between abduction and disposal of the body. It was all guesswork on our part.

In the back of my head— only because I didn't have the stomach to voice it— I was hoping that the amount of torture Kimberly Forest could endure before her body finally shut down would be a deciding factor in her fate. As much as it sickened me to consider what was probably being done to her, even as we sat here looking across the parking lot from which she'd been taken, I was hoping she had a strong constitution.

And, more importantly, an even stronger will to live.

"Okay, I need to go over there," I finally said, reaching for the door handle. "Just wait here."

"I'm going with you, then," Felicity said.

"That's really not necessary," I objected.

"Aye, don't start with me, Rowan," she returned.

"Don't either one of ya' start," Ben announced. "We're all goin'."

I didn't argue. It wouldn't have done me any good. Instead, I just continued lifting the lever and unlatched the side door, then slid it back on groaning tracks. Once we had all climbed out of the vehicle, and Ben had locked it up, we began wandering in the direction of the light standard.

"Just so I know, are ya' gonna go all Tee-Zone on us, Row?" Ben asked.

"If we're lucky, yes," I replied.

"Fuckin' lovely," he muttered. "What about you, Felicity?"

"We'll see," she said, the tone of her voice offering no assurances whatsoever.

"So whadda we do if ya' both start floppin' around like a coupl'a fish?"

"If we say anything then take notes," I offered.

"Yeah, great," he replied. "What else?"

"Try not to let us hit the asphalt too hard," Felicity returned.

"Yeah," Ben muttered. "Coupl'a fuckin' comedians aren't ya'."

We stopped talking but all smiled and nodded as we met a young couple heading in the opposite direction. They gave friendly nods in return, continuing along their way as they passed us by. A moment later, to our backs, we heard the clipped 'whoop' feedback of a car's locks being unlatched by a remote key fob.

"Jeez," Ben exclaimed as he looked around the busy parking lot. "It's five freakin' P.M. on a Thursday. What's with the crowd?"

"You don't shop much, do you Storm?" Constance asked.

"Why would I?"

"Oh, I don't know," she replied in a sardonic tone. "Clothes.

Shoes. Underwear without holes in them."

"My undershorts are just fine, thank you," he returned.

Somewhere in the distance, I heard the driving thrum of heavy metal music blaring, or at least that is what I thought I was hearing. I glanced around, looking for the source, all the while having a sudden attack of déjà vu.

"Boxers or briefs?"

"None of your business."

"So, I guess your wife did all the shopping for you?" Mandalay contended.

"Pretty much, yeah," he agreed.

"Yeah, well you've been on your own for a while now, and you said your divorce is going to be final in a couple of months."

"Yeah, so?"

"Yeah, so you'd better learn to shop. Either that, or get yourself a girlfriend who wants to do it for you."

"You volunteerin'?"

"Yeah, right," Mandalay replied, actually laughing as she made the sarcastic remark. "In your dreams, Storm."

"Maybe," he casually snipped. "But I'm pretty sure the woman in my dreams is taller than you."

I glanced over at Felicity and saw that she seemed to be handling the conversation well, considering. There was a time when I personally would have been almost livid about the insensitivity of their exchange in light of what was happening. To be honest, it still bothered me a bit, but to a large extent I had grown used to this sort of thing. I knew that the jokes and nonchalant conversations were just a defense mechanism that most anyone in their profession quickly developed. It was either that or the job would eat them alive, and I certainly couldn't fault them their sanity. I suppose in a way I was a bit jealous that I couldn't turn off the horror and hide behind the mundane as easily as they.

"I'm betting she has a set of thirty-eight double-D's too," Mandalay baited my friend with a note of disdain.

"Nope."

"Excuse me," she chided. "Forty-fours then."

"Nope. Not really all about the boobs," he replied with a shake of his head. "I'm more of a leg guy."

Constance grew quiet for a split second. The pause would have been almost imperceptible except that time seemed to be expanding all around me. When she spoke again, I could have sworn I picked up a hint of surprise in her voice, but then, the growing roar in my ears was making everything sound odd.

"Really?" she said, voice phasing through a shallow echo.

"Yeah, really." Ben's languid words flowed in behind hers.

I was just getting ready to call out to everyone that something was wrong when the thrum ended with an unceremonious crash, and the world around me phased into solid reality. I caught myself as I stumbled

"Row," Felicity asked, taking hold of my arm. "Are you okay?"

Ben and Constance stopped dead in their tracks and turned the moment she asked the question.

"Yeah," I replied, nodding. "Must be some residual dizziness or something from the seizure earlier."

"You sure, white man?" Ben asked.

"I think so."

"That's not what I asked you," he replied.

"Okay, yeah, I'm fine."

"Rowan..." Felicity began.

"Really," I told her. "Whatever it was, it's over now. I'm fine."

Ben looked me over as if he were sizing up a suspect, then muttered, "Okay."

My friend turned and started walking again. We all fell in step with him.

"So, I take it Albright is still running the investigation?" Constance asked, changing the subject.

"Yeah," Ben nodded. "You don't think she'd miss a chance to score points with the mayor, do ya'?"

"It figures," Constance replied. "But I was hoping maybe she'd handed it off to an underling by now."

"She did," he said. "While it was cold, but she took it back before the poor bastard had a chance to finish his first cup of coffee this mornin'. Now she's right back in the fuckin' limelight."

"Okay, so what if we hit on something here? How are you going to get it past her?"

"I was hopin' you'd tell me," he said.

"Me?" she asked. "I'm not assigned to this anymore."

"Yeah, well you're one up on me. I'm flat out banned from it."

"So what does that have to do with me?"

"Your badge is fancier than mine."

"Dammit, Storm," she admonished. "You know if you keep butting heads with Albright, you're not going to have a badge at all."

"Yeah, I know. That's why you're here."

"Well I don't know that there's going to be anything I can do," Constance offered.

Ben turned to face her and said, "Well, it's either that or we find the fucker and I just cap 'im myself."

"I'm not listening," she replied without missing a beat.

"Yeah, well," he said. "This has gotta stop."

"I agree with you," she told him. "But turning into a vigilante is not the way to do it."

"Sometimes I wonder," my friend mumbled.

We came to a halt as a group, standing to one side of the traffic lane behind a row of cars. Twenty feet to our left was the concrete base of the light standard.

"I'm still not listening," Mandalay told him again.

"Good."

Ben looked across the parking lot, twisting in place as he scanned the area, an intense frown digging a deep furrow into his face.

"Some rent-a-cop is probably watchin' us on the camera right now," he finally said while looking over his shoulder.

"More than likely," I heard Constance reply, her voice starting off at a normal tone then suddenly stretching into a stream of Doppler distorted syllables.

It was happening again. A sharp pain sliced through my ribcage before I could even open my mouth, and I felt my chest instantly tighten. Still, I tried to speak but found that I had no breath.

A choppy drone that vaguely resembled Ben's voice fell into the humming void behind Mandalay's. "Guess you better do whatever you're gonna do before security shows up. Okay, Row?"

The parking lot was starting to spin away, whirlpooling from my sight in a psychedelic swirl, like multiple colors of paint pouring down a drain. My heart was hammering in my chest, and suddenly nothing made sense to me any longer.

I didn't know where I was.

I didn't know who I was.

I didn't know what I was.

But, for some strange reason, I did know I was in trouble when I heard a vaguely familiar voice. It was loud; distinctly feminine, possessed of an Irish lilt, and unmistakably anguished as it echoed in my ears, "Ground! Dammit Rowan! GROUND!"

CHAPTER 31:

Something is biting into my side.
Pinching flesh.
Tearing skin.
Freezing.
Burning.
I'm not sure which.
All I know is that it hurts.
I cannot breathe.
I want to breathe, but nothing seems to work.
I think my brain is saying to breathe, but maybe it isn't.
My chest is tight, and I can feel myself shaking.
Or at least I think I can.
I just don't know anymore.
Nothing is making sense.
Nothing is certain except the pain.
Nothing at all.
Nothing…

I returned to the here and now in a single, horrendously painful, fraction of a second. The only warning that I was about to cross the veil yet again was the sudden feeling that I was being jerked backward, as if by a hand hooked into my collar. After that, it was all over. An entirely new kind of pain tore through my body as I gasped for air. I felt for all the world as if I had just slammed face first into a concrete wall.

My eyes snapped open and an unfocused mottle of contrasty greys took over my field of vision. My ears were filled with the sound of a car alarm blaring, and a ball of agony throbbed inside my head, keeping perfect time with it.

My sight faded quickly in, returning to something near normal, even if it was still no more than a black and white rendition of reality.

My head was hanging forward, and I noticed that I was leaning against something. At first glance, it looked like the back of a black sedan, but of course, color wasn't something I could readily identify at the moment. Still, unless I missed my guess, the car was ground zero for the obnoxious honking and warbling.

"Rowan!" Ben's voice wove its way through the raucous noise, filtering into my ears. "Rowan! Breathe!"

I looked up and blinked. It took a moment for me to realize I was staring into his face as he was steadying me. I fought to focus on him as light suddenly bloomed around me in a bright flash, chasing the shadows in a chaotic game of tag. Color began seeping into my world as if being slowly dialed in with a control knob.

I felt a hot breath suddenly explode from my lungs, and I coughed as I sucked in the cool, autumn air.

"Storm!" Agent Mandalay's voice threaded through the racket with more than a hint of urgency.

Out of reflex, I sent my eyes searching for the source of the cry. Ben maintained his grip on me but twisted around to look as well. As I rolled my head to the side and glanced past him, I caught a glimpse of Constance struggling to hold my wife's violently shaking form.

The memory of her first experience with such ethereal channeling was still fresh enough for me to get a hollow feeling in the pit of my stomach just at the sight of her seizing. Lucidity rushed in where once there was confusion, and the words "Dammit Rowan! Ground!" reverberated inside my skull. I instantly realized what had happened. Felicity, in an attempt to ground me, had taken my place on the other side.

I didn't know how far I had gone, but I did remember that the hold on me had been one of the strongest I had ever felt. Tearing me away from it meant she had been left with no choice but to release her own ground in this plane; and, because of that, now it was she who was grappling with the horrors on the opposite side of the dark threshold.

I couldn't remember exactly what had been happening to me

before I was wrenched away, but I knew it wasn't good. What I did recall was that at the very least, I was in horrific pain, and at the very worst, I was a scant few steps from taking up permanent residence in the domain of the dead.

In either case, I simply wasn't going to allow it to continue happening to her.

I heard myself screaming 'NO' as I broke away from Ben and threw myself toward my now posturing wife. I managed to sidestep my friend before he even realized what was happening, and a few steps later, I was hooking my arms around Felicity, taking the brunt of her weight from Agent Mandalay as she continued to shudder and jerk. I began settling downward as I cradled her, kneeling onto the asphalt parking lot.

"Dammit, Cerridwen, you bitch!" I said aloud, almost yelling; rancor was thick in my voice. "Leave her alone! Do you hear me?! Leave… Her… Alone!"

Never, and I do mean never, in my history as a practicing Witch, have I ever had a spell work in full the very moment it was cast. Especially when it was cast as a demand and not a request. And, even more importantly, when I didn't even realize I was casting one to begin with.

Of course, strong emotion is the most powerful energy one can muster, and the words themselves are nothing more than a vehicle for that energy. Sometimes, I suppose being painfully direct about what you want is the only way to communicate with The Ancients.

Still, as much as I would like to take credit for what transpired the moment I recited the angry demand, I am fairly certain my position with the Gods is not one of absolute favor. If it was, I'm sure I wouldn't be doomed to this particular destiny. Therefore, any demand I would make would be certain to fall on deaf ears, and I fully suspect this end result was mere coincidence.

However, you couldn't convince Ben Storm that it was anything short of magick.

Even as the last syllable was leaving my mouth, Felicity ceased her violent shaking and fell limp in my arms. She gasped once, her chest rose as she drew in a deep measure of fresh air, and then she began to breathe normally. She was unconscious, but that was probably for the best at the moment.

Strobe-like amber luminescence was now flickering across us in the pre-dusk dimness of the overcast afternoon. I felt a presence beside me and looked up to see Ben's incredulous face staring back down at us as he leaned forward.

"Damn, white man, I dunno who the hell Kara is," he said, just loud enough for me to hear. "But I think she's afraid of ya'."

"Special Agent Mandalay, Federal Bureau of Investigation." Off to my left, I heard Constance almost yelling the formality, and I looked over to see her face to face with a mall security guard. She had her badge case open and displayed in her hand, and the older man was giving it a close look.

I hadn't even noticed the truck pull up, but considering that the alarm on the car had yet to reset itself, I shouldn't have been surprised that I hadn't heard it. The security vehicle was equipped with a flashing light bar, so that explained the yellowish disco lighting that had suddenly appeared.

I looked around and noticed a small crowd of shoppers had gathered several yards away. There was plenty of the standard pointing, gawking, and leaning close to one another in order to compare notes as they speculated about the scene. I didn't have to hear them to know what they were saying. I'd stared back into crowds like this before. It was all just a part of the human dynamic, and where there was public strife there would be onlookers with off-base opinions.

"Seizure," Constance was shouting to the security guard. "Fell against the car…"

The last two words of her sentence belted out across the parking lot, piercing the suddenly low-level ambient noise as the car alarm reset with a clipped burp of the horn and settled into silence.

"Fell against the car and set off the alarm," she continued in a normal tone.

"She an epileptic?" he asked.

"Something like that," Constance replied.

"Would you like for me to call paramedics?" the guard asked, glancing past her at Felicity's motionless form, still cradled in my arms.

"Rowan?" Constance called over to me.

I shook my head. "No. We just need to get her home so she can rest."

"You sure, sir? She doesn't look so good," the officer leaned around Constance and spoke directly to me, a slight southern drawl to his voice.

I nodded quickly. "She'll be fine. We've been through this before."

Neither of us was lying. We just weren't telling the whole story. Fortunately, the security officer didn't seem to notice.

"If you say so," he replied. "But I'm gonna have to get your names and such for my report."

"Detective Ben Storm, SLPD," my friend offered, flashing his badge. "Listen, do you mind if I go pull my van up so she has a place to lay down."

The guard looked over the top of his glasses at the gold shield, then glanced around, inspecting the thruway. He finally nodded as he pointed to a freshly vacated slot a few cars away, "Yeah, go ahead. Just pull in over there so you're not blockin' traffic."

Ben took off at a jog, and the security officer turned his attention back to us. "A Fed and a city cop," he grunted and then looked over at me. "You got a badge too?"

"No sir," I replied. "We're both civilians."

"Good," he grunted again. "I was starting to wonder if y'all were out here about the abduction this morning. Wait here while I go get my clipboard."

Constance looked over at me as he turned his back to us and she asked, "Are you sure she's okay?"

"She should be. It's over now," I replied and then paused before adding. "For the moment, anyway."

"So, what happened?" she asked, her voice just above a whisper. "You started falling, she starting yelling something about the ground, and the next thing I knew she went stiff as a board."

"I slipped over to the other side," I replied quietly, not bothering to correct her perception regarding what Felicity had said. "I'm pretty sure she decided to rescue me, and since Kimberly Forest is her friend, she had an even stronger connection than me. So…" I allowed the rest of my speculation to remain unspoken.

"Damn, Rowan, I don't think I'll ever get used to you two."

"Don't worry," I offered. "I don't think we'll ever get used to us either."

"You said your name was Mandalay, right?" the security officer asked as he stepped back over to us, clipboard in hand. "So, how do you spell that?"

"Here," Constance said, reaching into her pocket and withdrawing a business card for him.

He took it from her and slipped it beneath the holder on the metal clipboard, then began writing, pausing now and again to glance at the cardboard rectangle.

"Rowan…" Felicity's faint voice wafted into my ears.

I looked down and saw her eyes fluttering open, so I shifted my arm and brushed the hair back from her face.

"Hey," I replied simply.

I had settled from my original kneeling position and was now fully seated on the asphalt. It wasn't the most comfortable of places to sit, and on top of that, it was cool enough to be leaching the warmth from my body right through the seat of my pants. I imagined Felicity was faring no better, since she was laid out across my lap with her lower half splayed onto the hard surface as well. I was glad Ben had gone to get the van.

"He's hurting her, Rowan," she whispered.

"I know, honey," I said, gently rocking. "I know."

"No," she spoke again, her voice still a weak thread. Her eyelids were falling back down as she continued. "I remember..."

"You remember?" I asked.

"Yes..." she whispered again, her voice barely audible as it trailed off, and she drifted back into a hazy sleep.

"Hey, Kemosabe," Ben's voice came at me from above. "Let me give ya' a hand."

I looked up and saw my friend in front of me. He knelt down and slipped a large hand behind Felicity's shoulders, then began gently lifting her up into a sitting position as I supported her neck. I pushed back and twisted my legs around, dragging myself up to my knees again and slipping my arms around her torso. Once Ben had helped me get her up off the ground, and I lifted her into my arms, he ran ahead to open the side door of the van.

I carried her the thirty-odd feet to the vehicle, and my friend was already waiting for us.

"How's she doin'?" he asked as he helped me settle her into the seat.

"She woke up for a second," I told him hurriedly. "And she said that she remembers."

"Remembers what?" he asked as he carefully reclined the seat several inches while I buckled her in.

"Something about what she saw on the other side, but I'm not sure exactly. She drifted back off before she said anything else."

"Shit," he muttered and then looked at me. "Okay, let's get rid of this rent-a-cop and get 'er somewhere comfortable so we can talk."

"I really don't want to leave her alone right now," I said.

He gave me an understanding nod. "Yeah, I know what ya' mean. You stay with 'er, and I'll handle it."

My friend took off at a trot, covering the distance quickly with his long-legged gait. I watched as he repeated the same action Constance had with the business card and continued talking to the officer as he wrote.

The wind was picking up, and the chill in the autumn air was beginning to take on an unpleasant bite. I looked back to check on Felicity and noticed her body was twisting away from the open door, most likely out of reflex, reacting to the drop in temperature. I stepped over and slid it partially shut to shelter her from the breeze.

When I turned back to see what was going on, the security officer was gesturing toward me. Ben was saying something to him, but I couldn't make it out at this distance. The officer started waving me over, and Ben began to jog in my direction.

I took some tentative steps, meeting my friend a few feet away from the van.

"He says he's gotta see your ID," Ben grumbled, shaking his head. "Jeezus, I hate wannabe cops."

"He's just doing his job, Ben," I replied, but I wasn't any more excited about the situation than he.

He jerked his head toward Mandalay and the officer. "Go ahead. I'll stay with Firehair."

"Okay," I returned, starting toward them while reaching for my wallet.

I only made it three steps before Felicity began to scream.

CHAPTER 32:

It no longer mattered whether Felicity's sudden disconnection from the other side of the veil had been the result of magick, luck, or pure coincidence. Whichever it was, it had obviously worn off.

Ben was already yanking back the side door of the van as I was turning in place. For a brief moment, I froze dead in my tracks, as the image that greeted me brought back a flood of fear-tainted memories.

Felicity's back was impossibly arched as she bucked and strained against the shoulder harness. Her hands were clawed around the armrests and her forearms planted firm, pressed along the lengths as if permanently cemented there. She convulsed and fell back into the partially reclined seat, tossing her head to the side while twisting against the unseen bonds. Her normally beautiful face was flushed deep red, and her features were twisted and carved deeply with lines. The fissures joined in a maddening tangle to form a horrid mask of pain. The muscles and tendons of her neck were visibly bulging, tensed to their limits, if not beyond.

For the second time in my life, I felt my blood turn instantly to ice as her tear-filled eyes met mine, and she wailed uncontrollably. The scream was one of pure agony— an unearthly sound I begged the Lord and Lady to never make me hear again. But, they weren't listening. When Felicity regained her breath, the grating banshee cry came again, this time coupled with the barely intelligible words, "Please! No!"

I was somewhere around a half-dozen or so steps away from the van when I turned, but I made it back to the open door in three.

"Whadda we do?" Ben yelled at me, fighting to be heard over my wife's pained cry.

"I have to ground her," I yelled back, reaching in and clamping my hand around her thin wrist. It had worked for her; I could only hope that it would do so for me. Unfortunately, I was all too aware that she was the one who had the bond of familiarity with Kimberly Forest, not I; and, such a connection was something that would be not be easily overcome.

An arc of pain immediately shot up my arm, causing me to tense as it joined with my other near forgotten aches, bringing them each back to the forefront. I shuddered but held tight to my wife's arm.

Her flesh was cool and clammy to the touch. I feared the intensity of the torture was taking a heavy toll. Ethereal or not, as far as her body was concerned, it was the real thing, and it was sending her into shock.

Her scream had faded to a nasal whine, punctuated by small cries at irregular intervals. With each cry came a violent jerk of her body as she fought to retreat from whatever unseen torture was being inflicted.

I looked over at my friend and saw that he was trying to maintain a stolid expression, but his eyes betrayed the fear and concern I knew he was feeling.

"Promise me something," I said to him.

"What?"

"If this works…" I stopped mid-sentence and swallowed hard as a sudden lance of pain ran like fire along the nerves in my arm. I gathered myself and rushed to continue, giving my head a quick jerk toward my wife. "If we end up swapping places, don't let her touch me."

"But…"

"No buts," I said, cutting him off with a hard shake of my head. "Promise me you won't let her die, Ben."

He stood looking at me, the fear now far more obvious in his eyes as my words began to sink in. When he didn't respond, I knew he had a full grasp of what I had just said.

"Promise me!" I demanded again.

He swallowed hard and gave me a quick nod. It was all I needed.

I turned my attention back to Felicity, struggling to form a solid ground as I shunted everything from her I could. I gritted my teeth and blinked back the tears that were welling in my own eyes, not sure if they were solely from the pain, my concern for her, empathic response, or all of the above.

Harsh shadows shifted in and out of my vision as ethereal darkness tried to fall, and I did my best to let it. Bright blooms of light fell in behind the contrasts, blinding me for sharp instants like the burst of a camera flash. I pressed myself forward, ignoring the growing intensity of the pain even as I heard myself begin to groan in the face of it. But, for each step I took toward the veil, I was shoved back the same, returning in part to cold reality.

My senses were expanding, as I stood on the edge of two worlds, unable to take a firm foothold in either. My frustration was growing, but more than that, my gut fears were beginning to overwhelm me.

By now, Agent Mandalay and the security officer were almost immediately at my back. I could feel them close, and I heard their voices as they argued.

"What's he doing to her?" the officer was saying.

"Stay back," Constance told him. "He knows what he's doing."

"That doesn't look like an epileptic seizure to me," he pressed.

"It's going to be fine," she replied, but I could hear the trepidation in her voice, and I'm sure he could too. "Just stay back."

"I'm calling the paramedics," he returned. "There's something wrong here."

Felicity continued to whimper as she writhed in the seat. Again, her jade green eyes locked with mine while she shook through a shallow tremor. Her mouth opened as if she was trying to say something, but no words escaped, only the high-pitched gurgle of absolute physical torment.

She tried again, attempting to force a word through her trembling lips, "B-b-b-bbbbb…"

I wasn't sure if the person trying to speak to me was Felicity or the channeled Kimberly. I shook my head and tried to shush her as I continued struggling to ground.

She kept shaking, her motor reflexes no longer cooperating as she persisted in her attempt to speak. In the end, she managed only to make a convoluted noise that sounded vaguely like 'hmmm'.

Then, without warning, her head snapped back as she once again arched against the safety harness, her guttural howl piercing the crisp afternoon air.

"THIS ISN"T WORKING!" I screamed in bitter frustration.

I was beginning to lose the battle, and I knew it. A feeling of panic was spreading rampantly through my chest, fighting to assume control and reduce me to a blithering idiot. I loosened my grip on her wrist and twisted my palm toward her pulse point then quickly clasped it tight once more, seeking a better connection. I could feel my feet getting hot, and I was beginning to dance from one foot to the other as the burn intensified.

I looked around, searching for nothing in particular but everything in general, all but begging for an answer to fall from the ether. My own fear was taking hold, and I knew I couldn't afford to let that happen. I had to think, but emotion was building an impenetrable storm front in my brain, and all rational thought seemed to be trapped behind the squall line.

As I continued shuffling in place, I panned my anxious gaze around. My feet felt as though they were on fire now, and I wasn't sure how much longer I could stand it. When I happened to look down, I saw the thick, rubber soles of my shoes.

Whether by actual realization or simple reflex, I kicked my right toe against the heel of my left shoe and began yanking my foot upward. I struggled against the tight laces of the ankle high tennis shoe until I managed to pull my foot free and then quickly plant it against the asphalt.

Coolness seeped upward through my sock but was immediately overtaken by the heat. I closed my eyes and concentrated as best I could on forming the connection between earth ground and myself. In my mind's eye, I could see a shaft of light, extending from me and leading down into the center of the earth. Or, at least I thought I could. I wasn't sure anymore because nothing was changing.

I opened my eyes and saw that Felicity was still writhing against invisible bonds. When I looked closer, I saw that patches of blood were starting to spread where her shirt was pulled taut across her chest.

In my clouded mind, I began wondering if I had done the unthinkable when I had made my cursing demand of Cerridwen. I was no longer thinking clearly, and the idea took vicious hold. I snapped my head to the side and squeezed my eyes shut, unable to look into Felicity's tortured face any longer, distraught by the belief that I had brought this upon her.

Emotion joined with pain, and I felt hot tears running down my cheeks. I blinked hard, and my blurred vision fell upon the back of the passenger seat inside the van as I allowed my head to hang. My body was beginning to shudder with the first wave of sobs, and I was losing control. I stared forward, continuing to blink as tears formed and overflowed onto my cheeks.

It was then that the ether finally gave up the answer.

In front of me, peeking from the top of the pocket on the back of the seat was a small silver dome, fitted with a ring. Extending from it, wrapped by bailing wire, were faded yellow-tan bristles expanding horizontally into a triangular fan.

It was a whiskbroom.

Felicity's attempt to stutter a word ran through my brain and joined with an arcane thought that had somehow managed to escape the muddy swirl that was supposed to be my rational mind. At its root, magick was a simple thing, and sometimes the simpler the better.

I reached out and plucked the broom from the pocket, flipped it over so that the bristles now pointed upward, and plunged it back into place.

"Goddammit, GO AWAY!" I screamed.

And, for me, the day turned into night.

Light became darkness.

Then consciousness became a distant memory.

The diesel engine of the life support vehicle was thrumming away at idle, sending a gentle vibration through the floorboards. The back door was hanging open, and looking outward through it, I could see the emergency lights flickering across the cars on the parking lot. To my right, in the cab, the two-way radio would occasionally burp with static and a stream of tinny voices, too faint for me to understand, before falling back into momentary silence.

True to his word, the security officer had called paramedics, and they had arrived within moments of my losing consciousness. When I awoke, I had a throbbing headache but other than that, seemed none the worse for wear. Felicity, too, was showing little or no signs of distress from what she had just been through, other than the fact that she was growing more anxious with every moment that passed. I suspected, however, that we were both running on residual adrenalin and the effects would eventually catch up to us. Fortunately, it was nothing a good, long sleep wouldn't fix.

"I told you we don't have time for this!" Felicity spat, her voice an audible indicator of her agitation. "We have to go!"

"I just want to check you over," the paramedic calmly told her.

"What for? How many times do I have to repeat myself?" she demanded. "I'm telling you that I'm just fine, then."

"Felicity, just let them check you out," I said, looking over in her direction, only to have my head gently turned back forward by a latex-gloved hand and a penlight unceremoniously shone into my eye.

"Ma'am," the paramedic tending my wife said, trying to calm the auburn-haired tempest in front of him. "Listen to your husband. We just want to make sure you're okay."

"I've already told you I'm okay," she snipped, her faint Celtic lilt taking on the hard edge of a full-blown brogue. "That should be good enough for the both of you."

"Ma'am," he appealed. "You have blood all over your shirt."

From the corner of my eye, I could see that he was motioning toward her chest with his gloved finger.

"I told you those are just stains."

He shook his head. "They don't look like stains, ma'am."

"Aye, and your point?"

He gave a shallow laugh as if he couldn't believe he was having the conversation. "Ma'am, that's fresh blood. Usually where there's blood, there's an injury."

My wife raised an eyebrow and cocked her head at the young man.

"You're wanting to see my chest?" she asked with a perturbed bob of her head. "Is that it?"

Before the paramedic could reply, Felicity crossed her arms and ripped her shirt upward. In a single motion, she pulled it quickly over her head with a snap, revealing that she was braless underneath.

Tugging one arm loose from the sleeve, she reached up and pulled her long hair back over her shoulder with the free hand, then thrust her chest outward.

"There," she said, glaring back at the startled paramedic. "Are these what you wanted to see, then?"

I was free to look over at them now that most eyes were focused on my half-naked wife, instead of tending to my impromptu check-up. Just as she had been telling him, there was nothing to see— in the way of injuries that is. The young man in front of her, for all his training and clinical experience, was so taken aback by her unabashed display that his face was running through every imaginable shade of uneasy.

Ben was standing outside the door with the county police officer who had responded along with the life support vehicle. My friend nervously cleared his throat and turned away.

The uniformed cop continued to watch, expression never changing. He nodded then quipped, "Nice tattoo."

"Thank you," Felicity replied out of reflex.

I sighed. "Put your shirt back on, Felicity."

"But you said for me to let them check me over," she replied sarcastically.

"Felicity…"

"Aye, all right, it is a bit cold, then," she retorted, then directed herself to the paramedic. "But I suppose you can see that for yourself now, can't you?"

"Go ahead and put your shirt back on, ma'am," he stuttered.

She let go of her hair and slipped her arm back into the sleeve, then lifted her arms in a reverse of her earlier display.

"Honey, leave the poor guy alone," I appealed. "He just wanted to make sure you're okay."

"And so I am," she spat. "And, why are you on his side? I'm your wife."

She finished pulling the shirt back over her head and then tugged it into place.

"Hey," I said. "I seem to recall being in the same position a few months back, and you weren't anywhere near as forgiving."

"That was different," she told me as she untucked her spiraling curls from her collar and brushed them back.

"How?" I asked, a note of incredulity in my voice.

"Because it was you and not me."

"I see," I replied with a nod. "Well, at least I was a little more cooperative."

"That's not my recollection."

"I didn't do a strip-tease."

"I was just being cooperative, then."

"How? By embarrassing everyone?"

"No," she returned. "I'm simply trying to get us out of here."

"Ben and Constance are waiting," I told her. "It won't take long."

"I don't care," she snapped. "Kimberly hasn't the time to wait."

With everything that had happened, I had completely forgotten that she had told me she remembered something from her excursion into the ethereal plane. I looked over at her and met her gaze.

"Do you still…" I started.

"Aye," she shot back, her voice deadly serious as she nodded vigorously. "And, right now, we're in the wrong damned place to do anything about it."

CHAPTER 33:

"What the hell was all that with the strip tease?" Ben asked as he backed the van out of the parking space.

"I still can't believe you did that," Constance added, but you could almost hear the giggle in her voice.

My wife replied in a matter-of-fact tone, as if the answer was obvious, "Getting us out of there."

"By takin' your damn clothes off?"

"Aye, it worked didn't it?"

"It embarrassed the kid," Ben replied.

"And he couldn't wait to get rid of me then, could he?"

"Yeah, maybe. I guess."

"Then it worked."

"You know they're gonna be tellin' stories about ya' don't ya'?"

"Aye, let them talk. They'll be giving someone else a rest then," Felicity remarked, then turned her attention to more pressing matters. With her next sentence, the deadpan delivery was gone and impatience suddenly underlined her words. "Have you found the map yet, Constance?"

"Still looking," Mandalay called back to her.

The first thing Felicity had asked for when we climbed back into the van was a Missouri highway map. She gave no explanation other than that she needed the map, and she needed it right now.

Agent Mandalay continued rummaging about in the glove box, extracting all manner of Chinese take-out menus, receipts, and even Ben's backup weapon. All the while, he was making haste for the nearest exit, looking to put some distance between Northwoods Mall and us.

I, for one, had absolutely no objection to that maneuver.

Eventually Constance extracted a wrinkled wad of semi-folded paper, gave it a quick glance, and then started to set it aside with the rest of the detritus.

"That's it," Ben announced before she dove in again.

"This?" she asked, holding it up. "For real?"

"Yeah, for real."

"How can you tell?"

"Just give it to her, will'ya'?"

"Well, I guess it's a good thing anyway," she muttered in reply as she handed the sample of origami-gone-bad back to Felicity. "Because I think something's alive in there."

My wife took the wad of paper and began looking for a free corner so she could unravel the map from itself. She reached up to click on the courtesy light but was met with nothing more than darkness and the popping noise of the switch.

"Bulb's shot," Ben offered.

"Obviously," she returned, her irritation plainly audible. "And I can't very well read this in the dark now can I?"

"Hey, you wanna chill?" he barked. "I'm workin' on it."

"Benjamin Storm!" she snapped in return. "Don't you understand? We simply don't have time to waste!"

"What did you just call me?" my friend asked, giving a quick glance back over his shoulder.

"That's what she does when she gets serious," I offered. "Uses your full name, just like her mother."

Ben shifted his eyes back forward and immediately slammed on the brakes, narrowly avoiding a rear end collision with a sports car. I couldn't help but noticed that Constance instantly reached for the shoulder harness, pulled it across her chest, and stabbed the metal finger into the catch at her side.

"Yeah, well stop it, Felicity," Ben called over his shoulder. "That just didn't even sound right comin' outta you."

"Hey, just be glad she didn't use your middle name," I explained. "She does that when you're in trouble."

"Dammit, will you two quit joking," Felicity demanded. "I'm serious."

"I know you are," I replied.

"Look, Felicity," Ben replied as he turned the van toward the main exit. "I know we don't have time. Trust me, I said it myself earlier, but a lotta shit has happened in the past two hours, and I'm still tryin' ta' get my bearings here."

"Kimberly is being tortured!" my wife appealed, her voice rising slightly. "Don't you get it?!"

"Goddamit, Felicity, yes! Yes, I get it. Isn't that what I just said?" Ben growled. "Jeezus H. Christ, you're worse than Rowan when it comes ta' this shit!"

"Felicity," Constance voiced, stepping into the role of mediator. "While neither Ben nor I can fully understand what you are going through, we do have a grasp of what's happening. We're on your side, but you are going to have to calm down."

My wife huffed out a frustrated sigh and sat back hard in her seat. "Aye. I know. But the son-of-a-bitch is killing my friend."

"Not if we can help it," Mandalay replied with a note of compassion. "I promise."

Ben angled the van toward the merge lane and shot forward into traffic, cutting off a small sedan in the process. Horns blared, but he continued wedging his vehicle into the flow of traffic anyway.

"Yeah, fuck you too," he muttered as he shot an angry glance out his side window.

The light ahead of us winked yellow and my friend punched the accelerator, making the left hand turn onto Northwoods Drive just as it switched to red.

"Over there," Felicity sat forward and exclaimed. "On your right. The gas station!"

"What?"

"The gas station," she repeated urgently. "Pull in and get under the light so I can read the map!"

Ben jerked the van over into the next lane and then quickly hooked it into the lot. He pulled off to the side, out of the way, and rolled beneath a bright streetlamp. Felicity was already out of her seat and climbing over me to get to the door before we had come to a stop.

I convinced her to wait a second while I levered it open and slid it back. She pushed past me the moment the opening was wide enough for her to fit through then continued spreading out the tattered map, which was literally falling apart in her hands.

Ben switched off the engine and yanked the keys from the ignition to kill the warning buzzer, then tossed them into the console.

"I'm going to go use the restroom and grab a coffee," Constance announced, pushing her door open. "Anyone want anything?"

"Make that two," Ben told her, reaching for his wallet.

"I've got it," she replied. "Rowan? Felicity?"

"I'll come with you," I told her unbuckling and climbing out of the seat. I squeezed past Felicity, who'd yet to answer, and put a hand on her shoulder. "Honey, anything?"

"What, oh, yes, a water," she chirped absently, intent on studying the faded and torn rectangles of paper. Then, almost as an afterthought she added, "And maybe a new map too."

I gave her a nod that I suspect she missed entirely, and then skirted around the nose of the van, following after Constance. Since we were parked along the far outer edge of the station's lot, near the street, the store itself was a good thirty-five yards or better from us. Mandalay waited a moment for me to catch up, and then we fell in step with one another, strolling across the near deserted expanse of asphalt.

"Is Felicity going to be okay?" she asked.

I looked over and saw sincere concern in her face. "I think so," I replied. "This case is really the first time she's been through this sort of thing from my perspective. I think we're both having a little trouble adjusting to the change of roles."

She nodded. "Makes sense. Okay, so clear something else up for me. What was that whole thing with the whiskbroom? That some kind of WitchCraft thing or just a sudden attack of Obsessive-Compulsive Disorder"

"It really is a spell actually," I replied with a slight chuckle. "It's meant to get rid of unwanted guests. Basically you just take your household broom and turn it bristles up. If the magick works, the unwanted guest will leave."

"Don't they get a little suspicious anyway when you scream 'goddammit go away'?" she asked with a grin.

I laughed. "Yeah, well, I have to admit that was my own addition. But I guess there are some instances where that could work without the broom."

Traffic was dying down out on the main road. I glanced at my watch and based on the time figured that it must be a dinnertime lull. Besides us, there were only two other vehicles on the gas station lot. One parked on the side of the building, and another with its lights on and sitting in a space near the front door.

An undulating breeze whipped along the lot, weaving its chill around the light standards and gas pumps as we walked. It swished through as if on a whim, caressing us with its gelid fingers, and then left as quickly as it had arrived. I found myself suddenly wishing that I had brought a jacket.

Still, the prickly cold that was running along my spine remained, even after the calm had returned. I shuddered at the feeling, my mind beginning to entertain the idea that it had not been an effect of the wind at all. As the hair on the back of my neck began to rise, I realized that my mind was apparently on to something, because it dawned on me that the sudden chill had come directly from Constance.

"You have got to be kidding me..." Mandalay said in a soft voice, more than a little incredulity wrapped around the sentence.

"About what?" I asked, confused.

She didn't answer, but she was beginning to slow her pace.

We were a little better than halfway to the door when I shot a curious glance in her direction. At that same instant, her arm came out in front of me, extended like a barrier. Her steadily slowing footsteps now came to a complete halt. Her expression was deadly serious, and her eyes were locked straight ahead.

"Go back to the van, Rowan," she told me in an even tone.

"What's wrong?" I asked, confused by her sudden change of demeanor.

"Go back to the van," she repeated.

She moved fluidly, and her arm was no longer in front of me. Following the motion with my eyes, I noticed she was slipping her hand beneath the folds of her blazer. As it disappeared under the fabric, I heard a quiet snap. She continued speaking in a no-nonsense voice. "Tell Storm to get you two out of here and call for backup."

Her hand was now filled with a forty-caliber *Sig Sauer*, and she was starting once again to advance on the storefront. I looked past her, through the large windows and at the brightly lit interior. It took a moment, but my eyes finally fell on the correct target, and I saw for the first time that which had not escaped her finely honed attention.

"Go! Now!" she hissed over her shoulder as she started to jog, angling toward a blind spot near the front door.

CHAPTER 34:

I was approaching the van at just under a dead run. Even though I couldn't see them, I could still hear Ben and Felicity bickering on the opposite side of the vehicle.

"Felicity, that's not much to go on," I heard Ben say as I reached the front corner and started to hook around.

"It's better than nothing at all, Ben," my wife snapped in return, her voice a mix of frustration and urgency, both vying for dominance over her tone.

I whipped around the front of the van and almost slammed directly into her. Her back was to me, and she was holding a scrap of paper up into the light of the streetlamp above, animatedly tracing a route with her painted nail as she spoke, "I'm telling you if we…"

"Whoa!" Ben barked, cutting Felicity off mid-sentence as he grabbed her arm and yanked her to the side. His other arm came up in a flash and brought me to an unceremonious halt as my chest thudded against his outstretched palm. "What the fuck, white man?!"

The impact had knocked the wind from me, and I sputtered as I tried to catch my breath. "Constance… Backup…"

"Do what?" he asked.

I sucked in another breath and pointed back toward the station. "The store's being robbed," I blurted. "Constance needs backup."

"Oh Gods!" Felicity exclaimed, shuffling to look past me. "Is she okay?"

"Jeezus!" my friend rumbled at the same instant, stepping forward and looking over the front slope of the van as he reached for his sidearm. "Is she inside? Forget that, I see 'er. You got your cell phone?"

"Aye," Felicity spoke up.

"Stay here outta sight and call nine-one-one," he instructed. "Tell 'em what's goin' down, and let 'em know they have two off-duty cops on the scene."

"What are you going to do?" I queried.

"If we're lucky, nothin'," he replied as he drew his sidearm and began scanning the area.

"What do you mean nothing?" Felicity asked, shaking her head.

"Just make the call," he returned quickly, starting toward the near side of the station, then stopped and muttered, "Awww, goddammit, not now…"

I peered past him and saw a car rolling to a stop in one of the spaces at the front of the store. I could see Constance crouched in a blind spot near the entrance, any view of her from the inside being blocked by a pair of back-to-back payphone pedestals. She was trying to motion to the person in the newly arrived vehicle to stay put but to no avail. Either the woman had yet to see her or simply wasn't paying attention, because she got out of the car and started toward the front door without a care.

Behind me, Felicity was already speaking to the 9-1-1 operator, quickly reciting the name and location of the gas station. Ben started moving, taking off at a fast clip into the shadows before cutting suddenly to the left and aiming for the side of the station.

Constance was gesticulating with as much fervor as she could while still remaining hidden from the interior of the store. The woman had actually gone several steps along the sidewalk before looking up, and she now noticed the gun-wielding federal agent. Of course, having no idea who Mandalay was, she froze in place and began to scream.

Ben was just hitting the corner of the building and fell to a crouch at the side of an ice machine, arms cocked with his *Beretta* firmly gripped and aimed in front of him.

As the woman's first fear-filled cry broke the quiet atmosphere, the old metaphor about 'hell breaking loose' was instantly invoked. Her fading wail was punctuated by a muffled pop, and that was followed rapidly by two more. The woman snapped her head to the side, looking in what was apparently the direction of the noise, then stared into the store through the windows. She immediately broke into a second scream. A fleeting second later the metal-framed door flew open, and a young man bolted through. I couldn't see his expression at this distance, but I could tell simply by the way he moved that he was panicked. In one hand, he had a paper bag and was clutching it in a death grip; in the other, I could see a dark object that I assumed to be a pistol.

He was heading directly for the car that had been parked in front of the store when we first arrived. He had almost made it to the door of the vehicle when he hesitated and looked back toward the screaming woman.

As the young man stood there, I caught my breath and felt my pulse beginning to pound in my temples. I couldn't have looked away if I had wanted to, so I watched, unblinking, the fate which was about to be revealed.

Constance came immediately up from her crouch, weapon stiff-armed before her as she moved forward, closing the gap. She couldn't have been any more than twenty feet from the young man, and she kept her pistol aimed at his center mass. Ben was stepping out from the shadows, moving in behind her, but still had quite a bit of distance between him and the situation.

"Stop!" Constance announced in a loud voice. "Federal agent!"

Startled, the young man jumped and spun toward her, throwing his arm up at the same instant, pointing it wildly in her direction. There was a loud pop and burst of fire from the pistol in his hand, and at the same instant, the front window of the store sparkled with an instant spider web crack.

Before the report of his gun had even reached its peak, the first of three bright flashes erupted from the muzzle of Constance's *Sig Sauer.* The rest followed in unison with a resounding trio of sharp cracks. The young man jerked backward with each impact and then fell, disappearing from my view behind the vehicle.

The bystander was backed against the windows, crouched down with her hands over her ears as she shook her head violently. She had fallen silent, apparently too frightened to scream any longer. Constance advanced forward carefully but quickly; her sidearm was still in hand, aimed with great purpose at the ground in front of her. Ben was a few feet behind and to her right, circling in with his own pistol stiffly pointed at the downed felon. I watched as they both moved in, Constance all but disappearing from sight on the opposite side of the vehicle while Ben's head and shoulders remained visible over the line of the roof.

Behind me, Felicity had stopped talking, but I could hear the thin strain of a tinny voice wafting into the air. I looked back to see her staring past me at the now quiet scene. The cell phone was resting against her shoulder and she slowly pushed it back up beneath her hair.

In a calm monotone, she said, "Aye, I'm still here." Then added simply, "Yes... She shot him."

A moment later, in the near distance, a siren suddenly began to wail, and I looked over to see flashing red lights barreling down the thoroughfare, heading in our direction. Glancing back to my friends, I saw that they had moved back up onto the sidewalk. Ben holstered his sidearm and then reached into his pocket. A second later, he carefully slipped a cord over his head then unclipped his badge from his belt and attached it to the bottom of the loop.

Constance was now leaning against the payphone pedestal, her head hanging and her doubled fist pressed against her lips. I watched as Ben looked over at her, shot a glance up to the shattered window and then brought his eyes back to her. He reached up and began rubbing the back of his neck. I could see his lips move as he said something to Constance. A moment later, I saw her head slowly bob in the affirmative.

And then, I started breathing again.

Bright white flashes punctuated the flickering red lights that fell across the front of the convenience store. The area was cordoned off with yellow plastic tape, and evidence technicians were snapping photos and setting out numbered tent cards next to shell casings on the ground.

A handful of local officers were now on the scene, from those in uniform, to plainclothes detectives. At present, one of the uniformed officers was directing a white SUV toward a parking place. As it passed us, I could see that it was emblazoned with the words SAINT LOUIS COUNTY CORONER.

Constance was locked in conversation with one of the detectives, occasionally motioning toward the pay phones or the suspect's vehicle. Felicity and I had been told to wait with the van. Initially, one of the officers had asked us some cursory questions and then said that we would eventually need to give statements since we had been witnesses. That had been a little better than thirty minutes ago, and lag time was not sitting well with Felicity.

The longer we were forced to wait, the more agitated my wife became. So, I wasn't at all surprised that when Ben finally broke away and walked over to check on us, she greeted him with a hand cocked on her hip and an attitude to match the pose.

"We have to go," Felicity announced, her words leaving no room for negotiation.

"We ain't goin' anywhere for a while," Ben said, giving his head a quick shake.

"How long is 'awhile'?" she asked.

He shrugged. "I dunno. As long as it takes."

She stared back at him with a hard look and then shook her head, speaking tersely. "We simply don't have time to wait around, Ben."

He looked back at her, then drew in a deep breath and pinched the bridge of his nose between his fingers as he closed his eyes. You could almost see him mentally counting to five. He slowly let out the breath and then opened his eyes.

"Let's try this again," he announced. "I came over here to tell you two that ya' should prob'ly get comfortable. 'Cause we ain't goin' anywhere for a while."

My wife continued glaring at him defiantly. He raised his eyebrows and glared back at her.

"You were here," he finally said, motioning to the scene behind him. "You saw what happened, right? Or am I just imaginin' that?"

"Aye, we saw it. And your point?"

"Felicity, there are two dead bodies over there," he explained, hooking his thumb over his shoulder again. "The clerk and the kid who shot her."

"I understand that," she replied, "But what about Kimberly?"

"What do you want me to do?" he asked as he splayed out his hands, palms up in resignation. "I can't help that we stumbled into a fuckin' armed robbery. Believe me, I wish we hadn't just as much as you do."

"Can't we just give our statements and get out of here?" I asked, trying to help defuse the tension between them.

"I wish it was that easy," he replied. "But one of those dead bodies over there has three government-issue, forty-caliber *Hydra-Shoks* in it, courtesy of Mandalay. There's no way to just give a statement and walk away from that."

"What about us?" Felicity pressed. "You didn't shoot anyone and neither did we."

"I was backing her up, and you two were witnesses," he replied.

"Can't you just get them to hurry up?" She was almost physically shaking from her frustration.

"I'm a city cop, Felicity. This is the county, and I'm not with the MCS so it ain't my jurisdiction. Besides, you don't rush this kinda shit. Not when people are dead. You know that."

"So, how is Constance anyway?" I interjected, trying to change the subject.

"Holdin' up," he replied, pursing his lips and casting a glance back her way. "It's never easy… Especially when it's a kid."

"How old was he?"

"Got no ID yet, but he looks like he can't be more than fourteen."

"Too young," I muttered.

"Tell me about it," he replied and then reached up to his neck.

"Ben," Felicity appealed again, her voice softer but no less demanding. "We have to go. Kimberly can't hold out much longer."

"Felicity…" His voiced trailed off for a moment, obviously tired. "You don't even know for sure where she is."

"I showed you on the map," she replied.

"You showed me the Chain of Rocks Bridge to the other side of the river," he returned.

"But it has to be somewhere close to there."

"Yeah, but where?" he asked. "Twenty-five mile arc? Fifty-mile arc? Huh? What are we gonna do, go across the bridge, start yellin' 'er name and hope she answers?"

"Dammit, Benjamin!" she snipped. "There's a way to find her, I know it, but we have to go!"

"What way? How?"

She shot me a furtive glance. "You wouldn't understand. Just… We need to go!"

"Try me."

"There's no time for explaining!" she insisted. "We have to go!"

"Okay! Fine! Whaddaya want me ta' do?"

"Get us out of here."

"Okay, how?"

"Tell them about Kimberly."

"Tell 'em what?"

"That she's out of time!" she spat. "That she's going to die if we don't do something!"

"So, lemme get this straight. You want me to go to the lead detective and say, 'hey, the little redheaded Witch over there says we gotta go now, 'cause she saw a kidnap victim in her crystal ball' is that it?" he asserted.

"I thought you believed me," she snarled.

"I do, Felicity," he shot back. "I've always fuckin' believed you two."

"Then just trust me!"

"I told you, I do, but right now what I believe doesn't mean shit to these cops!"

"How do you know if you don't try?!" my wife demanded.

"You know better than that. You think tellin' 'em some *Twilight Zone* crap is gonna fly? Gimme a break."

She glared back at him for a moment, then stepped around him and started across the lot. All she said was, "Well if you won't do it, then I will."

CHAPTER 35:

S he didn't get very far.

It took Ben less than two full steps to catch up to her and clamp a large hand around her arm, stopping my petite wife dead in her tracks.

"You don't wanna do that," he told her.

"And why not?" she demanded.

"Because I doubt they're gonna be as understanding as I am, for one," he retorted. "And for two, they're liable to put your ass in a rubber room. Want some more?"

"We'll just have to see what they do, won't we." She offered the question as a rhetorical statement.

My friend shook his head. "No. No we won't."

She tugged hard, trying to pull away. "Let go of me!"

"Dammit, Felicity, don't make me cuff you to the fuckin' van," he barked.

"You wouldn't dare!" my wife returned angrily.

"Watch me," he growled.

"*Fek tù!*"

"Yeah, right back atchya'."

Felicity twisted harder, still trying to pull away. She struggled for a moment, and having no success, she suddenly cocked her leg back then kicked him hard in the shin. Ben winced as he let out a stifled yelp but still maintained his grip on the auburn-haired firestorm. When she tried to repeat the attack, he shuffled quickly out of the way, causing her to miss and almost lose her balance.

He responded to her near fall by pushing her against the front corner of the van and steadying her there. Stepping back, he held my wife at arms length and then simply glared at her without so much as a word.

Felicity started her struggle anew and found herself locked in an even tighter grip. She looked over and called out to me. "Rowan?!"

From the tone of her voice, I knew she was appealing for help, and that was going to be a problem. I had been purposely staying out of the middle of this for the most part. I knew Ben wouldn't hurt her, although I wasn't entirely sure about the reverse. I also knew better than to get in front of Felicity when she was on a mission, and that put me in a quandary, because with everything that had happened, I could plainly see what Ben was up against.

Of course, the fact that they were both too stubborn to admit fault didn't help. In truth, I had seen this coming. As on edge as we had been the past few hours, this altercation was all but a forgone conclusion. And, it came as no surprise that it was between the two of them.

As usual, life was an obstacle course, and unlike the movies, you couldn't always make the hurdles in a single, graceful leap. In fact, you usually fell flat on your face and skinned your knees before moving on. Even worse, some of the bars were set higher than others, and this particular one was starting to look more like a wall.

Now I was caught with my back against that barrier, knowing exactly how my wife was feeling at this very moment but also fully aware of how police investigations worked. I didn't like the situation any more than they did. But, in the end, we had no choice in the matter, and that was an irrefutable fact.

"Honey, Ben's right," I told her. "There's nothing he can do."

"You're taking his side?" she almost pleaded.

"I'm not taking anyone's side," I explained. "I'm just telling you how it is."

"That's fine!" she snapped. "I said I'd do it myself then."

"Okay, but tell me this," I said. "What makes you think they're going to listen to you if they won't listen to him?"

She stared back at me with anger, anxiety, and a host of other emotions dancing in her eyes. I could tell she was on the verge of declaring one of the Gaelic epithets she kept in her arsenal of curses, but I could also see a look of resignation behind her molten gaze. As impetuous as she could be under the right set of circumstances, she was also one who subscribed to logic. Even though it was obvious that she didn't want to admit it, she knew we were both correct.

A long moment passed with nothing said, then she literally shrieked, venting her frustration into the night with an audible burst.

"All right!" she said. "Let me go."

"You gonna calm down?" Ben asked pointedly.

"Yes, damn you, now let me go."

My friend slowly released his grip on her upper arm, a tentative look filling his face. She jerked it away and began rubbing the spot where he had been clamped on. I could tell by the way Ben had positioned himself that he was expecting her to bolt, but to his surprise, she stayed put and simply glared back at him.

"Sorry if I hurt ya'," he apologized.

She answered him in a flat tone. "Aye, you did."

"Yeah, well that fuckin' kick wasn't exactly pleasant either," he offered in reply.

"Be glad I actually like you then," she returned flatly. "With someone else, I would have aimed differently."

Ben shook his head, then said, "Listen, just stay here and calm down. I'm gonna see what I can do, but I'm not makin' any promises."

"Thank you," Felicity said.

"Yeah, well don't thank me yet, I'm prob'ly not gonna get anywhere."

"For trying, Ben," she returned. "Thank you for at least trying."

"What are we going to do, Rowan?" Felicity asked.

She was parked in her seat, and she had reclined it even farther than it had been earlier. The light of the streetlamp above was filtering in through the tinted windows, bringing a dim glow to the interior that made her pale complexion look just that much more ghostly. She had her eyes closed, and she was slowly massaging her temples.

"Wait, I guess," I replied. "It's all we can do."

"I'm having a hard time with that," she said.

"I know, me too," I agreed.

Ben had been gone for almost half an hour now. We had watched the goings on for a while but finally lost sight of him after he followed one of the detectives into the convenience store. Apparently Constance was already in there, because she had disappeared long before he did.

We waited expectantly, milling around in front of the van and watching for any sign of his return. However, when he didn't come back out of the building for several minutes, it became obvious that his earlier assessment had been the correct one. We weren't going anywhere for a while.

We eventually gave up the anxious vigil and climbed into the van to escape the chill of the night air. We were both pushing the limits of exhaustion, and it felt good to have someplace reasonably comfortable to sit. Had it not been for the emotional fuel we were both burning, I suspect we would have fallen asleep where we sat.

I yawned and then asked, "So how's your head doing?"

"Killing me."

"Yeah…" I murmured. "I know the feeling."

"What about you?"

"Dull ache," I answered. "But you seem to be taking the brunt of it."

"Yes I am," she muttered.

We fell quiet for a few moments, and I rested my eyes as I listened to her breathing. Her respirations seemed to cycle, coming shallow for a measure, then deepening, and even holding on occasion. She was obviously fighting with some pain, and she reminded me of myself when I was dealing with the lingering effects of channeling.

She suddenly drew in a deep breath, but instead of simply exhaling she spoke. Her words were offered as a matter-of-fact statement, devoid of emotion. "Kimberly is going to die."

"You don't know that," I told her.

"Aye, I do. I can feel it. She can't take much more."

"She might have a better constitution than you give her credit for," I offered. "You never know."

My wife remained silent with the exception of repeating the series of panting breaths. I continued watching her as she worked through the pain and began to wonder about what she was experiencing. There was a very guarded feeling about her, but I'd paid little attention until now.

"Felicity, you aren't still connected with her are you?" I finally asked, trying to keep the concern out of my voice.

She gave a slight nod of her head. "Yes."

"Exactly how connected are you?"

"Enough to know. To feel."

"So, what are you feeling?" I pressed.

"Pain" was her single word answer.

"You're sure it's not residual?" I mused. "From earlier?"

"No, it's definitely new," she replied, still not opening her eyes, then murmured in a disgusted tone, "He's hurting her again, the *braidean*."

I continued watching her, and for the first time noticed that she would occasionally twitch. "Have you stayed connected the entire time? I mean ever since the seizure earlier?"

"On and off," she said. "More on than off, lately."

"Are you having trouble grounding?"

"No."

"Then why are you..." I let my voice trail off, falling silent for a moment, and then proceeded forward with a new question. "Are you doing this on purpose?"

"Aye."

"Felicity, that's dangerous." This time I couldn't hide the thick rush of anxiety that spread its cold fingers through my chest.

"You should know," she chided.

"This isn't the time for that," I told her.

"She needs me, Row."

I stared at her for a moment, furrowed my brow as what she said sank in, and then half-asked, half-stated in earnest, "Honey, tell me that you're not trying to ground out her pain."

She didn't answer.

"Felicity, talk to me," I insisted

She swallowed hard, then let out an involuntary whimper before sucking in a breath and letting it out slowly. Still, she refused to answer.

"You are, aren't you?" I demanded.

"Aye," she finally said.

"How bad is it?"

She winced, then rolled her head to the side and opened her eyes. They were moist with the tears she was barely holding at bay. "It's not good."

"Then you're going to have to stop it," I urged.

"I don't know if I can anymore."

"Gods, Felicity…" I muttered.

"I know…" she replied softly. She took another deep breath and then shuddered for a moment. "At least it's not as bad as at the mall."

"Maybe I did some decent magick for a change," I offered.

"Aye, maybe so…" she said and then paused to swallow hard once again before adding, "I think maybe it helps being away from where it happened too."

Her words rang like a bell inside my skull, awakening my grey matter from its tired slumber. Muddy thoughts parted, allowing a clear and frightening idea to advance forward. I dwelled on the sudden revelation for several minutes as we sat in near silence, the only sounds being those of Felicity's labored breathing.

I finally interrupted the quiet atmosphere with the calm statement of two simple words, "Stay here."

I turned in my seat and jerked the side door of the van open, then climbed out onto the lot.

"Where are you going?" she asked, her voice cracking with the next wave of pain she was channeling.

"To get you out of here," I replied.

With that, I shut the door then set off for the convenience store.

"Whoa, whoa, whoa," Ben said to me, waving his hand in front of me. "Tell me again, she's doin' what?"

"Channeling Kimberly Forest's pain," I repeated.

I had made it almost three-quarters of the way across the lot before I was stopped. Not that I hadn't fully expected it. In fact, I was surprised I had made it as far as I had. It took some finesse, but I managed to convince the uniformed officer that it was imperative that I speak with Ben, sooner and not later. He called over to another officer, who then went to deliver the message. A moment later, my friend came out the front door and looked over in our direction with an air of annoyance.

We were now standing on the lot where the officer had stopped me, a light wind rising and falling around us.

"So if she's all *Twilight Zone* again, what are you doin' talkin' ta' me?" he asked, concern welling in his eyes as he started to take a step toward the van.

"It's not exactly like that," I said, holding out a hand to stop him.

He halted and looked at me with his head cocked to the side. "Well then, what 'exactly' *is* it like?"

"She's purposely channeling Kimberly on a limited level in order to help her cope with the pain that's being inflicted." I explained.

"So she *is* kinda la-la then?" he asked.

"Somewhat, yes." I nodded.

"And she's doin' it on purpose?"

"Exactly, but that's not the point. She's telling me that Kimberly can't take it much longer, and that means she won't be able to either."

"You're not tryin' ta' say…"

"Yes," I exclaimed. "I'm trying to say she's going to end up killing herself."

"Well fuckin' tell 'er to stop."

"She's beyond listening, Ben."

"Well explain it to 'er," he replied.

"Understanding isn't the problem," I told him. "She's connected and that's that."

"You mean she can't stop?"

I shook my head. "I don't think so. The connection between them is too strong. When she more or less hijacked it earlier, she made it a part of herself. Combine that with the fact that she knows Kimberly... She's just not letting go."

"Felicity?"

"Either of them."

"Well, then, what about some hocus-pocus," he pressed. "Like ya' did earlier."

"I could try, and I will, but I doubt it's going to do any good. I probably just got lucky earlier," I said and then looked away for a moment before adding, "Besides, that won't help Kimberly Forest."

"Well whadda we do?"

"We have to make it stop."

"Okay, how?"

"By finding Kimberly and ending the torture."

He shook his head and reached up to smooth his hair. "Rowan, even if I walk in there and tell 'em to fuck off, we're leavin', we still got no idea where she is."

"That might not be a problem."

"Come again?"

"Felicity showed you something on the map, right?"

"Yeah, the other fuckin' side of the river," he answered in conjunction with an animated nod. "Like I said earlier. Not much help."

"Well..." I started and then looked away, ashamed of what I was about to say.

"Well what? Did she remember somethin' else?"

The thought I was about to voice was the one that had struck me when I was back at the van. The very notion that I had considered it then, made me ill. The fact that I was now about to verbally suggest it, made me want to vomit.

"Right now Felicity is totally connected with her. She's more or less like an ethereal metal detector," I replied. "Only instead of metal, she's tuned in to Kimberly Forest. If I'm right, the closer she gets to her physically, the..." I stopped and swallowed hard, mutely damning myself for the words that were coming out of my mouth.

"What, Row?" Ben urged.

I took a quick breath and blurted the offending sentence, "The closer she gets to her physically, the more intense the pain will become."

CHAPTER 36:

"**L**isten, I don't know how you handle investigating a shooting in the city," the detective said. "But in the county, we make damn sure we dot all the I's and cross all the T's."

We were standing on the periphery of the crime scene, away from the physical investigation, which was still in full swing. The lead detective had come out to talk to us and was now positioned with his arms crossed and a stony look on his face. His proverbial five o'clock shadow had already gone several hours past maturity, and it made his countenance just that much more severe.

His suit was rumpled, and the knot of his tie was pulled down at least three inches. The top button of his shirt was undone, revealing an indelible ring around the inside of the fabric. A stain, coffee from the looks of it, browned a small patch of his shirt around mid chest.

Simply by his appearance, he painted a picture of a long day that was just getting longer with each passing minute. It was obvious that he was beyond tired and in no mood for anything that was going to stand between him and bringing an end to the shift.

Unfortunately, even with the nondescript expression he was forcing onto his features, I got the distinct impression that having something else piled on him, such as our irregular request, had just gone a long way to sour his demeanor even more.

"We do the same thing," Ben replied, annoyance in his voice. "So let's not even go there."

"Fine," the county detective replied. "So we don't have much to discuss, do we?"

"Look," Ben outlined. "Alive and in peril beats dead and growin' cold any day of the week. We both know that."

The detective gave him a curt nod. "Yes it does. I'll give you that in a heartbeat. So what you're saying is that you know where this kidnapped woman is?"

Ben looked over at me then back to the cop. "Not exactly."

"Can you maybe define 'not exactly' for me?"

"We've got a rough idea."

"How rough?"

Ben danced around the question. "A general vicinity."

"Major Case doing a search?"

"Not exactly."

"You're 'not exactly' sure of much are you?"

"It's complicated."

"Simplify it for me."

Ben shook his head. "It ain't that easy."

"Okay," the cop said with a shrug. "Like I said, nothing to discuss."

"We don't know where she is exactly, but we can find her," I interjected.

The detective thrust his hand out and held a finger up in my face. "Sir, I need you to stay out of this."

"He's right," Ben told him.

"Yeah, okay," the detective said with an air of skepticism, then pressed for more. "So if she can be found then why isn't the Major Case Squad handling it?"

Ben huffed out a sigh and reached up to smooth his hair. As his hand slid back and began working at the muscles on the back of his neck, he recited his own version of something I'd said to him many times before. "Look, I told ya' it's a long fuckin' story, and you'd think I was nuts if I tried ta' explain it."

The county cop regarded him with a raised eyebrow and then looked over at me. "Okay sir, now how is it that you're involved?"

At this point, I had no interest in skirting the issue nor making friends for that matter, so I replied, "I'm the long fucking story."

"Yeah? So would you like to tell it?"

"Not particularly."

"Jeezus, I wish Deckert never freakin' retired," Ben mumbled, mentioning the name of a former Saint Louis County homicide detective we had both worked with.

The cop turned quickly to my friend. "What did you say?"

"Nothin'," he returned. "Don't worry about it."

"No," the cop insisted. "Did you know Carl Deckert?"

"Yeah," Ben replied, shrugging it off. "We worked together a few times."

"Wait a minute," the detective mumbled, his forehead creasing with a nagging thought. He shook his index finger in the air and then cocked his gaze back toward my friend. "Ben Storm. Yeah. You worked those occult homicides with Carl a couple of years back, didn't you? The media freaks called you guys 'The Ghoul Squad'."

Ben nodded. "Yeah, that was me," he said, his tone uneasy. The reputation he'd gained from that case had never ceased to haunt him, courtesy of a local television reporter with a penchant for sensationalizing every story she did. It didn't help that she and Ben had been at odds almost from day one. Because of that, the notoriety didn't always work to his advantage— especially with other cops.

"Yeah," the detective said as he returned the nod. "That's been bugging me all evening. I knew I'd heard your name before."

"Well do me a favor," my friend said. "Don't hold it against me."

"Are you kidding?" the cop said. "Deckert couldn't say enough good about you."

"Well, he was a hell of copper himself."

"Yeah. Sure was. Too bad the heart attacked forced him to retire," the county cop mused and then glanced back over at me. "So that would make you the warlock, right?"

"Witch," I corrected him.

"Oh, yeah, right." He nodded. "Carl talked about you too. He thought a lot of you and your wife."

"Did he talk about us enough for you to understand why we have to go?" I asked.

"You know," he replied. "Carl Deckert was one of the best cops I've ever worked with. He had this way of cutting right through bullshit and getting to the truth. He could talk to someone for five minutes and tell you if they were legit or lying through their teeth.

Never seen anything like it."

The detective paused. I didn't know if he was waiting for a response or just sizing me up. I simply looked back at him wordlessly.

"Makes sense now," he finally said, looking over at Ben.

"What's that?" my friend asked.

"Why Major Case isn't hot on this with you," he explained. "What with the 'church lady' running things.'"

"Yeah, 'zactly."

The county cop reached into his pocket, withdrew a business card and handed it to Ben. "You know, I have to apologize. I really hate to inconvenience you Detective Storm, but it's getting late, I've got a witness to interview, and a ton of paperwork to do.

"Do you think you would mind coming in tomorrow to give your statement instead of tonight? And, maybe you could bring Mister Gant and his wife along as well?"

Ben gave him a nod. "Not a prob, just one thing. We're gonna need the Feeb to come with us."

"The shooter?" the cop asked. "Now that's really pushing it. What do you need her for?"

"Because," my friend replied, "if we're right about this, we're gonna be crossin' state lines."

"Are you sure you want to do this?" I asked Felicity.

"Aye," she replied, pulling herself into a sitting position and fumbling for the adjustment lever on the side of the seat.

I was kneeling next to my wife, and I slipped my arm in behind her for support as the seatback popped upward into place. I helped her lean back into the cushion, then reached over and pulled the safety belt across.

"I'll be honest," I continued while fumbling with the buckle on the harness. "I'm not comfortable with it. In fact it scares the hell out of me."

"Join the club."

"I almost didn't even suggest it," I said. "You know, it makes me sick that I'm putting you in danger."

"You aren't."

"Yes I am. I'm asking you to do this," I argued. "But I just don't see any other way."

"Tell me now, Row, do you really think you're the only one who thought of it?" she asked, her voice fractured and weak.

"Are you saying this has been your grand plan all along?"

"Something like that."

"So why didn't you say anything?"

"I did," she said then shuddered with a wave of pain. "Sort of."

"So this is what you meant earlier when you said there was a way to find her?"

"Aye."

"So why didn't you just explain it then?"

She grimaced slightly, then crossed her arms and began to gently rock in the seat. The motion was so shallow that she barely even pressed against the shoulder harness.

She looked over at me and asked in a quiet voice, "Would you have gone along with it?"

"At that point in time, no," I replied.

"But you are now," she stated rather than asked.

I answered anyway. "Like I said, only because I don't see any other way."

"Me either."

"You know," I said. "What you did was reckless."

She allowed herself a small chuckle, and then closed her eyes tight as she winced. "So are you the pot or the kettle?"

"Yeah... I know." I muttered, unable to refute the idiom then added, "You know this isn't right. I'm supposed to be the one dealing with this. Not you."

"She's my friend."

"That still doesn't make it right."

"Aye, but it does," she told me. "It's your turn to rest."

"You call this rest?"

She gave another shallow chuckle. "Aye, what is it I've heard you say? Welcome to *my* life."

"Yeah..." I muttered. "Something like that."

"Are you going to be able to handle this, Row?" she asked me after a brief moment.

"I don't know yet," I admitted.

"You have to," she said, nearly pleading. "I need you to."

The driver-side door opened, creaking and popping on its tired hinges. A rush of wind blew in through the opening, bringing a quick chill to the interior of the van. I looked over my shoulder to see Ben climbing in. A moment later, the passenger door levered open as well, and Agent Mandalay quickly filled the other seat.

"How is she doing?" Constance asked, turning toward us before she'd even closed the door.

I twisted to the side and turned to answer, but Felicity spoke before I could, her strained tone an audible barometer of her condition. "I'm fine."

"Are you sure?" Constance insisted.

"Aye," Felicity answered with a shallow nod. "But I wouldn't mind getting this over with, then. Soon."

"I can understand that."

"What about... What about you, Constance?" my wife inquired, breathing through a stab of pain mid-sentence.

"I'm okay," Mandalay replied. "Not a scratch."

"I'm sorry," Felicity said.

Mandalay cocked her head to the side and looked at her with a befuddled expression. "For what?"

"That you had to shoot him," she replied. "I know it's hurting you. I can feel it."

Constance fell silent but continued to hold my wife's gaze with her own. Her expression told me that she hadn't expected anyone to see past her femme fatale façade.

"You ready to roll back there?" Ben called over his shoulder as he started the van and gunned the engine.

"Just drive," my wife instructed.

"Yeah, I'm workin' on it," he replied, then directed himself to Constance. "Door."

Mandalay continued to sit motionless, distant introspection in her eyes.

"Yo, Mandalay," Ben repeated as he poked her shoulder with his index finger. "Door."

"What?" Agent Mandalay broke from her rearward stare. "Oh, yeah. Okay."

He started the van rolling forward even as Mandalay was pulling the door shut and then hooked it into a tight turn. I was still kneeling next to Felicity, and I braced myself against her armrest as Ben whipped the vehicle around, heading us back out onto the main thoroughfare.

"Row, get in your seat," Felicity told me.

"I'm fine right here."

"No you aren't," she returned. "Ben is driving."

"Jeez..." my friend muttered.

"She knows you," Constance quipped, her voice still somewhat distant.

"Don't you start too," he replied, then over his shoulder he asked, "Two-seventy to Illinois, right?"

"Aye."

"Ya'know, you never did say why."

"Just a feeling."

"Jeez... I gotta be nuts..." he muttered, then asked, "It's a strong feeling, right?"

"Very."

"Good, 'cause my ass is hangin' way out on this one."

"Like it hasn't before?" I asked.

"Not as bad as this," he responded, and I knew he was serious. He paused, then asked, "Okay, so across the bridge and then where?"

"I'll let you know when I know."

"I thought this was a strong feelin'?"

"It is," Felicity replied. "And we'll be counting on some more when we get closer."

"Yeah, great. So, what do I do if ya' start goin' la-la on us?"

She answered without hesitation, "Drive faster."

CHAPTER 37:

"P... p... pleee... pleasssse..." Felicity whimpered pitifully as tears streamed across her cheeks. "H... hel... hellpp meeee..."

"Hold on," I whispered, struggling to keep my voice from cracking with the bitter fear that was constricting my throat. There was dampness on my own face, and I knew that I was silently weeping for myself as well as her.

I was doing my best to keep her grounded, but it was no longer doing any good. Her connection with Kimberly Forest was so deeply ingrained that they had all but become one person. As a matter of fact, I wasn't even sure which one of them I was talking to at any given moment.

"I... I... I can't..." she stuttered, her voice a thin whine as her body tensed.

She groaned, sending out a low, unearthly sound that instantly set about rending my heart with unimaginable fury. Her back arched, and her body began to actually vibrate.

I watched helplessly as she shook. She was twisting violently in the seat as her face contorted into a mask of pure torment. I had to steel myself against everything I was seeing and feeling, otherwise I knew I would spin into an emotional crash. I didn't know if I was doing her any good right now, but I knew for a fact that I would be worse than useless if I lost control; I would be a liability.

I was out of my seat and kneeling next to her once again. This time, however, she was in no condition to object. Her hand was clamped around mine, squeezing my fingers until they had gone almost completely numb. Even as she shuddered through the waves of pain, she never let go.

Neither did I.

As we both suspected would happen, her pain had gradually intensified the closer we came to the Chain of Rocks Bridge. Each mile that ticked away had brought with it a new level of torture that she would fight to endure. And, each time she would seem to bring it under some modicum of control, it would suddenly advance another notch up the scale, forcing her to begin the struggle once again.

As I said, this is almost exactly what we had expected to happen, so it came as no shock. We were as prepared for it as we could be under the circumstances, or so we thought— because, it was what we had not even considered that now blindsided us with the force of a locomotive.

Once we had crossed the river, those gradual increases immediately transformed into hastened attacks, unfolding themselves geometrically. Within minutes, the ethereal torture had vaulted to such a degree that the waves were overlapping one another. She could no longer cope, and she was reduced to a state of constant agony. The frightening speed at which this occurred caught us both unaware and completely without recourse.

And, it only got worse.

Within five minutes of crossing the Mississippi, Felicity had moved even beyond simple agony. And, by the time we started over the short expanse of the Canal Bridge, she was delirious.

"We have to be close," I said as I looked over my shoulder at Ben, the rampant anxiety beginning to consume me. "She can't take much more."

"Can't you do anything to help her?" Constance asked.

"Don't you think I've fucking tried!" I snapped, then immediately caught myself. "Gods... Constance, I'm sorry... It's..."

She cut me off. "I understand, Rowan. Don't worry. What can we do to help?"

"Find this prick and kill him," I blurted.

"We'll be coming up on Route Three in just a minute," Ben announced. "Should I keep going or turn?"

"I don't know," I answered quickly and then twisted back to my wife. "Felicity... Honey... Talk to me..."

Her chin was pressed against her chest, and her eyes squeezed tightly shut. She was literally squealing, as if a high-pitched scream was caught in her throat, escaping only in a thin stream of torturous noise. She snapped her head back suddenly and cried, "NO! PLEASE! Noooooo!"

The sound following the words was an unintelligible, raw scream, and it set a new benchmark for horrifying.

"Felicity!" I called her name, my voice raised sharply in both pitch and volume.

There was enough feeling left in my fingers for me to know that her nails were now biting deeply into them. I watched her through watering eyes as she struggled to move her head against some unseen restraint. The way she was postured, it looked as if something— or someone— was pressing her head back into the seat and twisting it to the side.

Suddenly, the sickly-sweet odor of singed flesh filled the cabin of the van, and as I looked on, a roughly circular, dime-sized burn appeared on her cheek.

"You sonofabitch!" I cried out. "Stop it! STOP IT!"

"What's happening?" I heard Constance ask.

"Turn or straight, Rowan?!" Ben called back to me again.

"I don't know, dammit!" I barked. "Just go straight... no, turn... Straight... Gods! I don't know!"

A second burn began to eat into my wife's ivory skin, and out of reflex I reached for her cheek with my free hand. My anger was seething and I had become blind to everything. Control was no longer a conscious option for me. Overwhelmed with the intensity of my emotions, I was no longer concentrating on the ground I had been attempting to maintain.

My fingers brushed Felicity's cheek, and there was the thin sound of sizzling flesh once again. I yelped in surprise as a blistering divot appeared on the back of my hand.

Constance's voice sounded again as she exclaimed, "Oh my God..."

"What the fuck is goin' on back there?!" Ben asked, confused urgency in his tone. "Mandalay, what's happenin'?!"

"Rowan!" Constance called out.

Her voice hit my ears as a pounding echo. My body was beginning to tense in a mirror image of my wife's as I inadvertently plugged myself in to her ethereal connection with Kimberly Forest. I forced myself to move against the constricting tendons, feeling them burn with the resistance.

"Heee'sss looosssiinggg itttt, Sstoorrrmmmmmmm!" Mandalay's voice stretched through time, a languid stream of sound.

Ben's words rumbled through the van, following hers in a repeat performance of the elastic speech. "Sssstaaayy wiiittthhh usssss, Rooowwwwaaannn!"

I struggled to keep my eyes focused on Felicity as I sought a new ground. I jerkily pulled my hand away from her cheek and saw a new burn forming. I reached for her again, but it didn't matter. I was no longer simply brushing through the ethereal sphere; I was joining with it. Hot pain lanced my own cheek as I became yet another surrogate victim.

"Roooowwwwaaaannnnn!" Mandalay's voice flowed around me.

I tried to turn toward her as agonizing pains began helping themselves to every inch of my body.

A low thrum was starting in my ears, driving and rhythmic. As it grew louder, percussive beats fell in with the heavy tune, slamming mercilessly against my eardrums.

When my eyes finally fell upon Mandalay's face, I could see that it was painted with fear. She was moving in slow motion, her mouth making shapes I was unable to decipher. I knew she was trying to say something, but I could hear only the angry music.

I started turning back toward Felicity and saw darkness beyond the windshield. In a flash, I caught a glimpse of dull green and reflective white, as the exit sign for Route 3 was struck full by the headlights. Then, as quickly as it appeared, it fell from sight.

I continued to twist until I once again faced my wife and saw a grimace of pain still warping her features. The pounding, heavy metal thrum drove through its crescendo, reaching a deafening climax.

Felicity's head was tilted back and her mouth stretched open wide. I could tell by the cramping muscles in my face that mine was doing the same.

I think we were both screaming, but I couldn't be sure, because a moment later, my consciousness escaped, leaving me to a world of peaceful darkness.

"Row! C'mon, white man, wake up!" A man's thick voice filled my ears.

I was drifting in a dreamlike stupor, somewhere between partially conscious and just plain dead. At least, that is what I assumed. All I knew is that I was no longer in pain.

"She's breathing." I heard a woman's no less frantic words nearby. "Strong pulse, but she's unconscious."

The sound of an approaching car filled in behind her voice, growing louder with each second. This was odd to me, but I endeavored to ignore it. I was comfortable, and I wanted to stay that way.

After a moment, the speeding vehicle seemed to be right behind me, and then just as suddenly, its sound began to fade in the opposite direction. A burst of cool wind whipped around my ankles, reaching cold tendrils up my pants legs.

"Felicity?" the woman's voice was calling behind me. "Felicity, can you hear me?"

"C'mon, white man!" The male voice hit me again and was immediately followed by a palm slapping hard against the side of my face.

As soft as I'm sure it actually was, the blow was magnified by my disconnected state. I jolted into a semi-awake funk, snapping at least partially back into the land of the conscious. When I opened my eyes, I saw Ben's concerned face staring back at me. He was hunched over in the darkness, arms outstretched to steady me. I looked around and found that I was sitting on the floorboards in the open door of the van with my legs hanging out.

"Rowan, talk to me," my friend said.

I was confused. I didn't remember stopping nor could I understand why I was sitting here in the door. And, if Ben was standing in front of me, then who was driving? Things had made more sense when my eyes were closed, so I decided that's what I should do.

"No way," Ben said as he shook me. "Wake up, Row. Talk to me."

I opened my eyes again and blinked, then tried to concentrate as my brain wandered through the murky fog that was overwhelming it. I started catching bits and pieces of mental impressions as they flashed to the forefront of my mind. Before long, they became fleeting images and feelings— darkness, fingernails biting into my hand, Constance trying to say something to me that I could not hear, a burn appearing on my wife's pristine cheek...

"Felicity!" I immediately yelped, looking frantically about.

Lucidity struck like a mallet to the back of my head, and I tried to leap up from where I was sitting. My brain was starting to work, but my motor reflexes were still a few steps behind, so I stumbled as I tried to stand.

"Whoa, Kemosabe!" Ben steadied me before I could fall onto the asphalt shoulder.

I twisted away from him, turning toward the van. Seeing my wife still belted in her seat, I climbed in through the door. Hunching down on my knees, I scrambled across the floorboards, almost knocking Constance over in the process.

"She's not coming to," Mandalay said to me as I pushed my way in next to her.

I reached out to Felicity and brushed a tangle of auburn curls from the side of her face. My still somewhat jangled brain was hoping that everything it was remembering had been unreal. Nothing more than a frightening product of an unchecked imagination left alone to play with the contents of a tortured subconscious, namely mine.

Unfortunately, it knew full well that the sadistic nightmare had been all too real. When my eyes fell on my wife's uncovered face, I saw that the circular burns were still there, horrific blemishes standing out against her pale skin. I noticed my own cheek tingling and began to remember even more. I looked down to see a charred divot in the back of my hand and suddenly felt very ill. If these stigmata were appearing on Felicity and me, I didn't even want to imagine what was actually happening to Kimberly Forest.

My wife rolled her head to the side, whimpering quietly as if struggling with yet another nightmare inside. She murmured something unintelligible and then turned her face away from me.

"Felicity?" I cooed softly, taking her hand in mine as I felt my eyes beginning to water and burn.

There was a tiny spark of a connection, something tenuous but definitely there. I held her hand and focused on it, letting it reach for me as I reached for it.

After a few moments, she turned back to me, still whimpering, and then slowly opened her eyes.

"Felicity? Honey. Are you okay?"

She stared back at me with pain and confusion wrinkling her features. Her eyes searched my face, and I got the definite feeling that she didn't recognize me. As she looked at me, tears began welling and overflowing onto her cheeks. She locked her gaze with mine, and in a frightened, pleading voice said, "Come back... Please. Help me... Come back..."

CHAPTER 38:

"**N**orth or south?" Ben queried.

"If you were going to torture someone, you'd want some seclusion, right?" Constance asked in return.

She was hunched forward, using the dim light from the glove box to illuminate an Illinois highway map. Fortunately, this one was in somewhat better condition than its Missouri counterpart, though not by much.

"Depends on who and why," Ben returned flatly.

"Seriously."

"I was."

My friend had already turned the van around at the first emergency vehicle median crossing he had come upon. We were now headed back the way we came and rapidly approaching the Route 3 exit. Since Felicity, or Kimberly through her, had begged us to 'come back', it stood to reason that we had missed the mark. As there was nothing between there and crossing back into Missouri, the state route seemed to all of us the most logical place to go.

"Well, Route Three south takes you straight into Granite City," Mandalay continued, ignoring his snide reply. "North takes you up to Wood River and Alton. However, there's a several mile stretch of farmland before you hit the first town, which is Hartford."

"Yeah," Ben replied. "That would definitely give the asshole some breathin' room."

"Do you really think a farmer would be doing this?" I asked.

"Who says it's a farmer?" he answered with his own question. "Could be an asshole who wanted to get away from the city. Besides, don't you remember Ray and Faye Copeland?"

"Sounds vaguely familiar," I replied. I wasn't in a mood to search my grey matter for obscure memories, and to be honest, I really didn't care. But, he was intent on explaining anyway.

"They were an old couple in Chillicothe, Missouri," he replied.

"Livestock farmers. Back in the early nineties they were convicted of murderin' five transients and buryin' 'em on their property."

"They were a bizarre serial case," Constance added, spouting off details that she had tucked away. "They kept a log of the transient workers they hired, and next to each of the murdered men's names was an X. Also, Faye made a quilt out of the victims clothing. While they were only convicted of the five homicides, there's a pervasive belief that they were responsible for more."

I simply replied, "Oh," and left it at that.

"How'd you remember all that?" Ben asked. "You had to be in like what, junior high?"

"I was in my first year of college, Storm," she answered with an annoyed tone. "Besides, I studied the case when I did a psych paper on Serials."

"Jeez, what don't you remember?"

"Usually, my car keys."

"Oh, so you *are* human."

"Uh-huh, but don't tell my SAIC or you'll kill my rep."

"So, white man, how's Firehair doin'?" Ben switched subjects.

"Okay, for the moment," I answered. "Not exactly good, but she seems to be holding her own."

Felicity had continued drifting in and out of lucidity, occasionally whimpering my name, then in the same instant looking at me as though I were a complete stranger. All of this was punctuated by fits of quiet sobbing and choking pleas for help. At the moment, her head was tilted back and her eyes were closed. She would moan quietly every now and then. From all outward appearances, she looked to be working through a fevered dream.

The one fortunate circumstance was that the excruciating attacks seemed to have stopped. When they would return was anybody's guess, but I was mutely begging for never.

"What about you?" he queried.

"I'm fine," I told him, but my voice was clearly betraying my distraught mood every time I opened my mouth.

"Yeah," he returned, unconvinced. "It's gonna be okay, Row."

"Uh-huh," I grunted.

He didn't press the point. We simply traveled in silence for a moment or two before Mandalay spoke up.

"Okay, Storm, do you have a plan?" she asked, shifting the subject yet again.

"You mean other than shooting this bastard?"

"Exactly."

"Not yet," he admitted. "You?"

"Well, we're probably going to need backup at some point, assuming we find what we're looking for," she offered.

"Yeah," he replied. "I know. I'm gonna hafta call Albright too."

"We have to find her," I insisted, throwing myself back into the conversation. "He's going to kill her and Felicity in the process!"

"I know, Rowan," Mandalay told me. "And we will find her. Right now we're just speculating about procedures."

"Okay, here we go," Ben announced.

I turned to look out the windshield and saw that we were veering off Highway 270 onto the exit ramp for Route 3 north. I immediately turned back to check on Felicity but found no change.

"What if, and this is a big 'what if'," Constance began, "we aren't able to locate Kimberly Forest? Is there anything at all you can do to protect Felicity?"

"I don't know," I replied, twisting back around to look at her. "I've never seen this happen before."

"What about you?" Ben asked. "You go freakin' *Twilight Zone* all the time."

"Not like this," I replied.

"So why do ya think she's not... you know..."

"...In pain right now?"

"Yeah."

"My guess is that the asshole got off, and he's taking a break."

A hush fell over us all on the heels of my comment. What I had said wasn't something new. Even the FBI agent at Quantico who'd worked up the profile of this killer had commented that the torture was probably the acting out of a psychosexual fantasy. I guess hearing it said aloud, as opposed to reading it in a report, simply made the sick concept a little too personal.

"Let's hope it's a long one," he said.

"Yeah," I agreed, my voice cold and flat.

The sullen quiet crept in again. I looked out into the darkness as we merged quickly onto Route 3 and started north. The morbid atmosphere in the van continued to bloom, eventually becoming more than my friend could bear.

"Friggin' dark out tonight," he finally said. "Must be the clouds."

"Wouldn't matter if it was clear," I offered. "It's a crone's moon."

"Do what?"

"Crone's moon. The darkness prior to the new moon," I explained.

"That something special?" he asked.

"It's a time of introspection," I replied with a humorless half-chuckle, given the circumstances. Then I paused before adding, "It can also be a time of some very serious dark magick."

"I thought Witches didn't do black magick."

"I didn't say black. I said dark."

"There's a difference?"

"A big one."

"They're arguing..." a thin and very weak voice came from behind me.

I turned slowly back to Felicity and saw that she had lolled her head to the side and her eyes were open, staring directly at me. Her cheeks were still damp with tears, and she looked exhausted. Her features were drawn and severe, telling me that she was still dealing with a healthy amount of pain.

"Felicity?" I asked.

She gave her head a barely perceptible shake. "No... Felicity is coming for me."

The voice was my wife's, but the inflections were someone else's entirely. Gone was her Celtic lilt, something that even at its faintest was still perceptible. The pattern of her speech was now fully Midwestern American, and even more specifically, south county Saint Louis.

"Kimberly?" I asked out of reflex.

"Yes…" she whimpered, the single word coming out as a dying whine.

I pressed forth. "Who's arguing, Kimberly?"

"They are…"

"Who are they?"

"The ones who hurt me," she whimpered.

I felt like I was talking to a small child who couldn't reason through a general question. With the sense of urgency I was feeling, I was having trouble maintaining my patience and in the end I couldn't keep the insistent tone out of my voice. I shook my head at her and snapped, "Who, Kimberly? Who is he arguing with?"

Felicity's face contorted with a look of fear, and she simply whined. I immediately damned myself for losing control.

"Ssshhh," I shushed her softly as I reached out and stroked her hand. "Ssshhh… Kimberly, I'm sorry. It's just that this is important."

"Is Kimberly Forest actually talking to you?" Constance asked, incredulity underscoring the whispered question.

"I think so," I quietly replied over my shoulder. "Or her subconscious mind at least."

"Jeezus…" Ben muttered, then asked in a louder voice. "Is she sayin' that there's more than one of 'em?"

"Who is that?" Kimberly asked, a new thread of fear weaving through her words.

"It's okay, Kimberly," I replied. "He's a police officer. He's coming with me to help you."

"Help me!" she pleaded, calling out with a fleeting burst of energy. "Please, help me!"

"She could hear me?" Ben asked.

"Apparently," I told him.

"Pleeeeaaaasssseee…" she whimpered.

"That's what we want to do," I soothed as I turned back to her.

"Can you ask her where she is?" Constance pressed, still keeping her voice low as if she was afraid she would interfere.

"Please help me…" Felicity's voice whined again before I could answer.

"We are," I told her. "We're coming with Felicity to get you."

"Please…"

"But, listen to me carefully," I continued, struggling to keep calm. "We need your help. We're trying to find you right now, but we don't know where you are. Can you tell us?"

"I don't know…"

"Can you tell me what you see?"

"It's dark," she replied.

"Okay," I said. "Are you in a house?"

"I think so," she sobbed. "They come down stairs to hurt me."

"Did you see the house from the outside?"

"No…"

"Nothing?" I pressed.

"No…"

"So much for that," I barely heard Constance whisper to Ben.

"Kimberly," I said. "You have to help us find you. Is there anything at all you can remember?"

"They're arguing again…" she replied, totally bypassing my question.

"Ask her who," Ben called out.

"Who is arguing?" I asked, completely forgetting the earlier exchange.

"They are."

I sighed and quickly reformulated the question. "Kimberly, can you tell me who is arguing with who?"

"Her…" she said. "He's arguing with her."

"Her?"

"Yes, her…" she moaned.

"Who is she?" I asked.

"The dyke," she muttered. "He's upset about what she did to my face."

"What about it?" I asked.

"He's upset that she burned my face," she whined. "He keeps saying 'You don't hurt face.'"

"That must be why the torture stopped," I offered to Ben and Constance.

"If we're lucky maybe they'll fuckin' kill each other over it," Ben mumbled.

"Ask her if she remembers hearing or smelling anything that might help?" Constance whispered.

I relayed the question.

"Sometimes the music…" she told me.

"What kind of music?" I asked.

"Death Metal."

I flashed on the driving thrum that had accompanied the onset of several of my episodes. I'd heard of the particular genre she mentioned, but was unfamiliar with it, that was until now. It would seem that the angry music not only had an explanation, it had a name.

I was just about to press her for more when I heard Mandalay's voice, noticeably louder than before.

"Watch it, Storm," she instructed.

"I see 'em," he returned.

"Wait a minute… Is that…" Constance's frightened voice trailed off.

"What the fuck…" Ben sounded confused. "How the hell did she…"

I turned to see what was happening just as he exclaimed, "Jeezus H. Christ!"

The van violently lurched as he yanked the steering wheel hard to the right. I fell sideways as I twisted, crashing hard against the side of the passenger seat. The van shuddered and there was the sickening sound of locked brakes and rubber squealing against asphalt as we careened off the side of the road. In the split second before we slid nose first into the ditch, I caught a shadowy flash of what had just put us there.

Directly in the middle of Route 3, with a single palm pressed stiffly out toward us, was a petite woman with pale skin and long, spiraling, auburn hair.

CHAPTER 39:

"Everybody okay?" Ben called out, voice not quite frantic, but carrying a definite edge of concern.

"Yeah," Constance replied, nodding her head vigorously.

We hadn't crashed so much as we had simply skidded off the road. The van was angled diagonally into a shallow drainage channel, causing us to pitch forward and to the right. We were shaken up, but that was about it.

The headlights were now cocked at such an angle that they were shining against a grassy embankment. The autumn-paled vegetation was now reflecting some of the light back, bringing a dim luminance to the interior of the vehicle.

"Row?" he inquired.

"I'm fine," I returned, pulling myself up using the back of Constance's seat for leverage against the odd angle.

"So did everyone see that, or am I goin' fuckin' nuts here?" Ben was continuing to talk even as he braced himself against the steering wheel and twisted around in his seat. I could see in his eyes that he was searching for Felicity. I got the impression from my friend's sudden silence that he actually wasn't expecting to see my wife still securely belted into her seat.

As soon as I had made it to my knees, I was turning to check on her myself. While I wasn't at all surprised to see her sitting there, I was relieved that she didn't seem to have been knocked around too badly. Her heavy-lidded eyes were half closed, but she appeared to be conscious and was even looking in my direction.

"I saw her. She was..." I heard Constance reply hesitantly, her voice tainted with awe. "But now she's..."

"What the fuck was that?" Ben almost demanded.

I heard the query but was otherwise occupied. I scrambled over to Felicity's seat and gently touched her arm. I wasn't quite sure how to address her at this point, but I knew the last person I'd spoken to had not been my wife—in spirit anyway. And, even though voices were being shared through the ethereal connection, whether or not physical experiences were as well was still a mystery. I hedged my bet and simply asked, "Are you okay?"

"I'm fine," my wife replied, ignoring the chatter in the front of the van. Although her voice was somewhat weak, her unmistakable Irish brogue was fully intact and thick as ever.

"Felicity?" I asked.

"Aye, of course. Did you bump your head then, Rowan? Who else would I be?"

I smiled for what seemed the first time all day. "Nice to have you back," I said.

She gave me a puzzled look. "You're sure you're all right?"

"I am now," I told her.

"Hey," Ben called out again. "One of you wanna answer me? What the fuck was that?"

"A glamour," I answered without turning.

"Ya mean like that time when you made me see a spider crawlin' on my shoulder?" He referred back to a bit of impromptu hypnosis I'd once used on him to prove a point.

"Pretty much."

"What's he on about now?" Felicity asked. "What glamour?"

"Yours," I replied.

She wrinkled her brow and gave her head a slight shake. "What are you talking about?"

"He's talkin' about you standin' in the middle of the fuckin' road," Ben interjected sternly. "You scared the shit outta me. You coulda' got us all killed."

"What?"

"You. Road. Swerve. Ditch," he replied, each word punctuated succinctly by a sharp gesture of his hand.

"Like I said, a glamour," I explained. "All three of us just saw an apparition of you standing in the middle of the road trying to flag us down."

"No wonder I'm so exhausted then," she said. "Although I can't imagine why I'd do such a thing."

"It's good to see you haven't lost your sense of humor."

"What do you mean?"

"So I guess this means we're close, huh?" Ben interjected with a huff.

"I'd say that's a safe bet," I replied.

"Close to what?" Felicity asked.

"Close to finding Kimberly Forest," Constance told her.

"How so?"

"Are you sure you're okay, Felicity?" she asked.

"I think so," my wife replied, trying to look past me. "I've a few pains I can't explain, but mainly I'm confused." She unlatched her safety harness and pushed herself forward. "Rowan, help me sit up."

"I'm not surprised," I told her, fumbling for the lever and easing the back of the seat upward. "Given what you've been through."

"Aye, I had a seatbelt on which is more than I can say for you," she said quickly. "Now what's this about being close to Kimberly? Can somebody please tell me what's going on?"

"What are you..." I gave her a puzzled look as my voice faded. "Felicity, do you remember anything that's happened?"

"Aye, we're supposed to be going across the river to look for Kimberly, and apparently Benjamin just ran us off the road."

"Hey, don't blame me," my friend instructed then popped his door open. The key alarm hesitantly blipped and then began a sickly buzz. "All right, since everyone's okay, I'm gonna check outside and get an idea of where we are." Before climbing out, he cast a glance back over his shoulder and directed himself at my wife. "And you, stay put, will'ya?"

"It wasn't actually her, Ben," I offered. "You know that."

"That doesn't make it any less fucked up," he replied.

Mandalay said, "Storm's right, you guys. That was too weird."

"Yeah, I'll give you that," I said. "But trust me, I've seen weirder."

Ben continued, "Weirder or not, lemme tell ya', two of her is one too many, 'specially if one of 'em is in my head." He looked back to Felicity again and said. "Like I said, no more hocus-pocus."

That said, he pushed the door fully open, climbed out, then carefully eased it back shut.

Felicity let out a frustrated shriek and suddenly appealed, "Dammit, will somebody please tell me what's going on?"

"Honey, we've been in Illinois for better than forty-five minutes now."

"Really?" she asked, the look on her face deeply serious. "Then where have I been?"

"Mentally? With Kimberly, I'm pretty sure."

She grew quiet and looked as if she was trying very hard to remember. In many ways, I was relieved that she couldn't recall the last hour; because it was one I suspected would be better left forgotten. I knew for a fact that it was a memory I, myself, wanted desperately to erase.

She finally muttered, "I suppose that would be why the glamour then."

"Yeah, I'm thinking so."

She pressed, "Then where are we now?"

"Route Three," I told her. "A couple of miles north of Two-Seventy."

"Is that where she is?"

I nodded. "She's probably close by. And, judging from your little out of body display, I'd say VERY close."

She started up out of the seat. "Then we have to go get her."

"Slow down," I told her, leaning forward and gently pressing her back. "We're working on it."

She looked back at me and suddenly furrowed her brow. "Let me see your face."

"What?"

"Let me see your face," she repeated. "What happened to your cheek?"

I reached up and touched the burn, wincing slightly as my fingertips came in contact with the blistered flesh. At this angle it was hidden in the shadows, but when I had leaned forward she had apparently noticed the blemish.

I turned so that she could see it, then said, "Same thing that happened to yours and Kimberly's"

Felicity mirrored my motion, gently pressing around the wounds on her own face. She closed her eyes and let out a pained sigh. "Gods…"

"I know, honey," I said. "But it just may be the thing that buys us enough time to get her out of there alive."

"How?" she asked sullenly.

"For about the past ten minutes, Kimberly Forest has been speaking through you," I replied.

Before I could go on to recap the preternatural conversation, the driver's door of the van opened with a pop and a groan. A moment later, Ben climbed back into his seat and pulled the door shut.

"Okay, looks like we've got a farmhouse about fifty or so yards off the road," he told us. "Lights are on, but that's all I can really see at this distance."

"Nothing else?" Constance asked.

"Nada."

"So where does that leave us?" I asked.

"Pretty much nowhere," Ben replied.

"There's nothing we can do?"

"Legally, no."

"But if Kimberly is in there…" Felicity started, urgency now fueling her.

He cut her off. "That's the problem. We got no way to know if she's actually on the property."

"But, can't you…"

"No," he interrupted her again. "I can't."

"Dammit, you don't even know what I was going to say," she spat.

"Doesn't matter," he snapped back at her. "We're between a rock and a hard place."

"Felicity, he's right," Constance offered. "We need reasonable cause to enter the property. We can't just kick the door in like they do on TV."

"I thought you could enter if you had a suspicion that someone's life was in danger," I said.

"We can," she replied. "But we don't have that, not a reasonably explicable one anyway."

"Well, can't you call someone and get a search warrant or something?" my wife appealed.

"Again, based on what?" Ben asked, turning in his seat to look back at her. Then he added, "Like I've told ya' before, the *Twilight Zone* stuff ain't gonna cut it."

"If I remember correctly, you're the one who asked us to help this time," she snipped.

"Yes I did," he returned. "And I'd freakin' do it again."

"Then listen to me!"

"I am, but what happens if we get in there and they've moved her?"

"They haven't."

"You got physical proof?"

"I know they haven't."

"I wish that was good enough, but it ain't. Look, we just gotta be sure we can make it stick, okay?" he explained.

"Then what do we do?" I asked.

Ben puffed his cheeks and blew out a hard breath. "We try ta' figure out a valid reason for entering the premises."

"We could try 'consent once removed'," Constance offered.

"Entry by deception?" Ben queried.

She nodded. "It's weak, but it might fly."

"Weak ain't the word for it. We're not officially workin' this case," he argued. "Prosecutor is gonna want to know why we did it."

"Hey, it didn't start out that way. We have car trouble," she replied. "It's a true story. I go knock on the door and ask to use the phone. I get in, look around, and we go from there."

"Yeah, besides the fact that you'd be lyin', even if you gain entry, what are the odds you're gonna see anything that'll get us anywhere? Felicity... Kimberly... Crap... Well, whoever it was said she was in the basement."

"Maybe I'll hear something."

"Jeez, Mandalay, that's stretchin' it. If you..."

Ben's sentence was interrupted by Felicity as she suddenly let out a sharp yelp. We all turned quickly to see her tensing as she gritted her teeth. However, before any of us could say a word, there came a startling pair of sharp raps on the driver-side window.

CHAPTER 40:

Apparently, the hiatus was over.

Felicity groaned as she entered into a new round of ethereal torture. For the moment, it seemed no worse than it had when we first began this expedition, which at least made it tolerable. However, I suspected it wouldn't stay that way for long, and that was not something I was willing to let happen. I simply wasn't going to sit by and watch her suffer through this again, especially when we were this close.

Ben twisted his body back around and began cranking down the window. A fresh gust of cool night air swept inward, this time bringing with it the distinct smell of a burning cigar riding along the chill.

There was a brief spate of silence, and in that moment, the van filled with a disturbing unrest. The feeling struck me hard, actually competing with Felicity for my attention.

"Are you folks okay," a husky voice finally asked. The timbre sounded odd and not quite identifiable in gender. I immediately flashed on Kimberly's reference to 'the dyke' and wondered if one of her tormentor's was standing only a few feet away at this very moment.

I tried to see around my friend, but in the darkness, caught only the orange end of the cigar as it glowed briefly then disappeared from view. I felt a stab of pain in my cheek and knew immediately that my fleeting thought was confirmed.

"Yeah," Ben replied with a quick nod. "We're fine."

There was a barely perceptible but very distinct change in my friend's mood as soon as he began talking to the person. It wasn't something I could audibly detect in his voice, but I could definitely feel it emanating from him. It would probably have gone unnoticed but for the chaotic energy coming from outside the window. All of my senses were triggering— both natural and supernatural.

The voice came again, "Heard you skidding all the way back up at the house."

"Yeah. Saw somethin' in the road and swerved."

"Probably a dog. We get a few strays around here. Lucky all you did was skid. Could have been worse."

"Yeah," Ben agreed. "Lucky."

"Do you need a hand?" the voice asked with a tone that sounded more annoyed than concerned.

"Nah," Ben replied, shaking his head. "I think we've got it under control."

"Are you sure? You've been sitting here for a while," the voice observed.

"Yeah, I know…"

Ben was interrupted as Felicity let out another sudden yelp. This time it morphed into a quiet but prolonged whine. I looked back at her and saw that she was leaning forward in the seat with her arms crossed.

"She okay?" Ben instantly called back to me, voice flat.

This time his tone was an obvious cue. I wasn't sure what to say, so I simply replied with, "Yeah. She's fine."

"Good" came his equally emotionless reply.

"What was that?" the voice asked.

"A friend," he said. "She wasn't wearin' her seatbelt, so she got knocked around a bit."

"She doesn't sound good."

"She'll be fine."

There was a tense silence for a moment, and then the voice spoke again, "Sure you don't need a hand?"

"Yeah, I'm sure."

"Okay then." There was another pause before I heard the less than sincere words "Be careful."

"Thanks."

I heard footsteps as the owner of the genderless voice began walking away. Ben was already cranking the window upward and had his head cocked so that he could watch the side-view mirror. I leaned farther forward and tried to see what he was looking at.

He held out his hand to Mandalay and made a quick gesture then glanced over to her and whispered, "You clear over there?"

Constance shot a glance out her window then shook her head and returned quietly. "No. I don't think so."

"Shit!" he muttered.

"What's going on?" I asked, dropping my voice to a whisper as well.

"I'm pretty sure she's the one on the surveillance tape," he said as he continued watching the mirrors, then after a moment, he levered the van into reverse and gunned the engine.

There was a momentary hesitation as the tires spun then took hold. The vehicle gave a slight buck and then jumped backward, rocking with a creak and groan as it rolled back up onto the highway.

"Nooooo!" Felicity whined, and then asked in a pained voice. "Wh-what are you doing?"

"Gotta move," my friend announced.

My wife continued pleading, "But, Kimberly..."

"...Is in there. I know," Ben hissed, cutting her off. He kept the van slowly rolling backward then came to a stop. "Mandalay, can you see 'er?"

"Not really... Wait... Yeah, there she is. About twenty feet up the driveway. She just looked back. Okay, now she's moving again."

"Can you see if she's armed?"

"...Something on her belt... Could be a cell phone... Not sure."

"You call it. Whaddaya wanna do?" he asked quickly.

"It's not good," she replied, shaking her head again. "Go around and we'll call for backup."

"No!" Felicity demanded. Her voice was still holding a pained edge but had grown far beyond a whimper.

"Not with you and Rowan in the van!" Ben hissed. "It's too dangerous!"

"Nooooo!" Felicity cried out again, but this time she was moving.

I felt a hard thump as she swivel-hipped out of the seat, striking purposely against my back and driving me off balance. I pitched forward and fell between the front seats and into the center console. A split second later I felt her sneakered feet stumbling over the backs of my legs.

Ben suddenly exclaimed, "Goddammit, Felicity! NO!"

But he was too late. The next thing I heard was the grating sound of the van's side door as it began to quickly slide. I twisted to grab for my wife, but she was too far out of my reach. The door continued moving by sheer momentum, as she shot through the second she could fit. It locked back in the open position with an angry thump that I could barely hear over Felicity's impromptu war cry.

"*TÚ SAIGH!*" My wife spewed forth a hateful sounding line of Gaelic. "*Umarlaid! Nach bu tù an t-urra isg!*"

Constance immediately kicked her door wide and bolted from the van in pursuit of the red-haired banshee. I was just pushing myself back up from the console as Ben levered the van into park, yelling back to me, "Stay here!"

He jumped out of his own door, and I heard the commotion grow outside.

"STOP! Federal Officer!" Constance was screaming.

"POLICE!" Ben bellowed behind her.

Their official demands were underscored by Felicity as she continued to wail, "*Tù saigh! Teasd!*"

This time I recognized all three of the Gaelic words, 'you', 'bitch', and 'die'.

I scrambled toward the open side door and rolled out onto the pavement, pushing myself up and forward the moment my feet hit the asphalt. I knew I should follow Ben's instruction and stay with the vehicle, but I couldn't keep my legs from driving me along behind them.

The odd angle of the van at the mouth of the driveway allowed at least some of the light from the headlamps to project up the gravel expanse. In the furthest reaches of the diminishing luminance, I saw a tangle of fiery auburn curls flash as my wife literally tackled the woman.

The suspect had had enough time to turn and see the screaming redhead running at her, especially since stealth had been a non-issue for Felicity. Still, even though she took a hard swing at her, my wife was short enough to duck it as she came in low and drove the woman to the ground, tumbling to the gravel with her.

Felicity was still shrieking, her voice a hoarse blend of unintelligible epithets and unearthly tortured sounds. She had landed on top, but the larger woman was fighting back immediately. She already had a handful of my wife's hair and was yanking her head back hard as she struggled to get away. Felicity responded by releasing her grip around the suspect's waist and flailing her arms out, impacting the heel of her fist hard against the woman's chin.

Ben and Constance were rapidly approaching them, with me bringing up the rear. I wanted desperately to jump into the fray and rescue Felicity, but logically, I knew that was the last thing I should do. I simply remained out of the way behind my two gun-wielding friends and fought to keep myself from responding to the gut reflex that was demanding I take action.

The woman was stunned by Felicity's blow but still managed to swing her own fist, glancing her knuckles against my wife's upper cheek. Felicity's head snapped, and she fell back. She was no longer on top of the woman, but she remained undeterred by the punch. She continued scrambling about and flailing her fists as the woman pulled her by the auburn mane.

My wife twisted, pulling up to her knees and forcing her shoulder up from beneath. With a quick lunge, she fell forward and drove her elbow hard into the woman's side as she was rolling toward her and trying to gain footing.

Before any more blows could be thrown, Ben and Constance were upon them, weapons drawn.

"POLICE! STAY DOWN!" my friend bellowed.

The woman rolled back and held her free hand out in plain view.

Felicity continued to punch, and the suspect threw her arm back up to protect herself from the unbridled attack. Mandalay took up a cover stance, and Ben quickly holstered his weapon then skirted around to pull Felicity off the woman.

I watched as he wrapped a large hand around the suspect's wrist and bent it back, breaking her grip on my wife's hair. My friend immediately took Felicity by the arms and started pulling her up. The woman tried to take a last swing at her, and Constance moved in closer, screaming, "STOP!"

My wife wasn't listening either.

She was still screaming at the top of her lungs, spewing Gaelic curses, mixed with colloquial Irish, and even a spate of English profanities. Ben was yelling at her to calm down as she struggled, still trying to swing. He managed to get her up to her feet, but before he could back away, Felicity bucked, using him for leverage as she kicked her leg out and brought the back of her sneaker hard into the prone woman's chest.

She was already swinging her other leg around, taking a second kick and aiming for the suspects face when my friend wrapped her in a bear hug and jerked her away. My wife continued twisting in his arms, kicking her legs against him and screaming as he carried her to the side.

Seeing that Ben had Felicity somewhat under control, Constance immediately stepped in between them, *Sig Sauer* stiffly aimed at the suspect on the ground.

"On your stomach! Nose to the ground!" Mandalay yelled to be heard over the continuing commotion. "NOW! Let's go!"

The woman was still trying to catch her breath after the kick Felicity had landed into her chest. Still, she did as she was told, rolling slowly over.

"Extend your arms to your sides, palms upward," Constance directed.

I took a moment to look off to the side. Felicity was face down on the grass herself. She was still screaming, but her curses were now directed at Ben as he held her down and applied handcuffs to her dainty wrists.

The scene was surreal. The darkness surrounded us, with only the distant light of the van's headlamps casting any illumination whatsoever. Wherever their dimness fell, oblique shadows were moving in angry, stilted motions. There was something very disconcerting about the whole thing, and I knew there was more to it than just what I could see in the physical plane. As I stared at the tableau, I began to get a very bad feeling.

I shook off the sensation and started toward my wife. I could hear Constance behind me, barking orders to the suspect. "Spread your legs, toes pointed out."

Ben had finished restraining Felicity, and he turned away from her, stepping past me without even acknowledging my presence.   He now had his weapon back in hand and stiffly aimed forward at the suspect.

I glanced over at them and saw him give Constance a quick nod. She re-holstered her weapon and then quickly reached beneath her jacket and produced a pair of handcuffs. She moved in swiftly, lowering herself down and placing her knee in the suspect's upper back.

"Left hand in the small of your back, palm down," she ordered. "Now."

The suspect complied, and in a deft motion, Mandalay slapped the metal restraint around the woman's wrist.

I turned and kept stumbling toward my wife who had ceased her screaming but was still cursing at Ben in at least one language. Without warning, she suddenly stopped and turned her face toward me. I was still a few steps away, but I halted dead in my tracks as our gazes locked. There was no mistaking the intensity of the fear I saw in her face, and a second later I heard the rushing buzz of electricity in my ears. She didn't have to say a word for me to know that she was hearing it too.

The hair on the back of my neck began to rise and was followed by the follicles along my arms rotating upward as well.

I started toward Felicity but then hesitated. Something unseen drew my eyes away, and I looked up at the lights of the house farther up the gravel driveway. Behind the ethereal crackle there was another sound. Muffled, but distinctly there. It had most likely been there the entire time but had remained unnoticed in all the commotion. I concentrated, listening as hard as I could and realized that it was a small gasoline engine droning along.

I stared into the distance, trying to pin significance on the newly identified sound. Somewhere in the back of my head, I was being told that it was supposed to mean something. But, that meaning was eluding me.

I turned back to my wife, and her eyes were wide with the rampant fear. As I started to take another step, her face suddenly contorted into a pained grimace, and her body stiffened.

All at once, Ben and Constance started yelling. I heard them, but I really wasn't paying attention, so it took a moment for me to realize that their shouts were directed at me.

I didn't really understand what they were saying, and I didn't have time to find out because I was running as fast as I could directly toward the farmhouse.

CHAPTER 41:

Four months had passed since I had even seen Brittany Larson's autopsy report, but here I was running through the darkness, speeding toward The Ancients only knew what, and that document was the reason. It had suddenly become as clear in my mind as if I had only just read it. And, of all the horrors it outlined, the one that came immediately to the forefront was the cause of death: suffocation.

What was standing out even more than the one word conclusion was the why: the technical jargon of the postmortem that explained what had brought about the fatal asphyxia. And, what it all boiled down to was that she had been electrocuted to the point that she could no longer breath.

Everything meshed in that instant. In relation to the electrocution, the bizarre ethereal seizures and the metallic taste in my mouth had been a given for some time. But now, the sound of the small engine made perfect sense. I knew that it could be only one thing. A generator.

I ran toward the house, my skin crawling with each footfall. I didn't even want to imagine what I might see upon entering, but I knew I had no choice.

I couldn't keep my mind from flashing on the fact that eight months ago I had done almost exactly the same thing. I had recklessly run into an abandoned building in an attempt to save a member of my coven from death at the hands of Eldon Porter. But, in the end, Millicent had died anyway.

This time around, I simply could not accept that outcome.

Kimberly Forest's life was not the only one hanging in the balance. The simple fact of the matter was that there were three lives at risk. If Kimberly died, Felicity would follow her beyond the veil in total, with no way to return. The strength of the connection between them made it an inevitability we had both foreseen.

And the third life, well, that would be mine. Being unable to save

Millicent had turned me into an emotional wreck. I knew without a doubt that losing my wife would kill me.

I veered off the gravel drive and aimed for the front of the house, driving myself forward with all that I had. Even with the electric buzz crackling in my ears, I could hear the sound of another set of feet pounding behind me. Intermixed with it all was Ben's angry voice demanding that I stop. I suspected he would overtake me very soon, and my only saving grace thus far had been the miniscule head start.

The house's porch occupied a space that was carved from the front corner of the building. I reached the foot of the stairs just ahead of my friend, whipping quickly around a wrought iron support trellis in an attempt to dodge him. The maneuver bought me a few scant seconds.

I took the concrete steps two at a time, vaulted myself onto the landing and burst through the front door with absolutely no regard for safety or stealth. I simply didn't have the luxury.

As I shouldered through the door, I found myself standing at the entrance of what appeared to be a living room. The space spread out before me, roughly a 16-by-20 rectangle. At the far end of the room was a doorway on the left wall. However, that was pretty much all that I managed to see before a large hand clamped onto my shoulder and yanked me back outside.

I stumbled backward, off balance and unable to compete with the force Ben was applying. He thrust me back forward at an angle, driving me away from the doorway and into the wall face first. I knew he was angry, and the severe lack of gentleness he used in planting me here was testimony to that fact. However, I didn't care. We would have to sort it out later.

"Dammit, Ben!" I screamed.

"Shut up!" he barked.

I twisted to look over my shoulder, trying to wriggle away. I could see that he had placed himself between the opening and me. He was holding me against the wall with one arm, and the other was extended stiffly toward the doorway with his weapon aimed. His eyes were searching, and the way he was postured made me realize that he was just as intent on shielding me as he was in keeping me from re-entering the house.

He spoke quickly, still not looking away from the open door. "Jeezus, Rowan, Felicity's all seized up back there! What the fuck do you think you're doin'?"

"Stopping this bastard!" I spat, still struggling to break away. "Let me go!"

"Leave this to us, Rowan! Backup's comin'."

"There's no time!"

"Didn't you hear me?!" he demanded. "Felicity's all *Twilight Zone* or somethin'!"

"Dammit, Ben, he's killing them!" I shot back. "They can't take anymore!"

"Jeezus H... You mean...?" His response came as what I was trying to tell him finally broke through. Still, his voice held an edge of indecision, as if he were weighing all options in relation to what I'd just said.

"HE'S KILLING THEM, BEN!" I repeated, screaming at him.

"Dammit, stay here!" he shot back.

My friend pushed away from me and immediately disappeared through the open door. I knew he was violating one of the most basic of police procedures by entering the dwelling without backup, but he realized there was no choice. Even so, now four lives were in jeopardy.

I twisted away from the wall and started toward the opening myself, but for some reason, I hesitated at the door. I wasn't sure if it was a conscious decision or not, but I stood there watching as my friend systematically worked his way inward, firearm positioned and ready.

There was no way I could simply stand by and watch. We had wasted enough time already, and I feared that it had been too much. I started to step across the threshold once again and felt myself inexplicably stop, unable to press forward.

My brain was in overdrive, rifling through every option it could assign to the scenario.

I considered running back to Felicity and trying to hijack the connection from her, just as she had done with me. It would most likely mean trading my life for hers if Ben was unable to stop this monster from killing Kimberly, but that was something I was more than prepared to do. I even went so far as to start in that direction, but by the time I reached the bottom of the stairs, my grey matter was telling me it wouldn't work. I hadn't been able to seize the connection from her even when I had myself halfway together. There was no way I was going to be able to do it when I was this close to panic.

As usual, my gut was repeatedly offering the same suggestion— go back up the stairs and run into the house. However, the small shred of logic I still possessed kept rejecting the idea. It knew that doing so was likely to get me shot. Still, even that was a risk I was willing to take.

Somehow I knew it wasn't the logic that was stopping me. It was something else. And, that 'something else' was becoming very insistent that I listen.

The sound of the engine was still droning in my ears, creating a backdrop for the incessant electric crackle. The meanings behind the two sounds had already started making me physically ill, and I could feel my sanity slipping as the panic continued threatening to take over.

I reached up and covered my ears with my hands, trying to listen to the 'something' that wanted to tell me what to do. I pressed my palms hard against the sides of my head in an attempt to drown out the torturous sound of the engine. I squeezed my eyes shut, fighting to concentrate as I struggled to ignore the noise that simply would not go away.

My skin was beginning to burn with the prickly sensation of unrelenting gooseflesh. I could feel static surrounding me, and random muscles in my body were beginning to spasm. For one brief moment, I even found it impossible to take a breath.

What seemed an eternity was truly no more than a few brief seconds, but in that time, my frustration level grew beyond containment. I was fighting to concentrate, to ground, and simply to keep my sanity. Unfortunately, I feared that I was losing them all.

I wanted to scream, to literally shout out a demand for the drone to be quiet so that I could think. I was on the verge of making the desire a reality when the 'something' reared back an ethereal fist and planted it between my eyes.

Realization didn't creep in— it sucker punched me.

I dropped my hands and listened, tracking the sound of the engine as it hummed into the night. I twisted quickly, focusing right and then left. The echoing sound seemed to be coming from the other side of the house, but I couldn't pinpoint an exact direction.

A quick glance told me that on my right, there was lawn and darkness. I took a step forward and looked to my left. There was more lawn and a large tree. Beyond them, I could see illumination from what appeared to be a dusk-to-dawn light high atop a pole. And, behind that was a large shed, bordered by a walkway. I didn't even bother weighing the options. I was already moving to the left, so I just kept going.

I darted around the corner and ran between the side of the house and the tree, skirting quickly around a cinder block well housing. As I came out of the shadows, the light seemed overwhelming, casting a harsh glare across the back of the house.

I kept moving, rounding the second corner and continuing along the walkway at a fast jog. My head kept swiveling, eyes searching frantically for the generator. The drone of the engine was growing louder, so I knew I was on the right track.

On my right was a screened-in porch. The walkway ran parallel to it for two-thirds of the length and then made a quick diagonal turn, leading up to a single stair and door. On my left was the shed. It ran the full length of the walkway and beyond, ending a few feet past the corner of the porch.

I picked up my pace and then suddenly stumbled as an ethereal spasm hit my leg, causing me to jerk uncontrollably. I fell hard on the concrete walk, raking my hands against the rough surface. A stab of pain bit into my knees, but I gritted my teeth and pushed myself back up.

The spasms were coming more frequently now, and that only served to heighten my fear. My connection with Kimberly Forest was nothing compared to Felicity's, so I could only imagine what they were going through. The one positive thing I was able to attach to the convulsions was that as long as I was experiencing them, it meant that they were both still alive.

The decibel level of the small engine increased with each unsteady step I took until I reached the corner of the oblong shed, whereupon it leapt dramatically. I shot a glance to my left. The large shed was blocking most of the light from the dusk to dawn sentry; however, enough was filtering into the expanse of the backyard to reveal a smaller wooden shed some forty to fifty feet away. My eyes caught a flash of motion, and I saw a flat rain cap flapping in the air where it was hinged atop a vertically mounted exhaust pipe.

I immediately raced for the small structure, limping and stumbling the entire distance as I struggled to deal with the spasms. I was only a few feet away when my entire body froze. I felt my heart jump as I struggled to breathe. My jaw began to clench and blood filled my mouth as I gnashed my already tortured tongue.

With a hard jerk, I fell face first onto the lawn.

CHAPTER 42:

I purposely tensed my body and snapped my head back. I couldn't allow myself to succumb to the unearthly torture that was ravaging me. I pushed myself up and for a moment, simply knelt in one place. My brain was a tangle of scattered impulses, and I suddenly realized that I couldn't remember where I was or even who I was.

Confusion had overtaken me, and I was frightened. I didn't know why. All I knew was that I was afraid. I shook my head, furtively glancing about. There was a loud noise thrumming in my ears, and it was making my head hurt.

Something in the back of my brain kept telling me that I was supposed to be doing something important, something that couldn't wait. I just had no idea what it was. I tried to concentrate, but the noise was pounding in my head, and it wouldn't let me think. I knew that if I was going to be able to remember, the noise had to stop. My eyes fell on the shed, and something told me that it was the source. If I could make the noise stop, then I would remember what I was supposed to do. I just knew it. I pulled myself to my feet and started moving.

My left hand was twisted into a tight claw, my own fingernails digging deep into my palm. My forearm was hugged against my chest and was shaking violently. My right hand was threatening to do the same thing. I didn't know what was happening to me, but I knew I didn't like it at all.

I stumbled against the small shed, and the noise was now louder than ever. The smell of exhaust was thick in the air as I leaned against the structure, and warmth seeped into my body from the wooden walls.

I pitched myself to the side then reached out with my right hand to grasp the handle on the shed door. I tugged and it moved a pair of inches then snapped back. I tugged again with the same result. I looked down and saw a hasp held securely in place by a padlock.

I yanked on the door, throwing my full weight into the attempt and achieving nothing. I was angry now. I wanted the incessant thrum to stop. I braced myself and kicked the door hard, managing only to send a lance of pain through my foot and up my leg.

I felt myself screaming, but the sound mixed with the maddening drone to become a single, painful chord. I stepped back from the shed, pitching to the right as I stumbled. I stood there screaming at it to stop, but it wouldn't listen to me.

My heart was racing now, and the pain in my head was becoming almost intolerable. As I stood there bellowing at the small building, my eyes fell on a sheet metal vent screwed into the side of the wall. The noise was pouring from it, and I stepped forward, infuriation driving me into a frenzy. In my rattled brain, the inanimate building was provoking me, and I'd had all that I was going to take. I did exactly what my emotions wanted me to do. I attacked it.

I swung my fist hard, slamming it directly into the slotted porthole. The sharp ribs bit into my hand, slicing nearly to bone, but I felt the vent move. I brought my hand back and drove it into the galvanized metal sheet again. This time not only did I feel it move, but I heard the sharp sound of cracking wood against the backdrop of the drone. For a third time I drew my arm back. In the dim light, I could see blood dripping from the ragged cuts, but I ignored it. I launched my fist, twisting my torso and throwing my weight behind the punch.

The sound of splintering wood snapped in the air, and the clatter of the sheet metal vent falling inward added itself to the cacophony. My body fell forward as my hand, and then arm, followed the vent covering in through the rectangular hole. I landed on my knees, and my hand automatically began groping the hot interior of the shed.

I jerked my arm back as an intense burning sensation started against the back of my hand, but I immediately thrust it back in and began to feel around once again. I didn't know what I was looking for or even if I would recognize it by feel, but I had to make the noise stop.

The hair on the back of my neck began to rise once again, and I felt my body beginning to tingle. The muscles in my chest were working into a spasm, and my breath caught suddenly in my throat.

My teeth started to grind, and I felt myself shaking.

The burning sensation returned to my hand and I flinched. Trying to ignore it, I forced my arm farther inward, pushing my shoulder into the opening. I continued to grope, and my hand brushed against something flexible. It was the first thing, other than hot metal, I'd felt, so I wrapped my tortured fingers around it and pulled as hard as I could.

There was a cough then a sputter, and the noise stopped. My body instantly relaxed of its own accord, and the hot air that had been trapped in my lungs expelled in a loud huff. I sucked in a breath and fell back on the grass, panting as the tension left my body.

Brand new pains began reporting in to my central nervous system. However, these were all very real and surprisingly, almost welcome. At first, I didn't even want to move. I just wanted to relax and take in the cool night air. But, my brain was starting to clear, and I heard myself mutter the name, Felicity.

All at once, I remembered where I was, who I was, what I was doing, and even why. Also in that instant, the only thing that mattered to me was getting to my wife. I scrambled up to my feet and started back across the yard, heading toward the lighted path.

Ahead of me was the back of the house. In the shadows of the screened-in porch was a slanted bulkhead. I hadn't noticed it earlier, but from this angle it was an obvious protrusion extending out from the foundation. I could see light seeping out between the crack where the doors split, and I wondered to myself if it was an entrance to the basement.

I didn't have to wonder for very long.

I'd made it all of five steps across the lawn when the left hand door of the bulkhead pushed upward then fell to the side with a heavy thump. Light poured out of the opening, and a second later, the right hand door flopped over. Finally, the silhouette of a head popped up. It was slowly followed by a shadowy pair of shoulders and then a torso, as what appeared to be a potentially very large man came up from the depths of the cellar.

In my single-minded quest to shut down the generator, I hadn't given any thought to what would happen once I did, other than bringing an end to the torture. I didn't even consider that the monster that was doing this would come to investigate. I suppose in the back of my mind I was counting on Ben to have subdued him by now, but the truth was, I didn't know how much time had actually elapsed. Ben might not have made it into the cellar yet, and in fact, there might not even be an interior entrance at all.

My first thought was to run in the opposite direction and hope that I could skirt around the large shed, avoiding him altogether. Unfortunately, my body wasn't taking orders from my rational brain.

My gut, however, was a different story. It was back in full control, and it issued its own set of commands. Fear and anger joined forces, requesting an immediate adrenalin dump from my nervous system. Free of ethereal influences for the moment, it complied posthaste. As the hormone injected itself into my bloodstream, I let out a bloodcurdling scream and rushed forward as fast as I could.

The man looked up, obviously startled as he saw me barreling toward him. He hadn't quite reached the top of the stairs when I took my final step, launching myself into the air for the last few feet. He let out a surprised yelp followed by a heavy groan as I slammed full force into him.

He stumbled backward down the stairs, flailing his arms and grabbing at the stone wall. I glanced off of him, ramming my shoulder into the opposite wall and then fell to the second stair with a heavy thud. I was stunned, but then so was he, or so I thought. As he continued stumbling backwards, I pulled myself upward then pushed off against the wall, throwing myself into him again.

This time, he was much more prepared and threw a large arm up to block my attack. He managed to regain his balance just as I struck and pressed his huge forearm out against my chest. Upon impact, the air was forced from my lungs in a violent huff. With an almost animal-like growl, he thrust his arm to the side, flinging me down the stairs to the slab floor.

I hit hard, rolling across the rough concrete and landing in a heap. I was fighting to catch my breath, and a few more new pains were added to the smorgasbord of aches my body was experiencing. I rolled to the side and looked up, seeing that the man had fully regained his balance and was coming back down the stairs. I'm not sure if it was the angle at which I was seeing him, the damage he had just inflicted, the situation, or all of the above, but he looked huge. He was certainly taller than Ben, and I was sure half again as broad. Suddenly, my original thought about running the opposite direction was looking far better than the option I had chosen.

I pushed myself up to my hands and knees as he lumbered down the last stair. As my head came up, I looked across the dim cellar and saw a nude woman bound in a chair. Her feet were positioned in buckets, and she was covered in bleeding wounds. There was a set of what appeared to be jumper cables clamped to her, one lead attached to her left hand, the other biting into the flesh of her right, upper arm. Her head was lolled to the side, but I couldn't tell if she was dead or merely unconscious.

The giant wasn't interested in letting me find out. Before I could pull myself to my feet, a massive hand clamped around the back of my neck. I swear I could feel his thumb and fingers almost meeting one another as they wrapped around to press into my throat. I felt myself lifting upward, and before I knew it, I was completely suspended several inches above the floor.

I couldn't see him, but I was kicking as I hung there, swinging my legs in an attempt to inflict any kind of damage I could, which considering the situation was probably none. With a hard thrust, he tossed me forward, and I smashed against a metal storage unit.

Rusted coffee cans, jars, and countless other unidentifiable items scattered across the floor with a horrendous crash as the unit toppled. I came down hard on top of it, taking a sharp blow to the ribs as well as hammering my forehead against the edge of one of the shelves.

I was disoriented from the blow to my head, and I was tangled into the now twisted braces of the shelving unit. I struggled to pull free, but I felt like I was going to pass out at any moment. I suddenly had a very bad feeling that I was going to die. There were no two ways about it. I didn't stand a chance against his hulking size.

I heard a grunt and the sound of shuffling feet behind me. Panic issued its own demand for adrenalin, and I started frantically trying to extricate myself from the tangle of bent metal. My left arm was free, and I sent my hand searching for a weapon, anything at all that I could use to defend myself. It brushed against something that felt like a handle, and I automatically wrapped my fingers tight around it.

A moment later, I felt the large hand against the back of my neck once again. Before he could clamp on, I twisted, flailing my left arm out and swinging along with it whatever it was I had managed to grasp. I had no way to aim, so I simply stretched out as far as I could when I swung. As I rolled, I saw the jagged end of a broken soda bottle raking across his face.

He let out a pained roar and stumbled back a half step. I let out my own yelp as I yanked my right arm free, feeling flesh scrape against broken glass and jagged metal. I continued to twist and tried to pull myself back to my feet. I only managed to make it to a squatting position before he came at me again.

I swung the bottle, but he made a lumbering sidestep, and I barely grazed his arm. He grabbed my left wrist and squeezed as he pulled me up by my arm. My hand opened, and the bottle fell from it, clattering to the floor. His other hand slammed hard into my chest, and I felt myself once again lifted off the floor, literally swinging from my arm as he used it to pivot me around. At the last moment, he let go, and I flew several feet.

Somehow, my feet touched first, and I tried to backpedal but to no avail. I stumbled and continued with the momentum, slamming my back into the door of an upright freezer. I hit hard, rocking it back and falling to the floor in front of it. The door swung open, and a good portion of the contents spilled out on top of me. Abject horror welled up from the pit of my stomach, as amid packages wrapped in butcher paper, was a woman's severed head, her clouded, dead eyes staring coldly back at me.

I broke my gaze away, looking up as the shadow of the giant fell over me. His face was bleeding, and that just made him look even more frightening.

I had nothing left. I couldn't even bring myself to move. I knew I was about to die, and it crossed my mind that the Dark Mother hadn't even bothered to show her face. If I hadn't been so paralyzed with fear, I might have laughed at the irony. I'd been cheating Cerridwen for so long now that I'd grown to expect her presence at every turn.

And now, at the moment I was about to finally lose the war, she wasn't even going to be here to usher me across the bridge.

I closed my eyes and waited for the inevitable. My heart was pounding in my ears, and I felt the hot breath of the giant as he bent over me. After a moment, I heard him shuffle away, and then I thought I heard whimpering.

I slowly opened one eye and saw him sitting on the floor in front of me, a scant few feet away, a severed head cradled in the crook of his arm. He was staring at it lovingly, cooing and whimpering softly as he used his free hand to stroke the hair.

I heard shuffling and slowly pushed myself up and looked back to the stairs, my eyes drooping as I struggled to remain conscious. Standing a few feet away was Ben, his pistol stiffly aimed at the large man. My friend's face was a mask of sickened disbelief as he watched on.

I heard him slowly mutter, "Jeezus fuckin' Christ…"

The sounds of footsteps thudded above us, creaking on the floorboards in a strict, determined search pattern as backup arrived and entered the house.

Monday, October 7th
2:43 P.M.
St. Louis, Missouri

CHAPTER 43:

"I still can't believe it," Ben said, looking over at me. "She seemed like she was okay."

We were sitting on my deck, looking over the back yard. Leaves were layered in a spotty carpet across the lawn, piles built up here and there. A wheelbarrow and a pair of broom rakes were still lying exactly where Felicity and I had left them in a rush just a few days before. The cover on the compost pile was thrown back, corner flapping in the gentle breeze. Again, just as we had left it.

The sky was grey with a heavy stratum of clouds. It had rained the night before, but it hadn't been a major storm front, just a quiet, gentle sprinkle.

A cold, endless, and depressing October sprinkle.

The loamy smell of the damp leaves filled the air, providing an earthy backdrop to the pungent aroma of our cigars. I continued staring out across the lawn, absently thinking about work I needed to be doing and finding a million excuses to avoid it.

"Hey, white man," my friend prodded quietly. "You hear me?"

"Yeah," I replied quietly, my voice a thin whisper. "Me either."

I brought my cigar up and tucked it in the corner of my mouth. I puffed, but nothing happened. I pulled it out and regarded the business end without emotion. I stuck it back between my teeth and reached into my jacket pocket for a match.

My right hand was still wrapped in gauze. Several stitches had been required to close the wounds across my knuckles. There was a hand-shaped bruise square in the center of my chest that had already cycled into several bright shades of purple. My entire body was sore. I didn't even have to move to feel the aches, and the damp air wasn't helping. But, it didn't matter.

I was finding it hard to really care about anything right now.

I fumbled with a wooden match, trying to strike it using my bandaged hand and succeeded only in breaking it in two. Ben reached over and took the box from me, ignited a match, then cupped it in his hand and held it forth so I could re-light my cigar.

I puffed carefully, using my left hand to twist the stogie as I drew on it, then pulled it away and inspected the end, blowing a gentle stream of smoke at the glowing coal.

"Thanks," I muttered.

"Not a problem," he returned as he shook out the flame and flicked the charred wooden stub over the railing.

"I need a drink," I announced.

"No you don't," he replied.

"Yes I do."

"Trust me, white man," he returned. "You don't. 'Specially not right now. Give it some time."

We continued sitting in silence for several minutes. Several feet beyond the deck railing a small flock of birds were pecking at the ground around one of the feeders. Out of the corner of my eye I could see Emily, our calico cat, stalking them.

"Just doesn't seem right," he said.

"Can we talk about something else?" I asked, swallowing hard after the words.

"Yeah," he said, paused, then offered, "Albright's pissed."

I couldn't say much for his choice of new topics, but I went along with it anyway. I didn't have the energy to do anything else.

"Like I care?" I replied.

He nodded. "Yeah, I know. Guess it was to be expected, huh."

"She making life hard on you?"

"A bit, but I'll survive. I always do."

"Yeah. You do."

"By the way, talked to Mandalay this mornin'," he offered. "She asked about ya'."

"She okay?"

"Yeah. Needin' ta' talk. The shooting at the gas station was the first time she'd ever had to kill anyone."

"And it was a kid."

"Yeah."

"She in trouble?"

"A little. She's on administrative leave. They aren't too hot on the fact that she left the scene, but considerin' the circumstances she'll come out okay."

"Good."

"They were brother and sister, you know," my friend said, switching subjects again.

"Yeah, you told me."

"Yeah," he said with a nod. "Guess I did."

I shifted in my chair, trying to get comfortable. I wasn't succeeding.

"They tested the brother," he offered. "Got an IQ of fifty-two."

"Too bad," I murmured.

"Why do ya' say that?"

I looked over at him, unable to muster an expression and simply said, "Because with an IQ that low, our judicial system will let the bastard live."

"Yeah, prob'ly," he answered, and then sighed before continuing. "The sister is the real sick one."

"They're both sick, Ben."

"Yeah, but the sister is the one behind the whole mess."

"Is she mentally challenged too?"

"No."

"Good," I replied. "Then they can execute her."

"Yeah, I'm sure the prosecutor will push for it." He paused and took a puff from his cigar, rolling the smoke around on his tongue before letting it out in a slow stream. He tapped the ash then looked back over to me. "Regular fuckin' torture chamber they had down in that basement. Crime scene guys said they actually had some kinda current-slash-voltage regulator or somethin' hooked up to the generator. Kinda like a homemade electric chair."

"Yeah, they were real experts weren't they," I grumbled.

"I guess," he replied, then added, "Apparently electrocution is pretty painful. The sister liked ta' see how much the victims could take. That's her kink. Inflictin' pain."

"You've got an odd view on changing subjects. Do we really have to talk about this right now, Ben?" I asked.

He frowned and looked away then muttered, "Yeah. I know. Sorry."

After a short, uncomfortable silence, he spoke again. "So whaddaya wanna talk about?"

"Nothing."

The heavy silence fell between us again as I puffed quietly on my cigar. I watched on as Emily continued creeping slowly toward the blissfully unaware flock of birds.

"So, what about the brother?" I asked, reopening the wound of my own accord.

"I thought you didn't wanna talk about it?"

"I changed my mind."

"Okay, so what about 'im?"

"He was torturing the women too."

"He was just doing what his sister told him to do," my friend said with a mild harrumph. "Still doesn't get that he was doin' anything wrong."

"What about the heads?"

"There were fifteen total," he replied. "From four different states so far. They've identified all of 'em except three. Missing women dating back six years. We're still tryin' ta' get 'em ta' tell us where the rest of the bodies are buried."

"I meant why did they keep them."

"Oh. Yeah. Well, it seems big brother thought they were pretty, so he wanted ta' keep 'em."

"Gods…" I murmured.

"Yeah."

"Any idea why the scattered grave sites?"

"Not yet."

I turned my head slightly and watched Emily as her tail twitched and her hindquarters danced in preparation to attack. She suddenly uncoiled and sprang forward, missing her mark but sending the flock noisily into the air.

Ben huffed out a breath then asked, "So, what time are you going to the funeral home?"

"About three-thirty," I replied.

"That's comin' up pretty quick."

"Yeah, I know."

"You know, it ain't your fault she's gone, Row. You did everything you could."

I didn't answer.

"So... You gonna be okay?"

"Yeah."

"You sure?"

"Yeah, I'll make it."

I thought I heard a noise and turned to see an auburn-haired vision standing in the open back door. Her hair was pulled up in a loose Gibson girl, neatly pinned in place. She was clad in a solemn black dress and pumps.

"Aye, Rowan," she said softly. "Come in and change. We have to leave soon."

"I'll be right there," I told her with a nod.

She looked back at me sadly. Her soft face looked like it had been brushed with a tasteful amount of makeup, but it still couldn't hide the black rim around her eye nor the bruise on her cheek where she'd taken the punch. Fortunately, the burns on her opposite cheek had completely disappeared, as had mine. Would that all injuries healed as quickly and completely as the ethereal ones seemed to do. In that same vein, it was too bad that the emotional scars of the supernatural would never really fade.

I continued to watch as she turned and disappeared back into the house. When she was out of sight, I turned back to the yard and puffed on my cigar.

"Yeah," Ben muttered again. "The Forest woman really seemed

like she was gonna make it when they took 'er outta that basement. I guess she'd just been through too much."

"Yeah," I replied quietly.

"Jeezus, Row, I know it sounds bad, but I'm glad it was her and not... Ya'know... And... And I hate ta' say it, but I'm just glad she lasted until after the *Twilight Zone* thing fizzled out... Ya'know? And Firehair didn't... Well... Ya'know..."

"Yeah, Ben. Me too," I muttered. "Goddess help me. Me too."

EPILOGUE:

H e closed the door of the attic office then sat down at his desk and pulled out the lower drawer as far as he could. The twisted corner of a plastic shopping bag was peeking out from underneath a stack of paper. It had been tucked in the back of the file drawer for over a week now. Out of sight but never out of his mind. Now that the dark moon had come back around, he was ready for it.

He pulled the bag from its hiding place and shut the drawer, then he pushed his keyboard and mouse aside, clearing an area on the surface of his desk. He emptied the contents out onto the space and set about opening an oblong box. After a few moments of struggling with twist ties and string, he managed to extricate the toy from the package.

He sat the 12-inch fashion doll on his desk and propped her against the face of the computer monitor. Her plastic skin was pale ivory and her nylon hair a cascade of long, spiraling, red curls. He looked past the doll at a framed picture of a woman and was amazed yet again by the resemblance, just as he had been when he saw the doll in the store.

He shook his head and began to fiddle with the other items that had poured from the shopping bag. A packet of salt, a black candle, some clear cellophane wrap, and a spool of purple ribbon. He didn't have long to do this. She would be coming home soon.

After quickly preparing his space, he lit the candle and began to meditate, breathing in through his nose and out through his mouth. He wanted his mind clear and focused, because for this to work, there was no room for even the slightest doubt. He dropped into a relaxed rhythm and eventually opened his eyes.

Reaching out, he lifted the doll and began carefully wrapping it in the clear cellophane. Once he was satisfied, he began to weave the purple ribbon around the plastic-encased poppet, criss-crossing it as he went. With each lace, he murmured to himself, "Never again. With this shield, I bind you from harm, Felicity Caitlin O'Brien."

When he finished trussing the doll, he gathered the trash and stuffed it into the shopping bag. Then, he picked up the doll and set out for a place to bury it.

With luck, he would put it in a place where she would never find it.

ABOUT THE AUTHOR

Author of the best selling *Rowan Gant Investigations* series of suspense-thrillers, M. R. Sellars began reading at age four, and writing shortly thereafter—he hasn't stopped since. The product of a liberal family, from an early age Sellars was exposed to many different religions and belief systems, both mainstream and obscure. To this day, he remains an avid student of the religious diversity that surrounds us. Not one for remaining "in the broom closet," Sellars often gives group lectures on request in order to help dispel the many myths and misconceptions that surround the practice of Witchcraft, Paganism, and the Wiccan religion.

A self-described "long-haired hippie activist tree-hugger," Sellars studied Journalism and Literature as well as Computer Science throughout high school and college, winning many prestigious awards for writing during his academic course. Although his first love was the written word, fate quickly led him to his vocation of more than twenty years as a senior level Electronics Technician and Internet Systems Administrator. Even with his hectic dual career, Sellars finds time to indulge in his hobbies of hiking, camping, nature photography, and cooking. A classically trained, accomplished gourmet chef, he can often be found 'playing' in his favorite room— the kitchen.

M. R. Sellars has been an honored guest and speaker at numerous public libraries, community organizations (both Pagan and Non-pagan), and at national events such as the annual *Real Witches Ball* in Columbus, Ohio; the *S.P.I.R.A.L. Pagan Unity Festival* in Burns, Tennessee; *Gathering of the Tribes* in Virginia; *Festival of Souls* in Memphis, Tennessee; *Florida Pagan Gathering*; and the annual *Heartland Pagan Festival* and *Pagan Pride Day Celebration* in Kansas among numerous others.

An avid member of several environmental stewardship organizations, Sellars resides in the Midwest with his family where their home is known to be a safe haven for neglected and abused animals. The novels in the *Rowan Gant Investigation* series: *Harm None (2000), Never Burn A Witch (2001), Perfect Trust (2002)*, and *The Law Of Three (2003)* have all spent numerous weeks on various bookstore bestseller lists, and *The Law Of Three* garnered the St. Louis RFT People's Choice Award soon after its debut.

At the time of this writing, Sellars is working on several projects, as well as traveling on promotional tour.

For more information about M. R. Sellars and his work, visit him on the World Wide Web at www.mrsellars.com.